EPITAPH

THE NECROMANCER THANATOGRAPHY
BOOK TWO

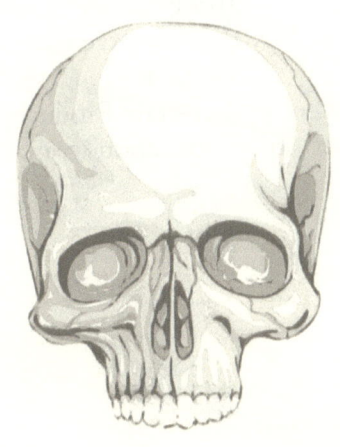

SHANE SIMMONS

ISBN: 978-1-988954-13-4

Epitaph
Copyright © 2019 by Shane Simmons
All Rights Reserved.

Published by Eyestrain Productions
eyestrainproductions.com

Prologue

Aptitude Test

"SO, DO I HAVE THE GIFT?" I asked, eager to be validated, reassured that I had some talent, some hidden ability that everyone else was simply too blind to see, too narrow-minded to appreciate.

"Not a bit of it," he said firmly.

I must have looked crestfallen. My hopes were dashed. For one shining moment, I thought my life had purpose, meaning, direction. A direction to where, I had no idea, but I desperately wanted it to lead me somewhere. And now?

But he wasn't done. There was more, and he looked quite saddened by it.

"You have the curse," he told me. "In spades. You poor dumb bastard."

And I, in my naiveté, in my youthful exuberance, in my wretched inexperience, took this as good news.

Chapter One

A Drop in the Ocean

THREE YEARS, FOUR MONTHS, and eleven days was how long it took to put Humpty Dumpty together again. Even with all that time spent reconstituting myself, I never located all the pieces. Not even close. So what finally washed up with the surf and flopped onto the beach that night was a malformed, translucent blob that looked more jellyfish than human. I knew what it must have felt like for our ancient ancestors to come crawling out of the ocean and take their first steps into a whole new world on fins that were never built to walk around on dry land.

I dragged myself through the sandy muck until I was just past the tideline and sure another wave wouldn't come and sweep me back out to sea. Then I collapsed in the dirt for a good long rest, well deserved after the last leg of my journey back from the dead.

"That sucked," were the first words I spoke aloud with my ill-formed vocal chords, choked with salt water. There was no one around to hear me, and they wouldn't have been able to understand me if they had been.

I had no notion of where in the world I might have landed. That's the problem with burials at sea. The ocean is a big place, connected to all the other oceans, and you can get lost very easily—especially when your burial at sea was in the form of cremated ashes, scattered into the wind and waves.

Imagine, if you will, the most tedious jigsaw puzzle in the history of the world. That's what I had been up against for three long years. My consciousness, drifting around, picking through untold trillions of gallons of water, trying to identify and link tiny particles of dust that used to be bits of my body. Time became an abstract notion, and my incorporeal mind was reduced to nothing more than an obsessive collector of minutiae—a myopic assembly line for the fragmented debris of a dead machine, each piece almost too small to see.

I saw the sun rise through actual physical eyeballs for the first time since my last death. They were gelatinous and bubble-thin, but I could sense light with them, and see the surrounding beach behind a veil of haze. With much effort, I flopped over again and began to crawl towards what I thought might be plant life. It took me at least an hour to travel ten feet, but I eventually felt grass under my newly formed fingertips. Sticking my face into the tangle of greenery, I gummed at the blades, trying to break them down enough to swallow and consume the nutrients I needed to start rebuilding my body.

Nobody was around to witness my agonizingly slow rebirth. That suited me fine. It would have been humiliating to be seen like this. I felt like a wad of mucus somebody had spat onto the ground after a week-long head cold.

Wherever I had found myself, it was remote enough for me to graze in peace, like the primordial blob I was, for the next several days. Once I was able to rise to my flapping, viscous feet and get a look around, I dared to take my first few steps forward in search of more substantial sustenance to help me form an acceptable body. I waited until nightfall to embark. Sunlight, dim as it had been since I'd first arrived, was painful to my membrane skin.

It's difficult to say how far I had to walk before I stumbled upon an object I could discern and recognize with my still-forming eyes. It was a road sign. I tried to read it, but my vision remained dim. Squinting at it didn't help since I could see right through my eyelids. Eventually I had to walk up to the sign and read it one letter at a time from only a few inches away. I got through the "B" then an "R" and an "I" before the sign became washed out. Bright light reflected off the surface I was trying to study, blinding me. My body cast no shadow to mute the brilliance. The approaching headlights cut through me like I wasn't even there. In fact, I was barely there at all, so thin and insubstantial were the building blocks of my body. I didn't feel like a man so much as a lightly penciled outline of a man. A car flew past me a moment later and the light faded away. I doubted the occupants even saw me at all, and if they had, they would hardly have known what they were looking at.

Once my vision cleared, I resumed the tedious task of trying to read what the sign had to say. Following the contours of each letter, I made out an "S" a "T" an "O" and finally an "L." There was more writing below, indicating some distance away, but I was already too exhausted to attempt it.

Bristol. I was x-number of miles away from Bristol, which could only mean I had landed in England, a whole ocean across from where I'd started. Washed up on the south shore, London was an achievable journey away, even in my current shaky state. It couldn't have been a coincidence. Instinct above and beyond the whims of the currents had brought me here. Even with my mind lost to the intricacies of fusing incinerated soggy ashes back together amidst a torrent of fathomless sea, my subconscious had a destination in mind. On some level, I knew I would have to come ashore in a place that would offer me shelter and salvation, from the one person who would know better than anyone how to help me finish rising from my watery grave.

Θ

I didn't like my odds of hitching a ride to London. My fingers were only stumpy half-digits and I barely had any thumbs to stick out at all. As I made my way along the side of the road, none of the sparse traffic seemed to notice me. Practically a ghost, I wished I looked as solid as one. That would be something. At least I'd be recognizably human.

As the sun started to rise, I knew I would have to get off the highway. By daylight, someone could spot me, freak out, and call the authorities or worse. I didn't fancy getting dissected by public-health officials in biohazard suits, intent on figuring out what I was, what was wrong with me, and if it was catching. Before I could make plans to crawl into a ditch or a gutter and wait for the cover of darkness to move on, I spotted what must have been a truck stop. Whether it was offering fuel for the lorries or food for the drivers, I guessed most of them were on the way up to London for pick-ups or deliveries. I crawled into the back of the first one that had an open flatbed and wormed my way under the tarp that was tied down over crates of produce inside. The boxes were full of oranges, destined for fruit and vegetable shops somewhere up the road. A slat on one of the crates was broken and, after enough poking and prodding, I was able to get a single orange to roll out.

By the time a driver came out of the truck stop and took the wheel, I had been sucking at the exterior of the loose orange for ages without breaking the skin. There were no teeth in my head to penetrate the citrus fruit, and my mouth was an ill-defined, quivering orifice that could do nothing but attach itself to one side of the orb and suck. I couldn't tell if I was drawing any revitalizing vitamins, but I kept at it as the truck backed out of the lot and turned onto the highway.

We were in the city before the sun could crawl above the skyline. Whether it was the weekend or a week day, it was still too early for most people to be up and about. The streets were virtually unpopulated, the traffic thin. I hoped it would stay that way just a little longer, until we were across the Thames and closer to the safe harbour I was shooting for. I counted myself lucky when everything turned dark all around me. It was difficult for me to spot landmarks with my too-new eyes, but I calculated we must have entered the Blackwall Tunnel. That meant we would be in the east end once we came out the other side. I released my orange, still unbreached but crinkled from dehydration, and prepared to abandon ship.

That final leg of the trip was the worst. Knowing I was in the right neighbourhood, but with no indication the truck was likely to stop there, I had to throw myself out the back and onto the hard pavement. In my fragile state, I was afraid I would burst apart all over the road, and send a body that was more water than flesh cascading down the nearest sewer grate. The impact distorted and warped my rubbery form, but there was nothing close to real bone to break yet. I was able to crawl to the curb and work myself back into some semblance of a mobile lifeform before any subsequent vehicles flattened me out like chewing gum.

While the light was still faint and there were few people to notice, I hobbled off the highway and climbed an exit that let out next to a block of flats. Tucked away behind them was a small park, fairly barren and strewn with garbage. There were a few clumps of trees around the edges, and enough unkempt brush to hide me. I crawled under a canopy of tangled branches and plastic bags that had become caught in them in the wind. There I spent the day as just another bit of abandoned human waste, mixed in with the rest of the park trash, letting the hours go by until it was dark again.

It drizzled that night—my final night living as an amorphous pariah in the wilds. I was glad for it. Fresh water, polluted by the city air or not, was welcome, absorbing into my nascent body as the London rain ran down my barely extant skin. The body I was growing would need much more than that, but every bit helped, and it was important I remained hydrated. Once the foul weather and late hour had driven enough people off the streets, I came out of my hiding place and tried to navigate by memory and what street signs I could focus on.

Canning Town was close, and it was still the maze I remembered from my youth. I wandered the residential streets for hours, trying to find my way and getting lost repeatedly. Each time I was sure I had wandered right back out of the district, I would spot something familiar that would refresh my sense of direction. So many of the row houses looked the same, I walked up the path of a dozen different ones until I finally arrived at a door that bore the number that was forever burned into my mind. I had to bear down on the doorbell with as much force as I could muster, putting all of my weight behind it, in order to make one of my malleable digits push in the button and make it ring.

I didn't think I could manage it a second time, and was relieved when the porch light snapped on. There was a long wait before I heard the locks unlatch. The door swung in moments later and I saw a familiar face that had grown even more venerable than I remembered it. Though the power of perceptible speech still eluded me, I hoped my physical state would speak for itself.

The old goat recognized me straight off, despite my being a marginally opaque monster. He looked me up and down, hardly surprised to see me after so many years, and said at once, "You look like you could use a cuppa."

Chapter Two

Bad Influence

I HESITATE TO CALL Oliver Franck a mentor, but he taught me a lot when I first came to him looking for answers and, I suppose, guidance. After several unproductive years in university and a worthless degree that I ended up using to line my sock drawer, I decided to round out my education by backpacking through Europe, the way young bohemians are supposed to in their early twenties. The grand plan included hitchhiking my way through every seedy hostel on the continent, zigzagging through places like Paris, Barcelona, Berlin, Prague, and Rome. I wanted to soak in diverse cultures, see classic architecture, view great art and, let's be honest, bed exotic women.

With my whole itinerary set and my sense of adventure maxed out, I landed in Heathrow and promptly never made it out of London.

Stopping by a randomly selected pub for a pint, in an effort to tick off the most important cultural immersion to be had in the United Kingdom, I happened to strike up a conversation with an elderly local. Figuring a chat with a geezer over a few stouts was as Londonesque an experience as I was likely to get before hopping across the Channel to more fertile foreign grounds, I let him drone on endlessly about footie, shitty weather, and the parasitical royals.

This fellow, Oliver, waited until last call to casually mention he was a necromancer.

"What's a necromancer?" I asked in my blissful ignorance. "That has something to do with death, right?"

"It means controlling death," he said, and I felt the levity of the evening sucked right out of the room.

I knew then that our meeting was not so random. He had sensed something about me, sought me out, and drew me in before I had any idea what he was after.

"I have a knack for dealing with death," he explained, "an affinity for the dead and the risen. And you, my boy, have been dead before. More than once, am I right? Yet here you are, back and no worse for wear."

"How do know you that?"

"I can sense it. I felt you coming, before your plane even set down. Being attuned to that sort of thing, I couldn't ignore it. It worried me. I didn't know what sort of unstoppable, unkillable entity was landing on my doorstep, but I knew I was the only one currently available to deal with it. And I'm hardly up for that sort of thing at my age. You don't know how relieved I was to find nothing more dangerous than a kid on holiday. Still, it's quite a power you have tucked away there."

It was something I didn't like to talk about back then. My uncanny abilities had failed to win over anyone who'd seen them in action back home, and my family had spent much of my childhood being shunned or chased out of town by superstitious zealots or the merely freaked-out.

"You know what?" I said, "Let me get this last round and I'll be on my way."

The old man had been generous, paying for our drinks all evening. And I had been happy to let him, saving my modest pool of cash for the next stops in my itinerary. Nevertheless, I got up to settle the final bill at the bar, eager to extract myself from the conversation that had taken a turn I didn't care for. I never returned to the table and, instead, offered Oliver a polite parting wave as I stepped out the door.

I wasn't more than a dozen paces away from the pub before he caught up with me. The short jog had him out of breath, and I felt obliged to stop and let the old fellow get his wind back.

"We need to talk," he told me.

"We've been talking all evening," I said.

"We've been bullshitting all evening. I bring up a real topic and you run."

"There are some topics I'm not comfortable talking about, bullshit or otherwise."

"Fine," he said. "I'll talk, you listen. There are things you need to hear, and things you need to see."

Oliver reached into his pocket for something. Stupidly, I waited around to see what it was. What he held out in front of him looked like a tool of some sort—but just the handle of one. I was still trying to guess what it was when he popped the knife on the switchblade and I saw the streetlight above us glint off the sharp steel edge. Before I could ask him what it was for, he showed me, plunging it into my heart.

☉

Oliver was right. I had died before. Many more times than I even knew back then. But that was my first time getting murdered. I probably should have been more pissed off about it, but once my consciousness crawled back into my body and got my punctured heart beating again, I was mostly curious.

Looking around, I saw I was no longer on the street where I'd fallen. This was a house—small, quaint, British. I sat up and found I had been left lying on a couch, with a bath towel set down under me to catch the blood as it seeped out of my chest wound and trickled down my side. The towel was spotted, but with a stopped heart failing to pump blood, there hadn't been much to contend with, and the couch had been spared an unsightly stain.

Now that my heart was keeping time again, fresh blood began spilling out of the slit in my chest. I wadded up the towel and applied pressure. The cut would seal soon enough, the bleeding would stop, and whatever wounds Oliver had inflicted on me would heal quickly once I'd had some food and drink to replenish the damaged tissue.

As if cued by that very thought, Oliver arrived and plunked down a tray of tea and biscuits on the coffee table in front of me.

"There we are," he said, "back already. Right as rain and with time enough to boil a kettle."

I didn't bother asking where I was. It was obviously his home. I was more concerned about the logistics of the move, and who else might have seen me die.

"How'd you even get me back here by yourself?" I asked him.

"I called over a couple of my mates to help carry you."

"They must be good mates to help you move a body."

"I told them you were drunk," he said. "Most bodies found lying around on the pavement are only drunk. I left the knife in so you wouldn't bleed so much."

"Considerate of you."

"And practical. I didn't want you coming back from the dead until I had you inside."

"So what am I then? Your prisoner?"

I made a point of checking my wrists and ankles to make sure I wasn't shackled to anything.

"The door's unlocked. So are the windows if you'd care to sneak out that way. Nobody's holding you, but you need to stay just the same."

"I'm not hanging around here with you," I told him, deciding the time was finally ripe to start getting cross. "You murdered me!"

"Don't get all sore about it. We both know it wasn't going to do you any harm."

"It still hurt and it ruined my shirt."

"Don't be such a baby. I'll buy you another t-shirt. One with a good band on it."

My shirt had a tear through the centre of the rock-group logo, and a big red stain that didn't match the colour scheme. It was merchandize from a small-time band back home. I'd bought it a year earlier after one of their club appearances, partially because I wanted to support them, but mostly because they were obscure enough to make me look cooler than the other kids who were all wearing name-brand rock-group t-shirts.

"You sound like you want to be my sugar daddy."

"This isn't a pick-up. But if you play your cards right, I might just teach you a thing or two."

"I already have a travel guide in my bag."

"I'm not talking about which bloody tube station to get on or off, or where to find the fucking London Bridge!"

"Arizona!" I practically shouted, pleased with myself for knowing that particular bit of geographical trivia.

Oliver slapped me across the face. Not terribly hard, but hard enough to get my attention.

"I'm offering you an opportunity here, boy," he said, losing his patience. "You need to learn, and I have lessons for you if only you'll stick around and listen."

"I have a room booked for tomorrow night in a Paris hostel," I protested. "They're expecting me and I don't want to lose my bed."

"You don't want to do that," Oliver insisted.

"That sounds like a threat," I said, warily.

"It is. You ever been to Paris? It's full of French arseholes."

There was a moment of silence while I considered his words and toyed with his offer. That was when I heard footsteps. They were crossing the floor upstairs, right above our heads.

"Who else is here?" I asked.

"No one," said Oliver.

I tracked the passage of the interloper as he plodded towards the stairs.

"It sure sounds like somebody."

One heavy thud after the other, each stair creaked in turn, and I felt dread at the coming introduction.

"Well," conceded Oliver, "I suppose he qualifies as 'some body.'"

I turned and saw the man who had just arrived to join us. His face was sallow, which matched the rest of his emaciated body's complexion, and his head was cocked to one side, at an angle that would be uncomfortable to anyone who could feel anything. His jaw yawned open, revealing browned teeth jutting out of receded gums. They propped up a blackened tongue that looked like a cutlet of meat that had spoiled and then dried out too much to finish rotting away. What hair he had left was white and stringy, and dangled down across his face and shoulders as a torn spider web might. Two foggy shrivelled eyeballs were set back deep in their sockets, fixed on nothing in particular, at two decidedly different points in the room. For so grotesque a vision, he was surprisingly well dressed, in a cheap but clean suit. A carefully folded handkerchief poked out of his breast pocket, next to a blandly clashing striped tie that was done up in a tidy but lopsided nicky knot. He wore no socks, but his loafers were freshly polished, their toes pointing in at each other on the end of bent and crooked legs. If not for his obvious state of undeath, he might have been presentable enough for a middle-management job interview. The only incongruous fashion accessory was the pine-tree-shaped air freshener dangling from a lanyard around his neck.

"What the fuck is that?" I shouted, my voice approaching a shrill cry.

"Don't go wetting yourself. That's just Shambler. He's my zombie."

"You have a zombie? Like a walking-corpse zombie?"

"Yeah."

I took a second look at Shambler. He said nothing, remaining as still as the grave he wasn't lying in.

"You're telling me he's dead?" I asked, though the answer would have been obvious to anyone at a single glance.

"Does he look well to you? Of course he's bloody dead. He couldn't be a proper zombie otherwise, could he?"

"What are you doing with a zombie in your house?"

"Where else would I keep him?"

"But why is there one in here at all?"

"I made him, of course."

"You *made* him?"

"Well, raised him from the dead, reanimated him, set him to work," Oliver specified modestly. "He helps me out with simple household chores. And he's cheaper than buying a dishwasher."

"Who was he?" I said, still marvelling at Oliver's handiwork.

"Jehovah's Witness. Long time ago now. He came by, trying to save my soul or convert me or some such. I told him souls aren't things you can save, and you can't convert anyone from nothing to nonsense. He wasn't having it, so I invited him in for a more in-depth theological debate. Poor bugger had a heart attack and dropped dead right there, that spot next to your feet. I hope it wasn't something I said. Anyway, there wasn't a stitch of identification on him, and he never did give me a name. Some necromancers are good at talking to disembodied spirits and getting information, but that's never been one of my strengths. What was I to do?"

"Didn't you call an ambulance or the police or something?"

"And have them poking around in here, asking questions about what it is I get up to in the privacy of my own home? No thank you!"

"Surely he had family or friends looking for him? People in his church?"

"I kept an eye out for notifications, missing persons. I even called around to every Kingdom Hall—as they call them—seeing if they were short one evangelist. Nothing. Eventually I gave up and decided to put him to good use. No point letting him spoil all over the carpet."

"I guess not," I conceded.

"At any rate, I won the debate. Jehovah's Witnesses are convinced there's no afterlife in store for most of us."

"You certainly proved him wrong."

"So what do you think?" said Oliver, after he let me stare in silence for a good long stretch.

"It's disgusting," I concluded, but sounded anything but disgusted. I know I should have been repulsed, sickened. The only corpses I'd ever seen up to that point had been my own—from the outside, looking in. And yet, face to face with a dead man, I wasn't put off. I was fascinated, intrigued.

"Want to know the trick?"

Despite myself, and any sense of morality or basic humanity my parents and society at large had instilled in me over the years, I had to admit I did.

Θ

I lived with Oliver and Shambler for a full year, picking up what I could, learning the trade, and having my mind and talents expanded. Come the end of my tutelage, I had spent most of my summer-job nest egg on essentials like food, clothing, and pints. The rest of my European jaunt was a bust. There was barely enough left to pay for air fare back home. By that time I had badly overstayed my visa, and I was informed, in no uncertain terms, that the authorities didn't care to see me back in the United Kingdom for a good many years. They didn't need any accidental illegal immigrants like me hanging around past their allotted time and taking good-paying British jobs away from their citizens. I considered explaining to them that necromancy was a rare occupation, and that Britain, with its thousands of years' worth of dead buried underfoot everywhere, was in sore need of more professionals who could manage the problems that inevitably cropped up in the face of so many corpses and not-quite-departed spirits. In the end, I sagely decided to say nothing, and accept my banishment by the customs agents.

In theory, my visa faux pas should have been long forgotten and forgiven, but I had never attempted a return trip, and had hardly stayed in touch with Oliver outside of the occasional phone call or letter. Still, I shouldn't have been surprised that he recognized me now, standing in his doorway. He could always see right through me, even before that night when he could literally see right through me. I expect he knew I was coming, exactly how close I was, and had timed the kettle to come to a boil precisely on my arrival.

The effort of getting to Oliver's house had been monumental. Liquid was dripping down my embryonic body. I wasn't sweating so much as seeping. But without me having to say a single intelligible word, Oliver knew what to do. He led me into his house—which I could tell, even through my clouded eyesight, hadn't changed significantly since the day I left—and sat me down on the same couch I had found myself on the first time he had "invited" me into his home. Without straining me with conversation or questions, he poured cup after cup of tepid broth down my throat, until we had graduated to something resembling a weak soup. Then he put me to bed upstairs in the guest room I had once lived in, covered me with enough bedding to keep me warm without crushing my frail form in coziness, and left me in the dark to sleep and heal.

Θ

I slept through the night, the day, and the following night. When I awoke to a new morning, I found there was more of me to get out of bed than I had expected. I looked like a massive fetus, but that was a step in the right direction, towards something unmistakably alive.

There were small nubs of enamel popping out of my gum line. It hurt like hell, and I was reminded what it must be like to be a teething baby. Still, I was thankful for them. At last I was able to bite—or at least nibble—and chew. There was a breakfast waiting for me on a tray next to the bed. Nothing too challenging— but there were slices of fruit, some sort of bread pudding and, for sorely needed protein, a mushy dollop of canned meat that didn't demand more than a thorough gumming.

When I was finished, I cleared my throat and attempted a word that might be understood by someone other than myself.

"Hello?"

My voice was raspy and weak, but it was a voice.

I got out of bed and wandered around the house, taking careful steps so as not to stress the new bones that were forming in my feet. The place was empty—except for Shambler which, as far as conversation went, was very empty indeed. With his pet zombie busy sweeping the floor, Oliver was keeping out of the way in the back, working in his garden. I found I had just enough manual dexterity to pour myself a cup of tea left over from the first brew of the day. With the cup in hand, pushing the limit of the weight I was able to safely lift, I joined Oliver outside. His tiny plot of land was sprouting four rows of shoots that had barely begun to break the surface. I couldn't tell what he was trying to grow. Snails, by the look of the dominant lifeform in the yard.

"I never understood you and the gardening," I wheezed.

"I like to grow things, nurture life."

"That's a little ironic, don't you think? Considering what it is you do."

"That's not irony. It's balance."

He picked an invading snail off of his freshly weeded soil and tossed it over the neighbour's fence with a disapproving click of his tongue.

"A man needs a hobby," he told me. "You have a hobby?"

"No."

"You should get a hobby. All death and no play makes Jack a morbid boy."

"How do I look?" I asked.

"Absolutely horrible," Oliver told me candidly. "Much better, but horrible. At least now you look human. What the hell happened to you?"

"I got killed."

"Again," Oliver sniffed.

"Bad this time. Very bad. Nearly permanent."

"In your dreams."

My skin was still too tender for clothing, but I had a sheet wrapped around me and pulled over my head. It helped keep me warm. There was hardly any circulation in my body worth noting, and I was completely hairless. These things would return in time, but my patience ran thin. I'd been out of the loop for too long, and I was eager to reconnect with the world and find out what I'd missed.

I held my hand up in front of my face and looked for any sign of skin tone that would suggest I was starting to look publicly presentable. There was none. I was as white as a sheet of paper.

"I've gone from looking like a blob of snot to looking like a wad of pus, so I guess that's an improvement."

"You'll get your colour back," Oliver assured me. "You always do. I can see a hint of it already."

"Where?" I asked, parting the sheet and looking down at my body. I immediately regretted it. No man should have to see his genitalia in mid-growth, respawning from a blank slate. It looked like one of Oliver's sad little sprouts.

"Your eyes," said Oliver. "I can see some flecks of green in them. Well, one of them."

"Just one?" I asked, dismayed.

There was a tin watering can sitting on a deck chair. I stooped down to check my distorted reflection in the polished surface. It was hard to say for certain at this early stage, but it seemed my one white eye—the one that had had all the colour knocked out of it by a well-meaning but ill-advised bullet—was not regaining its old colour. Even after the complete destruction of my body and a painstaking regeneration, that one scar still remained.

"Shit," I said. It felt good to swear aloud again after years of only being able to think it.

"Fuck," I added, and felt better still.

Even with no body hair and scarce blood flow, it was colder out than it should have been.

"What time of year is this?" I asked. I was sure I knew the year, but not the season.

"We're just heading into autumn," Oliver told me.

"Little late to be growing your garden."

"There's always something to plant, even late in the year. These are radishes coming up. They'll be ready to eat before winter arrives."

"Hey, Ollie!" I heard a voice call out.

It was Oliver's next-door neighbour, peering over the partition fence between properties. I turned around so he wouldn't see my pale, premature face.

"Whose flipping dog was that, barking in the middle of the night?"

Oliver looked up from his garden.

"I didn't hear anything."

"Sounded like it was somewhere in the block. And a big bastard, too."

"I couldn't say."

"Last thing I need is to have to pick up some stray's shit in my yard. People who don't look after their animals, am I right?"

"I suppose so," said Oliver.

"Who's your friend?" asked the neighbour, and I knew he was talking about me, even with my back to him.

"Just a guest."

"Don't he talk?"

"Not much, no. I like quiet guests."

"Him and that other fellow you always have over."

I figured he was referring to Shambler without realizing the seldom-noticed zombie was more than an occasional visitor. He was a live-in servant, if not full-fledged roommate at this point. I was worried I would have to say something with my weak, whisper of a voice, but the man from next door was distracted a moment later.

"Fuckin' hell," declared the neighbour, and dipped out of sight behind the fence. He popped back up again, holding a curled shell between his fingers.

"Do you get snails like this all the time? I come out back and all I hear is crunch crunch crunch underfoot. It's a pestilence of the blighters!"

"Can't say I do," said Oliver.

"You using some sort of pesticide to ward them off?"

"That's probably it."

"Fuck going organic, am I right? Napalm the wee bastards."

"Mmm," Oliver said, as though he agreed.

The man blustered back inside a moment later, leaving us alone.

"Charming fellow," I wheezed.

"He talks a lot, but he's just the right level of incurious I like in a neighbour," said Oliver. "Come inside before we have to explain you to someone more observant."

Oliver rose to his feet, flung a final snail over the fence, and led me through the back door. Shambler was done with his sweeping and was now mopping the floor in the kitchen at his languid zombie pace. His slow, deliberate strokes hardly seemed an efficient or effective way to accomplish an end, but he was a tireless worker, and everything he was tasked with got done eventually.

"Look who's home for a visit," Oliver said to Shambler.

The zombie took it as a command and looked up from his duties. If there was a hint of recognition or interest in his blank stare, I missed it.

"Hello, Shambler," I said anyway.

"Uuuuuuuuugggggggggghhhhhhhh," moaned the zombie, taking his time to emit the long grunt. Perhaps it was in response to my greeting, but there was no way to say for certain.

"He's getting talkative in his old age," I said. "That was nearly two syllables."

"Want some lunch?" Oliver asked me.

"I just had breakfast."

"You're a growing boy," he said. "Growing back from nothing at all. I need to fatten you up."

Before I could stop him, he was frying up whatever he had on hand in a pan on the stove.

"You'll eat some more, perk up a bit, and then you can tell me how it was you came to this sorry condition."

Θ

By the time I was done getting another real meal in me, I was
feeling considerably better. My voice was returning, for one. It
was still hushed and raspy, but it wasn't so tiring to speak anymore. I was able to share a truncated version of my not-so-
recent adventures with Oliver, who listened like I was recount-
ing a comedy of errors that was too ridiculous to laugh at.
Mostly he sat there shaking his head, until I realized he wasn't
showing dismay or disbelief about everything I'd been through.
It was disappointment.

"What's wrong?" I finally asked, as the day stretched into
evening and I couldn't take the look on his face any longer.

Oliver got out of his chair and approached me.

"You're a dabbler, you are," declared Oliver, and smacked
me across the back of the head. Hard. My skull was still too soft
for that sort of treatment, and the blow didn't leave a mark so
much as a dent.

"Ow!" I declared, letting my pain be known.

"Don't fucking dabble in it if you've got the stones to do it
right!"

"I do what I can with what I have," I said.

"No, you piss about and half-ass things. The talent you have
and what do you do?"

"I try to make a living."

"And you can't even do that properly! At least if you sold
out to make some money... That I would understand. I
wouldn't respect it, but I'd understand it."

"I've had my share of success in the business," I said.

"Oh, have you now?"

Oliver sounded unconvinced, and I was determined to
show him I'd made good. It was only then that I remembered
that, in fact, I had.

"I'll have you know, I've actually become fabulously wealthy," I announced.

"You don't look so prosperous."

"This was only a minor setback," I insisted, referring to my current lack of cash, possessions, or a fully functional body. "Just before my untimely demise, I came into a fortune. It should still be safely squirrelled away in Switzerland."

"You become a fancy millionaire digging up the dead then?"

Oliver didn't sound impressed, and likely thought I was lying through my brand-new set of teeth. He knew it was a tough business, and after decades at it, he'd had about as little luck monetizing it as me. Nevertheless, I doubled down. The figure of my discovered fortune was still rattling around inside my freshly reconstituted brain.

"Millionaire?" I scoffed. "Try multiplying that by ten."

"Billionaire, is it?" Oliver scoffed right back at me.

"I said multiply by ten, not a thousand. Ten million. I have over ten million dollars in the bank."

"The fuck you do!"

"I'll show you. Do you have an internet connection?"

"Of course I don't have a bleeding internet connection. You see how old I am, don't you?"

Oliver was an even bigger technophobe than I was. No internet, no cell phone. He probably had a landline, but considered it a passing fad.

"Fine, we'll go out. I'm sure there must be an internet café around here somewhere."

I wasn't really ready to go outside again, and I certainly wasn't ready to be observed closely by anyone. But it was late, it was dark, and a pair of sweat pants, a hoodie with the hood up, and sunglasses had me nearly completely covered. It may have been premature to pass myself off as a normal human in public, but pride demanded I show Oliver how wrong he was about me as soon as possible following our argument.

"C'mon, Shambler. Want to go walkies? Walkies! There's a good boy," said Oliver, popping a hat on his companion's dead head.

Any worry I had about drawing attention was alleviated by the zombie third-wheel Oliver was bringing to the café with us.

"Are you sure no one's going to notice him?" I asked. I was compelled to make my concern known. The last time I had taken a zombie for a walk, I did it with a sizeable degree of stealth and fear of discovery.

"What's to notice?" asked Oliver.

"The way he walks, for one. He looks like a zombie."

"He looks like an alcoholic. Plenty of those in the neighbourhood. Besides, I need to air him out every now and then. And he could use a good stretch of the legs to keep him limber."

Θ

The nearest internet café was only six blocks away, and Oliver correctly called it: nobody gave us a second glance. Oliver looked like a harmless old man, Shambler looked like a drunk, and I looked like a pasty chav bringing up the rear, trying to decide which of the two I should rob.

At the café, I gave Oliver instructions on how to go about buying us a short block of time on one of the computers. Once we were at our assigned station, we sat down while Shambler stood hovering between us. I was getting the feeling back in my fingertips and was able to poke my way around the keyboard until I brought up the website for The Benziger-Obrist Kantonalbank in Zurich. The login information and account number I had stumbled onto years earlier was still branded into my synapses. How could I ever forget the details of my greatest recovery operation?

"Would you like to be amazed in dollars or pounds?" I asked, poising the mouse cursor over the exchange-rate buttons.

"Wealth always seems to sound better in dollars," said Oliver, bracing himself for the big reveal. I could see he was starting to believe, was anticipating being impressed. For people who deal in real mysticism like us, this was the sort of magic trick that could still amaze.

I clicked through to the account and unveiled the current balance as it stood, with another few years of interest piled on top of it. I expected to see eight figures, but there were only two, and they were both after a decimal point. There was currently eighteen cents left in the account. And it was all mine.

"So how much is that in pounds?" Oliver wanted to know. "Or should we add it up in pence?"

I checked the account history and saw that the entire fortune had all been transferred out to some other account at some other bank. First in dribs and drabs, then whopping great chunks, until the last few hundred thousand vanished in the blink of a digital eye over a year ago.

"Mind if I crash at your place for a little while longer?" I asked.

"I should start charging rent," Oliver scoffed.

"Will you accept a cheque for eighteen cents? I'm good for it."

☉

I slept poorly that night, though it wasn't my financial woes that interfered with my rest. Easy come, easy go was my well-reasoned position on that. It hadn't really been my money in the first place, and now it indisputably wasn't. Not so many days ago, I was dead and gone and beyond financial worries. Being subject to monetary concerns again was strangely reassuring. It reminded me I was alive once more.

Even so, I lay there in bed, troubled by the twinge of back pain I'd long suffered, and feeling anxious about my future now that I had one again. I wondered if the back pain was part of my anxiety. Surely it was all in my head. The root cause of my pain should have been burned away in the fire and subsequent cremation that had destroyed my body. But it lingered, returned again like the one white eye. Some marks can't be erased.

I was still awake to hear the pub crowd let out after last call, the loud alcohol-fuelled chatter, the starting engines of drunk drivers headed home. And also, in those early hours, the distant howl of some large animal, making its presence and its displeasure known to all within earshot.

Chapter Three

A Dog's Breakfast

"LOOK AT THIS! Didn't I tell you? Fuckin' dog shat right on my lawn."

I recognized the booming voice of Oliver's neighbour. It was right under the window of the guest room at the front of the house. Crawling out of bed, I pulled the curtain aside so I could see what was going on.

"A dog did that?" said Oliver below, looking over at the throw-rug's worth of lawn belonging to the next row house over.

"What else?"

"A horse perhaps?"

I saw the mound of excrement they were discussing. It was piled high, but didn't look much like the oat-and-straw road apples you'd ever see fall out of a horse.

"Come off it," said the neighbour, "there ain't no horses trotting up and down the lanes here. Besides, I heard it barking and howling again last night, didn't you?"

"Slept like a baby," said Oliver. "I must have missed it."

I got in the shower rather than listen to any more of the exchange. I'd been at Oliver's for a week, and my hair was coming in. It was still mostly peach fuzz, but I shampooed it anyway, like that might provoke quicker growth.

I was discouraged by how long it was taking me to bounce back. Of course, I'd never attempted to regenerate my entire body from virtually nothing before. My teeth were finished growing and I could eat properly at last. Things were beginning to speed up, though it amazed me how much food had to be consumed to replace every single cell in my body. It amounted to a lot of meals and, worst of all, it was British food.

I threw on a bathrobe and came downstairs to find Oliver salting the threshold of the back door. He had the top of the shaker unscrewed and was pouring a narrow trail from one side of the door frame to the other, muttering something I didn't recognize in a language that sounded like Polish to me.

"What's up, Oliver?" I asked.

"Just keeping pests out," he said.

"You getting snails inside now, too?"

"No, not yet. But a barrier of salt will keep all sorts of nasties away."

I nodded like I accepted what he was saying at face value. Snails weren't likely to cross a line of salt. Not without shrivelling up and dying. But then, salt could act as a stop sign for things far worse than garden-invading mollusks. What I'd heard him muttering seemed to be an incantation, and unless I was way off, Oliver was casting some sort of ward. He repeated the ritual at the front door as well.

"Are snails going to bust in from the street as well?" I asked.

"You never know."

"You should call an exterminator to get rid of them all."

"Or a Frenchman," Oliver commented.

Having poured the final grains out of the vessel, he screwed the cap back on.

"We need salt," he said, tossing me the empty shaker.

"Great," I said. "How am I supposed to choke down your cooking now?"

"Go out and pick up some groceries, you lazy bastard."

"Looking like this?"

"You're coming along," he declared, after judging how much my appearance had improved overnight. "Won't be long now, you can get back out into the world, reunite with your friends, move forward like nothing happened."

"I'm not so sure about that," I said. "A lot of time has passed. Too much time. They must all think I'm gone for good. And it's never easy coming back when everyone you know thinks you died for real."

"You've managed it before."

"Not since I was a child. Even then it involved major relocations—a whole new life with new people. I don't want to have to start over."

"These friends of yours back home, they know about what you do, what you're capable of?"

"To varying degrees, yeah."

"Give them a try. They'll adjust."

I was unconvinced. Adjust people too much and they break.

"Have you ever died?" I asked Oliver.

"Do you think I'd still be here if I had?"

"I mean died and come back."

"I've never tried. And I wouldn't if I could. One round of all this is quite enough for me."

"I can't even count the number of times I've died," I lamented. "I used to think I was keeping track, but it turns out I've been dying over and over again since the day I was born."

"And how do you feel about that?"

I had to think about it for a good long while before I concluded, "Lonely."

Oliver nodded like he knew exactly what I was talking about.

"A strange talent keeps everyone at bay. The stranger it is, the more strangers it creates."

"Ever hear of anyone else with my condition? Someone else in the business maybe?"

"You've met other necromancers. Have you ever met one who can do what you do?"

"No."

"Me neither. Maybe it's time to consider whether this unique talent of yours wasn't a gift, but a curse."

"You mean an actual curse? Something maliciously intended by an outside party?"

"I do."

I gave the notion a moment to sink in.

"I've been able to die and come back since I was a kid. Who would have had it in for me back then?"

"Who can say? You were the one who was mucking about with time travel. That leaves too many possibilities open. Too many points in your life an enemy can strike at you. Rule number one: stay the hell away from time travel."

"You never told me that."

"I'm sure I must have."

"I didn't even know time travel was possible until I was already travelling through time! It wouldn't have come as such a surprise if you'd let me know that could happen."

"I suppose it slipped my mind. It's such a rare event, and there were so many other things to teach you about."

"How long have you suspected I was cursed?" I asked Oliver.

"Day one," he recalled after some contemplation.

"You could have said something."

"All young men feel like they're going to live forever. In your case, that feeling appears to be right. Would you have believed me if I'd told you that was a terrible thing? Do you believe me even now?"

"I'm not sure," I admitted.

"You've got some sort of perpetual afterlife situation going on. I don't envy you."

Oliver's outlook had changed with the years. He hadn't always been so pessimistic. I was the pessimistic one.

"Since when are you so down on the afterlife?" I asked.

"Since I survived long enough to get this old. Now the less I hear about life after death, the better."

"The company you keep seems to be a constant reminder," I pointed out, watching Shambler do his chores at a molasses pace.

"Does that look like a life to you?"

"That's what you called it when you said you'd won your afterlife argument with him."

"I don't remember saying anything of the sort."

"So you don't believe in one anymore?"

"Oh, we both know there are plenty of lingering spirits and such. You could always chat them up easier than me, but I know they're there. Do I want that for myself? I should fucking say not," Oliver spat. "Having lived a whole life, why would I want more tacked on at the end? Afterlife? Aftertaste more like, and a bad one at that. It sits in your mouth, reminding you of what you just ate. It might have been fine when you were actually eating it, but now the taste is just a reminder of what once was. And the longer it sits your mouth, mixing with your acids and your enzymes, it starts to go sour, until it doesn't taste anything like the delicious meal you once had. It tastes bitter and old and you can't wait to wash it away with a long drink of water."

"Or a pint of beer," I suggested.

"Now there's a thought!" said Oliver, brightening up. "Care to pop 'round my local?"

It was still light out. There would be people in the street, more in the pub.

"I don't know if I'm up to seeing people yet. Civilians, I mean."

"It's more a matter of if they're ready to see you." Oliver looked me over again and added, "You're more or less present-able now. You look sickly, but you don't look dead, so there's a start. Let's try you out in mixed company and see if you can pass for human. Besides, a good stout or two will help put hair back on your chest."

Θ

"It's a tad cruel, don't you think?"

"How so?" asked Oliver, who was blind to my point.

"I thought Jehovah's Witnesses don't believe in Christmas."

"He's non-practising."

For the holidays, Shambler was outfitted in a more festive set of clothes. Oliver had tucked him into a tacky reindeer-themed woollen sweater and a Santa hat. The pine-scented air freshener around his neck was the usual brand, but this one had been altered with a number of coloured pens to look like a Christmas tree decked out in a rainbow of bulbs and decorations. He looked very holly and jolly.

"Nuuuuuuuurrrrrrrrrgggggggggghhh," Shambler moaned, almost but not quite in time with the Christmas music that played over the radio.

Days, as they tend to, had become weeks, and the weeks had stacked up on each other until they were months. By the time Oliver had harvested his late-season radishes, I'd been fully healed. Now, weeks beyond that, we were having the last of them as part of our Christmas dinner. I felt like a bird that had outgrown the nest, but Oliver failed to push me out, refused to force me to fly before I was ready. Maybe he just liked the company. I was rather more chatty and challenging than

Shambler, and I could run certain errands that were beyond the zombie help—like going out for lottery tickets and beer.

I set Shambler to tidy up after dinner while Oliver and I, at his insistence, sat down for a sacred tradition.

"Scrooge. Alastair Sim. The best," stated Oliver as the movie started.

"How many times have you seen this?"

"I watch it every year. Have done since my family could afford a telly."

"A horror movie about ghosts and death," I said disapprovingly. "Can't you watch normal Christmas movies like everyone else?"

"Like what?"

"I don't know. Like *White Christmas* or something."

"I fucking hate Bing Crosby. Child-beating wanker."

"Something else then. *It's a Wonderful Life*."

"Oh, you mean the one about the fella who wants to commit suicide on Christmas Eve and gets shown a vision of his own personal hell until he repents? That normal Christmas movie, then?"

"Bad example."

"You ever notice how many Christmas movies are about horror and violence and end times?"

"Aside from the three million adaptations of *A Christmas Carol*, no."

"Run through a list of Christmas movies sometime, you'll see for yourself. Violence, violence, violence, death, horror, mayhem. Merry Christmas."

"I'm sure they've cut off my cable by now."

"This will always be my favourite, though. It was the first movie I ever saw, just a few years after we immigrated and I was old enough to nip off on my own. It was magic."

"Wait," I said, "you're not English?"

"I wasn't born in Blighty, no."

"Your accent says otherwise," I informed him.

"My parents were Czech. I was a Czech. For the first six years of my life anyway, during the war. We got out just as the guns fell silent, before the Soviets streamed in and claimed the whole country as their own. London is where we landed, and after trimming a few syllables off our name, Londoners we became. Or, at least, I did. My parents struggled with the language to the end."

"And there I was, back when we first met, thinking I was having such a Londonesque experience, sharing pints with an authentic cockney geezer."

"I'm as authentic as they come. More so. After the things I saw in the war, I embraced life here, let me tell you. Before I was ten years old, I was more English than cricket. It helped give me some distance from the homeland, which is exactly what I needed at that age."

I'd done the math before and calculated Oliver had been around for the war. I figured he'd spent his childhood on the receiving end of The Blitz, never guessing he'd experienced a much more personal war in one of the hottest hot zones of mainland Europe.

"What was it like," I asked, "being right in the middle of it so young?"

"I don't have many strong childhood memories from before our arrival in England. What I have are visions scored into my infant brain. Things no one should have to witness, least of all a child."

Oliver wasn't watching the television any longer. His eyes were fixed on the supernatural rehabilitation of Ebenezer Scrooge, but it was no longer registering. He was decades in the past, reliving a memory that was always replaying in the back of his mind.

"The thing I remember best happened in the last year of the war. At that point, my whole life, I'd known nothing but a world with men at each other's throats. Bombs and bodies, infernos and dismemberment. Even at such a young age, it was compelling somehow. Children who are forced to deal with death too early react in strange ways. Survival mechanism, I suppose. Me, I embraced it, obsessed over it. I wanted to understand it, not realizing most adults grow into old age and never figured it out."

There was a catch in his voice before he continued, like he was contemplating whether to go on or not. But the memory loop was already clocking forward, with or without him, and he continued to narrate it aloud. My being in the room was almost incidental.

"We'd all heard about the truckload of Jews they'd shot and buried by the side of the road. My village was close by. Close enough to have heard each shot fired into the men in the ditch, one after the other. I can still hear them echoing through the strip of woods that separated our village from the road. No one left their house that day. No one wanted to get involved. Everyone feared there were more than enough bullets left for them. But me, stupid child that I was, I wanted to see for myself. The next morning I was up before anyone else. I dressed myself—a new trick I'd only recently learned—and then I was out the door."

Oliver had to wet his throat with a swig of beer before his mouth could catch up with his recollection.

"The road had been trampled to mud overnight by all the refugees leaving the burning city a few miles off. By the time I arrived on it, they were all gone. There was nothing but footprints through the puddles and personal belongings abandoned in the dirt. Everything was such a mess, I could hardly spot where the earth had been piled over the corpses. I would have passed it by completely if not for the man."

"What man was this?" I asked, suddenly worried I might already know who.

"The man who rose from the dead," said Oliver.

I said nothing, not wanting to prompt him, not wanting him to continue.

"That mass grave opened up in front of me, just a crack, just enough to spit one of the dead back out. First his hands, then his head, then a whole torso. He came crawling out of the mud, right at me, all covered in blood and filth. And then he spoke. And do you know what he said to me?"

"Boo," I said, because I knew.

"As a matter of fact, that's exactly what he said. Good guess. He weren't no ghost though. No, not that one. He was a real, honest-to-gosh dead man who'd come crawling out of the grave to live some more."

"What did you do?" I asked, even though I remembered it well.

"I ran. I ran as fast as my little legs could carry me, all the way home. And once I was home, I hid under the covers and didn't come out again until night had fallen and I was starving to get some bread into me. My parents thought I'd fallen ill, but I never felt better. I felt alive like I never had before because I knew, for the first time, that death wasn't all there was. Death could be defeated. And that moment, on that day, set the course for the rest of my life."

I wanted to tell Oliver how sorry I was—for the war, for the awful childhood, and for a life-changing moment that should never have happened. But it was too big a notion to express.

"I didn't dare set foot on that road again. Not until my whole family was forced to take it, trying to make it to the British lines ahead of Stalin's army. My father always told me, he'd rather I be dead than raised a communist."

Oliver smiled at the thought of the existence behind the iron curtain he'd been spared and took another drink.

"Once we were here, life moved on, and I went from being a little Czech kid to a big British boy. For years I thought maybe what I saw was some childhood dream, or a flight of fancy, or some such made up shite. But it happened. I knew it happened, and I thought I was the one who must've done it. And that's when I started down this path. I wanted to see if I could make it happen again."

I tried to broach the subject that weighed on me as delicately as I could.

"You ever consider that maybe it wasn't you—that little Czech-kid you—who raised the dead that day?"

"I don't suppose it matters now, does it?" said Oliver. "I chose my path, I followed it here. And here is where we are."

"I thought I'd chosen my path, long ago. Now I'm not so sure," I pondered. "I feel like somewhere out that door is the life I'm supposed to be living. And maybe it's not full of dead bodies and ghosts and ghouls and shit like that. Maybe I have been cursed, and the best way to uncurse myself is to ignore it all and go live a normal life."

"A normal life," Oliver echoed.

"Yeah."

"Is that what you want?"

"Don't I?" I asked.

Oliver turned to the screen for a moment, to watch Alastair Sim beg the Ghost of Christmas Yet to Come for another chance, and downed the last of his beer.

"Be the man you were meant to be, Rip Eulogy. If that's your name, wear it, and fuck all the rest."

It was the first time Oliver Franck ever said my professional moniker aloud. He'd laughed at me the day I came up with it. He'd held it in contempt ever since. Too showy, too literal, too silly. Why operate under such an obviously false name? What was wrong with my real name? Of course, this was before he'd told me he'd lived his own life under an assumed identity—one that was less fake, less show-biz, but no less a fabrication.

Neither of us were who we were born to be. Our names, our occupations, were a choice.

It was nice to hear him say my name—what had become my real name for all intents and purposes. It flowed off his tongue naturally. And it was also the last time I ever heard him say it.

Θ

I had a difficult night, neither restful nor refreshing. Normally I'm not troubled by dreams, good or bad, but I remember sensations and images that can only be described as nightmares. I thought my routine dealings with corpses and living-dead creatures had immunized me against any sleepy-time terrors more stressful than scenarios concerning public nudity or missed school exams, but apparently even necromancers aren't exempt from all the hair-raising horrors a subconscious mind can throw at them.

It was the heat I remember the most, like a blasting vent blowing into my face in waves I thought might peel the flesh right off me. By the time I woke up, the pillow was drenched with sweat and my face was still dripping. When I felt my forehead, my hand came away wet, but also sticky. My hair was slicked back and my skin felt like it was glazed with a layer of mucus. I wondered if it was a residual effect of recovery—my new body's final effort to expel some of the impurities it had been forced to work with during the initial stages of regrowth, before I was able to feed it better construction material.

Whatever I might have secreted in my fevered sleep was gone and I no longer felt so hot. In fact, I had become quite chilled in the wet bedding. A warm shower fixed me right up, and the slimy film on my skin washed away down the drain easily.

I came downstairs, dressed for breakfast, to the distinct smell of nothing on the stove. Most mornings, Oliver would have been in the middle of a frenzied fry-up, but there was no activity at all. Resigned to a morning of cereal flakes in slightly expired milk, I went looking for Oliver and found him exactly where I thought he might be—sitting in his armchair in front of the television. After a few beers and a late-night Christmas-themed film fest, he'd dozed off and never made it to bed. I was about to offer to pour him his own bowl of breakfast cereal when I noticed he wouldn't be joining me in the kitchen nook.

Oliver had been decapitated in the night.

I wanted to summon his spirit back at once so I could ask what happened, but I needed the physical remains of a brain to do that. There was no brain. There was no head. It looked like it had been chewed right off. By a messy eater no less.

"Did you do this?" I asked Shambler, who was in the corner of the living room, staring at a random point between me and his later master. He had nothing to say, nothing to grunt.

I didn't blame him for his lack of response. It was an offensive question. Zombies get a bad rap when it comes to eating people—brains in particular. Popular culture has some pretty weird ideas about the dead. It's a cruel bias that makes racism seem quaint. The fact is, zombies don't eat people, or body parts, or anything at all actually. The cliché arises from times they've been expressly ordered to chew on somebody's fingers or bite off a nose. A loyal zombie is compelled to obey. Ugly anecdotes told by witnesses who didn't understand the mechanics at work get repeated over and over again and, the next thing you know, a simple misapprehension is a lucrative multi-media cottage industry.

No, Shambler didn't do it. He probably only watched stupidly, unable to stop it or intervene without a command to do so. And poor Oliver, taken by surprise, was too busy getting eaten to issue an intelligible demand of his loyal servant.

A quick search of the small home revealed no culprit, but the point of entry and exit was obvious. The back door was splintered and barely hanging on its hinges. I looked for evidence of what had come and gone in the night, but the remaining swirls of blood tracked across the floor were few and indistinct. Shambler had mopped most of them up in the wake of Oliver's death.

I didn't know who or what had done this to my friend, but I knew whose fault it was: mine.

With Oliver asleep in his chair, and me keen to tuck myself in, I had handed off to the help. In my haste to order Shambler to tidy up, I hadn't been specific enough about my wishes. I only wanted him to do the dishes. Instead, he'd spend the night cleaning the house and, most damningly, sweeping the floor. In the process, he had swept up Oliver's lines of salt that had been dutifully maintained and replenished for months. With the ward brushed into a dust pan, its effect was spoiled. Oliver had never shared what it was he'd been trying to ward off, and I hadn't asked. He'd never been candid about any of his projects or sidelines in all the time I'd known him, and I had trusted him to have things well in hand. Now that I needed to ask him what was going on, it was impossible to do so. There had been something more sinister than snails he didn't want crawling into the house. Whatever it was, it wasn't St. Nick. This thing didn't come down the chimney, it broke through the back door, suddenly and violently. And I had slept right through the attack.

I stepped outside into the chill morning air to see if there were any other hints or clues for me in the yard. There was no snow on the ground to capture prints, but the grass was lightly frosted from the winter night's temperature plunge. Embedded in those morning crystals, melted into the light layer of ice, I could see animal tracks. Each paw print was as big as my own foot.

Chapter Four

Night Terrors

BAILING ON OLIVER'S BODY and the scene of the crime seemed a cowardly move, but I saw no other option, really. I couldn't explain what had happened to him, to bureaucratic authorities least of all. As far as they would be concerned, I was some undocumented illegal, landed in the country unannounced, and a prime suspect in a grisly murder the tabloids were going to adore. I didn't even want to think about what they'd make of their other person-of-interest—a zombie ex-Jehovah's Witness who had died and vanished decades earlier. Maybe they'd have better luck identifying him than Oliver had, but any answer on that front would only lead to more unanswerable questions. It all seemed a terrible mess best avoided.

Plus there was some gigantic head-hunting hound prowling the neighbourhood that might come back for seconds at any moment.

It was time to go home. I was fuzzy about how exactly I was going to accomplish this with no money or passport, but first thing was first. Something had to be done about poor old Shambler—masterless, rudderless, lost. I considered putting him down myself, but that felt wrong. Mindless zombie servant though he was, I'd long regarded him as a real person, even though he was hardly anything more than an ambulatory appliance. He felt like a friend, almost as much as Oliver had. The two would forever be associated in my mind and, sentimental as it seemed, I didn't want to part with both of them at once.

"Off you go," I told Shambler that night, long after the sun had set and the streets had cleared. "You're free. No more orders to follow. Go live your life—such as it is."

He'd always followed my commands if Oliver wasn't around to outrank me. In that moment, the old necromancer's corpse-companion looked to his headless master for instructions that would belie my own. None were forthcoming. At last he turned and plodded out the open front door and into the street. He stood in the road for a long while, forced to decide whether to wander off left or right. It was the most complex decision he'd had to make on his own in years. Left finally won the arduous mental coin flip, and away he went, to a future fate that, I'll admit, didn't look so bright. The pom-pom of his Santa hat bobbed behind him with each liberated step.

☉

I would have taken Shambler with me if I could have, but I wasn't confident my fledgling plan to escape across the ocean was going to work out for one body, let alone two. Early the next morning I raided Oliver's wallet and the emergency stash of cash he kept in a shoe box in his bedroom closet. There were supplies to be purchased, arrangements to be made. I wanted to be gone by the following day at the latest.

Popping by for a visit with Oliver's loud neighbour was at the top of my list. Since I'd moved in next door, we'd hardly done more than nod a greeting at each other, but I was hoping I could prevail on him being neighbourly enough to do me a favour. I didn't have to ring his bell on my way to the office-supply shop. He was already outside, fuming.

"You see this?" he said to me before I could even offer a greeting. "I swear I wouldn't mind so much if only I could catch him at it."

The man was standing over the latest offering that had been deposited on his lawn. The copious pile of enormous turds reeked from where I stood. I approached regardless.

"I'd love to get a look at the mutt so I'll know whose dog it is what thinks my house is its own personal toilet."

"I'm guessing it's not the Chihuahua at the end of the block."

You could have buried half a dozen Chihuahuas in the mound.

"I just want to know what they're feeding the fucking thing," said the neighbour.

I already knew no one was feeding it. It was helping itself to whatever it cared to. Attuned as I was to the presence of necrotic remains, I could tell the animal had gorged itself on a variety of urban wildlife and domesticated pets—possibly that very Chihuahua at the end of the block. Plus there was something else in the mix. Even at a casual glance, I spotted shards of chewed-up bone that had to have been from a large skull. And judging from the curvature, it hadn't belonged to any animal.

"I was wondering if I could ask you for some help with a little errand," I began, switching subjects.

"What's that, then?" he asked, suspicious about how little the errand might be compared to how big a pain in the ass it might become.

"I'm leaving—moving on—and I'm not going to be around to help out Oliver anymore," I began. "The thing is, he's got a package he needs to post tomorrow. It's kind of big and fairly heavy, and I worry about a fellow his age trying to carry it himself. I was wondering if you'd be able to run it down to the post office for him if he leaves it out on the front steps."

"I supposed I could manage that for Ollie, sure," he said, after a quick think about it.

"Well then," he added, "I guess if this is goodbye, I should know your name to wish you bon voyage."

"It's Bill," I lied.

"Reggie," he replied, offering his hand for a shake. "Good to know you, Bill."

I started to head down the path, but Reggie called after me.

"Say Bill," he said, "maybe you could return that favour in advance..."

Reggie stepped inside and disappeared behind his open front door. He returned a moment later with a folded garbage bag and a trowel and tried to hand them to me.

"If you wouldn't mind," he said, looking down at the mess on his lawn. "The big bugger could have just as easily done it on your lawn, don't you think? Share the burden and it don't seem such a burden no more, I always say."

I smiled thinly and accepted the bag and trowel.

"True enough," I agreed.

$$\Theta$$

I had communicated with brain matter in poor and degraded conditions before, but never as trace elements in dog shit. The only way to know if such a thing were possible was to try. I've never felt like such an idiot as I did standing there, on a moderately busy residential London street, discreetly chatting with an enormous pile of excrement. If I weren't so keen to find out what had happened, so eager to share a final word with Oliver, I would never have lowered myself to attempt it.

"Oliver?" I asked the heap of stinking waste. "Are you there? Can you hear me?"

"No," was the distinct thought that penetrated my mind.

"No, you can't hear me?"

"No. Not. There."

I was definitely picking up hints of consciousness from trace morsels in the scat, but it was muddled, indistinct, like it had been divided too many times.

"Where then?" I asked, hoping to identify where a greater concentration of consciousness, better able to carry on a conversation, might be found.

"Inside," was the only answer offered. I was only getting a trailing end of Oliver's thoughts, from what few grey cells made it out the ass-end of the beast that ate his head right off his shoulders.

"Inside what?"

I could feel the connection fading. There just wasn't enough to go on. What brain matter was left was too diluted, distilled, drained of what had once made Oliver Oliver.

"Gwyllgi," was that last thing I heard before the line went dead. It was gibberish, useless. He was too far gone. Or maybe I was just rusty.

I finished scraping the muck off the grass and into the trash bag before tying it off and dropping it at the curb.

Whatever unnatural thing Oliver had run afoul of, it wasn't my problem. Friends or not, he must have known what he was up against and chose not to share it with me. It wasn't my place to seek vengeance against something I knew nothing about and understood even less. Gigantic man-eating devil-dogs sounded like a problem for animal control, not an out-of-practice necromancer who wasn't even on his home turf. I resolved to distance myself from the situation and hope the dispute—whatever it was—had ended with Oliver's life, and a final territory-marking squat on the neighbour's lawn.

Θ

I spent Boxing Day fitting myself for boxes. I needed something large enough to fit in, but sturdy enough to make the
trip without coming open at an inopportune moment due to
mishandling by postal workers spread across two continents.
Having weighed myself on the bathroom scale, I also tried to
judge the dimensions of the package I would be posting. When
I calculated the total of how much shipping would cost, I
bought several rolls of stamps at a corner shop to cover it, with
a few extra just to make sure my package wouldn't be rejected
for insufficient postage. It was a costly affair, and ate most of
Oliver's reserves. Air mail was out of reach, but surface mail
suited me better. I expected less scrutiny for crates leaving by
ship. The last thing I needed was some paranoid security-
obsessed airport agent plucking my box out of the back of a
loading bay for a random inspection, and taking a peek inside
for contraband or anything else not specifically listed on the customs slip.

I purposely didn't punch any air holes in the box and, in
fact, went out of my way to seal all the cracks with packing tape
from the inside. The plan was to suffocate myself within the first
couple of hours of transit so I wouldn't have to make the long,
uncomfortable journey stuck in a physical body that would still
need to go through certain biological necessities before I
reached my destination. Once I was out of my body, I could tag
along as a spirit, within quick reanimation distance of my physical remains.

I would have preferred to have been long gone already, but
my escape scheme required me to wait for the post offices to
reopen on the 27th. Until then, I was trapped in Oliver's house,
with his headless body and no real options. Out of cash, I
couldn't even check into a hotel room if I'd wanted. There
wasn't much to do but barricade myself indoors, hope Oliver's
personal demon didn't come back for another helping, and
clock the final hours before my departure.

The back door was the highest priority, if for no other reason than to keep the cold out. It was a broken, splintered mess, but I propped up what I could, pushing it back into its frame and taping it in place with extra adhesive strips to seal the more prominent gaps. It wouldn't hold up to anything stronger than a stiff breeze, but it did its part to keep most of the heating inside the house where it belonged.

After making sure all the windows were properly shut and locked, I decided to pour a couple of new salt lines by the front and back doors, just in case. I knew a few warding incantations, but I didn't know which one Oliver had used, and had no clue if any of mine would be appropriate. Rather than undo any lingering effect of Oliver's spell that might still be in play, I restricted myself to replacing the reagent element of his ward, and hoped it might shore up that line of defence for one additional night. There was no use in my doing more and screwing it up any further than I already had. Any supplementary supernatural precautions I took against another nocturnal visitation would have to be my own original material. But by the time the sun had set, I'd come up with nothing. Without knowing what I was trying to fend off, there was no way to guess an appropriate countermeasure. Until I saw it face to face—assuming it had a face at all—I wouldn't know what to throw at it. And even then, I was assuming I would recognize this whatever-it-was when I saw it. There was no guarantee of that. I'd seen heaping tons of weird and twisted beings in my time, but that didn't make me an expert on all things unnatural. Some creatures of the night are common, some are rare. And still others are wholly unique and beyond my ability to deal with until I've had time to study the problem. Whatever this hungry hound was, it didn't sound like it was going to sit around long enough for me to make a thorough evaluation before it tried to gnaw my head off. If it came bursting through the door again that night, I didn't expect to have more than a couple of seconds to spot it, identify it, and defend myself against it.

Sleep wouldn't have been a prudent move, and was impossible anyway. I settled in for the night sitting in the chair opposite Oliver's remains, much as we had been sitting on our last night together. If not for the missing head and the mess of dried blood and dog drool, we might have been having a pleasant conversation. As it was, I let the TV do the talking, turning it to a channel that had a time code in the corner so I could watch the long night pass. The blather about current events I felt completely disconnected from filled the silence, but mostly stretched the time, reminding me how long it could take to say absolutely nothing of value whatsoever.

It was two in the morning when the beast first made its presence known. The thud on the roof was so loud, I thought someone had dropped a cinderblock on it. Moments later, there were footsteps— a set of four, with the scratching report of long claws gripping the shingles with each stride. The television and single lamp switched off without me even touching them, and a heavy thud out back announced that the creature had made landfall in Oliver's yard. Fleeing out the front door seemed an obvious option, but I wasn't willing to wager I could outrun my visitor on only two legs.

The remains of the back door creaked and rustled as they were pushed in. The animal could have shredded them in a moment and entered at will, but this was a gentle prodding. The renewed ward may have been holding, or at least discouraging. I rose from my chair and crept close to the kitchen in time to see one of the tape seams tear away from the splintered wood it was stuck to. An enormous black snout pushed through and probed the empty space beyond, sniffing and snorting. Billowing clouds of vapour erupted from the twin stovepipe nostrils, even though the winter air wasn't nearly cold enough to account for so much streaming breath.

I swallowed my panic. Sticking around had been a calculated risk. Incorrectly, I had bet that the visits would end with Oliver's death. Even so, now that the beast had returned, I still clung to the hope that it was only back to finish feeding on his corpse—that this siege was still strictly between Oliver and his haunting hound. Best, I resolved, to just get the hell out of its way.

A door in the kitchen led down to the cellar, so that's the route I took. I knew that would leave me cornered, with no avenue of escape, but I opted for a defendable barricaded position rather than the open peril of full retreat.

The snorting nose poking inside seemed to track me as I crossed the narrow stretch and slipped into the basement. No sooner had I closed one door behind me than I heard the mangled ruin of taped-together wood slowly tear away from its frame and collapse onto the linoleum. The dog was inside the house.

A latch on the cellar-side of the door allowed me to lock it, but could hardly be expected to withstand more than a few hard knocks before the short screws tore right out. I descended the stairs and pulled the chain on the bare overhead bulb to light the way. It flickered badly before finally agreeing to cast a dull glow. Oliver's basement was familiar to me, but I hadn't been down there since the days of my original tutelage under him. There was no way to anticipate what he might have in stock. Like any senior citizen, his home was filled with items he'd owned for many years, interspersed with new ones that were added to replenish what got used up regularly. Oliver's cellar had functioned as both deep storage and a pantry—not a cook's pantry, but a necromancer's. Rather than new bags of sugar and old cans of soup, apples still reasonably fresh, and shrivelled potatoes with eyes that had grown into long stocks, there was a vastly different selection of produce and ingredients.

Dusty jars brimmed with preservatives and contained a wide array of necrotic tissue and body parts, saved from long-forgotten biopsies, autopsies, and medical studies. Other items were stored more loosely after being appropriately dried, mummified, or ground into powder. Oliver was always in the market for inexpensive bits and pieces. You never knew when a spare ear or toe might come in handy for a job. Regardless of how uncommon such a demand might be, Oliver came prepared, and was rarely caught shorthanded of hands when one was needed. I would argue with him that it wasn't worth keeping such a comprehensive inventory, year upon year, for every what-if scenario that might never come up. But, I had to admit, he almost never had to run out to get a key element of an essential ritual in the middle of a gig. For my own part, I preferred to suffer the occasional inconvenience of having to make an impromptu graverobbing side-trip while working a case, rather than turn my home into an anatomy archive. It came down to a matter of style.

I might have spent the better part of the day in the cellar, ducking under the low-hanging beams, and cobbling together some sort of deathly deterrent to another home invasion, but it would have been a fool's errand. Oliver's filing system was abysmal, and only he knew where everything was. Besides, if there was any ammo in his arsenal better suited to deal with the problem at hand, he would have already used it to save himself. Now, however, with a man-eating monster loose in the same building, giving the inventory at least a cursory glance seemed time well spent.

I could hear the hound pacing around upstairs. It sounded impatient, agitated, and not the least bit interested in wolfing down Oliver's cold leftovers. Each time it passed back through the kitchen, it paused at the cellar door and scratched at it like any household pet that wanted access to a forbidden room. But these scratches were done with dagger claws, and I could hear the wood splintering under the assault. He would dig a hole right through the moment he committed to getting in.

Mentally leafing through a file of half-remembered spells and incantations I had never had cause to use, I couldn't match anything that came to mind with the reagents in stock—disorganized bounty that they were. Oliver seemed to have at least one of everything, a few items in bulk, and a number of doubles whenever natural anatomy offered parts in pairs. I was trying to remember one defensive ritual I'd read about, that could put the jar of pickled fingernails to use, when I spotted the skeleton.

Finding a human skeleton in among a necromancer's possessions was hardly unusual. I myself had a skull running the minutiae of my business back home. What struck me about the disassembled pile of bones in a box was that it was incomplete. So many of the bones came in pairs, left and right, I couldn't help but notice there was only the one femur. Maybe the other one had been pressed into service, used up, ground down, consumed or otherwise spent in the service of one of Oliver's jobs. It wasn't important. What was important was that the one remaining femur drew my attention and suggested a solution to my problem—a staggeringly stupid solution, so foolish it could work.

Give a dog a bone, is the thought that sprang to mind.

It seemed a long shot, a ridiculous notion to risk my latest life on. But it was the only thing I had going for me. A dog, a wolf, a hound—whatever it qualified as—my hope was that it liked the same things as the rest of its canine cousins. A femur, the longest, strongest bone in the human body, seemed like it might be the right size to tempt it. I only hoped it was big enough for the big boy.

As the snorting, clomping interloper upstairs made another circuit of the house, I crept back up to the door and cracked it open. The remains of the back door lay crumpled on the floor, and I was able to step over the debris and out into the yard without being noticed. I knew the beast would have my scent in a moment, once it made another pass, but my plan was to lead it away to where a real distraction could be arranged. All I had to do was survive for a few blocks.

I opened the lane gate and got ready to make my move. Running was pointless, and would only make me a more tempting target. The animal's focus had to be captivated by the treat I was offering or I was sunk. Tapping the head of the bone on the fence, I whistled like I was summoning a friendly pooch to play.

"Here boy!" I encouraged, "Here! Come get the yummies!"

Piercing red eyes appeared in the darkened kitchen and peered out through the gaping hole in the door frame. I didn't stick around for a better look and backed away down the lane, waving the bone back and forth like a flag. The sound of the heavy padded paws stepping across the hardened soil of Oliver's tiny garden was distinct in the lane that was otherwise silent with the winter chill and late hour.

I withdrew to the far end of the passage that ran behind identical rows of houses in time to see a dark figure push through the back gate and prowl after me. I rapped on the sidewalk with the femur and whistled once more, but I already knew I had the creature's undivided attention.

How it had crept around the city undetected was made evident as we worked our way down the road. Each porch and street light blinked out as the hound approached, and remained dark until it was well past the spot. The dog, itself pitch black, was further obscured by the darkness that answered to its presence, and not a single source of illumination failed to shrink away from it, as though in terror. I could hardly tell it was there at all, but for the steaming breath that billowed up out of the shadows, and the dimming of electric lights that tracked its progress.

I kept whistling and waving the bone, like it was just a game we were playing, hoping the dog would be patient enough to wait for the chew-toy I promised. If he wanted, he could take it from me, along with my whole arm, at any moment he cared to.

The walk to the brick wall at the north end of the district was a short one, but felt like the longest stroll of my life. It bordered the neighbourhood, acting as a barrier to both foot traffic and sound. Beyond it was the constant drone of vehicles passing along the A13 at all hours of the day and night, cutting their way through the heart of London. Once we were close enough, and I was satisfied I had pushed my luck to its limit, I made my move.

"Fetch!" I shouted, and hurled the femur end over end over the wall. A black mass, indistinct in the darkness that enveloped it, launched forward, straight at me. I ducked, sure it would split me in two and leave me splayed across the street as a top and bottom half, loosely connected by my spooled-out entrails. There was a discernable breeze as it leapt past me and bounded not over but through the brick barricade and into oncoming highway traffic. No sooner did the sound of shattered mortar settle, than the racket of swerving cars, honking horns, and screaming brakes rise to replace it. Metal impacting metal was next, one after the other, as a dozen car pile-up began to daisy chain down Newham Way with a series of fender benders, blown tires, and whiplashes that would be the talk of the morning traffic report. Nothing exploded or burst into flames, which I was grateful for. I had hoped to turn the thing dogging my heels into an unfortunate roadkill statistic, but I hadn't counted on how much disruption and possible death his sudden appearance in the middle of the A13 might cause. Thankfully, I could detect no new casualties entering the ether in my vicinity. Unfortunately, that also meant my ravenous stalker had survived the string of accidents and impacts and was still out there, somewhere. I could only hope he'd be satisfied with his bony reward until morning.

As the first emergency vehicles began to converge on the site with flashing lights and bleating sirens, I returned to Oliver's and resumed my vigil. For the rest of the night I heard nothing more, except for what could only be interpreted as the sound of gnawing, remote but still unsettlingly close.

Chapter Five

Dead Letter Office

FTER A LONG, SLEEPLESS NIGHT filled with constant peril and the threat of being eaten alive by some horrible canine monster from the abyss, I was looking forward to spending some time dead again. It sounded wonderfully restful. I also liked the idea of putting an ocean between myself and the black terror that was lingering around Oliver's tiny row house. Whatever it was, it was a physical entity, large and heavy enough to put dents in the shingles on the roof. As such, it was unlikely to walk on water or swim the whole Atlantic. And I couldn't imagine anyone selling the thing a plane ticket so it could keep coming after me. With the Christmas holiday over and the post offices open again, it was time to get the hell out of London.

Setting all my shipping material outside, I shut Oliver's front door for the last time and stepped into the box. Once I was sure there was no one on the street looking my way, I nestled down into my bed of packing chips and closed the box flaps over my head. A tape dispenser was my sole piece of luggage, and I used it to finish sealing the inside of the box with several layers of packing tape. Settling down, I breathed deeply, hoping to exhaust the supply of oxygen inside and pass out quickly. After several minutes, the atmosphere grew unpleasantly humid, and

I saw the walls of the box were beginning to buckle as the air thinned. Each breath I took was shallower than the last, but unconsciousness and death eluded me. I finally had to invent a Plan B on the spot, stuffing my mouth full of Styrofoam peanuts until I mercifully choked to death.

It took a few hours for Reggie, the neighbour, to discover the box. My consciousness hovered impatiently nearby, concerned that someone might spot the tempting package and help themselves to it, hoping to score some expensive merchandize—a late Christmas present that had come in the morning's mail and been left unsigned for at the door. It would be terribly awkward for all involved if they dragged their stolen goods away only to find a freshly dead body inside once they cut open my cardboard sarcophagus.

Reggie sized up the package scornfully. It was doubtless larger and heavier than he had anticipated. He took careful note of how much of the exterior was plastered with postage stamps—ultimately deciding it was enough that he wouldn't have to pay for any extra at the post office. With palpable reluctance, he fulfilled his promise and dragged the box, grunting and straining, to his little compact car that was designed to fit down narrow European streets and not, for instance, transport large boxes. After awkwardly jamming it into the boot, he employed a kick or two to shove it in far enough to tie down the trunk lid with a bungee cord. I realized then that I should have marked the box "fragile" in large unmistakable letters. But the package survived the manhandling and manfooting with only minor dents and dings to its frame. There was no likely damage to the precious mortal-remains content that, so far, was pristine if you didn't count the handful of Styrofoam crammed into its esophagus.

The short trip to the post office was a precarious balancing act, with the unwieldy cargo hanging out the back of the car and only a single elastic cord to keep it in. One sharp turn, or an encounter with a random pot hole, threatened to send it tumbling into the road at any moment. I kept envisioning my corpse breaking free of the box on impact, becoming exposed for all to see, before getting mashed under the wheels of the next wave of traffic. I drifted in the wake of the vehicle until, with great relief, I saw Reggie pull over into a parking spot just a few doors down from a sizeable Royal Mail branch.

Unwilling to mule the package much farther, Reggie went inside and managed to convince a clerk to come out and help him carry it the rest of the way. Before he laid a hand on it, the clerk confirmed that the appropriate shipping forms had been filled out and taped to one of the box flaps. The list of contents was a string of plausible lies that went unquestioned, the affixed postage was deemed sufficient, and at last my makeshift coffin was set down in a back room to await the next truck out.

Θ

Whenever I end up as a disembodied consciousness, it's always tempting to wander off and explore, unencumbered by the usual limitations of a physical existence. But my body was on the move, and it wouldn't do to lose track of it. If I didn't see which truck it got packed into or, much worse, which ship it got loaded onto, I could condemn myself to a long and miserable search. And I'd spent far too much time and effort regrowing that body from the scantest of resources to go and misplace it now.

From branch to truck to depot to sorting room, I hugged my body close. Any closer and my spirit would have been back inside, reviving it. Another truck, another depot, another round of sorting, and I at last found the ship that would usher me back to my target continent. It was a typical cargo-container vessel—huge, rusted, and nondescript. My remains would be filed among the many hundreds of cargo pods, only a few of which housed Royal Mail deliveries. The rest contained exports and products from around the U.K., bound for North American shores, which would reciprocate with their own retail crap headed right back to consumers in Europe. There was so much tonnage of stuff setting sail every day, shipping out and shipping in, I was confident my tiny bit of contraband—one medium-sized parcel with a slowly spoiling corpse—would go unnoticed in the regular flow of trans-Atlantic commerce.

It was dark when we left with the evening tide. Keeping so focused on the location of my body, I wasn't entirely sure where we were leaving from, and the view of the world at large is always obscured when observed from the ether. Once we had cast off, and I was certain where my corpse would remain for the duration, I allowed myself to float around on deck and get my bearings. The lights of England's shoreline faded away as we left from what I judged to be the Southampton docks. Rounding the Isle of Wight, we were soon in the Channel, with the sea yawning open beyond.

By the time we were several days gone, I had settled into a routine. I would spend most of the light hours doing circuits around the deck, observing the ocean, and being grateful I was no longer out in it trying to find and cobble together bits of scattered ash. With no body, my regimen didn't amount to exercise. Being dead, it couldn't make me any healthier. But it kept my incorporeal mind occupied. Come the darkness, I would haunt the lower decks and observe the crew going about their duties. I made no effort to interact with them, despite the temptation to amuse myself with a ghostly jest or two. Manipulating the physical world from the other side was something I'd been able to do in some small capacity before, but I needed to practise if I was ever going to bump myself up to anything approaching poltergeist status. There was no use perturbing, troubling, or even terrifying the working stiffs making a boringly routine run across the Atlantic. They were good enough to be unwittingly taxiing my corpse across thousands of miles of inhospitable water. The least I could do was refrain from supernaturally pranking them to alleviate my own boredom. Instead I restricted myself to working on small items, away from the notice of living humans. I considered it a great success whenever I was able to move a single coin of loose change half an inch, or push a precariously placed sheet of paper the rest of the way off the edge of a table. My power to affect the physical world when I wasn't technically in it amounted to little more than a light nudge, but I cultivated it so that it would at least manifest more naturally, without so much taxing mental effort that my spirit was left drained.

The only time I ventured out on deck after nightfall was the lone evening when the full moon came out in a cloudless, clear sky. As spectacular as that sight can be on the open water, with a canopy of brilliant stars stretching from one horizon to the other, it wasn't the romance of this vision that drew me up from below deck. It was the howling.

Rising above the relentless white noise of the churning ship engine and the waves breaking across the bow, there was another sound that carried through the steel bulkheads and down into the hull, as if trying to drown out any whale song from the deep through a combination of volume and intimidation.

I knew I wasn't the only one who heard it—that this wasn't an invention of a bored mind made even more desperate for input by the lack of any sense of touch, taste, or smell. The crew heard it too, and the sound frightened them. Their immediate reaction was to check the engine and other mechanics of the vessel—the moving parts, the pumping pistons, the turning screws. Surely such an unexpected, incongruous noise so far out to sea had to be something gone wrong with the propellers. It couldn't have been an impact with something in the water, like another ship, floating debris, or a North-Atlantic iceberg. That would have been felt throughout the ship. This terrible noise, rising and falling in pitch, was experienced more internally, like a basic instinct from our early primate history. It was a lingering evolutionary trait that told us to beware the predator, even tens of thousands of years after man had built civilization around himself to insulate all he held dear from the wilds that still viewed him as just another link in the food chain—a meal to be plucked from the herd, torn open, bled out, and devoured raw so another corner of the savannah soil could be stained red.

Maybe it was the same instinct that kept them all from going up on deck to see if the source could be found there. Better to stay inside, behind layers of steel walls, and look for a practical cause that could be dealt with, rather than step outside and face whatever it was the least evolved parts of their brains were warning them against. Being dead, and unable to get any more killed, I was the only being onboard to answer the call. Even then, I did so with great trepidation. Was it possible that my stalker had stowed away, pursuing me even in death? If so, it had managed to remain hidden among the fields of cargo containers throughout a week-long voyage, resisting the urge to feed on any of the crew, cleverly avoiding discovery as it waited for landfall and the next act of its hunt. It was behaviour that seemed beyond any beast, but then it had already proved itself to be no mere animal, no typical predator, and not even any sort of classifiable creature a zoologist would be qualified to weigh in on with an informed opinion.

I passed across the deck slowly, using the rail as a guide even though I couldn't touch it. I was determined to do one orbit of the ship, up to the bow by the starboard side, down to the stern by port, until I was satisfied there was nothing to see. Not for one moment did I think that was a thorough enough search, but if I did that and came up empty, I could convince myself that I had done all there was to be done under the circumstances.

The stretch to the bow was uneventful. The ship cut its straight path through a still sea, and the moon lit the way as well as any spotlight might. Other than wind and water and an engine that was in perfect operating order despite all the crew currently working on it, there was no foreign sound. The unnerving drone that had risen to such an ear-splitting pitch before sinking back down to a bone-vibrating rumble had ceased and not reoccurred for the better part of an hour. I held my position at the cutting edge of the vessel and stared across the water to a horizon that offered no reassuring city lights or land pending. There was nothing expected to come into view for at least another week, and I hoped the one disturbance, real or collectively imagined by superstitious sailors and the one ghost among them, would not reoccur.

I turned back to roam the opposite side of the ship, and that's when I saw it, quite some distance away, but aboard the cargo mule with me. Perched atop the highest point of the stacked corrugated-metal containers, caught by the fierce glow of the moon, was a huge shaggy silhouette, at least eight feet in length, with its ridged back of fur standing up like a fan on sickles across the length of its spine and down its erect tail. Red eyes glowed in the dark, piercing the night and the ether alike, shining so bright they appeared to be on fire. It threw its head back and howled once more through a maw of uneven razor-teeth, wagging its forked tongue like a wind sock against the billowing exhale of superheated breath.

The sparse crew of sailors would huddle close together in the common room that night, from the moment they were off duty until the first morning light. They would nurse coffee cups and flasks as they compared notes about the terrible noise they had all heard in the early hours of the long night. Few would get any sleep before the next shift, and by the time the sun rose again, they would all be telling themselves the same lie about a distant discordant ship's horn aboard a boat no one had seen as lights on the horizon, noted as a blip on the radar, or heard as chatter on the radio. For my part, I spent the rest of that night huddled inside my box with a corpse that looked infinitely more restful than I felt. I could say I was guarding it, but that's not true. I was hiding.

I kept an eye out over the course of the rest of the journey, but never conducted what I would qualify as a proper exploration. I didn't know, even in my current state, if the creature would be able to sense me, sniff me out, do me harm. For the most part, all I did was make daily checks on my body, confirming it was where I had left it, unmolested, undiscovered, untaste-tested. If the hound was truly confined to the physical world, maybe it was the stink of my slowly spoiling body that had allowed it to track me this far. If that was the case, it didn't seem interested in digging in for a meal as it had done with Oliver. Maybe, like a bear, it didn't fancy dead meat. Perhaps it needed a current occupant in order to enjoy its snack, and was waiting patiently for me to revive.

The weather was cloudy and the seas choppy for the rest of the trip. The moon did not reappear and tempt the creature to come out of hiding to serenade it. I was never so glad to see land again than when I came up on deck one grey morning and saw an equally drab and grey skyline of a familiar city that promised a port and an opportunity to unburden the ship of all it held—my body and my spirit included. Whether the hairy stowaway was still onboard, or swimming to shore on its own terms now that landfall was imminent, I didn't see or hear it again. And that was enough for the moment.

Θ

I'd lost track of my body as the ship was unloaded and postal pods were bundled into the back of mail trucks, but I knew where it would end up before long. The physical world is only a distorted shadow of itself when viewed from the other side, but if you know a location well enough you can navigate by key landmarks that remain prominent, even through the afterlife filter.

I floated up and down familiar streets until I got my bearings and made my way to the central post office. It was a large old government building, with an absurd amount of masonry and Romanesque pillars, denoting the importance the institution once held before modern technology made most of the communication that went through the mail seem about as efficient as smoke signals. Recognizing the building at once, I passed through to the interior and began searching for one particular department. The place was thick with offices filled with paper pushers pushing tons of pulp where it was meant to go each and every day. What I was looking for was the one place where the constant movement of letters and packages, postcards and parcels, came to a standstill and stagnated. Every major post office had one, and I found the local delivery cul-de-sac in a vault in the basement. It was tucked away deep in the guts of the building, away from the hive of activity on the floors above it, forgotten by many, ignored by those who knew of it. It was a place of stillness that seemed to be hiding on purpose, out of a sense of shame, or a reluctance to further embarrass a system that promised a certain degree of competence, if not efficiency, for the low price of a single postage stamp.

This was the dead-letter office, where the undeliverables went to die. Stacked on shelves, filed in bins, stuffed in sacks, were the many thousands of items deemed lost causes by the sorters who had to pick through whatever the automated machines couldn't read or identify. Sometimes the scanners were thrown by smudged ink or crumpled paper, and it was up to actual humans to figure out the intended address on the box or envelope. Usually they could decipher it with basic intuition, but there were times when it was impossible—when the writing was too cryptic, or outright non-existent. Such mail, with an illegible destination, would be returned to sender, unless that address was also unreadable or absent, in which case it would be deemed a dead letter, rubber-stamped as such, and sent down to the pits for further classification.

There were other occasions when a package had a perfectly legible destination, neatly printed across the front, that didn't correspond with any actual address in existence. In my case, I had purposely sent my box to an impossible number on a fictional street with a postal code that was pure fantasy. With no return address in the corner, it too was destined for the dead-letter office, just as I had planned, arriving there within forty-eight hours of making port.

Before being permanently tucked away in that final vault of ignominy, there was always one last-ditch effort to determine the origin or destination of a questionable bit of correspondence. Postal forensic specialists would invoke a special exception to privacy laws in such cases, and open the letter or package in an attempt to identify it based on the contents. This was a time-consuming process, and the backlog was enormous. My intention was to revive and escape long before anyone scrutinized my wayward mail too closely.

One night, once the unionized staff had worked their allotted hours and left for home, I triggered my revival, slipping back into my body and jumpstarting my brain. My first sensation was distress. I flailed around inside my box, unable to cry out or breathe, until my punches and kicks ruptured the cardboard and allowed me to spill out onto the floor. Immediately I began violently vomiting up a puddle of packing chips, coughing uncontrollably for several minutes until my lungs and stomach were clear of Styrofoam fragments. I remained on my hands and knees, breathing deeply and letting the blood flow once more, until my heart stopped pounding and assumed a more moderate pace.

I was alive again, home again. It wasn't the most dignified arrival, and I didn't feel like a triumphant hero returned, but I was back, and that was good enough for me in the moment.

As far as my many returns from the dead went, my body was in above average condition and nicely intact. Nevertheless, I expected I looked rather grey and sickly after spending two weeks deceased. Salty sea air and a tightly wrapped tomb had kept serious decomposition at bay, but something had to be done to improve my appearance for public consumption. Except for a small cleaning-crew shift that came and went in one hour flat, I had the building to myself. I resorted to some small acts of vandalism and theft in order to shore myself up, breaking the glass of a vending machine and helping myself to all the sweets and chips inside. I then cleaned out the change bucket and fed the coffee machine quarters until I'd gotten enough liquids into me to rehydrate the flesh that had drawn tight over my bones.

Come the next business day, I remained in hiding until there were enough regular customers sending and picking up packages for me to infiltrate their ranks and leave like I had only popped in for a moment to see which dead celebrity had just been honoured on the latest commemorative stamp.

I was able to hail a cab at the very next corner. That only took a few moments. Deciding where I wanted it to take me was a much lengthier task, so I instructed the driver to simply drive until I could make up my mind.

Chapter Six

Monuments

"**W**HAT HAPPENED TO THE CEMETERY?" I asked as the cab, still directionless, turned up another boulevard from a cross street.

A few years can change a city. Not drastically, but noticeably if you haven't seen it in a while. There are always demolitions, new construction, repaved roads, updated signs. Businesses and restaurants close, new ones open. Once-vibrant streets get boarded up in tough times, while dodgier neighbourhoods get gentrified by upwardly mobile bohemians. It's a living breathing organism, ever-changing, never stagnant. The cemetery, a vast field of graves and tombs in the middle of town, there since before the sprawl spread all around it, was shockingly absent. Buildings are torn down and built up again all the time, but cemeteries rarely are. People tend to get queasy and sentimental when it comes to relocating their dead. It takes a lot of money and sway to make it happen.

"Gone," answered my driver.

"Gone?" I echoed back. I had done a lot of business there in the past, and I guess I can get sentimental about such things, too. Sure, there were other graveyards around, but none as old and atmospheric as the Algonquin grounds had been.

"Dug up and transplanted so they could build this thing," the cabbie said, looking up at the skyscraper that now occupied most of the open land that had once capped the top of the boulevard.

"It's huge," I said, ducking my head so I could look out the car window at the many storeys that stretched high into the sky. The roof of the cab cut off my view of the peak.

"Tallest tower in town," I was informed.

"I guess a lot has happened since the last time I was here."

"Not so much," said the driver. "The economy is still in the toilet. Who the hell has enough cash to build a monstrosity like that, I don't know, but it's the only new bit of construction of any note. They've torn down more than they've built lately. Unless you count parking lots with a pay booth as new construction, which I don't. Laying asphalt and sticking a tiny wooden shack on it so you can charge people to leave their cars for a flat hourly fee isn't urban renewal, if you ask me. My old man was in construction. He laid a lot of bricks in this town. He'd be sick to see how little has changed since the last time he broke ground."

"Does he still live around here?"

"He doesn't live around anywhere anymore. He was in Algonquin Fields, but now that it's been turned into Algonquin Tower, he's out in the new cemetery in the north end."

"North end where?" I asked, trying to guess at the plot of real estate I would likely be commuting to for work.

"You play golf?"

"No," I said.

"Good. Because they tore up the golf course and filled it with graves instead of greens."

We drove in silence for a few minutes as the cab circled around the city's one major addition to the skyline and back down the boulevard.

"You decide where you're heading yet?" asked the driver, who was happy to run up the fare, but likely preferred a determined destination rather than endless meandering.

There was no avoiding it. Eventually I would have to reconnect with people. I gave him an address and hoped my first stop wouldn't be a disaster.

☉

I stood outside the apartment building for too long. The cab wasn't waiting for me. I didn't tell it to wait, and the driver wouldn't have if I'd asked. He wasn't pleased to have his metre settled with fistfuls of loose change pilfered from a vending machine.

I was trying to compose what I would say after so long. Being dead for years is a good excuse to not pick up a phone or send an email. But I had been alive again for months now and had made no attempt to let Rebecca know I was back and well. She was my closest friend, yet I hadn't wanted to speak with her, and certainly didn't want to face her now. Of all the people I knew who must have moved on with their life in my absence, I worried she had probably moved the farthest away.

I should have guessed that the move wouldn't have merely been mental, but physical as well. When I finally mustered the courage to buzz her number, I saw that the name "Rebecca Stone" had been unartfully whited out, and the name of a new tenant written in on the card inside the call box.

I rang for the superintendent instead.

☉

"You're back. Of course."

The tone walked the line perfectly between disdain and boredom. I expected nothing less from Reynaldo the Wise, who instantly transformed himself into Reynaldo the Fuckhead the moment I walked in the door. I hadn't expected the see him at Wilbur's Wonderama, but his unwelcome presence seemed inevitable in retrospect. Of course I would bump into the person at the very bottom of my reacquaintance list first.

"Surprised to see me?" I asked, spreading my arms in the doorway so he could get a good look.

"No," said Reynaldo, and raised two fingers to his temple as he closed his eyes. "I foresaw it—in a vision."

"Sure you did," I grumbled, unconvinced—but not completely unconvinced.

"It took you long enough to rise from the dead. Are you slipping?"

"Let's see you resurrect yourself from ashes scattered at sea," I said. "Go on, I'll time you."

"I would sooner win that competition by not dying at all."

"Where's Wilbur?" I asked, wanting to replace Reynaldo with a friendlier face as soon as possible.

"You don't know, of course," he said, and sounded genuinely solemn.

Wilbur had been neither young nor all there, but somehow I had expected him to last, unchanged, like the magic shop he had owned and run for decades.

"When did this happen?" I asked.

"Not so long after you left," Reynaldo informed me. "He went out on a career high note, which would have pleased him. The notoriety he achieved helping you with your grand-finale stunt put him right back in the public eye. Nothing boosts waning celebrity like an arrest record. He even got one more television special out of the deal. Strictly local, but I'm sure you can stream it online somewhere if you're curious."

Between Wilbur and Oliver, the sage elder voices in my life were being silenced quicker than I could cope with. It's not like I had logged a huge number of hours with either of them since setting up shop as a freelance necromancer, but somehow I'd always found it reassuring knowing that they were there, that I could go see them whenever I wanted and get my ear talked off about the old days. Now they were both gone, and the sagest person I had left in my life was an insufferable, egomaniacal medium competitor I couldn't stand.

"At least the Wonderama is still here," I noted.

"You're welcome," said Reynaldo.

"What do you mean?"

"There was an estate auction. I bought it as-is and maintained it just as it was. The books were a terrible mess, but I've managed to turn it around so it brings in a modest profit. It's a hobby, really, but it pays for itself, which is always the best kind of hobby."

My stomach turned. The idea that this cornerstone of the stagecraft community was now in the purple-fingernail-polish hands of Reynaldo made horrible, sickening sense. The Wonderama had always been something of a hangout for him. Who else would have him? Now that it was his, there was no getting rid of him.

"Let me know if you need a discount on anything," he said, sounding magnanimous. I knew an insult was coming. "Wind-up chattering teeth, glow-in-the-dark fangs, rubber spiders. Whatever it is you use in that quaint boutique business of yours."

"I can always use spare body parts," I said. "Care to donate one of your chins to the cause while I'm setting up shop again?"

"There are limits to how much I'm willing to assist the competition," Reynaldo sneered.

He stepped behind the counter and pulled a small packet off an impulse-buy rack.

"Perhaps I could interest you in some Sea-Monkeys? I'm sure with your typical level of care and compassion you could kill them all off in short order. That would give you some dead matter to start with."

I ignored his generous offer of brine-shrimp eggs in cryptobiosis and focused on an engraved plaque hanging between the cash and the bulletin board. One square foot of wall space.

"What's this?" I asked, reading the dedication.

In memory of Rip Eulogy.
Kind of creepy, but a helluva guy.

Some dates followed that were completely fictitious. Nobody knew when I was born, my deaths were many, and my final demise proved to be not so final after all.

"Do you like it?" asked Reynaldo. "Wilbur wrote it himself."

I had recognized the sentiment and the language straight off.

"I'm amazed you keep it up," I said.

"I thought it would be disrespectful to take it down."

"Thanks, Reynaldo," I said, making the mistake of fleetingly being touched.

"To Wilbur," he clarified. "Of course, now that a memorial has proved to be completely pointless, I'll be happy to toss it in the bin."

I'd had my fill of Reynaldo and cut to the point of my visit. I had hoped to ask Wilbur, but the backup proprietor of the Wonderama would have to do.

"I'm looking for Rebecca," I said. "She moved out of her apartment years ago. You seen her?"

"Not since your funeral," shrugged Reynaldo. "What possible reason would I have to socialize with your friends?"

"Wilbur was a friend," I reminded him.

"Wilbur was a beloved local celebrity. I grew up watching his show like everyone else. His was a legacy I was pleased to carry on. As for the rest of your associates, there's simply no reason for our paths to cross."

"Tom must still swing by the shop," I suggested.

"On occasion, but it's rare. I understand he's been on the road with his act quite a bit of late. When he's in town, I sell him the occasional prop. Things that can be swallowed, manipulated internally, and brought back up."

"Of course," I said, all too familiar with Tom's regurgitation act.

"I offered him Sea-Monkeys as well," said Reynaldo. "If he could find a way to swallow the packet dry, hatch them in his stomach, and vomit them into a fish bowl, he'd have a magnificent act."

"Maybe for the front row," I said. Reynaldo was used to intimate audiences of one or two at a time. He had no concept of performing for a room of spectators. "Sea-Monkeys are too small to play to the cheap seats."

"I defer to your expertise," he bowed. "I, for one, never play to cheap seats. A seat at my table is a very expensive ticket indeed."

All this talk of Tom's regurgitation act made me want to puke the vending-machine junk food I had shored myself up with. Or maybe it was just Reynaldo. I turned to leave.

"There's one more thing," he called out, interrupting my departure.

Reynaldo disappeared under the counter before coming up again with a simple cardboard box in plain brown wrapping, neither particularly small nor very large. He set it down and it appeared to be quite light.

"What's that?"

"It's yours," he said. "Wilbur left it to you. I expect it was mentioned in a clause in his will. Or maybe he still believed you would come back one day, even in the end. At any rate, this is your inheritance."

"What is it?"

"Not money."

"Did I ask how much?" I fumed. "No, I asked what it was."

"I don't know, I didn't open it. Something sentimental, probably. Don't pawn it."

I tucked the parcel under my arm and turned to leave.

"Even after all I went through, the last few years without you have been great."

"Let me know if you ever need another break," said Reynaldo. "I'll happily toss you back in the ocean."

Θ

Tracy's number was still the same, but it was her answering service that picked up. I figured she was probably out on a job, so I bought a newspaper and checked the obituaries. There were a few funerals scheduled for that afternoon, but they mostly seemed to be for beloved family members who would draw their fair share of mourners. I was looking for some unloveable S.O.B. who needed a professional moirologist at their service to provide the tears no one else could muster.

There was one businessman going in the ground who looked promising. His photo in the paper certainly made him seem like an unlovable prick. And his business had been a used-car dealership. Someone had run him over in his own parking lot—probably on purpose. He certainly had a face that would make you want to hit the gas if you saw it poised in front of your hood ornament. It was just a guess, but it was a solid one, so I hopped a bus. At least the buses weren't touchy about getting their fare paid in nickels, dimes, and quarters.

The funeral wasn't at that fancy new cemetery in the north end that had eaten up an entire golf course. This was a west-side semi-suburban place that catered to various ethnic community pockets clustered together in areas that were easily identified by the preponderance of culturally specific restaurants and cafés. Munsif Khoury was the name of the decedent, so I felt safe skipping the Jewish and Greek Orthodox sections of the yard. The Muslim quarter would have been obvious, even without reading the Arabic etched into the markers. Their graves ran against the grain of the rest in the plots, allowing their occupants to be laid to rest on their sides, pointing south-east towards Mecca.

There was only one burial happening when I arrived, so I assumed it was the one I was after and hung back to see if I could spot Tracy in the crowd. It proved an impossible task. The ceremony was strictly religious, and a lot of the women, standing separate from the men, were wearing burkas, black and uniform. Tracy, counter to her usual performance at funerals, was playing it low-key, if she was there at all.

Once the *Janazah* prayer was finished and the Imam had wrapped things up, the mourners made their way out of the yard. The women all moved together in a cluster, their covered heads bobbing in a synchronized dark tide. But then one of the burkas froze in place, letting the rest of the sea of black flow past.

"You magnificent motherfucker!" I heard a familiar voice squeal.

One of the anonymous women broke off from the pack and threw herself into my arms. Tracy, as per her usual shtick, had managed to embarrass me in three seconds flat.

"Um, ultra conservative religious occasion, Tracy. Dial it down," I pleaded.

She released me, but proceeding to beat my chest with her fists. It was a playful, happy gesture, but it still hurt.

"How the fuck? How the fucking-fuck? You were ashes! Ashes in a box!"

We were drawing a lot of uncomfortable stares from the departing mourners, but nobody said anything.

"Did I mention I sometimes, kind of, sort of, rise from the dead?"

"We swap freaky stories all the time and you skip that detail?" said Tracy, sounding betrayed. "What the hell, Rip?"

"I have to be careful about sharing information like that. People lose their shit."

"Of course people lose their shit! It's fucking awesome! You're like some weirdo zombie superhero!"

"I am nothing like a zombie," I protested. "Trust me on that. I know some zombies. I'm not saying zombies aren't good people. But they have their thing and I have mine and it's not the same at all."

"Thank fuck you're back," said Tracy. "It has been boring as shit without you."

"Apparently," I agreed. "I came looking for you and I couldn't even pick you out. I was expecting more of a scene."

"It's a Muslim thing. Very subdued, very modest funerals. My client was a used-car dealer."

"So the obit said."

"He sold the community so many lemons, he was worried no one would turn out for his funeral. I was just here to fill out a burka at a reduced price. No tears or wailing required. He needn't have bothered. The community turned out for him anyway, even in the cold."

"He had a bigger send-off than I did," I noted.

"Maybe if you butter up your own community a bit more, you'll get a better showing at your next funeral."

"Yeah, well, I'm trying to touch as many bases as I can now that I'm back."

"Have you seen Rebecca?" she asked me.

"No, I was hoping you'd know where she is."

I couldn't see Tracy's eyes well through the mesh, but I could tell she was looking at me like I was stupid.

"You sure didn't look hard."

"She moved out of her old apartment. The super couldn't remember where."

"Have you been back to your place yet?"

"What's to go back to?" I shrugged. "I'm guessing most of my stuff ended up in a dumpster. Even if the place has any vacancies, it would be weird moving into a different apartment in the same building."

I could hear Tracy snickering at me under her burka.

"Just go home, Rip."

Θ

Of course it made perfect sense.

We'd both lived in dumps, but mine was a higher class of dump—a rent-controlled dump. All Rebecca had to do was move right on in and continue paying my rent like nothing happened. It wasn't like I'd been officially declared dead or anything. As far as the management knew, I was still living there, with a new sugar momma who was covering my bills for me.

"Rebecca Stone," read the tag in the directory, right next to my old apartment number. I rang and waited.

"Yes?" came a voice over the speaker. The tone was instantly familiar and suddenly I was at a loss for words. I had no idea what to say, so while she waited for me to respond, I pressed the button again.

There was a pause before I was buzzed in. Rebecca probably figured I was an inarticulate delivery man, or that the speaker was on the fritz again. I took the elevator up the three floors and approached number 306 at the end of the hall. Rebecca didn't see me coming. The spyhole in the door was still out of commission three and a half years later. Presumably it was Rebecca who had whimsically covered it over with twin Band-Aids in the form of an "X." You could still see the scorch marks around the edges.

I set my parcel down on the welcome mat, mustered my nerve, and knocked. The door swung in a moment later, like Rebecca was expecting a quick exchange with a courier. She was on a call, with her phone propped between her ear and shoulder. It only took one look at me for her to stop her conversation in mid-sentence, drop her shoulder, and let her phone fall to the floor. The glass screen cracked on impact and the call disconnected. She never looked down to assess the damage.

I still couldn't think of anything to say to her by way of reintroduction, so I smiled—a halting half-grin that I hoped looked apologetic, but probably appeared shy, awkward, and dimwitted. Maybe the end result was charming. I never found out because the next thing I knew, Rebecca had punched me squarely in the face.

Chapter Seven

Dearly Departed

"WHAT TOOK YOU SO LONG?" Rebecca demanded, coldly.

The blow to the face had been more shocking than damaging. Rebecca was no streetfighter or bar brawler. Her punch had briefly flattened my nose, but had failed to break it or even draw blood. It stung a bit, but not as much as the harsh, disapproving expression etched in her face.

The façade didn't last. Her lips were quivering before she made it to the end of her question. The next I knew, she was draped around my neck and blubbering down my back with great soggy sobs. She held on tight as a noose and wouldn't let up for the next ten minutes as she poured out years of pent-up grief, punctuated by unexpected relief and—dare I say—joy at seeing me again.

Tracy would have been envious of the display.

Θ

"I thought you'd never move out of that place," I said about an hour later, after a torrent of apologies from the both of us and a quick summary of how I was miraculously alive again.

The explanation seemed necessary despite the fact that I had yet to fail to rise from the dead.

Having helped Rebecca find her old apartment in what seemed like a relentless and fruitless ordeal to pick just the right place, lasting weeks, I thought she had rooted herself to the spot permanently.

"You told me my building had rats," said Rebecca.

"I never said any such thing."

"My building had rats, Rip."

"I know. I didn't want to alarm you."

"And cockroaches."

"The rats have to eat something."

I was wandering around my old abode, taking in the new and the different. Rebecca had retained most of my furniture, but replaced a few of the more worn and banged up pieces with some of her own. The result was a mishmash of styles, or at least a mix of Rebecca's style countered by my aggressively neutral non-style. A stack of cards bundled in a crossed silk ribbon caught my eye. They were sitting on a new shelf that had been bolted to the wall.

"What's all this shit?"

They looked like greeting cards, but dour and muted.

"Condolences," said Rebecca. "From your funeral. I kept them all. I thought you might like to see them if you ever came back."

"You knew I was coming back?"

"No. But I thought I'd give hope a try."

"I've missed a lot," I said, feeling the need to state the obvious.

Rebecca agreed, adding, "Wilbur died."

"I heard. What happened?"

"A couple of years back," she said. "It was quick. He had a stroke and was gone the next day."

"I'm sorry I didn't get a chance to say goodbye."

"Well that shouldn't stop you of all people. You can go visit the grave for a chat any time you want."

I considered it, but only for a moment.

"No," I concluded. "Let him rest. He doesn't need me bothering him for no good reason."

"Have you seen anyone else?"

"Tracy and Reynaldo," I said.

"Glad to know who's on the list ahead of me."

"I went to them asking after you."

"Sure you did," Rebecca commented dismissively, but she knew it was true—and was flattered.

She came over and took another in a series of long stares at my face, like she had to repeatedly convince herself that I had really returned.

"You need a shave," she noted, patting the long stubble that covered my face. "Any day now and that thing's going to turn into a real beard."

"Like it?" I asked.

"No. It makes you look old."

Rebecca picked at a few unruly strands.

"And you're going grey," she commented.

"Must be all that salt water."

Our eyes locked for a while. A long while.

"There's something I've been meaning to ask you," I began.

Rebecca waited to hear it.

"I left a note for you."

She raised her eyebrows and slyly commented, "How romantic."

"It was an account number and a password. Did you find it?"

"No..."

Rebecca looked confused. It hardly sounded like a heartfelt bearing of my soul, confessed in posthumous parting.

"I figured as much," I said. "You wouldn't have moved in here if you had. You'd be in some luxury beach house where winter never happens."

"What are you talking about?"

"Keys to the kingdom," I bemoaned. "A digital roadmap to a hidden fortune that fell into my lap too late to do me any good. And now it's all gone. To where is anybody's guess."

"And you wrote this down on a piece of paper and left it lying around?"

"I thought I'd be back. At least, I thought I'd be back relatively soon. Not three or four years later. And I didn't just leave it lying around. I filed it away carefully. With someone."

"With who?" Rebecca asked, and it was only then that I understood the horrible stupid mistake I had made.

Θ

I half expected Gladys to have been sold off as an oddity in my absence. She was a magic trick nobody outside the necromancy craft, unfamiliar with osteo-reanimations, could explain. As such, she seemed destined for some circus sideshow, travelling carnival, or unseemly stage act. Or maybe just a museum—a stuffy institution that would take her in for further study and examination. They would quickly learn she was too cantankerous, too potty-mouthed to ever put on display, where she would doubtless pass her days insulting tour guides, bitching out security guards, and teaching small children on classroom field trips new and socially unacceptable language. Before long, they would give up trying to solve the puzzle of the talking skull with the indeterminable foreign accent, and file her away in a drawer in their stock room with all the other disused artifacts. Preferably one heavily lined with cork or cotton to muffle the expletive-laden complaints that would be shouted tirelessly and at full volume for the duration of her imprisonment.

But no. Rebecca, just about the only living person who got on with her at all, had kept Gladys out of a sense of obligation, if not outright friendship. The skull remained in my old home office, repositioned so she could gaze out the window at the uninspiring view with her empty sockets.

"You're roommates," I commented.

"I wouldn't go as far as that," said Rebecca. "It's not like she can do her fair share of the cleaning and cooking. On the other hand, she can't make a mess and doesn't eat."

"Oh, she can make a mess all right. Plug her into a computer, give her internet access or a phone line, and she can make no end of mess. Isn't that right, Gladys?"

I turned her around so she was facing me. The sound that came out of that skull, echoing out of her eye and nose holes, sounded like some vile, vitriolic cackle.

"I da reechist skall in da warld!" Gladys gloated. "Yoo wurk for me now, beetch!"

I wanted to wring her neck, if only she had one.

"I was going to retire on that money!" I yelled at her.

"You're too young to retire," Rebecca commented.

"That was the best part! I was going to skip all those years of work and annoying clients and go straight to the good part."

As I said it, I knew I was kidding myself. Even with all the money in the world and no clients being pains in my ass, I would keep up with the necromancy in some capacity. Oliver was right. It was who I was and there was no walking away from it.

Still, I felt like a sucker. Three and a half years earlier, I had only transferred enough funds from the recovered Higgins slush fund to pay my most pressing bills and get the business out of the red. I should have grabbed some mad money as well, stashed it in another account under my own name, or turned it into cold hard cash I could have squirrelled away in a safe deposit box or under a damn mattress. Now it was all gone, hidden, disappeared, and under the sole control of a vindictive and aggravatingly stubborn talking skull I bought on eBay and imbued with a random spirit simply because I couldn't make things work with any normal human secretary.

"In the morning I'm going to take that fucking skull down to the nearest crematorium and feed it to the bone grinder."

After hours of pointlessly trying to extract information, reason, or mere decency out of Gladys, I'd given up. Night was falling, and I had to figure out where I was going to crash.

"Don't be like that," said Rebecca.

"She embezzled all my money. Every last penny of it," I groused. "Okay, not every penny. She left me eighteen cents. But that just comes across as insult to injury."

"At least you know where it went and who has it."

"Knowing the thief who holds the purse strings is hardly reassuring. This is the same skull who hired a company of hitmen to assassinate me," I reminded Rebecca.

"Didn't she apologize for that?"

"She regretted it, but that's not the same as being genuinely sorry."

"Come on," said Rebecca. "It's late and we've both had a long day."

It was time for me to beg, hat in hand.

"I hate to impose, but if you could let me spend the night on the couch, I would be sincerely grateful."

"You're not sleeping on my couch, Rip."

"I have three quarters in my pocket and eighteen cents in the bank. It's this or a park bench."

"Come," she said, rising to her feet and offering her hand. "There's a queen-sized bed in the other room. Plenty of room for two."

"I don't know," I said, unsure. "I'm not great with beds."

True, I'd spent the last few months on the guest bed in Oliver's house, but I'd had a resurgence of my back problems as a result. Plus, of course, there was the awkward unspoken issue that Rebecca and I had never been in bed together—either for sleep or intimacy purposes.

"You prefer sleeping in a casket?"

"Is it here?" I asked, hopefully.

"Don't be an idiot."

I knew it was too much to expect that Rebecca had kept my old casket around as a novelty coffee table or a morbid chest for storing linen. It wasn't her style. It wasn't anybody's style. Even undertakers would call it tacky. With a certain reluctance, I accepted the invitation. Exhaustion outweighed awkward. Twenty minutes later, we were side-by-side in my old bedroom with the lights out. It didn't take long for me to start drifting off. An arm across my chest, a hand on one shoulder, and a forehead nestled into the other, jolted me wide awake an instant later.

"What are you doing?" I asked suspiciously.

"I'm cuddling," said Rebecca.

I thought about the act of cuddling and everything it could mean for several long moments in the dark.

"It's weird," I said at last.

"*You're* weird."

I could hear Rebecca sniffling and thought she had started crying again. It took me a while to realize it wasn't weeping.

"What?" I asked.

"You smell funny. Have you been dead recently?"

"Yeah," I admitted.

"For how long?"

"I had to spend a couple of weeks dead so I could book cheap passage as a piece of freight. I only got up again yesterday."

Rebecca promptly uncuddled me and rolled over.

"Damn, Rip, take a shower."

"I just had one."

"Take another. Or no cuddles."

"Suits me," I said, and rolled over onto my side so my back was to her.

"You're washing these sheets tomorrow," she told me.

Θ

"How did you find the mattress? Firm enough for you?"

Rebecca had caught me in mid-stretch after a solid night's sleep. Arching my back, I waited to hear a bone or two pop, but there was nothing. My muscles were loose and there was no familiar ache.

"It was okay," I reported. "Back's good."

"It never occurred to you to try a new mattress? Your go-to default was a casket?"

"I knew it would work," I said from experience.

"I would have tried sleeping on wooden planks before I went with a coffin."

"One came up and the price was right."

"I think you just wanted to sleep in a coffin."

"They're much cozier than you'd think."

Rebecca went into the kitchen to finish scooping out her grapefruit.

"If you're so hung up on it, you can drag it out of storage and stick it in a corner somewhere," she said. "Just throw a table cloth over it during the day so I don't have to look at it."

"You kept it?" I asked, surprised.

"I kept all your crap. Or at least the crap that wasn't so crap it needed to get thrown away as a health hazard. Anything that's not up here is down in the basement."

Θ

I went to have a look after showering and eating. As instructed, I took the bedsheets down with me to run them through a cycle in the laundry room. My death-soiled clothes were mixed in with the load, which left me with exactly no wardrobe. All my old clothes had fallen under Rebecca's definition of health-hazard crap and had been gotten rid of. I think she just wanted all the closet space for herself. In the meantime, I was stuck doing laundry in her bathrobe.

With everything in the wash, I checked out my apartment's storage locker. It wasn't much of a locker—with only a rusty combination lock left over from high school keeping things secured. The walls were spaced slats of wood, allowing anyone to poke their nose in and take inventory. As such, none of the tenants kept any valuables down there, though break-ins still happened from time to time. Usually this only occurred when rent was due and someone was desperate to sell something—something not necessarily belonging to them—to a pawn shop. Years earlier, I caught the guy who used to live in 412 after he'd busted into my locker, hunting for valuables. It wasn't much of a sting operation. I'd found him curled into a fetal position at the back of the row, muttering to himself, two days after he'd gone poking through some of my disused boxes. The things he'd seen in there had bent his perception of reality to the breaking point and turned him into a bit of a gibbering madman. I didn't call the cops on him, figuring he'd been punished enough. Instead, I helped him back to his apartment, heated up a can of soup, spoon-fed him, and put him to bed where he lay shivering under the covers. The only intelligible thing he said to me the whole time was to beg me to leave the lights on as I left. I checked in on him a couple of days later, but he'd already moved out.

Down the dimly lit corridor, I found the locker with my apartment number painted across one of the slats. I had the combination written down somewhere Rebecca must have discovered, but I couldn't remember it off the top of my head after so long. I thought I might have to go back up to ask her what it was, but I tried pulling on the lock first. It opened easily. Typical. Rebecca probably had trouble remembering the number too, so she left the shackle looped in place without pushing it back into the case. It looked locked enough to fool anyone who wasn't actively trying to break in.

The locker was twice as stuffed as I'd left it, full of my possessions that Rebecca had exiled from the apartment. The bulkiest item by far was the casket, which stood on end at the back, leaning against the wall. It was dusty from its years of basement banishment, but had survived the move unscathed and would polish up again nicely. As well as I'd slept that night, I attributed it mostly to exhaustion. I was looking forward to getting some proper rest in a familiar boxy enclosure that I wouldn't have to share.

Pulling open the lid, I inspected the interior to make sure Rebecca hadn't weighed it down with any additional items, using the space for even more storage. So far, I hadn't spotted much from my home-office days, so I expected to see file folders of old cases, bubble-wrapped jars of tissue samples, and maybe a few stacks of the mortician trade journals I used to subscribe to. But there was nothing—there wouldn't have been room.

The casket was already occupied by a body.

I slammed the lid shut when it opened its eyes and glared at me.

Θ

I was back in the apartment two minutes later. Rebecca was surprised. I'd only just left.

"There's a bit of an infestation I have to deal with downstairs," I informed her.

"Don't tell me this building has cockroaches, too," said Rebecca, concerned she'd relocated from one pestilent apartment to another.

"Worse."

"What could be worse?"

"Vampires."

Rebecca sounded profoundly relieved. "Oh good. Because I thought you were going to say rats."

I considered that for a moment.

"Depends on his transmogrification skills."

I started hunting through the hall closet that was filled with all things Rebecca and nothing familiar.

"Where's my tool kit?" I asked.

"Your what?"

"The satchel with all my stuff in it."

"Oh," she realized, "your murse."

"Yes."

"I threw that thing away years ago. It stank of I-don't-know-what."

"It sure didn't take you long to start chucking out all my best stuff."

"I know I should have kept it for you in a shrine honouring your memory, but Rip, stink is stink."

"I'll have to improvise," I said, wondering how exactly I was going to do that and coming up empty.

"Are you serious?" asked Rebecca, who usually knew better than to ask when it came to these sorts of things.

"Most of the time," I assured her.

"About there being vampires in the building?"

"Just one," I said, rummaging through the pantry cupboard for ammunition and finding nothing but useless canned tuna. "As far as I counted. It seems to have taken up residence in my old casket."

Something was nagging me. You'll find vampires tucked away in all sorts of crawlspaces and attics, behind false walls and up chimneys. Anyplace dark and quiet, but near enough to people for them to feed is good. But the ones who set up camp right inside an abode, right under the noses of their prospective victims, can't just do it for the sake of a short blood commute. There are rules governing supernatural beings, and the rules must be obeyed.

"Rebecca," I asked, delicately, "did you invite a vampire into the building?"

"No," she claimed, but it sounded like a guilty fib.

"Rebecca..." I cautioned her.

"I didn't invite him!" she protested, but then added, "I may have buzzed him in."

"That's as-good-as when it comes to vampires! They'll accept any invitation, formal or implied."

"I didn't know it was a vampire! It was just some creepy dude, for all I knew. He asked about you, which is what most creepy dudes seem to do, and then I thought he went away."

"What have I told you about buzzing in strange entities?"

"I buzzed *you* in."

"And you ought to know by now, I qualify as a strange entity. You need to check and confirm."

It was an oft-repeated lecture. Always screen arrivals at the door via the intercom unless you know exactly who it is. Otherwise you could let in just about any unwanted guest or intruder—from a snake-tongued demonic succubus intent on draining you, body and soul, to Girl Guides selling addictive cookies. I knew all too well from past errors, and they had been equally difficult to banish from the premises.

"I've seen you buzz in people without confirming who's at the door," she said, calling me on my sometimes lax approach to my own rules and guidelines.

"I only do that when I'm actually expecting someone."

"Well I was expecting a package."

"In the middle of the night?" I scoffed. Vampires don't keep the nine-to-five hours of most service workers.

"I thought the courier guy was running late."

"How long ago was this?"

"Two or three weeks, maybe," Rebecca guesstimated.

"Has anyone in the building gone missing?"

"I don't know," she said, thinking back. "The neighbours aren't exactly neighbourly, but I've noticed a spike in vacancies lately. You don't suppose some of the occupants got..."

"Eaten?"

Rebecca sucked in a deep breath of air through gritted teeth, embarrassed.

"My bad."

I opened the apartment door.

"All right, you stay here, I'll shoo it away."

"You're going to shoo away a vampire?"

Rebecca didn't sound convinced.

"Unless you want to do it," I offered, generously.

"I'm sure you've got this."

"Things could get ugly once I flush him out. Don't answer this door to anybody but me."

"How will I know it's you? The spyhole's broken."

"Whose fault is that?"

"You're never going to let that go, are you?"

"I'll knock three times and say, 'It's me.'"

"Everybody knocks three times and says, 'It's me.'"

"Yeah, but I'm the only one who's actually going to sound like me."

I left before our circular conversation could do any more laps around the track.

Θ

A word about vampires: Yuck.

Oh I know, they're all so very Euro-sexy. Smooth talkers with smouldering bedroom eyes and supernatural powers of darkness and seduction. If they're not devastatingly handsome, they're boobtastic, with just the right hint of bisexual switch-hitting if you happen to be into that sort of thing. As walking cadavers go, they make necrophilia quite socially acceptable, even trendy. And did I mention their glorious fashion sense? Each and every one of them seems to know exactly how to fill out a designer suit or fetishistic period-bustier. They embody how we like to picture the deathstyles of the beautiful people. Cold boring graves aren't for them. They're the afterlife of the party, and party they do—all night every night—cruising for that special someone they can gift with a love bite and perhaps even immortality.

If this is what you think vampires are like, you've never met one. I'm afraid movies, TV, and junk literature have poisoned your mind—the way these things tend to poison everything— for cheap entertainment and easy profit. I've seen my share of vampires. Real ones. And they don't live up to the hype.

First off, vampires don't have fangs, or even particularly sharp teeth. But they do bite. They bite at any extremity or artery that gets within chomping distance and promises to bleed profusely. When they bite, they go at it with such violent gusto, they dig deep and hit bone more often than not. As a result, they all eventually end up with a mouthful of twisted, chipped and broken teeth, which only make for even nastier bite wounds on future victims.

The blood they drink stagnates and spoils inside their immobile, non-functioning organs. They're dead after all, and the dead don't digest. Nevertheless, the old foul blood from past meals gets slowly pushed through the atrophied gastro-intestinal system by the slurping and swallowing of fresh blood. Eventually it has nowhere left to go, and the blackened oily collection of rotting plasma has to secrete all by itself, subjecting the host vampire to a routine trickle of tainted anal leakage. That's where the worst odour comes from. They may stink of the grave and smell like a corpse, but they themselves aren't actually rotting. It's their diet that rots, over the course of weeks, as it slowly works its way through their mortified guts. They reek of the tar-like mucus that runs down their legs from uncontrollable sphincters, and the fumes of decay that waft out of the shattered-tooth maws every time they open their mouth to take another bite of someone.

Still think vampires are sexy?

Getting rid of them is an unpleasant ordeal, and killing them is out of the question. They're not alive, they won't die, and they're damn near indestructible. Forget what you've heard. Nothing works.

Their tight pale skin is light-sensitive, and they'll tan and burn faster than a ginger Irishman, but even the sun won't destroy them. Crucifixes and holy water have no real effect, but Catholic guilt is more immortal than any vampire. If they were faithful in life, they're probably still God-fearing in death, and have likely mistaken their condition for the devil's work. Devout symbols that used to give them comfort now invoke fear and horror, but this is purely psychological. Religious icons can't harm them in death any more than they could save them in life. But hey, if they're a believer, go ahead and use it against them. So what if it's not fair play?

Vampirism is contagious if they're sloppy about how they eat, and their numbers have risen slowly but surely over millennia. Since they can't die, the world is chock full of them. Fortunately for us, unfortunately for them, most end up locked in coffins and buried under six feet of well-packed soil. They would like nothing better than to rise from their graves and feast on the living, but they're stuck. So they wither and starve over the years, the decades, the centuries. Don't feel bad for them. If you ever saw one coming for you, pity would be the very last emotion to cross your mind. And then they would suck you dry and throw your husk away like an empty candy wrapper.

I didn't fancy facing off against one my first full day back on the job. I wasn't even one hundred percent sure I was back on the job at all. Being home again felt like old times, but falling into my routine seemed a long stretch away. Doing battle with some graveborn monstrosity could have been exactly the push I needed, but having at it damn near naked was more of a challenge than I was looking for. I had returned to the basement armed with a mauve bathrobe, a pair of flip-flops, and no underwear. You could say I was going commando, but I didn't feel like a commando. I didn't even feel as tough and prepared as a rookie cadet. Three years out of the necromancy loop and the best I had managed so far was to sleep through my semi-mentor's murder and run away from a big dog. Now I was going to square off alone against a vampire of unknown age and power—an unkillable, unstoppable, undead force—looking like I'd just stepped out of the pool at a nudist colony. It wasn't shaping up to be a good day.

Everything was as I had left it. The casket lid was shut, the locker door open. My plan, such as it was, consisted mainly of talk. Since killing it was impossible, and fighting it was futile, I hoped to successfully evict it with the gift of the gab. Convincing a vampire that there were more fertile feeding grounds awaiting them elsewhere had worked for me before. It wasn't a great solution, of course. Mostly it just made the vampire someone else's problem, but provided that someone else was far enough away from me, I took it as a win.

I stepped into my cordoned-off storage space and approached the casket. Since the sun was up, it was sleepy time in nosferatu land. It was the only bit of reassurance I had that the occupant wouldn't come leaping out of the box and start chewing on me the second I opened it. If you have to talk to a vampire at all—and I don't recommend it—best do it when they're pooped out. Interrupting their nap will make them grumpy, but I'll take grumpy over hungry any day. At least they'll talk when they're only grumpy. The most you'll get out of them when they're hungry is some rather vulgar "num-num" noises as they tear out your throat and lap at your arterial spray as it fountains all over their ugly faces.

I knocked on the casket lid to announce myself.

"Wakey wakey," I said. "We need to have a chat."

I threw open the lid abruptly, showing no fear. Fear is a quick way to turn yourself into a light snack. There was no one inside.

"Yes we do," came a gravelly, hollow voice from right behind me, and I knew the vampire had emerged from the shadows elsewhere and stepped into the locker with me, blocking the door out.

I'll admit it. I screamed. So much for showing no fear.

"You scared the shit out of me!" I angrily barked at the bloodsucker that had intruded much too far into my personal space.

"I apologize," he said, which was a first. Vampires have a lot to apologize for. Their terrible table manners tops that list, followed closely by their permeating stench. But they always seem to be too busy feasting to be conciliatory.

There must have been a draft in the basement that put the vampire upwind of me. Now that we were in such close quarters, the smell didn't just announce his presence, it blared it like an olfactory fire alarm.

"You mind taking a step back there, big guy. Your deodorant just isn't cutting it today."

He took a step forward instead—a stiff, unliving gait that made my skin crawl. The vampire stood a whole head taller than me and, despite myself, I was intimidated into ceding ground. I edged back. Any farther and I would find myself standing in my vacant casket.

"I need you," he said, betraying a certain longing. If a vampire said anything to its victim before tearing them open, it was usually a bare-bones explanation like that. I braced for a bloodletting and another death I'd have to rise and rehydrate from.

"I am Marin Venerio Grissoni," he said, "and I require your services, necromancer."

I opened my eyes. Only in doing so did I realize I'd had them clenched shut.

"Huh?" I cleverly replied.

"I have travelled a great distance over much time to seek you out," he continued, "even though I heard you were deceased. I trust you are recovered now?"

This Marin was well spoken for a vampire. The accent was European. Not Euro-sexy, but cultured in a formal way that suggested English, perfect as it was, wasn't his first language. Or second. Or third. I took a closer look at him—as close as I cared to get in the dim light—and could almost see the man he had once been behind the grey flesh, sunken white eyes, and maw of tangled teeth.

"Uh, yeah. I'm just jim-dandy now. Thanks for asking."

"There is a pressing matter that connects us both. Threatens us both."

"Well, right now, I'm mostly concerned about you shacking up under the same roof as me."

"It was the best place to await your return," he explained.

"Was it also the best place to help yourself to a tasty human or two?"

"The world is an open buffet for my kind. Humanity is a swelling ocean of blood. I swim as the tide takes me, I drink my fill, and in so doing, I sustain myself through the ages."

I hate it when vampires get poetic about murder, so I got to the point.

"Have you been eating the other tenants?"

"I left the one living in your apartment alone."

"Big of you," I said.

"I thought she might be a partner or associate of some import, and as it was you I had come to see, it seemed prudent to not do anything that might disrupt your business."

"So you don't always think with your stomach. Good to know."

"Of course, if she is of no significance to you, I may indulge this evening. She looks quite delectable."

"Leave her alone, toothy. She's of plenty significance to me."

"As you will."

I looked around my storage locker turned vampire lair.

"So what did you do with all your empties?"

There was no sign of any vampire victims, sucked dry and tossed aside like squeezed lemons. The bloodsucker's eyes shifted to an old travelling trunk I'd had for years. I noticed the boxes of mementos and bags of old photos that had once been inside were now stacked next to it. Without another word, I scooched past the looming undead presence that was crowding me and opened the trunk for a look.

It had been a long time since I'd seen the remains of a vampire victim, and I still found it a touch disquieting. Drained to the last drop, they were nothing but wrinkled skin and dry bones wrapped around organs that had withered away to raisins. What was left behind looked like a rag-doll version of a human, devoid of any stuffing. There must have been as many as ten people crammed into the trunk, and it wasn't that big of a trunk.

I picked one up by the leathery scruff of its neck and looked into the mummified face that was pulled too taut over the skull. The deflated eyeballs that rested at the bottom of their sockets like popped balloons seemed to stare back. They still looked confused, betrayed, horrified.

"Is this Mrs. Rodriguez?" I asked, noting a few familiar features that reminded me of my second-floor neighbour.

The vampire gave me a non-committal shrug and said, "I did not know her name, but she tasted like a Spaniard."

The place should have been swimming with cops looking into missing-persons reports by now, but I'd already guessed what must have happened. Midnight moves by people who couldn't make rent were common enough. And my degenerate sleazebag superintendent would have been perfectly happy to sell off anything they left behind for some quick cash to supplement his free rent and modest wage. The fact that the departed tenants had left behind all their worldly possessions wouldn't strike him as suspicious so much as a happy windfall.

"Look," I began anew, "I'm still officially on sabbatical, so I'm not taking on any new cases. In the meantime, I think you've drained this address enough for the moment. I'm sure there are plenty of better spots for you to tap."

"We must work together," he insisted, "closely."

I ignored him.

"And you know what? As a parting gesture of goodwill, I'll take care of disposing of all these bodies for you. No need to thank me. It's the least I can do after you've come all this way from wherever it was you started out."

There was a furnace in the boiler room I could feed Marin's victims to. Since they were already dried out and folded away into modest bundles, they would burn easily. I didn't like covering up someone else's crimes, but dealing with human remains was, after all, my field.

"He is coming for us both," Marin insisted. "Necromancer and vampire alike, and he shall have us if we are not cautious."

"All the more reason to split up then, don't you think? Be a moving target, make it tough for him."

I didn't know who he was talking about and I didn't really care. If this threat helped me convince a vampire to get the hell out of my home, I'd happily use it without ever knowing what it was.

"You know of whom I speak?"

"I sure do," I said, even though I sure didn't. "In fact, I have him down in my agenda for a meeting right after you. He's swinging around for coffee and a chat."

"We must not be seen colluding!" Marin cried out, fearfully.

I ran with it.

"Right," I agreed. "I'll go and keep him distracted, you slip out the back. The sun's up, but the alley is nice and shady. Keep on the east side of the street so you don't get too sunburned and don't stop moving until you're far far away."

"I have better means of retreat," announced Marin, as he seemed to fade away right in front of my eyes. Before more than a few moments had passed, he had dissipated into a fine mist that drifted out of the locker between the slats and rolled across the floor as a low-hanging fog. It clung to the cement floor, thick enough to hide the entire surface from view, then seemed to decide on a direction and quickly filtered out through a number of cracks in the masonry and gaps in the woodwork.

My line of bullshit had worked. Marin was gone, frightened off, hopefully for good. But I was left troubled, not only by the unknown threat he'd referred to, but his entire demeanor. And especially his means of departure. Vampires have a long list of things they can transform themselves into. Bats are traditional, swarms of rats are common. I once saw one become a pile of hissing black beetles and scurry off in all different directions. But fog, that's a tough one. It takes practice, experience, and lots of time on the job. A vampire that can do fog is really fucking old. He's been around, he knows exactly what he's doing, and he knows all the tricks of the trade. A vampire like that doesn't end up living in a necromancer's basement—sleeping in the necromancer's own casket—without a very specific agenda. He knew the score, and I didn't even know the game we were playing.

Chapter Eight

Rebirth

I SPENT THE REST OF THE DAY second guessing myself. Had I been too hasty getting rid of Marin? Maybe I should have tried to hear him out, even though my patience for threats runs thin at the best of the times, and being in so tight a space with him and his stench made me feel like a condemned man trying to give one final interview from inside the gas chamber. I decided that since my ploy to get him out of the building had worked, I might as well stick with it and seal any avenue of return. That meant a trip to the fruit and vegetable shop around the corner.

Garlic works. In quantity. Vampires suffer from sensory deprivation. They're effectively dead and so are most of their senses. They probably couldn't stomach drinking so much blood if their pallets were up to snuff. They certainly couldn't handle their own stink if their noses were in proper working order. But garlic permeates. It's pungent in just the right ways to penetrate, and it panics vampires when they encounter a strong odour for the first time in years.

So far I had sprinkled mashed cloves in my casket, rubbed garlic juice around all the entrances and emergency exits in the building, lined the windows of the apartment with garlic scapes, and nailed a garlic braid of a dozen cloves to the door of my flat.

Rebecca had watched my preparations in silence, afraid to comment after her invitation gaff, but once I was done she tried to be helpful.

"What else can keep a vampire out?" she asked.

I went through my mental list.

"Rice is good, or really any kind of grain. The older the vampire, the more meticulous it becomes in time. Given enough years, they all develop obsessive-compulsive disorders, and will stop to count the number of grains left by an entrance."

Rebecca checked the kitchen cupboards.

"We're all out of rice. I don't suppose Hamburger Helper is any good?"

"No, but other things can work. Seeds are a safe bet, or..."

I tapered off.

"Or?" Rebecca prompted.

"Salt," I said.

Is that what Oliver thought he was up against in Canning Town? A vampire? It almost made sense. Some vampires can transform themselves into wolves or large dogs, which would explain what I saw. But even then, they drink blood, they don't eat heads. Tempting as it was to combine the two, the square peg refused to fit in the round hole. If there was a connection, I still couldn't make it.

Rebecca didn't notice me musing over recent events and their meaning.

"So are you going to kill him if he comes back?" was all she wanted to know.

"Nope," I said.

"Why not?"

"I can't."

"Are you having some sort of crisis of conscience? I mean, if vampires are as bad as you say..."

"They are. But I can't because it's impossible. Vampires don't die. Ever. The best we can hope for is that I talked him out of hanging around here anymore."

"So vampires can be reasoned with," she concluded, hopefully.

"Not really. But this one was different from the usual sort of blood leech I've encountered. He seems old. Really old. Maybe old enough to have remembered basic human interaction. Things like manners, restraint, negotiation."

"He was very polite to me at the door."

"He still wanted to eat you," I said. "He told me as much."

"Nice of him not to, though, don't you think?"

"Don't," I warned.

"Don't what?"

"Pity him. He was human once, but he's not human anymore. Don't think of him as a person—alive, dead, or undead. Don't think of him being the same species at all. This is a predator that does only two things. Kill and sleep. When it's awake, it kills. When it sleeps, it dreams of killing."

"But you talked to it. *Him.* I talked to him, too. There's a person in there."

"Only enough to keep up appearances long enough for it to close in for the next kill."

"If that's the case, why am I still alive? Why didn't he attack you?"

I couldn't answer that. There genuinely seemed to be something else on this vampire's itinerary. Something that wasn't about feeding.

"Are you done making the whole apartment smell like this inside of a shwarma wrap?" Rebecca asked, seeing I was finished with my precautions.

"I've done what I can," I said. "Hopefully he'll take the hint he's not wanted."

"Good," said Rebecca. "In that case, you have your first business meeting to get to."

"Since when?"

"Since right now."

"Look, I know you're anxious to see me get back to work, but I'm not ready for meetings and appointments and contract negotiations. I'm not open for business. I don't know when or if I will be. Besides, whatever you've booked me for, I'm going to be late if I'm supposed to be there right now."

"Well then, it's a good thing you only have ten feet to commute."

Θ

"I nat shur. I nat feenished lokking at applikints. I let yoo no."

"Don't give me that bullshit," I told Gladys, at the end of my humiliating job interview. "There aren't any other applicants!"

"Neecrewmincers ar a deem a doozin. I tak to dem all da time. Eef I hiar yoo, it oonly becass yoo eesy on da ayes."

"Oh great," I said. "I haven't even been hired yet, and already the boss is sexually harassing me."

"Say dat agin," Gladys demanded.

"You're sexually harassing me."

"Nat dat part! Da beet abat me been da bass."

"You're the boss?" I repeated.

"Fakkin rite I da bass! Say it agin."

"You're the boss."

It was a concession. A highly reluctant one. And it pleased Gladys, I could tell. If she had lips draped over her teeth, she would have pulled them back in an enormous shit-eating grin.

"Okey. Yoo gat da job."

Θ

"How did it go?" Rebecca wanted to know a few minutes later. I felt like I'd just gone ten rounds with the heavyweight champion and lost by unanimous decision.

"I've been hired on a probationary basis."

The words tasted bitter in my mouth.

"Did you negotiate a fair salary?"

"I was offered a livable wage."

It had been difficult trying to explain to Gladys what a livable wage in the modern western world was. She had never been alive in the modern western world—hadn't been alive at all in a very long time—and had forgotten about some of life's petty necessities. Like food and the price of groceries.

"Now that we've got the financials squared away," said Rebecca, "I wanted to talk to you about your uniform."

I was immediately confused.

"What uniform? I don't have a uniform."

"Gladys and I have been discussing that, and we've decided you need a uniform in order to present a certain professional image to the public."

"What, like a red shirt and a visored cap and a nametag that says, 'Hi, my name is Rip Eulogy. How may I serve you?'"

"Interesting suggestion. We'll take it under advisement at the next meeting of the board of directors. In the interim, I came up with something that better presents the image of a necromancer. It's all about branding, and you need to live up to client expectations when they're consulting with you about death."

"What the hell do you know about image branding?"

Rebecca cocked her head as she glowered at me, burning a hole through me with her eyes.

"I've been in marketing my entire professional career," she growled.

"Have you?" I said, genuinely surprised. News to me.

"For fuck's sake, Rip, you've known me how many years and you don't know what I do for a living?"

"Judging from the fumes that routinely come off of you, I always assumed you worked in a distillery."

"Cute," she sneered, scrunching up her face. I mirrored her expression back at her.

"I'll have you know," she added, "that this is a dry apartment. I haven't had a drink of anything in over a year."

"You're shitting me."

"It was getting to be a problem."

"I hadn't noticed," I said to be polite.

"I got myself into a twelve-step and everything."

"So you submitted to a higher power to overcome your addiction?"

"I had problems with that step. You're the one who told me there was no higher power to believe in."

"I guess I would know," I agreed. Being dead so many times, you'd think I would have bumped into one by now.

"Luckily the program has had a secular rewrite over the years."

"Things really have changed in my absence."

"Some for the better," said Rebecca.

"Still," I lamented, "I'll miss watching you drink yourself beyond the power of speech. I'll miss the silence most of all."

"Some things certainly haven't changed at all. You can still be a real dick."

"I'd raise a toast to consistency, but apparently that's not your thing anymore."

Rebecca parted the curtains on a window and looked down at the street below.

"Is it safe to go out?" she asked. "Or are there too many vampires lurking?"

"It's daylight," I said. "He'll make himself scarce for now."

"Good. We're going shopping. Whole new outfit for you. I'm thinking dark and retro."

"I hate shopping for clothes."

"Then I'll go by myself and you'll wear whatever I bring back from the thrift store."

"The hell I will."

"You'll wear it and you'll love it," Rebecca insisted.

I could tell, before she even selected a single stitch, that I would hate it.

"In the meantime, let's do something about that bush you're trying to grow on your face. It makes you look more like a Viking than a necromancer."

"I'll shave," I said.

"Not so fast," she said, assessing her semi-blank slate. "Have you considered a goatee?"

"I try not to consider any hair styles named after a barnyard animal, why?"

"I think it would look good on you. I think it would make you look sinister."

"Why would I want to look sinister?"

"You're a necromancer, dummy. People expect a necromancer to look sinister."

"People expect me to do the job they hire me to do," I said.

"And you can look sinister while you're doing it at no extra charge."

"Is it too late for me to call a placement centre and find myself some office-overflow work?"

"Sit," she demanded, grabbing a single dining chair and setting it down in the middle of the living room. So I sat.

Rebecca draped a table cloth over me and tied it around my neck. One dip into the bathroom for a razor, shaving cream, and a pair of scissors later, and the torture session began.

Θ

It was the longest haircut of my life. Rebecca's fine tuning seemed to extend to the precise length of every hair follicle on my head and face. Extra care was taken to get her envisioned goatee just so, like a sculptor being mindful not to chip too much off the marble block in case it turned out the lost nugget would be needed at a later moment of creative inspiration. It felt so exacting, I knew at once I would never be able to maintain it. Not unless Rebecca tackled me and forced me to undergo home-salon maintenance on a weekly basis. I didn't put it past her to do just that.

"There," she said at long last, stepping back and letting the overtaxed scissors cool off. "Have a look and tell me what you think."

Rebecca retrieved a compact mirror from her purse and opened it in front of my face. The reflective surface caught the setting sun through the window and bounced it back at me. I winced—not at the damage done, but the sudden bright light.

"Ow," I commented.

"That bad?" she asked.

"I don't know," I said, squinting. "I can't see your handiwork thanks to the last bit of redecoration you did to my face. My one white eye is light sensitive."

"Hmm," she said, not the least bit apologetic. "Let's see if we can work with that."

Rebecca went rummaging in her purse again and came up with a pair of flip sunglasses with small round wire rims. She left one of the shaded flaps down, but raised the other, unscrewed it, and removed it completely. When she hooked them over my ears, the tinted lens sheltered my damaged eye.

"Better?" she asked.

"I guess."

She held up the mirror again and I hardly recognized myself. Between the haircut, the goatee, and the ying-yang sunglass, I looked like a bass player from some one-hit-wonder alternative rock band. The obligatory weird one in the group who didn't speak during interviews.

"Seriously?" was my only critique.

"You're going to try," Rebecca told me patiently. "The right outfit to go with it, and we'll have a whole new you. Someone who looks the part. Everyone's going to wonder who the mystery man is, and you'll burn through your stack of business cards. No more scraping by. You'll be turning down contracts."

"I'm on a salary," I reminded her. "I'm scraping by regardless. What do I care about bringing in new business?"

"Work hard, do a good job, and maybe you can make partner one day."

"Partner in my own home office," I snorted. "Some promotion."

"You can keep the glasses. As for the rest, I'll have to see what I can dig up."

She went to the hall closet and rifled through the various coats and jackets inside.

"I'm not wearing any of your clothes," I told her.

"I happen to own some very stylish unisex outfits. Nothing that's going to fit you, though. I was hoping maybe there were gloves or a scarf we could use, but everything is too colourful. Too happy. We want grim. Basic black, matte, muted, dull."

Thwarted, she shut the door and started back, only to trip over the parcel I'd brought from the Wonderama. It had been left in the hall, forgotten, since our reunion.

"What's in this box I keep having to step over? Is it a present for me?"

"It's an inheritance. For me," I said. "Wilbur left it."

"Can I open it?"

"Enjoy," I instructed her, as I undid the table cloth from around my neck and stood up, shedding no end of stubble all over the floor.

"Oh," declared Rebecca once she'd torn off the wrapping and flipped open the lid of the cardboard cube beneath. "Oh my."

"What is it?" I asked.

Rebecca turned to me and smiled broadly.

"It's perfect," she said.

Θ

I was exhausted with Rebecca's makeover, and she was barely halfway done. After begging for an intermission, she gave me an hour to go through my office and take inventory of what was there nearly four years after I'd last had a chance to file things or put them in any order. Much had been moved or misplaced, but one key item remained front and centre.

"I'm glad you didn't throw Louie away," I said of the small jar of formaldehyde that was preserving the reassembled partial human brain within.

"I didn't exactly know what to do with him," said Rebecca. "I mean, he's still a person. Sort of. At least *you* can talk to him. Gladys too, when I pop him in her skull for date night."

"Are they still a couple?"

"Sporadically," Rebecca shrugged. "Who can really tell? A brain and a skull. I guess they complete each other. Sort of. Mostly they seem to bicker. I only hear the Gladys end of things."

"I bet that's an earful."

"It sounds pretty dysfunctional. On the other hand, maybe the fighting is their version of dirty hate-sex. Who are we to judge? At least they can say they've been a couple longer than anyone else I know."

I would have to initiate contact with Louie again, but put it off for a later time, once I was settled back in and mentally prepared to hear about the romantic woes of a former coroner, who got his brains sloppily scooped out, and then fell for a hot-tempered skull. Relationships are complicated. Some more than others.

I was barely through a single filing cabinet when inventory was interrupted by the lobby door bell.

"Check who that is before buzzing them in," I instructed Rebecca. The sun was still up, but a vampire visitation wasn't out of the question.

"Of course," she replied. "You've got me all paranoid now."

Rebecca hit the intercom button and listened.

"It's Tom," said the voice on the speaker.

"It's Tom," Rebecca echoed at me, and leaned on the buzzer to unlock the downstairs door.

"I hear he's been touring a lot."

"He's been looking for more gigs out of town if that's what you mean."

"Broadening his fan base?"

"More like trying to be elsewhere. Anywhere but here."

"Oh?" I asked, curious despite my natural distaste for gossip. "What's he hiding from?"

"Me, mostly," said Rebecca. "He still checks in. Like now. Making sure I'm okay and still off the sauce. But, uh, we had a thing for a while."

"A thing?" I asked, fishing for a definition.

"A thing that, like most things, ended."

"You going to tell me what happened?"

"What happened is I sobered up. I stopped drinking and a realized I was in a relationship with a guy who barfs up novelties and knickknacks for a percentage of the cover charge."

"And you're a professional woman with a professional career."

"Right," she said, not sounding so certain of this fact.

"In marketing," I added.

"You remembered. How sweet."

"I get it," I claimed. "I do. You're from different worlds, going in different directions."

"Exactly."

I could hear the elevator arrive in the hall.

"So... Is he still hung up on you?"

"Wouldn't you be?" said Rebecca, throwing open the door. Tom was standing right behind it.

"Hey," said Tom, flatly.

"Hey," Rebecca said back at him, equally straight-faced.

It was hardly a chatty exchange. There was a lot of unspoken history there. Three years' worth. I had missed it all.

Tom's eyes fell on me. He looked surprised but not shocked. Rather than greet me or say anything at all to me, he turned to Rebecca.

"He's back?"

"He's back," Rebecca confirmed.

"When?"

"Yesterday."

"And you're already living together?"

"I moved back into my own apartment!" I interjected into the conversation that seemed determined to continue like I wasn't even in the room.

"It's been a long time," said Tom more civilly. "How have you been, Rip?"

"Dead."

"Right," Tom caught himself. "Because of that whole... death thing. Gotcha."

"So what brings you by?" I asked. "I'm guessing it's not this big welcome-home party that's been blowing the roof off the place since yesterday."

"I was just stopping by to check up on Rebecca," he said, like he'd been caught doing something shady. "As I do. I've been on the road for the last couple of weeks."

"I keep telling you I'm fine," Rebecca told Tom. "I can take care of myself."

"No you can't," I interjected, and then said to Tom, "No she can't. You keep right on checking up on her."

"What is this patronizing bullshit I'm getting from both ends now?" fumed Rebecca.

"Rebecca," I explained patiently, "I believe today we already established that if someone's not keeping an eye on you, you do silly things."

"Has she been drinking?" Tom asked, concern suddenly spiking.

"Worse than that," I said. "She's been inviting vampires into the building."

"Remember the delivery guy who was asking about Rip last month?" Rebecca reminded Tom. She turned to me and mentioned, "Tom was over at the time. He saw him too."

Tom knew at once who she was referring to. Marin would be hard to forget.

"Right. The creepy one with the personal hygiene issues."

"Turns out...not a delivery guy," said Rebecca.

"We ran into each other in the lobby that night," recalled Tom. "He was on his way back out. Very polite, I thought. A real gentleman. Just, you know..."

"Creepy," said Rebecca, completing Tom's thought.

"And smelly," he added.

"With bad breath."

"And really crooked teeth."

Their description wasn't telling me anything I hadn't seen for myself, but it disturbed me just the same. Two potential victims in a row, and Marin hadn't touched either of them. In fact, he'd been unusually gracious and social with my friends. Even as he was plotting to set up residence in the basement and help himself to the other tenants in the building as he pleased.

"He was pretty disgusting," said Rebecca.

"Repellant," Tom concurred.

"But you kind of felt drawn to him anyway."

"He had a certain charm to him."

"Like a really butt-ugly guy you meet in a bar and would normally want to run away from but you don't because there's an underlying charisma—and then it's last call and the next thing you know you wake up in his apartment in the morning and can only find one shoe."

Rebecca, lost in thought, returned to reality when she caught Tom and me staring at her.

"Not that anything like that has ever happened to me personally," she clarified.

"It's what vampires do to get close to their victims," I explained. "They mesmerize you with superficial charm that makes you look past how repulsive they are, and that's how they get in. Like insurance salesmen and politicians. Don't fall for it."

"There was just something so compelling about him," Tom recalled. "I couldn't look away. And I could have listened to him for hours."

Again, it was the sort of charm only a very old vampire could turn on. The oldest vampire I had ever encountered in the past had been prowling for less than a century. There had been no charm to contend with. Only snapping teeth and swiping claws. It made me wonder how far back Marin's personal history stretched, but there wasn't enough data to make the calculation.

Tom drew me out of my thoughts a moment later as he poked one of my severed locks of hair on the floor with his toe.

"Who's shedding? You adopt a dog while I was away?"

"I was trying to give Rip some style," said Rebecca. "He came home looking like some shaggy mountain man."

"Right, the facial hair is new," Tom remembered. "I wouldn't have noticed otherwise."

"You need to see the whole effect," said Rebecca, handing me the modified sunglasses.

I reluctantly put them on to model her handiwork for Tom.

"What's with the half-shades?" he asked.

"It's my white eye. Too much light irritates it. This helps."

Tom nodded knowingly.

"Maybe it's the rims. It gives you a certain pirate-John Lennon effect."

Rebecca stepped away for a moment and then approached me from behind to set the hat on my head like she was crowning royalty.

"Ta-da!" she announced.

Tom snickered on cue. The hat was the final gift from Wilbur. It had been the sole contents of the box, without so much as a note to explain what it was or why it was now mine. There didn't need to be. I knew as soon as I saw it.

"A top hat?" asked Tom, not masking his derision.

"Yes, a top hat," insisted Rebecca.

"When I bought my stage tux in a vintage shop, there was a top hat for sale, too. I didn't bother because there's such a thing as taking it too far."

It had to have been the one Wilbur used on his old TV show for years. A pivotal prop in an act that had lasted for generations and delighted a million children. It had been home to many a deck of cards, hundreds of collapsible flower bouquets, and a long lineage of docile rabbits.

"It's not just any top hat. It's a magic one," I said, and then clarified. "Fake magic, not real magic."

There was nothing more mystical about it than a false bottom from which any number of props and small animals could be pulled. Even so, that at least promised to provide some handy storage space.

"It makes you look like an antique undertaker," Tom decided.

"Exactly!" Rebecca beamed. I'm sure she felt vindicated. I, for my part, still felt like a bit of an idiot.

There was a knock on the door and Rebecca, still smiling ear-to-ear, went to get it. Before I could stop her, she'd yanked it open, revealing Marin Venerio Grissoni filling the frame, blocking passage in or out.

"May I come in?" he asked.

"No!" I yelled, too late. Rebecca and Tom had already said, "Sure" and "Okay" respectively.

The vampire stepped across the threshold and into my home.

"Guys!" I shouted at them, and they looked apologetic, for all that was worth—which was nothing at all.

"Hold it right there, Snaggletooth," I said, blocking the undead interloper with one hand to his chest. I could feel his bony cold ribs right through his thick woolen coat. "You need to be invited in by the rightful owner and I'm it."

"You rent, do you not?" Marin asked.

"Well, yeah."

"Then is it not your landlord who is the rightful owner?"

"Don't go quoting technicalities at me. He didn't invite you either."

"I was invited in by the charming woman who dwells in this abode," he said, making eyes at Rebecca. Despite herself, she seemed flattered.

"Don't go getting all flirty with the lady. You're at least three centuries past being able to seduce anything," I reminded him, cruelly but accurately. He looked like shit, even for a vampire. At least he was better mannered than the newbies, who are terrible conversationalists that eat first and, at best, only comment on the meal after it's already dead and unable to respond.

"I apologize," said Marin, bowing his head ever so slightly, as an aristocrat from a bygone era might. "I do not wish to interfere with the virtue of your woman."

Rebecca and I both snorted, stifling a laugh. Not about the same thing, as it turned out.

"Virtue?" I asked.

"His woman?" said Rebecca.

"His then?" asked Marin, looking at Tom.

"We used to date," Rebecca explained. "And Rip lives here. But we're all just friends."

Marin's pale eyes rolled around inside his skull, from one face to the next, trying to sort things out.

"A difficult concept," he concluded. "The world is much changed from what I remember of being human."

"How are you even in here?" I wanted to know.

"I was invited. I entered," he explained.

I tore the braid of garlic off the door that was still hanging open and shoved it in the vampire's face.

"Doesn't this repulse you? Make you sick?" I demanded.

"As I have said, I am Marin Venerio Grissoni. I am dead now, but when I lived, I lived my life in Italy. And garlic," he said, cupping a bulb from the braid in one of his claw-like hands and inhaling its fragrance deeply, "is the most beautiful of all flowers."

"Well, shit," I said, wondering how many meals it would take to use up so many cloves that had proved otherwise useless.

"Might we speak now?" said the vampire, taking me aside. "I trust our adversary has left."

"What adversary are you talking about?"

"The threat I spoke of. He comes for us both."

"Right, him," I remembered. "He was never here. I strung you some bullshit to get you to leave, but obviously that didn't pan out because here you are again."

"It is essential we discuss our plan to evade his grasp. You are already marked," Marin said, pointing one of his split and filthy fingernails at my damaged eye. "I have not yet received The Mark of the Sighted One, yet I know I am selected. He will seek to destroy you and subjugate me. This must not come to pass!"

I wanted to give Marin a fair chance to bring me up to speed—it sounded like it might be important—but my heart wasn't in it. It had been a long day and I'd had my fill of garlic-loving vampires, Rebecca and her makeover assault, Gladys and her attempts to turn me into an indentured servant, and Tom haunting the apartment like the ghost of failed-relationships-past.

"Fuck it!" I announced. "I'm going out for a drink."

"A drink?" Marin asked expectantly.

"Not that kind of a drink!"

"I think I could use a few, too," said Tom. He caught Rebecca's eye and apologized, "Sorry."

"Don't mind me," she replied. "I'm on the wagon and I want no part of it. You have your boys' night out."

"I was planning on drinking alone," I began, but stopped when I caught Tom's expectant look. "Fine. You might as well join me."

"I, too, shall join, necromancer!"

The familiar bellow came from inside Tom's jacket. He pulled out his gutted pocket watch and I could see the tattered fish inside swimming loops around the aquatic enclosure.

"And of course you still have that damn thing," I noted. "Fine. Let's make it a team effort. You, me, Moby-Dick. Louie might as well come along, too. Right Louie?"

I grabbed the jar of brains on the way out the door. As soon as I touched it and said his name aloud, I felt Louie's presence and heard his thoughts.

"Rip? Oh my God, Rip, is that you? They told me you were dead!"

"Dead drunk before the hour is out if I can manage it," I told Louie.

I felt momentarily concerned about leaving Rebecca alone with Marin, but remembered she'd already been alone with him for nearly a month without incident. Still, I knew I should say something.

"Both of you, no juicing. I don't want to come back here and find out you've been enabling each other's addictions."

Rebecca looked insulted. Marin only looked undead. The rest of us were gone a moment later.

We were out on the street and less than a block away when a cloud of white mist formed directly in front of us. The street-lights had just come on with the dark, and the beam of light made the isolated fog bank glow as it drew in upon itself and formed a humanoid shape.

Marin finished manifesting in front of us and asked, "Might I attend the festivities?"

It sounded like a plea from someone who craved companionship even more than blood. I remained firm.

"Boys' night out is for living boys only."

"Half your party consists of a partial human brain and a dead fish possessed," he said.

"He has a point," said Tom.

I crumbled. I'd had my fill of bickering.

"Okay, you're in. First round is on you. If anybody passes out, that's not an invitation to suck them dry."

"I will refrain from feasting upon anyone in our company," Marin agreed as he joined us.

There was a little dive bar a few blocks away I had in mind. It was early and we would have the place to ourselves. I only hoped the group I was bringing with me didn't send the bartender screaming into the night. Who would mix our drinks then?

Chapter Nine

Last Call

THE BARTENDER WAS SURPRISINGLY COOL with his first customers of the evening. The place was enough of a dive that he saw all types. I was sure I had just brought in some types he'd never seen before, but he was jaded enough to think he'd seen everything, so I didn't try to burst his bubble. The closest he came to busting us was carding Tom before he served the first round.

Tom reached for his driver's licence when the bartender set it back on the bar, but I snatched it up first and gave it a read. Tom's full name was there in print. I had never heard it before. Since I'd known him, he'd just been "Tom." Or his ridiculous stage persona.

"Thomas Kincaid? That's your real name?" I asked, handing the card back flabbergasted.

"On my birth certificate and everything," Tom confirmed.

"You have a cool name like Thomas Kincaid and you went with 'The Amazing Barfo' professionally?"

"Barfo sells tickets. And he is amazing."

"Thomas Kincaid sounds like a proper magician. A class act, sophisticated, debonair."

"You've seen my act. Is there anything classy about it?"

"The tuxedo," I said, after some protracted contemplation.

"Exactly. I'm a regurgitator, not a mentalist. If you have a gross skill set, you sell it with a descriptive name. Isn't that right, Rip Eulogy?"

"Don't lecture me on how to sell my wares. I've had enough coaching for one day."

I set my top hat down on the bar and ordered a spiced rum. Tom just had a bottled beer, not even a draft. The bartender asked Marin his pleasure, but the vampire wanted nothing.

"Designated driver?" he was asked rhetorically. "Can I get you a soda water?"

"I will have something later," Marin assured him.

"No you won't," I said.

"Or not," he agreed.

The first three rounds went down quick and easy. Tom and I were feeling loose and relaxed within half an hour. We nursed the next three rounds over the following hour. Tom, not kidding around, switched from beer to scotch. That left us well and truly tipsy. The next three rounds got us shitfaced, and we wanted everyone else to join us in our drunken bliss. I poured a shot of gin into Louie's brain jar, which got him fucked up in short order. I accused him of being a lightweight, but I don't think I would have fared any better if someone started pouring alcohol directly on my grey matter. In no time, he was lamenting his rocky relationship with Gladys. I had started to tell him the epic story of my return from oblivion, but once he caught up getting as drunk as I already was, he was more interested in soliciting half-baked advice about his love life.

"Mixed relationships are still tough, even today. People can be so judgmental."

"A brain and a skull seem like a perfect match," I opined. "Two sides of the same coin."

"When I say people can be judgmental, I mostly mean Gladys. She can be..."

"Loud, obnoxious, insane?" I suggested.

"Critical," said Louie. "I mean, sure, those other things too. But it's the criticism I have a problem with."

"You're a brain in a jar," I reminded him. "What's to be critical of? That you watch too much TV? You don't have eyes. That you lie around on the couch all day? The only way you could do that is if someone put you there. That you don't have a job? You have more brains than the average barista, but not the hands to make those silly designs in the foam."

"In her defence, I will admit I have a lot of vivid sexual thoughts going on most of the time."

"Of course you do," I said. "You're a guy and you have nothing to do but think all day long, with no body to give you an outlet. You can't even plug into the internet, so it's up to you to run your own mental porn site. You ever ask Gladys what she gets up to online? I bet it's not so innocent."

I knew for a fact it wasn't so innocent—though her interests ran more towards murder and fraud.

"It's not just that. She also makes fun of my vocabulary. I'm just a partial brain, so there are a lot of things missing, and I don't always know the right banana for everything."

"Word," I corrected. "You mean the right word for everything."

"Exactly!" said Louie. "Banana. I'll try to remember that. No, wait, I lost it again."

"Look, Louie, Gladys is the last person in the world who should be criticizing anybody's language skills. You have to stand up to her."

"I have no feet to stand on."

"Put her in her place."

"I'm the one who gets placed. Specifically inside her skull, otherwise we can't talk."

"You think maybe it's time to split up with her?" I asked.

"I couldn't do that. I love her. It would break my heart."

"You don't have a heart, Louie."

"Of course I do, Rip. A heart isn't an organ in your chest. It's a state of mind."

Apparently Tom and Moby-Dick had experience being drinking buddies on the road with their regurgitation act. Tom had an eyedropper which he used to drip-dose the fish in his miniature aquarium. I'd been relating what Louie had to say about the ups and downs of romance, and it was catching. The moment Tom's pal become insta-soused by sucking a single drop of scotch through his gills, the lesser demon, Qixxiqottltoq, starting talking shit about his own woes through his puckering goldfish face.

"The she-fish will not spawn with me," moped Moby.

"What's he saying?" I asked, after the comment penetrated the seventh-round haze.

"I think he's bitching about some guppy slut who won't put out for him," Tom elucidated. "I made the mistake of bringing him to a pet store when I was browsing props for my act."

"I will fertilize all over her eggs," groused our aquatic companion. "This I swear!"

"Yeah, you go for it Moby-Dickless, ol' boy," I encouraged him. "Show her who's boss."

"What exactly possesses your fish?" Marin, the only sober one at the bar, wanted to know.

"I dunno," said Tom. "He says he's a minion of the Canaan-ite fish-god, Dagon. His right-fin man or something."

"Is he still trying to talk you into doing naughty things, Tommy?" I inquired.

"We have come to an arrangement," Tom said. "I carry him around, I feed him, I care for him, I change his water now and then. And in return he doesn't try to drive me mad by whispering soul-damning suggestions into my ear all night when I'm trying to sleep."

"You will purchase for me the she-guppy so that I may ravish her without mercy," said Moby-Dick.

"That wasn't part of our deal," said Tom. "You want extras like that, you have to hold up your end of the act better than you have been."

"You swallow me, I return. This is the bargain I uphold!"

"That part is all on me. What I need you to do is stop insulting the audience."

"They are cackling fools and imbeciles!" raged Moby-Dick. "This fact they must know, if they know nothing else!"

"I've seen your fans, Tom," I reminded him. "They're not exactly sophisticates out for a highbrow soiree at the theatre."

Tom kept trying to get his partner to toe the line.

"The talking-fish routine only works if you don't alienate the paying public!"

"What care I if they feel slighted by truth?" replied Moby-Dick. "They should tremble at the thought of Qixxiqottltoq's wrath, and bow before me in deference and fear!"

"Audiences don't respond well to contempt. And your shouting is throwing the timing of the gags off."

"You speak to me of humour? You say nothing amusing in your act!"

"There's more to comedy than telling jokes. It's about the physicality, the gestures, the nuance."

My chuckle echoed out of the drained shot glass in my hand.

"'Nuance,' says the Astounding Puke-Face," I laughed breathlessly.

"Amazing Barfo!" insisted Tom.

"Whatever," I said, waving him off.

"Just for that, I'm not going to tell you," he grumbled.

"Tell me what?" I asked, trying to keep a straight face. I felt a touch guilty for siding with a demonic fish against Tom, but my opinion of regurgitation acts hadn't improved in the last few years.

"You told me not to say." Tom shook his head, "I wanted to. I thought you should know, but screw it."

"When did I tell you this?" I asked, suddenly suspicious.

"Nope. Not gonna say," announced Tom in drunken stubbornness and fell silent.

I was getting that "Something freaky this way comes" feeling, and I didn't like it. I hoped it was just the booze talking, but my intuition was telling me other things.

The next three rounds were a mistake.

Marin had been off in the toilets for a long time, possibly evacuating necrotic blood but more likely scouting potential victims among the barflies that had been trickling in all evening. The party had reconvened in a booth because, drunk as we were, it had become too easy to fall off our bar stools. By the time he found us and squeezed in, I was on about how being a necromancer in the modern world sucked. It was an old complaint that only ever occurred to me and got spoken aloud when I was hammered.

"I might have liked being some Dark Mage," I said, "back in the golden age of magic and mysticism, living in a wizard tower, commanding a vast army of the undead."

"That's not real history," Tom slurred. "That's storybook stuff."

"Sounds better than making ends meet in a shitty apartment, doing freelance work for cheapskates and assholes, getting bossed around by a skull who can barely speak the language she's abusing me with."

"Mister Eulogy," Marin interrupted, "we must discuss the matter which presses upon us both at your earliest convenience."

"All right," I said, throwing back the rest of the current round I had only started sipping, "hit me."

Of course, now that I was soused enough to hear it, he was hesitant.

"Later perhaps, when you are less inebriated."

"That's the only reason I'm listening now, so you better go for it."

"Would you excuse us?" Marin asked Tom and Moby-Dick. They nodded as best a drunk and a fish could manage. Tom had bought a pitcher of beer for the table and was letting Moby-Dick swim around in it freely. It may have spoiled the beer, but at least it had shut the fish up.

Marin and I slipped into a smaller booth in the corner that barely sat two.

"We drinking buddies now?" I asked.

"I have had nothing to drink in many days," said Marin.

"Cutting down?"

"Trying to kill less," he stated earnestly.

"You certainly managed to go through plenty of my neighbours."

"A few small indulgences compared to my usual appetite."

"Since when do vampires give a shit about how many people they kill?"

"Since I have been asked to participate in mass murder so vast, the act of killing, even for my own sustenance, has begun to repulse me."

"You're right," I said at the first mention of mass murder, "maybe I am too drunk to get into it right now. I'd go home to sleep it off, but somebody's taken over my bed."

"Your woman shuns you?"

"Not her. You."

"The casket was your place of repose?"

"Of course it was mine!"

"I apologize," said Marin. "You may have it back if you wish. I will arrange for another location to shelter myself from the day."

"I don't want it now that you've filled it with your corpse-stink. Why did you come here anyway? I've been dead and gone for years. As far as anyone knew, I was going to stay that way."

"He told me you would return," explained Marin.

"Who told you?"

I had a sneaking suspicion who.

"I do not know exactly who or what he is. He did not give me a name. He only gave me his card."

I chased my sneaking suspicion with an easy guess.

"And there was no name or number on the card?"

Marin reached into his coat and removed a slip of card stock that had been tucked inside. He placed it on the table for me to see, but it was too dark to read in a dingy bar. I didn't have to angle the black-on-black print to the scant light so the glossy letters would show against the matte background. I already knew the name that would appear there if I did.

"The name on the card is 'Charlie Nocturne,'" I said. "You'd have seen that for yourself if you hung around in better-lit places."

"I have been aware of this entity for some time now. Through the years and the centuries, I felt I was being watched. Assessed."

"Charlie's still lurking around, trying to recruit for Team End Times?"

"Only recently was direct contact made, and in our brief exchange I was told of a plot to bring about the termination of all life," confirmed Marin. "It seems I am to play a pivotal role in the prophecy manifest."

"Why you?"

"I possess certain appropriate traits it would seem."

"So this is who you were hiding from, the one you wanted to warn me was coming for us," I said, staring down at Charlie Nocturne's calling card.

"Oh no," Marin said to my incorrect conclusion. "This Nocturne creature desires to use me for a purpose I want no part of, but there is another who approaches who is a much more pressing concern. Nocturne's plan has yet to be realized—may never be realized if we resist it. He is a concern for the future. I speak of a threat in the present. One who has already cut a swath of destruction around the world, and is here among us now, with more murder and destruction on his agenda."

"Is this why Charlie sent you to me?"

"He did not send me. Your name came up when he told me of his other recruits. He said you were the only one to elude the destiny he foresaw—that despite his being convinced you were the Death Incarnate he sought, you successfully refused the position, going so far as to die permanently to avoid it. He believed you would eventually return, however, so I came here to await you. I dared hope that you could help me escape his machinations, as you apparently have."

"But now there's somebody else in the mix. Somebody new."

Marin confirmed it.

"Your replacement."

"So Charlie has himself an emergency backup Death Incarnate. I guess I should be jealous."

"Another necromancer," said Marin.

"Like me?"

"No," he said, shaking his head. "Powerful. Dangerous. He kills the living as prolifically as he raises the dead."

Considering who Charlie Nocturne had recruited to play the role of War in his world-ending escapade, this guy sounded like a good match.

"What does he want?"

"My power and your destruction."

"What's he have against me?" I protested. "I may be back, but I'm minding my own business. Sounds like he's already landed the gig and he's welcome to it. I passed."

"You were the first choice," Marin reminded me. "That does not sit well with the one who has inherited the position. He seeks to eliminate you and all other conceivable competition so there will be no doubt who is the best and final choice for the personification of Death in this prophecy."

"What do you mean by all other conceivable competition?"

"Other necromancers have been removed from the field," Marin said. "I am aware of instances in Istanbul, Alexandria, Rabat, Madrid, and Lyon."

Suddenly, Oliver's demise didn't seem to be an isolated incident—a one-off case gone wrong.

"London," I added to the list, speaking softly.

"There is a trail to be followed. Not direct, but distinct, and it leads here."

"These other necromancers," I resumed after a long silence, "were all found decapitated?"

"I do not know the specifics of their various ends," said Marin. "Is that important?"

"Maybe," was all I said.

"There are other necromancers still spread across Europe, but they are all minor practitioners. The major players are gone. Rumours suggest the origins of the trail may lead all the way back to China. This I have not confirmed."

"You say he wants you. What for?"

"How better to personify death than to join the ranks of the undead?" Marin speculated. "He is human now, a mighty necromancer the likes of which I have never before encountered. Despite the power he already possesses, he seeks to also control the forces of the night as only the most venerable of vampires can. Consuming my essence will bring him all the wisdom of the ages it has taken me centuries to accumulate. With my strength flowing through him, he will be an unstoppable force."

"What happens if he gets to you? Won't that screw up our mutual friend's plan to have you fill a saddle as one of his vanguard horsemen?"

"Drained, spent, withered, I will only better embody the role Charlie Nocturne wishes to cast me in. For I, it seems, am to be his Famine."

After taking that in for a moment, I announced, "I need another drink. You?"

"Yes," agreed Marin. "But not the kind they serve here."

"Right."

"Allow me to buy you another round," he offered. "Inebriated as you already are, I sympathize with your desire to finish drinking yourself into unconsciousness after what I have told you."

He dug into a small leather purse that had probably held whatever wealth he had scrounged from his victims going back to the Middle Ages. He produced a few modern bills, stained with blood that had turned brown with age. It was a nice gesture just the same.

"You know, for a vampire, you're not so..." I searched for the right word.

"Smelly?" he suggested.

"No, you stink," I assured him. "You stink bad. 'Feral' was the word I was looking for."

"I am not a recent creation, as you might already suspect. After several centuries, one learns a measure of control. Even now, much as I would like to slice your hand off at the wrist and suckle deeply from the spurting stump, I choose not to, as I realize there are greater things to be accomplished by not indulging as my desires command."

"Nice of you," I said.

He dipped his head in a curt bow as I flagged the bartender.

Two more shots and I could no longer count how many I'd had. Math was beyond me. If it hadn't been for the table propping me up, I'd have been under it. It didn't keep me from talking shit, as drunks do. It sounded profound in the moment, stupid in retrospect.

"Being dead for a few years really changes your perspective on life," I mumbled.

"I have been dead for hundreds," said Marin, staring through a wall at a distant point in his past.

"Yeah, but you're not all-the-way dead, are you? You're half-dead, undead, all-fucked-up-dead, but not dead-gone-dead."

"Dead and gone is often preferable to undead and lingering."

"Yeah," I said, "but you can do some cool shit. That turning into mist thing—that's a good trick. Never seen that before. Bravo."

I tried to applaud, but my hands kept missing each other.

"I have only been able to accomplish that transformation for the last century or so," said Marin, sounding flattered. "It was difficult to learn."

"What else can you transform into? A wolf maybe?" I suggested, perhaps too suspiciously.

"I can transform myself into a great many things, but not the one thing I most desire to be: a mortal man who can breathe and feel and love."

I sputtered into my drink, trying not to laugh too hard and spill it.

"That line of shit work with the ladies?" I chortled, as I wiped my mouth with a napkin.

"No," he replied, his eyes sad, his face long.

"I didn't think so."

For a guy who wasn't boozing it up with the rest of us, Marin looked sadder than the saddest drunk in the joint. I thought getting him to talk about better times might cheer up the bloodsucker and take his mind off all the veins he wasn't currently tapping.

"Where are you from, originally? I mean other than Italy before it was even Italy. Back when you were a human walking around with the rest of us heart-pumping sippy-sacks."

"Venice," he said. "When it was its own empire, and the greatest seat of power in all of the Mediterranean."

"Ah, Venice," I echoed.

"You have been?"

"Nope."

"Pity," he said. "It remains to this day much as I remember it. A man-made jewel floating on a lagoon, propped up by a petrified forest of support beams—an engineering marvel stuck in time. It should have sunk to the bottom of the sea long ago, like Atlantis before it, but my Venice was too beautiful for men to let slip away into history and legend. They have preserved it and cherished it."

"You go back sometimes, take a gondola ride, eat a tourist or two?"

"Alas, the very structure of my home city is not welcoming to what I have become. The many narrow streets lead to many short bridges across many canals. And with the coming and going of the tide, the water below can be seen, at times, to run."

"Running water," I repeated knowingly. Vampires can't cross it for reasons that were arcane to mere mortals, myself included.

"As such," said Marin, "I can never return."

"That sucks," I said. Even drunk I caught myself. "Sorry, I didn't mean 'sucks' like vampires suck blood. I meant...I hate puns."

"I quite understand. And I agree. Such is the tragedy of my unliving state."

"I guess that means vampirism wasn't catching in Venice. How'd you get the bite?"

"You ask to hear my tale?"

"We've got an hour till closing," I said, consulting the clock over the bar. "I'll give you until they kick us out."

"I am Marin Venerio Grissoni," he began.

"I know that part," I interrupted.

I was too pissed to listen politely, certainly too pissed to process it at the time. Even now, my memory of what he said is fuzzy. It's taken some effort to piece together a reasonable transcript. When he began again, this is, more or less, what he said:

Θ

I am Marin Venerio Grissoni, and immortality will be the death of me.

The first time I rose from the dead was an inauspicious occasion. The Black Death was sweeping across Europe, and so many people were falling into early graves, no one noticed when one of the bodies got back up. What had caused the epidemic was a mystery. None would have believed microscopic bacterium, transmitted by fleas, riding on the backs of rats. The victims all sought solace in more plausible explanations. Like the wrath of God.

For my part, I did what I could to stem the flow of death, for I was a man at the time, and still held life dear in my beating heart. Day after day, I rose from my bed in a tiny rented room, ate a small meal prepared by the lady of the house, and then donned the implements of my profession. There were other tenants like myself in the building. Since her husband had died—not of the plague, but a common fever years earlier—the owner had offered every spare room, closet, and corner to merchants and traders as they made port. Had the sleeping arrangements not been so tight, the place might have been called an inn. I would have preferred an inn, but they were all closed to the likes of me, despite the many vacancies. Since the outbreak, there was little trust for outsiders or those who lived on the road. We were all suspect as the bringers of death and decay.

I was raised in Venice, but all of Italia was my home, for I travelled much, plying my trade, my calling. As Venice was its own republic and economic empire, the routes of commerce were many, and the traffic was thick. Passage to and from the floating city-state was simple to arrange, and the fleets setting sail along the eastern coast left many options to arrive at points all around the peninsula.

Each time I undertook a journey that would have me on the road or at sea for weeks or even months, I would bid a painful farewell to my beloved, Francesca. Many times we spoke of marriage and family, but I was still establishing myself, and she was perched on a level of society ever so tantalizingly out of my grasp. Our plans for the future were put off as I sought stability, for we assumed there remained much future yet to unfold for us.

The bodies were already piling up in Venice when I crossed the lagoon to the mainland, on my way to attend to business in Florence. My final words to Francesca before I left was to bid her to stay safe and well, to remain indoors as much as possible, and to avoid crowds in public areas. Then, as now, it was the soundest advice I could offer under such circumstances, and I prayed it would keep her until my return.

It was the spring of 1348, still early days for the plague, and it would be years before it burned itself out. I had hoped the situation farther down the boot would be improved. Milan, for one, was said to be a safe oasis of good health. But as I turned sharply south, the ravages of sickness and disease worsened, until I was faced with mass graves of blackened, pustule-laden corpses outside tiny villages and great city walls alike. Holes could not be dug, filled, and covered over fast enough, the supply of bodies was so constant. Often mere days, certainly no more than a week would pass, from first symptoms to horrid vomiting death. The grotesque growths on necks, groins, and armpits were everywhere. Often they were accompanied by stinking, seeping scars as victims, or those who had tried to save them, lanced the terrible boils to let some of the foulness out. Successes were rare, survivors were few, and the efficacy of the treatment questionable.

The Black Death took multiple forms. Those who were infected in the lungs presented different symptoms and proved especially doomed. Exactly how many manifestations of the sickness existed was hotly debated. Some victims in Florence, I noted, went from exhibiting no signs of illness whatsoever, to being found only a day or so later simply wasted away. Their bodies were not defiled by boils or blackened fingertips, but rather seemed to have been drained utterly. Few took the time to examine the corpses of the dead as they were rushed to the pits on carts stacked high, but the withered cases seemed to also bear bloodless wounds that were lost within the folds of their leathery dead flesh.

Daily, I wrote to Francesca, hoping those who bore my letters north survived long enough to deliver them to my love. Alas, I never returned to her. Rather, more accurately, what returned to her was not really me. For the man I once was, was dead before the month was out.

It wasn't the plague that took me. It was a predator, lurking in the shadows, using the tremendous numbers of dead to hide its own kills. Lore of the nosferatu, the vampyr, dated back to epochs far more ancient than the one I was born into. The stories were almost as widely disbelieved then as they are now, despite the rampant superstitions and religious hysterics of the age. Rumours of attacks and the fate of those gone missing were speculation at best, more rationally attributed to witchcraft than vampirism. I have since learned, however, that many of the forgotten who slipped through the infinite number of cracks in society may well have ended up as sustenance for the undead.

Had I known then what I know now, I would have recognized the many desiccated remains as castoffs from feedings. I have since seen many such shrunken faces, pulled tight and dry over gaping skulls and exposed teeth, in the aftermath of my own bloodlusts. At the time I was content to blame them on another branch of the Black Death that seemed to be coming for us all in one form or another. It was as the vampire lurking in Florence intended. While the end of days itself seemed upon us, who was likely to spot the work of a single prolific blood drinker amidst so much carnage? The terrible circumstances of the plague had left the creature free rein to indulge himself as much as he had ever wished.

I, myself, may have ended up as another emaciated corpse, dumped in a pit and covered over as an assumed victim of the plague—bubonic, septicemic, or pneumonic, it mattered not. Dumped and covered over I was, but my body went into the ground without ever being fully drained. There was nothing special about the attack I was subjected to. I was merely a convenient target, separated for a few moments from the rest of humanity after turning down the wrong street one night as the business of a long day was done. I never knew what hit me, and could only speculate long after I was dead and reborn. The vampire may have been operating outside of its usual narrow feeding grounds. Perhaps the alleys and tight corners had not been fruitful that night, and the hunter, having grown too accustomed to regular feedings, had allowed its hunger to drive it further afield, to a more travelled path. No sooner had the attack begun, and I heard the first of my open arteries painting the cobblestones underfoot, than my cries brought lights and eyes to the windows above. Caught in the act, the vampire vanished down the nearest gutter as a wriggling mass of mangy rats, leaving its murderous errand unfinished and its thirst barely quenched. By the time help was at my side, I had bled to death of my own accord, assuring the transmission of the curse that would see me become one such as the fallen who had robbed me of my life.

An apparent crime to even a casual observer, no one, it seems, was interested in investigating a murder in the middle of so much death. The city constables were only concerned with maintaining a degree of public order in the face of rampant chaos, not in determining the guilty party in a single random slaying. The authorities never even collected my body. It was, instead, directly transported to the pit currently being filled. My wounds, not made by any weapon, were never examined, and no alarm was ever raised by the fact that a visiting journeyman had been savagely mauled to death by tooth and claw.

My life was most certainly gone, but I was somehow not yet departed. My mind stayed trapped within, and I was acutely aware what it was like to consciously inhabit a corpse. I could not speak or move or control my extremities in any way. I was helplessly stuck, like I had been sentenced to spend eternity in the smallest possible jail cell—one no bigger than my own dead body.

It was only after the next setting of the sun, after my remains had been unceremoniously tossed onto a pile of plague victims, that I was able to regain control. The hole we were in had not been completely filled. The gravediggers, exhausted from their endless task, had only layered a few feet of soil over the day's casualties. They anticipated being able to tuck in another few dozen corpses before the space in that pit was exhausted. Had much more earth been stacked on top of me, I might never have escaped, strong though I felt when control of my limbs returned. I knew I was dead—or undead as the case may be. I did not struggle with this reality because my every waking thought was instead consumed by desire. The instinct was unambiguous. There was no period of discovery, no slow reveal of what I was being compelled to do. I knew at once what my new form demanded of me. Blood. Human blood. Rivers of it. A torrent unending.

Most of my kind give in immediately. They tear open the first vulnerable throat they spy, savage any human victim they can catch away from assistance or notice. The only consideration is blood, and the necessary privacy to consume it down to the last drop. But I was a man of letters, of books, of knowledge. I approached my predicament with a measure of wisdom that kept the raw instinct at bay. The folktales and ghost stories were known to me, and I suspected what I had become. It repulsed me. And I rejected it.

My first compulsion was replaced with a more conscious goal. I wished nothing more—not in life, not in death—than to return to my home, to my love. At once, I set about arranging it. Having not been dead long, I could pass for human far more easily than I could ever hope to now. Through written instructions and brief meetings with unsuspecting dupes amidst the shadows, I arranged the direct passage of a single crate back to Venice. Ensconced within that crate, I made the journey of several long days, hidden away from the sun, concentrating intently so that my thoughts remained focused solely on the hope of seeing Francesca again, and away from the repugnant needs the curse demanded of me.

On the evening I arrived at the shores of Venice, I could hear the familiar waves through the slats of the crate. A short paddle across the lagoon was all it would take to reunite me with Francesca. But the water was in motion at that hour. It ran with purpose, and I could feel the motion as an impenetrable barrier. I knew at once, even if I could figure a way across, the thousand canals would serve as an impenetrable maze. The layout of Venice would box me in and leave me at the mercy of the rising sun. Discovery was a certainty, with retreat impossible. Every avenue of escape would be thwarted by more canals on all sides—each an uncrossable boundary of water that moved regularly with the tide. Venice was a trap.

Even as the crate was being loaded onto a longboat, I could not bear the sensation of the water's movement beneath me. Left with no other option, I burst out of the box, sending the shoremen, the cart driver, and his team of horses fleeing in terror. That day, I sought shelter in a rocky cove, away from the light. For the first time since I came crawling out of that Florentine mass grave, I rested as only the dead can rest, and briefly—so briefly—I felt at peace.

The second time I rose from the dead proved more memorable than the first.

As twilight approached, I stirred in my stony hole. My eyes opened and I observed the distant towers and steeples of Venice. The sun had set and it occurred to me that in my slumber, I had formed a plan.

A message had to be delivered. If I could not get to Francesca, I longed to bring her to me. I was able to compose a short but insistent letter on a scrap of paper I found in my pocket. The nub of charcoal I used to write with made for difficult penmanship, but the end results were recognizably in my hand. I paid for it to be conveyed by a fisherman I encountered a mile or so down the coast as he checked his traps for crabs. He was wary of the dark stranger who approached his skiff at the beach, but the last silver grosso I had to my name, and the promise of another from Francesca when she received my note, convinced him to carry my correspondence to its destination.

Long hours passed, and most of the city lights were snuffed out for the night by the time the skiff returned bearing my beloved. Dropped off and left alone on the shore, I could see Francesca searching the dark for any sign of me. I savoured this moment of reunion I had so long anticipated, until finally I allowed myself to be seen by the grace of the rising moon. She recognized me by my shape and stature at once and came running to me. I felt tremendous relief at seeing her alive and well, unmolested by the ravaging plague. In my arms again, Francesca had delivered unto me everything I most desired. Everything I loved.

The kiss I laid upon her pale neck became a lick, then a bite, and then an awful gnashing. I think she cried out, but all I could hear was the wet viscosity as blood erupted from the wound. The blood was my desire, my love, my everything. Francesca herself was nothing to me now but the source of the sweet nectar I would squeeze out of her organs and into my wanton mouth, and wring out of her veins and arteries once the flow had been halted by the cessation of her heart. Even after I was done and satisfied, and Francesca had been reduced to a dry husk draped over the low-tide rocks, there was no remorse, no regret. I felt nothing, for I had no more feelings but want. Such was the low thing I had become.

A feast has never been so grand, and after I was satisfied, I slept as I never had in life, and have never again in undeath—for weeks of wonderful, dreamless, remorseless repose. It felt as though the hunger, the longing, the need would never arise again, nor I with it. But of course it did. It had to. And even in my merciful hibernation, I slowly became restless until I could rest no more.

The third time I rose from the dead, it seemed a matter of routine already. I found a meal in short order and drank my fill, but it was only a morsel in comparison to that first time—a single drop in a vast sea of want that would demand satisfaction with ever increasing frequency. Since then, I have risen from the dead every single night with the setting of the sun. The nights now number in the tens of thousands, but it no longer seems like a routine. It feels more like a damnation beyond religion or sin. This is not about survival, or continuity of existence. It is about hunger, raw and pure, and nothing more.

Θ

An insatiable taste for blood, a longing for human contact that had returned with advanced age, I could see how Marin could symbolically function as Charlie Nocturne's incarnation of Famine.

"Waking up in a mass grave is a lousy start to any day," I said in solidarity. It was the one part of Marin's story I could relate to. That, and mailing your dead body in a big box.

"Especially when the morning sun eats at your flesh and scorches you with agony on top of the anguish you suffer for what you have become," Marin agreed.

"Mondays. Am I right?"

"How did you know I first rose on a Monday?"

"Lucky guess," I said. "Mondays generally suck."

"Years and centuries have rolled by since that terrible Monday, burdening me with a wealth of time to contemplate my actions and regain some semblance of the man I once was. I feel I can now look back on my former life with a certain insight, and a firmer connection to past events that were lost in those early bestial days. Intellectually, I can once again grasp what it meant to be a mortal in love, holding life dear, and wishing to share it with another. I reflect upon Francesca, and it is my fondest wish to have her again at my side, with only the distance of a single touch or an intimate whisper between us. I picture this in my mind's eye, and I so very much wish it to be so. For if she were here now, no words would pass between us. There would be no need. I would merely lean in, as if to breathe sweet romances into her ear. And then tear open her throat with my bare hands all over again. I would part her soft pale flesh like a curtain and bathe in the explosion of delight that would erupt from within. Her screams would be music to me as I lapped and gulped and swallowed until I was sated—just as I was that first time I drained a human of every last drop."

"You're a real romantic," I noted.

"I am," he conceded, "Italian."

Last call had come and gone while Marin took his stroll down memory lane. I had missed it, but that was fine. I'd had more than enough for one night, and the last hour had allowed me to sober up a bit. A small bit. Out on the street again, we were among the final patrons to leave. Marin excused himself as Tom and I were shown the door.

"You going back to the apartment?" Tom asked.

"Where else am I supposed to go?"

"Nowhere I guess," answered Tom, before announcing, "Okay, I'm going to grab a cab or find a night bus or something. You coming Qix, old chum?"

Tom held up his pocket watch a few inches from his face to confirm Moby-Dick was safely back in his carrying case.

"Ferry me away from this foul den of degenerate human waste, slave!" he was commanded.

"At once, Your Highness," Tom replied, and flung the pocket watch on the end of its chain over his shoulder like a heavy load. He started to head away up the street.

"You treat her right," Tom murmured to me as we parted.

I may have nodded in response. The other possibility was that I was having a hard time holding my head up.

I heard the bartender locking the door behind us. It was only then that I realized how badly I needed to pee. Luckily, like all good dive bars, the joint came with its own narrow, filthy alley, and a choice of two walls to urinate on. I stepped off the street, leaned against one, unzipped, and let flow. The steady wet trickle seemed to continue, even after I was empty. I looked down and confirmed I was done, but still the sound persisted. Tucked away again, I turned to find the source of the noise and saw there was somebody lying on the pavement at the back of the passage, hidden away behind trash cans and a stack of crates full of empty bottles. This person was on their belly, not quite lying flat, but partially raised like they had been caught in mid push-up. Their back heaved rhythmically, and the wet sound rose and diminished like waves rolling in across a stony beach. It was slurping.

"Hey!" I shouted.

The vampire stopped feeding, raised his head, but refused to look back at me.

"Hey!" I shouted a second time and took a step towards him.

Caught in the act, he suddenly leapt to his feet and started to run towards the dead end of the alley. There was nowhere to go but up, and that's just where he went. After only two steps, his body distorted and shrunk away, until it was nothing but a black shape flapping away over the brick wall, losing itself in the maze of fire escapes and clotheslines between buildings.

"Of course he can do bats, too," I said to myself.

Marin had managed to behave himself all night, but once a bloodsucker, always a bloodsucker. Vampires don't starve like a normal human does, but the need to feed is ultimately as pressing. It can't be put off forever.

I approached his victim who was lying on her back in the alley. She had been in the bar that night. Just another random customer drinking, socializing, looking for someone to hook up with, or a safe place to pass out. She was young, but already had the sort of lines creasing her face that came with a lot of hard living and hard drinking. Her throat was horrendously torn open. Enormous bites had been taken and spat out in chunks, until arteries were flowing as freely as a faucet on full. There was so much flesh missing, her trachea lay exposed and I could see the white bone where spine met skull.

What blood hadn't already been consumed was now pooling under her in a quickly diminishing torrent. As I approached, her eyes snapped to one side and locked with mine. She couldn't move, couldn't speak, but those eyes told me plenty. Terror, confusion, dismay, regret—a bad life with a bad end.

"Oh shit," I said. "You're still alive."

If she could have cried for help, she would have. If I could have provided any help, I would have. But there was nothing to do for her. She had moments to live. The best I could do for her was make sure she didn't die of the bite. Drained completely, a vampire's victim won't rise again. Left in a mortally wounded state like that, however, the curse would spread. It was my fault, really. If I hadn't interrupted Marin's meal, he would have finished properly. Shamed into cutting it short, he'd left a big problem on his plate, and I was the only one who could deal with it.

I had killed a living human being before. Once.

Murdering Csaba Szabo had been an act of impotent vengeance, but entirely justified just the same. He'd been an evil man who had led a long life filled with acts of depravity and violence. I didn't regret killing him. I only wish I could have destroyed the entity he eventually became with as much finality.

This was different. This was a civilian—an innocent victim. Stuffing Marin's previous victims into my building's furnace was simple housekeeping. This was another matter entirely.

I consoled myself that the woman was dead already. Undead. She just didn't know it yet, hadn't gone through the transition. She'd have thanked me if she knew what she was about to become.

There were no convenient tools to help me get the job done, and there was only one way to do it. Her head had to come off. Unfortunately for her, luckily for me, the savage bite wounds already had the job halfway completed. It was only a matter of finishing.

I sat down on the pavement awkwardly, a few inches above her head, and placed my feet on her shoulders for leverage. Gently, I took her head in my hands, finding a good grip under her jaw. It seemed like a consoling gesture—and it was, at least in part. The woman tried to form words, but her vocal cords were in shreds. All she could do was bring her lips together and make a string of pleading "Muh muh muh" sounds.

The blood flow had diminished to a trickle, making what I had to do next a much cleaner job than it might have been. It also meant there wasn't much time left in which to do it. I tried to explain my actions to her as best I could.

"I've been in this situation before," I said, "cleaning up after a vampire. It was a long time ago, and I couldn't bring myself to do it. There were consequences. This is for the better, believe me."

What I had to do next was awful—the sort of thing I would never fully forgive myself for. I certainly wouldn't ever forgive the vampire that had compelled me to do it. Holding the woman by the base of her skull with one hand, and the underside of her jaw with the other, I leaned back and pulled as hard as I could, pushing her shoulders away with my feet. Her head tore from her spine as the remaining flesh and musculature stretched to the breaking point. After a few inches of resistance, the rest of the tissue failed at once, and the head popped off its spinal column with a moist crack.

The woman's heart made its last few beats, pumping the final dregs of blood out of her neck stump, and then fell silent forever. Breathing heavily from the effort, I lay on my back for a while, cradling the human head in my arms. I was grateful to have been drunk for the procedure. It had made it more physically taxing, but gave me the necessary distance from reality to carry through.

Sitting up again, I held the woman's head in my hands and looked into her face, memorizing the vampire's victim—my victim. She stared back. Her eyes blinked once, and never again.

I rose to my feet and surveyed the damage. For a decapitation, I'd managed to keep it surprisingly clean. There were a few streaks of blood on my clothes, but most of it had either spilled or been swallowed before I intervened. I was in no condition to dispose of the body. Inevitably it would be found and investigated, but I was content that I wasn't soiled enough to leave a trail of evidence.

I delicately placed the woman's head on top of her body to await discovery, and left the scene of the crime quickly and quietly. Just to be sure I wasn't tracking bloody footprints to my own doorstep, I walked a few blocks in the opposite direction of my apartment before looping back around a parallel street. Once I finished the circuit, I paused at my building's door and looked down the street at the distant red neon sign of the bar. It had been switched off for the night. No one else was around. The body hadn't been noticed yet, and probably wouldn't be until morning.

I expected to be sleeping the night off during the inevitable commotion of cop cars and police detectives. Marin would be as well. Either under my own roof, or hiding from me in some secondary location.

We would have words again. And not civil ones.

Fucking vampires.

Chapter Ten

Death Anonymous

"ONE NIGHT IN A ROW in bed with me, and then it's straight to the couch. I'm flattered."

Rebecca was standing over me where I had collapsed, face-down, on the couch. The setting sun was streaming in, and my head was throbbing to the beat of my pulse. I'd slept the day away.

"I came in late and I didn't want to wake you," I muttered, as I made the colossal effort to roll over and sit upright.

"You going to make a permanent decision about our sleeping arrangements, or do you want to try out the bathtub tonight?"

"I can't do another night on the couch. My back won't take it."

The ache in my spine had returned after a rough night in an awkward position. The only mercy was that the pain in my head dwarfed all other discomforts.

"Or you can go down to a local funeral parlour, splurge, and buy yourself a new casket. I'm sure Gladys will give you an advance on your salary if you suck up real nice."

"I don't know. I think maybe I'm done sleeping in caskets. I just spent weeks dead in a box and now the thought of ever getting a good night's rest, even with the lid up, seems unlikely."

"Don't tell me you've developed claustrophobia."

"If I feared closed spaces, I wouldn't be shacked up in this little apartment with you and Gladys."

"So it's the bed then. With me."

"I guess so."

"Try not to sound so excited about it."

I held my head in my hands and stared down at the floor-boards, but even that felt like too much sensory input. Closing my eyes didn't improve matters much. The bright afternoon shone red through my eyelids.

"You look dead," Rebecca noted. "Even by your standards."

"This feels worse, trust me," I groaned, rubbing my temples, trying to keep my hangover from cracking out of my skull like a newborn lizard out of an eggshell.

I'm good for a beer or three, but I normally avoid heavy drinking. I like to keep my inhibitions right where they are. If I let them slip, casting a spell for the hell of it, or reciting an incantation just to show off, starts to seem like a fun idea. And that never ever goes well. I tried to remember if anything like that had transpired and if there were consequences to deal with.

"I can't claim to be able to compare," she said, "but I know what waking up from a bender feels like. Let me fix you the world-famous Rebecca Stone hair-of-the-dog hangover cure."

Rebecca fluttered away to the kitchen while I made a valiant effort to get on my feet. I might have stayed on the couch, but nature called. The walk to the bathroom felt like running a marathon, and my piss smelled like you could set it on fire. By the time I flushed, Rebecca was waiting at the door with a brimming mug of something that smelled even more flammable.

"You sure that won't finish me off?" I asked.

"It'll get you up and about," she promised. "Like a zombie maybe, but better a walking corpse than one lying down on the job."

"Might as well," I decided. "I feel like I've already been through the 'apocalypse' part of a zombie apocalypse."

I took a sip. It tasted like gasoline. I took another sip.

"So how do you start a zombie apocalypse?" Rebecca casually queried.

"Give everyone a smartphone."

"No, seriously. Ever since I've known you, you've dropped the occasional zombie-apocalypse joke, like such a thing was actually possible. Is it?"

"You've been witness to a lot of supposedly impossible things," I reminded her. "Very few things are truly impossible."

"So it can be done then. How?"

"That's a trade secret. I start telling people and word gets out, the next thing you know somebody tries it for real and then it's a very big mess. One I don't want to have to clean up."

I made my way back to the living-room couch before braving another sip of Rebecca's hangover-remedy cocktail. She persisted.

"Is it catching? Like a contagion in the movies?"

"I certainly hope not," I said. "Otherwise I may have fucked the entire U.K."

I wondered how Shambler was doing, strolling the streets of London, his own master for the first time in decades. He was unlikely to cause any trouble on his own, but the world is a harsh place, even for the living with all their senses and consciousness in place. Who knew what it had in store for a poor, lost, ownerless zombie.

It occurred to me, not for the first time, that I might have used my powers to go probing into the shrivelled remains of Shambler's brain in order to determine who he once was. Oliver may not have been good at that trick, but I excelled at it. I never tried it while Oliver was alive. The relationship between a necromancer and his reanimated servant should be treated as sacrosanct. There had been nothing to keep me from sticking my nose in once Oliver was gone, but it didn't feel right. Who-ever Shambler had once been was many years in the past now. Shambler was who he had become, and that's who he would make his way in the world as now. Or not. The world was probably going to chew the poor bastard up—worse than it had Oliver—and then it would spit his necrotic flesh out rather than swallow.

"So what did you hard-drinking manly men get up to last night?" Rebecca probed.

I had to think about it for a while. My memory of events grew dimmer with each round.

"Talk mostly," I said.

"Bullshitting?"

"Some, I guess."

"Better than talking about your feelings or anything per-sonal, right?"

"Right," I agreed, hoping it would get her to stop. It didn't.

"Anything else?"

There was something else, and I had to concentrate really hard to dredge up the details.

"I think I killed somebody last night."

"Again?" was Rebecca's only comment.

"What do you mean, 'again?' You make me sound like a serial killer."

"Careful this doesn't become a habit with you."

"I know, I know. You saw me kill an old man once. Would it help any if I told you he had it coming? That was Csaba Szabo, big-time war criminal. Oceans of blood on his hands. Not my usual style, but let's just say it was a long time coming."

Rebecca recalled the event, years in the past now. Decades technically—an incident we were involved in before either of us was even born. Time travel plays havoc with the correct order of your memories, which is why I don't recommend it.

"Sure, seeing you drowning that old man freaked me out. But I have enough faith in you to know you had your reasons."

"So then what's the problem?" I asked.

"That wasn't the only thing Charlie Nocturne showed me about you. When I—passed back through him I guess you'd call it—it wasn't a direct return trip to Gallery Nowhere."

"No?"

"No. I got a look at the future. The distant future. Or maybe the near future. I don't know when, but you were there. I guess Nocturne was—or will be—as well. And there were three others. You were all on horses."

I didn't like the sound of that at all. I thought I'd gotten off the prophecy merry-go-round. Marin had told me as much. I've always found prophecies are best avoided. Of course, avoiding them isn't so easy. Actually, it's typically impossible. That's what's so aggravating about them.

"Marin, dammit," I said, remembering more about the previous night or, should I say, that early morning.

"Does he have something to do with this?"

"Plenty," I said. "Aside from him being fitted for a horse right next to mine, your pet vampire has a bad eating disorder. Just when I thought maybe, *possibly*, he might be the one nosferatu with a modicum of self-control, he goes and helps himself to some poor girl and doesn't even finish the job before flapping off into the night. I had to mop up after him. And that meant finishing off his victim before she turned into another one of *them*."

"Shit, Rip, that's rough."

"Rough but necessary. Being drunk helped. Notice any cops today?"

"There was some hubbub down the street when I went out earlier," said Rebecca. "A couple of patrol cars and an ambulance. They were taping off the area around one corner."

"I should burn these clothes," I said, looking down at my-self. "Forensics could have a field day."

There were a few blood spots but no major spatter. The stains were washable, but who knew what traceable fibres or other DNA I might have got on myself when I was taking care of Marin's scraps. I didn't fancy trying to explain to police that yes, I technically committed the murder, but I wasn't actually responsible for it.

"Lucky for you, your new wardrobe is ready."

There were a few large shopping bags by the door. I dread-ed what might be in them.

"Where's your hat?" Rebecca asked.

"Shit. I must have left it at the bar."

Or worse, I thought, at the crime scene.

"Oh, here it is," she said a moment later, stepping into the office.

I joined Rebecca and found Wilbur's top hat resting on Gladys's skull. Rebecca retrieved it for me.

"Geev dat bak!" Gladys complained. "Dats mine!"

For a fashion-obsessed skull, it must have been hard not having a body to wear clothes. Hats were her only option.

I noticed the retractable cap of her skull was ajar. Hinging it back, I looked inside and saw a squat glass jar resting in Gladys's bony interior.

"Looks like I remembered to bring Louie home, too," I said. "I was starting to worry I might have chugged him by mistake between rounds."

"What a night," I heard Louie thinking. "My brain hurts."

"You two getting cuddly?" I asked.

"He still peervart!" complained the skull.

Coming home drunk last night, Louie had probably kept Gladys up all night whispering sweet obscenities to her. I closed her cap and left them to it.

Back outside the office I told Rebecca, "I have to deal with this Marin situation. Somehow. I don't want to have to run all over town beheading half-drained victims because we're harbouring a vampire."

"Just after you left, he promised me he was going to quit," she said.

"He can't quit. Killing people, drinking blood—it's a vampire's *raison d'être*. It's all they have."

"We could try to give him something else to live for. Or unlive for, as it goes."

"It's pointless," I said. "Don't even try."

"I thought you might be more sympathetic towards him. It sounds like you two are in the same boat."

She wasn't wrong. Charlie Nocturne had Szabo. He wanted Marin. I thought I was in the clear, but if Rebecca's vision of that unknown future was correct, maybe I wasn't the free agent I thought I was.

"I don't want to be one of the horsemen of the apocalypse," I told her.

I must have looked vulnerable, weakened. Maybe it was just the hangover. Maybe not. Rebecca came over and gave me a hug, holding me tight.

"Obviously," she said.

I embraced her back.

"I hate horses," I said, my head on her shoulder, her hair in my face. "My parents took me on a pony ride when I was twelve. Damn thing threw me and I broke my neck and died in front of everyone. Very embarrassing. Very difficult to explain when I came back. We had to move again."

"Come with me," she said, taking my hand.

"Where?"

"To see all your goodies. You're going to love it."

Rebecca led me to her piles of shopping bags.

"I'm not going to love..." I began. "Oh, hey, that's neat. Where did you find it?"

Rebecca offered me her first thrift-store find. It was an antique medical bag—a physician's portable valise with a split-handle design from back when house calls were a thing. The edges were scuffed, but the leather body remained firm and intact. The interior was lined with all sorts of fancy compartments and pockets that would come in handy. At the bottom of the case were several familiar tools from my old kit, including lock picks, casket key, and my trusty derringer.

"I kept a few pieces that weren't junk," said Rebecca. "Stuff I figured might not be so easy to find again. Some things were old and broken and had to go, but I bought replacements for the staples I could remember."

Among the bulkier items was a new heavy-duty flashlight that made a fine substitute for the one I had broken on a ghoul's face long ago.

"Make a list of what else you need and we'll get your whole kit back in stock."

"I appreciate what you're trying to do," I said, putting the tools back in the valise and shutting it. "Really. But I don't know if I can do this anymore."

"Don't be a dumbass," said Rebecca. "What else are you going to do?"

What seemed such an easy choice for her still weighed heavily on me. Resuming work wasn't a simple matter of picking up where I'd left off. Too much had happened, none of it very encouraging. I tried to explain.

"Ever since I returned—even before I came back here, I mean—it's been one long string of disasters. London turned into a mess. This has been no better. My whole career has been about barely holding things together. Maybe I don't have what it takes. Maybe I never did. Maybe I'm just not very good at this."

"Rip," Rebecca said patiently, "you can rise from the dead. That's a pretty amazing talent right there, before you even get to all the other stuff I've seen you do."

"That's not a talent. That's a birth defect, an abnormality. Like the ability to wiggle your ears, or being born with a tail, or having six fingers on each hand. It's an accident and it has nothing to do with necromancy. All it does is give me an unfair advantage I didn't earn, and rarely put to any good use."

I was feeling sorry for myself. I expected Rebecca to call me on it.

"You know what your problem is, Rip?"

"People trying to tell me what my problem is."

I hoped my snarky response would cut her short. It didn't.

"Your problem is you've died too many times for it to teach you any important life-lessons."

I took a moment to process what Rebecca had said to me. Even on reflection it didn't make any sense. She kept going when all I offered her was a blank stare.

"Most people who have a near-death experience come away from it with some sort of personal revelation. Knowing their life was nearly over puts things in perspective. It gives them a better understanding of what's really important."

"I don't have near-death experiences. I have death-death experiences."

"Exactly! And they roll right off you because there are no long-term consequences. You get up again and life goes on. How can the threat of death, or even death itself, change you if you can just get over it, shrug it off, like a hangover?"

"This hangover doesn't feel so shruggable," I said.

"It will pass. Just like all of mine did."

"I don't know. I've seen some of your hangovers. And the mood they put you in. I'd say there were a few that had a profound effect."

"Only in the moment," Rebecca said. "Later that day, or the next day, or the next week, I'd have another drink. Even if I swore to every god in the phone book that I would never touch another drop if only the headache would go away, I'd forget my promise and have another drink."

"So what are you saying? Death is a hangover and there's some lesson to be learned there, but I'm too stupid to get it?"

"Something like that."

"Sounds like I need a twelve-step program of my own. Let me know if you hear about one for people with my condition."

"Nobody has your condition."

"True," I agreed. "And since nobody knows what it's like to be me, maybe everybody should refrain from offering unsolicited advice."

I sincerely hoped that last comment was mean enough to get her to shut up. It was. But the effect only lasted about five seconds.

"So what's your plan now that you're back? Sit around and mope?"

"I'm a necromancer," I reminded her. "Necromancers don't mope. We brood."

"You need a gig. Make the call."

"To who?"

"You have connections inside the police force. See if they have any unsolved cases you can shed some light on."

"I'm trying to disassociate myself from a murder that just happened. Getting reacquainted with the cops right this moment doesn't sound like a wise choice."

"Are you kidding me? It's your best option. You reestablish yourself as their go-to guy, they'll never suspect you."

"Cops suspect everybody of everything."

"Just make the damn call."

It sounded like an order. I didn't feel like being ordered around. Or prodded, or prompted, or pushed.

"I'm not ready."

"Sure you are," Rebecca insisted. "You've got your new kit and a fancy new set of duds that will make you look like a lean, mean mortician. You can do this."

"I'm rusty," I complained. "What if I don't have it in me anymore?"

Articulating the nagging notion that I may be washed up as a necromancer made it feel very real. It made me realize there may have been a less-tortured explanation for why I didn't try to connect with Shambler's dusty grey cells. Why I didn't make the effort to guide him home rather than let him go free range. Maybe it was because I was worried I'd fail at something that used to come so easy. My talk with Oliver's scatological remains had been fragmented and inconclusive at best. I'd been able to chat to Louie's partial brain just fine, but the connection was already there. He was an old friend. I wasn't sure I could do so well with less familiar corpses or their organs.

Rebecca, bless her, wouldn't let me stand on self-doubt.

"You owe me fifty percent of the rent. Get on it before I kick your ass out of here."

"I need more time."

"You had three years off."

"That wasn't exactly a holiday, you know."

Words weren't getting the job done, so Rebecca let a withering stare of disapproval do her dirty work for her. I cracked in mere moments.

"Fine! Fine!" I grumbled, tossing back the rest of the hangover cure and throwing my hands up in surrender. "I'll call the precinct and see if Frenz is working on anything I can help out with."

"No, you'll call all the precincts and make the rounds. Get Frenz to vouch for you at the other cop shops. Canvass, canvass, canvass that market!"

As a career coach, Rebecca sounded more like a task master beating a drum to set the pace on a slave galley. I could never row fast enough.

Θ

Rebecca kept on me until I'd broken the ice by making at least one call. After a few hours of further recovery, she forced me to model the outfit she'd assembled. Black shoes, black pants, black shirt, black pea coat. All that crowned with a black top hat and half a pair of sunglasses. At least the new socks and underwear she picked up for me were a different colour: grey.

She made me stand still while she took a 360-degree walk-around, surveying her work from all angles.

"Look at you, my big boy all grown up, ready to go out into the world on the first day of his whole new career."

"New career, same as the old career, only now with more bullshit," I groused.

"You look badass."

"I look like an idiot who got kicked out of a cosplay club."

The clothes didn't feel like a uniform. They felt like a costume with no party to attend.

"If that's your attitude, that's how you're going to come across. Believe you look like the coolest motherfucker in the joint, and that's who you'll be."

"Right up until the pointing and the laughing starts."

I was getting hot indoors with the coat and hat, so I hung them up and sat down on the couch. Getting off my feet after parading my necromancer accessories for Rebecca was short lived. The phone rang and I heard Gladys pick it up on her headset in the next room.

"Yooloogee, wat yoo want?"

Somehow I knew it was a business call. My first in years. I looked ready. I just didn't feel it yet.

"Reep! Peek ap da phoon!"

"Showtime," Rebecca beemed.

I grunted as I returned to my feet.

"Don't forget your hat again," she reminded me.

"It's not raining."

"Hats are for heads. Wear it. Own it. Be it."

Chapter Eleven

Dance of the Dead

"**D**ANCE CLUB DOWNTOWN. The Craven Image. Heard of it?"

"No," I told the precinct messenger boy who had called me back. It was later the same evening, after I'd rung them up and asked to be returned to the "active" list in a file that was called, often to my face, "Frenz's Freaks."

The mechanics of getting back in the loop as one of the police detective's consultants was vastly easier than I had anticipated. Apparently my old associate, Alan Frenz, had never even shuffled me to the rear of the file as one of the inactives. According to the clerk who took my call, the only alteration to my contact sheet had been a Post-It note with a question mark affixed to one corner. Frenz had me down as merely MIA, unreachable, not returning his calls—for years.

Detective Frenz wasn't in his office to talk to me himself. He was out on a case. I really didn't expect him or anyone else to return my call. Best case scenario, I figured there might be a little something thrown my way by the end of the month to test the waters, make sure my abilities were still up to snuff after so much time away from the front lines. I hadn't even tried dialling another precinct, as Rebecca insisted, to make an introduction and try to arrange a first face-to-face with someone in charge, before the phone rang and Gladys patched it through to me.

I asked for the address of the club. The Craven Image wasn't a familiar name to me, but it could have been a new venue that cropped up while I was lost at sea, or an old one that had recently reinvented itself. There were no details offered, other than the fact that Frenz had called in only minutes ago and asked for one of his stable of psychics and soothsayers to be sent down to a crime scene right away. He didn't specify which one. I figured my name came up because whoever had just altered the file had left my profile sitting at the top the stack.

The cab I took downtown let me off at the corner, half a block up from the address. The whole place was roped off, with barricades at either end of the street, and patrol cars and cops blocking all motor and foot traffic. The street itself looked like a discotheque of revolving red and blue lights shining across the façades of the buildings on either side. The effect came mostly from the squad vehicles idling with their flashers on, but there were also two fire trucks, three ambulances, and a few other nosey municipal cars looking to get in on the action, all of them lit up like it was Christmas again.

There were plenty of media as well. Bright camera floods spot-lit the gravely serious affiliate reporters on a grey winter day as they filed their stories for the late news, or offered live commentary on a story that was breaking big enough to go national. It seems there had been a massacre.

It took me ten more minutes to make my way to the door of the club. I had to explain who I was, and drop Frenz's name every few steps, to some cop or other who was part of the small army keeping absolutely everyone not directly involved in the investigation, or with emergency services, off the premises. Once I was through the final barricade, I marched up a stairway that was painted black, ceiling to floor, and lit by little more than luminescent designs and flourishes. The club itself was just as black-washed, but the house lights were up so the cops and paramedics could work. Nobody was getting much done, however. The cops were at a loss to explain the scene, and the paramedics were left with nobody to save.

I started to count the bodies, all tangled up and overlapping on the floor, but decided it would just be simpler to ask for a number. Even from behind, I spotted Frenz at once. He was standing a few steps away, hands on his hips, surveying the nightmare of paperwork, and probably trying to tally the number of pages it would amount to in his head. They, too, would be a tangled and overlapping mess before long.

"How many?" I said to him.

"Eleven," he reported, before he even turned to see who was asking.

It took him an extra moment to recognize me when he saw my face. A bit of a beard and a funny hat will do that, even to a seasoned cop.

"Christ Almighty, Rip!" he said at last, "I heard you were dead."

"You heard right."

I wanted to thank him for not shredding my file, considering the rumours of my death weren't greatly exaggerated, nor even slightly incorrect.

"How long has it been?" he wondered. "A year?"

"Closer to four," I said.

"And it took me all this time to start missing you."

"At least you got around to missing me."

"Where'd you run off to?" he wanted to know.

"I was out of town. On business."

"Years' worth?"

"It was very busy business."

Frenz didn't pursue it any further, which I appreciated. Personal details never strayed into our conversations. He'd only ever been interested in what I could do for him, not how or why I could do it. He remained in the dark about some of my more mysterious talents. Rising from the dead being one of them.

"When I asked them to send down a specialist weirdo, I figured it would be Reynaldo."

"He been filling in for me?"

"Yeah," confirmed Frenz, "but he's been underperforming."

"Oh, really?" I asked, trying not to be obvious about my delight, or my desire for juicy details.

"He's just not getting the same results anymore," Frenz said, shaking his head sadly at the decline of my top rival. "I had him on a case last year. Missing family. Four of them gone without a trace. One witness-slash-suspect. Should have been simple for him, but Reynaldo couldn't even determine if the victims were victims at all. Alive or dead, he refused to commit one way or the other. So no arrests and another open case littering my desk."

"I guess you get rusty doing daily palm readings."

"Anyway, now you're here," Frenz said, and his relief was palpable.

"So I am."

"What's with the getup?" he asked, looking my new work attire up and down.

"Supposedly, I'm rebranding."

"As what? A silent-movie villain?" he flicked the brim of my top hat with one finger. "You tie any pretty ladies to the train tracks I should know about?"

I switched the subject to business. These were billable hours I was happy to stretch out, but I didn't need Frenz poking fun at me fresh out of the gate and back on the job after so long.

"What do you have for me?"

"Bad one," he said. "You sure chose a hell of a time to come back. It doesn't get much worse in my business."

"I bet it does in mine."

"Those new shoes, too?" he asked, looking down at my footwear, black as the floor.

"Yeah, why?"

"Watch where you step."

As we approached the point on the dance floor where the bodies began, I could see the whole area, all the way to the back of the club, was pooled with blood. It was a shallow, still lake of crimson, with each body an island sticking out of the glassy surface. The floor looked like it had been repainted red, with only the uneven edges and the lack of "fresh paint" signs defying that impression. The coppery scent of spilled blood filled the air and drowned out the usual nightclub smells of alcohol, cheap perfumes, and sweat.

I stopped at the shore of the beach, as close as I needed to be in my professional capacity. The forensics team could wade through the blood in their boots to gather evidence. A dozen of them, despite their best efforts, were tracking red rubber-soled tread marks all over the club as they went back and forth between bodies. As the spilled blood slowly thickened and dried, their footprints across the pool took longer to fill in with still-viscous fluid.

"Were they all pledging the same fraternity or something?" I asked.

Each of the victims was dressed similarly, all in black, with only a tiny amount of wiggle room left for individual expression. I'm sure they thought they were terribly stylish and unique, but I would have been hard pressed to pick any of them out of a crowd, or identify them individually—boys or girls. I realized, with a certain self-conscious discomfort, that my new look would have let me fit right in.

"Goth kids," explained Frenz. "It's a goth club with goth bands playing goth music. Most of them ran when the killing started. We've been rounding them up for blocks in all directions and taking statements."

"Sounds like you have lots of witnesses. Why do you need me?"

"They were all stabbed through the heart."

"Am I supposed to have some special insight into a mass-knifing?"

Frenz tapped a member of the forensics team on the shoulder and was handed an evidence bag in return. He held up the clear plastic envelope so I could see inside.

"They were all done with one of these. One per victim."

I stepped closer for a better look. The murder weapon was bloody and had stained much of the inside of the bag, but once it was right in front of me, I could tell the weapon was a piece of wood. A stake.

"That's fucked up," I said.

"And that's why you're here," said Frenz. "You specialize in fucked up.

"I suppose I do. I should put that on my business card."

I would suggest it to Rebecca, my self-styled manager. New business cards were being designed as we spoke. Something more eye-catching than the bare-bones white-on-black contact information I'd used years ago, even though that contact information hadn't changed in the interim. I didn't much see the point, but apparently it was all part of my fresh marketing strategy.

"So this is exactly what I think it is for exactly what it looks like it's for, right?" Frenz sounded worried.

"I'd say so," I agreed.

"Are they all..." Frenz looked at his pile of goth victims, afraid to use the term he was driving at.

"Fashion victims?" I suggested.

"You know what I mean."

"No," I reassured him, "don't be silly."

Frenz breathed a sigh of relief.

"So none of them... I mean, they're not..."

"Are you kidding me?" I asked, nearly laughing in his face.

"You're the one who's supposed to know this crap!"

It had already been a long day, and Frenz was in no mood.

"Take it easy. None of them is going to pop fangs and take a bite out of your crew."

"Because things like that don't even exist, right?"

"I didn't say that," I told him. "But all you have here is a bunch of dead kids."

"What about the killer?"

I took the stake from Frenz, handling it through the plastic bag, admiring it.

"Quality workmanship," I said. "Nice finish, smooth grip, barbed point, needle-sharp tip."

"Does it looks like a pro?"

"Nope. Rank amateur."

"A rank amateur did all this?" asked Frenz of the carnage.

"I didn't say he wasn't prolific."

"But so many bodies..."

"A bunch of drunk goth kids dancing to shitty music and trying to hook up. Soft target."

"For who?"

"Someone who thinks he's fighting the forces of evil rather than the forces of bad taste."

"Great. So I have some mass-murdering crazy running around trying to stake anyone with a black wardrobe and too much mascara in the name of the greater good."

"Did any of the goths you rounded up have a description for you?"

"Nothing consistent. It was dark, it was loud, and it was chaos once the bodies started hitting the floor."

"Okay, how about I have a chat with the victims, and see if any of them got a better look. They're the ones who saw this guy close up."

"Where do you want to do this?"

"Is there an area backstage?"

"The club manager has an office."

"Perfect," I said. "I'll set up shop there. Have your guys bring them in one by one as they peel them off the floor, before they take them downstairs and load them into the meat wagon. I'll do a few minutes with each and then you can finish processing them."

Frenz weighed my request and nodded his approval. Doing this off to the side, away from the rest of his team, would be best. As usual, he could refer to me as a special consultant he'd brought in as an extra pair of eyes. No one else would have to know the specifics of why I was on the case, or what I was doing with the bodies.

I was shown into the nightclub manager's office. It stood in complete contrast to the rest of the venue. Simple, utilitarian, with plain white walls and beige office furniture. I set my doctor's bag down on the desk, but doubted I would need anything from it for the interviews. The coming exchanges promised to be straightforward, barring the usual afterlife alarm from newly deceased corpses who thought they'd had their whole lives ahead of them.

The timing of the case perturbed me. What were the odds that a wannabe vampire hunter would turn up in town right around the same time as an ancient master like Marin Venerio Grissoni? Take any random city, and there's bound to be one or two vampires lurking in the darkest corners, preying on outcasts who wouldn't be missed, hiding their victims' bodies away where they would never be found, and keeping a low profile. If you were determined to seek them out, you could probably find some. I wasn't so determined, and was content to let them be so long as they didn't ping my radar. It's not like there was much to do about them anyway—not for an experienced necromancer such as myself, and certainly not for some loon playing at being a slayer, who obviously didn't know what the hell he was doing. This live-and-let-die attitude had served me well, and I hadn't had to deal or interact with a single vampire for most of my solo career. Not since I'd left Oliver behind and struck out on my own. Now there was this slaughterhouse, obviously vampire-inspired if not directly vampire-related, coupled with the arrival of Marin in my life. It was a lot of the same tone, the same flavour, in a short period of time.

Θ

"That's not me."

"Look closer," I said.

The first victim I summoned back for a talk was in all-too-typical denial. Even as her manifested spirit looked down on the corpse in the gurney, she couldn't make the connection.

"That's not me!" she stubbornly insisted.

Her own mother wouldn't have recognized her with so much hair dye and makeup, but I expected she must have spent a lot of time in front of the mirror getting her look just so. She knew who she was looking at, even if she didn't want to admit it.

"No, that's not you," I agree patiently. "That's your body. The shell you used to inhabit. Now it's dead, and you're else-where."

"That's impossible. I have tickets to see *Stitches for Bitches* next Friday!"

It sounded like a band. Probably a popular one. What would I know? I had been out of the popular-music loop since my burial at sea. Honestly, I was out of the loop long before that.

"You can still catch the show," I assured the dead girl. "You won't even need the tickets. You can just float on in and observe."

That seemed to reassure her somewhat.

"Cool," she concluded. "I can scalp the tickets and probably come out on top."

I didn't bother to burst her bubble. If it put her in a better mood, she could believe what she wanted to believe until I got some information out of her. So far my ability to connect with the dead was as solid as always. It was a clear connection, no static. The reaching out, the summoning, the linking—it all flowed naturally. And it felt right. Intrusive, but right.

"Did you see the guy who stabbed you?"

"Only for a second. The strobe lights were on for the guitar solo of *Wendigo Spunk's* song 'Your Daddy Feeds the Worms Now.' Do you know it?"

Mercifully, I didn't.

"Sure," I lied. "Instant classic."

"Isn't it though? Anyway, I was in my sweet spot, just swaying out on the floor, like I wasn't even in my body. And then I really wasn't in my body. This guy came out of nowhere and started nailing, like, a tent peg right into my chest with a hammer."

Stake and mallet, it would seem, but close enough.

"Did he say anything to you?"

"Yeah, he did," she recalled. "He said, 'Die, unclean!' What the eff is that supposed to mean? I took a bath this morning and everything!"

"I think he mistook you for someone or some*thing* else."

"If I was going to kill somebody, I'd make sure I knew who I was killing first."

"There's not always time for that," I commented.

Regrets about last night were resurfacing. I'd killed a woman and didn't even know her name. She couldn't have told me while she was alive. Not with her throat torn out like that. But I could have taken a moment to chat with her severed head. Explain what had happened and why. Now I would never know who she was—would never be able to offer a proper apology.

"What was the big rush?" asked the goth girl. "He couldn't wait until the next song came on?"

"Did you recognize this guy?"

"Nah."

"Had he been hanging around lately?"

"Not that I noticed."

"What did he look like?"

"Just some guy. I couldn't say. Not with the strobes flashing in my face like that."

"What was he wearing?"

"Clothes."

I figured he hadn't come in naked. A bouncer would have stopped him.

"Just clothes?" I asked.

"A coat maybe? Like a rain coat?"

It hadn't been raining last night, but it was a good way to keep the blood off.

I tried my line of questioning from a number of angles, but goth girl gave me nothing to move on. There seemed little hope that anybody in the rest of the pile of bodies was going to be of much more use. Considering the racket of the music and the flickering-light effects that were happening during the attack, I could already guess no one had seen or heard anything revealing. The live witnesses were Frenz's best bet. If he was lucky, the person collecting cover charges would remember one guy in a raincoat among the hundreds he'd let in—from the moment the club opened to when it was emptied out in a stampede.

I dismissed goth girl and thanked her for what little she provided.

"Where do I go now?"

"Up to you I guess. There's a lot of ether to float around in, not a lot to interact with."

Her spirit lingered over her body, like she was looking for a way back in. It was an easy trick for me, but impossible, it seemed, for all other living things. And it wasn't something I could teach.

"I used to put on makeup to look pale like a corpse, but that's not how corpses really look, is it?"

Even through the makeup, the pasty grey flesh was showing through. The process didn't take long, and began to set in as quickly as rigor mortis.

"No," I agreed. "There's playing dead and there's real dead, and there's no mistaking the two."

"I was really into all this morbid stuff, 'cuz I thought it was, like, really cool," she said. "But death totally sucks!

"Live and learn," I shrugged.

She drifted off after that, never to be seen or heard from again. As was often the case, I was the last living person these kids would ever talk to. None of them seemed to grasp the finality of it all, and I didn't bother to point it out to them. They would figure it out in time, and then that long lonely purgatory of death would set in—continuing until they just faded away. Probably out of sheer boredom.

As predicted, all eleven victims had pretty much the same story to tell. Some had been aware that the massacre was underway before others, and had gone down trying to flee. A few got their stakes in the back. Front or back, it didn't matter. The wooden weapon still pierced their hearts and killed them in seconds. Too quick to allow much in the way of witnesses. By the time the song and the strobe lights were done, so was the slaughter, and the slayer vanished with the tide of panic.

The interviews ran long into the night, and Frenz had to make excuses for why the coroner wasn't getting his bodies delivered in a timely fashion. There wouldn't be much to get from an autopsy either. At least on my end, I was able to confirm the names and residences of each of the victims. Some were underage and had gotten in with fake IDs, so at least I could be of some service.

By the end of the night, trying to pick up the pace, I was interviewing multiple victims at a time. It was all the same redundant information. Even speaking as a small group, the final three couldn't jog each other's memories any more than I could speaking to the dead individually.

"Where are we supposed to go now?" was the recurring theme.

"Hey, let's go haunt my parents!" suggested one. "I bet they don't even know I'm dead yet."

I wished them luck with their post-mortem hijinks.

"You know," said the final soul to depart, "I was thinking about committing suicide just last week. I gotta say, this was a way more awesome way to go out."

"Well there you go," I encouraged him. "If you stick it out, don't give up, you never know what might be waiting for you around the corner."

Θ

"You're sure we don't have a vampire problem I should know about?"

I could tell Frenz felt ridiculous even invoking the term, but he knew I was the one to ask. Despite my earlier assurances, it had remained a necessary question that needed to be directly vocalized.

"Because it sure looks like somebody thinks we have a vampire problem," he added, watching the last goth-filled body bag leaving the venue, along with the first stack of evidence bags stuffed with stakes.

I could have mentioned Marin, but there was no point. Confirming the presence of one real vampire in town didn't necessarily have anything to do with a lot of pretend vampires getting killed.

"There were no vampires here tonight," I said. "Just a bunch of kids whose questionable taste in fashion and music got them killed."

"How can you be so sure one of them wasn't..." Frenz didn't want to say the word out loud again. Too many of his men were in earshot. He bared his teeth so only I could see. I knew a bad Bela Lugosi impression when I saw one and got the message.

"Vampires need to be invited in. A real vampire would never get past the doorman."

"What, they're not cool enough to get into a trendy club?"

"No, they're not."

Frenz accepted my assurance. He didn't need me to tell him that pop culture and reality were often at odds. He'd seen enough cop shows and monster movies to understand the difference.

"That still leaves us with a mass murderer on the loose with a really fucked-up M.O."

"None of the dead goths saw anything particularly helpful," I said. "Mostly they just confirmed what we already know."

"My guys are still talking to live witnesses, but with the shitty lighting, nobody got a better look at the suspect. No one remembers him coming in, and apparently none of the victims interacted with him before the killer started spreading their ribs. A raincoat is the best description we have, but we don't even know what kind or colour."

"Red is my best guess after spilling this much blood," I said.

"Thanks for coming down anyway, Rip," Frenz said, starting to give me the brush off.

"I didn't say I hit a dead end yet."

"So you got a lead after all?"

"Mind if I hang on to one of these?" I said, taking one of the individual evidence bags with a stake in it. It was one of the ones left abandoned on the floor. It hadn't actually staked anyone, and didn't have so much as a spot of blood on it.

"That's evidence, Rip."

"You have fifty of them lying all over the place," I reminded Frenz.

"They need to be dusted."

I already had the bag open and was pawing at the stake, touching it all over, gripping it in my fist.

"Oops, looks like I got my fingerprints all over this one and contaminated the evidence. Silly me!"

"Dammit, Rip!"

"So I can keep it, right?"

"Fine!" said Frenz. "But if you don't find anything, you know where you can stick it."

I wrapped the stake up in its bag again and stuck it in my valise next to my incomplete set of tools.

"It's been fun," I told Frenz on my way out.

"Call me if you get something," he said.

"And you call me if something else comes up. My office is always open."

I was out on the street again before I realized I'd meant what I said. It had been a lousy time for eleven innocent victims, but it had been a good night for me—good for business, good to be back in the trenches of necromancy, doing what I did best. What, I had to grudgingly admit, I loved.

I was, indeed, open for business once more.

Chapter Twelve

Headlines and Deadlines

BY THE TIME I GOT BACK HOME, the early morning news was filled with harrowing tales of The Craven Image Bloodbath. Frenz had managed to keep certain details out of the papers and off the TV—particularly the method of the mass murder. Reporters were left to wildly speculate. All of them assumed guns had been involved. While pundits made the media rounds and collected their fees for discussing tired talking points about gun control and automatic versus semi-automatic weapons, I had time to conduct my own investigation into the real culprit, who was a stabber rather than a shooter. The guns and ammo industry could shoulder the blame and spare wood-workers the heat until I came up with answers.

When she finally rolled out of bed half an hour after my return, Rebecca found me on the couch, in my underwear, shovelling breakfast cereal into my mouth, while I watched local morning-show hosts decry the events I had just witnessed as "shocking," "appalling," and "simply awful." Then it was on to the sports scores, a commercial break about feminine hygiene products, and the promise of a vital upcoming segment about a children's choir singing vintage advertising jingles for charity.

"How did it go?" asked Rebecca through bleary eyes.

"It went well," I said. "For me, not so much the victims. Eleven dead. It was a long night establishing contact with decedents."

"Did you make breakfast?"

"I got the box of Wheatie-Puffs down from the top shelf. You're welcome."

"Tern da channal, thees sheet sacks!"

An inane spot promoting adult diapers had provoked Gladys's ire. I'd relocated her to the coffee table so she could watch TV with me and get up to speed with the case I was on via the newsbreaks. Once they were done with their inaccurate spin, I would fill in the details moving forward.

"Okay," I agreed, grabbing the remote, "let's see what they have on channel three."

Local Three was another network affiliate with a morning blather show, almost identical in format to the competition. The hosts were such a carbon copy of their colleagues two numbers up the dial, it would have been hard to pick them out of a police lineup. They were a few minutes behind on their news coverage, and were only now getting to the headlines of slaughter and mayhem that were meant to help viewers better digest their morning eggs and toast.

Familiar footage of parked emergency vehicles, flashing lights, and police removing vast quantities of human remains from a crime scene followed. It was so familiar, it took me a few seconds to realize the vehicles were of a different design, the police uniforms didn't match, and the location of the massacre was far removed from where I'd spent the night. This was a whole new crime scene—not from anywhere around here, yet instantly recognizable once I knew what I was looking at.

International media had, at last, picked up the story of what was being called "The Canning Town Charnel House." The scene I had left behind at Oliver's had finally been discovered and investigated. What had, initially, been assumed to be a mundane suicide case, had exploded into a media circus once investigators discovered the inventory in the basement. How exactly they concluded that Oliver had blown his head off with a shotgun, when there was no shotgun on site and no brains stuck to the ceiling, I couldn't say. Maybe the police were feeding the media disinformation and half-truths, just as Frenz was doing an ocean away. Regardless, Oliver's demise was taking a back seat to the If-It-Bleeds-It-Leads angle that was eclipsing all other considerations. The quantity and variety of human remains being excavated from his home would have forensic departments across the U.K. pooling their resources for the next year just trying to identify, separate, and count how many bodies they had stumbled across. There was no mention of foul play, but already newsreaders, commentators, and vloggers around the world were speculating where this case might fall on the list of history's most prolific serial killers.

There was an interview clip of Reggie, the unknowing neighbour, offering the usual quote about how the suspected mass murderer had been a quiet man. A police sketch of a "person of interest," doubtless based on his vague memory and unflattering description of me, was flashed on the screen as detectives fished for additional leads.

Poor Oliver. What a legacy. They would have posthumously knighted him and given him a state funeral and national day of mourning if only they knew how much he had done to keep Britain safe from the onslaught of netherworld horror trying to push its way into their dull-normal reality. I guess he would at least be content that his actions prevented them from ever having to know.

"That your case?" Rebecca asked as she emerged from kitchen, helping herself to handfuls of dry cereal straight from the box.

"Kind of," I said, as the images showed British police loading another covered load of random human remains into the back of an ambulance. "Not the one from last night."

The next piece on the news was back to local events. The grand opening of the Algonquin Tower was only a couple of days away. It promised to be a gala who's-who event as all the movers and shakers in the city gathered to cut the ribbon and jockey for position in the ensuing photo-op.

"We should get you in there," Rebecca commented between munching.

"Me?" I said. "Why me? I'm nobody."

"Attending events like that is how you become somebody. You rub elbows and you raise your profile."

"I don't think the world is ready for celebrity necromancers."

"I'm not asking you to become a media darling. But there are a lot of big names at events like that. Big names with big money. Like the rich son of a bitch who paid to build that monstrosity. I bet they all have complicated estates to settle in their families. And I bet some of them could use a necromancer to help sort out what dearly departed grandad wanted. Stuff that wasn't covered in the will because he incorrectly assumed he still had a few good years left in him."

"Maybe," I said. "The morning mail hasn't arrived yet. I'm sure my invitation will be in with the phone and cable bills."

"There are other ways to get invited to these things—other than officially. Let me work on it. I'll make some calls, see who owes me a favour."

I set my cereal bowl down next to Gladys and got up from the couch.

"Before you make any of those calls, there's more pressing business to get to. I want you to get on the phone as soon as businesses open for the day. Call every woodworker and carpenter in town."

I opened my valise and retrieved the evidence bag tucked inside.

"I'm after a mass murderer. This was his weapon of choice."

I set the wooden stake down where Rebecca and Gladys could get a look at it through the clear plastic.

"This is only one. There were dozens more on the scene. He goes through a lot of these things, so he'll need to resupply. See if anyone has been mass producing them."

"You heading out early?" Rebecca asked.

I was on my way across the room—not towards the front door, but the bedroom.

"No, I'm sleeping in late," I said. "I was up all night communing with a pile of dead goths. Come wake me if you get something."

"I mak da call arund heer!" said Gladys, reminding me of her office jurisdiction.

"Fine," I agreed. "You dial, but Rebecca does the talking. I can't waste any time with them wondering if they got a wrong number from Timbuktu. You can be sure the cops will be making the rounds right behind us, but we have the jump on them."

I was determined to beat them to the suspect. Bringing this guy in—or at least identifying him before the police detectives figured it out—would go a long way towards keeping me at the top of the "Frenz's Freaks" list. Plus I wanted a big fat bonus for solving their case for them.

"How do you figure that?" Rebecca asked.

"No one around here gets unionized coffee breaks."

"I'm not your slave, you know."

"I nat sleeve! I da bass!" Gladys also reminded me.

"This cowboy with the stakes killed eleven kids. He'll kill again if we don't stop him. So do this for me or don't. I need to get some sleep."

I didn't wait around for any more backtalk and was under the covers moments later. As my head hit the pillow, I heard Rebecca and Gladys in the next room.

"Did he just guilt-trip us?" asked Rebecca.

"Ya, I tink so."

"Did it work?"

"Ya, I tink so," said Gladys, and then added, "Fakker."

I fell asleep with a smile on my face.

Θ

"Got it!" Rebecca announced, waking me from a deep sleep and holding a slip of paper in front of my face I couldn't focus on to read. "Three dozen 'wooden nails' made to order just last week. Picked up on the afternoon of the crime."

I checked the clock. I'd been permitted a whole four hours of sleep.

"Okay, I'm up," I announced unconvincingly.

"The place is on 49th, mixed in with the antique shops there. They make and stain wooden furniture to order. Mostly tables, chairs, dressers, that sort of thing, if you're into rustic. The guy remembered the order easy enough. It was a first for him, and he's been at it for nearly forty years."

"I don't suppose he offered up his unusual client's address."

"I asked. He said it's on file but confidential."

"I need cash," I said.

Rebecca got her purse and handed me a twenty to cover the cab.

"More," I said, keeping my hand out.

"You want to hire a limo to take you?"

"I need more for the bribe. It's confidential client information right up until there's enough money on the table."

"Will fifty do it?"

"Better make it a hundred in case your carpenter has ethics," I said. "And get Gladys to cut me a cheque for an advance on my salary. I'm tired of borrowing from you every time I need to leave the apartment."

Rebecca left me alone long enough to get dressed. Once I was back in my appointed necromancy uniform, I came out of the bedroom and asked her, "Has Marin dared to show his face around here again?"

Rebecca nodded. "While you were sleeping. I didn't want to wake you."

"I need you to stay away from him. He's not your typical vampire, but he's dangerous."

"I did just fine with him under the same roof for weeks."

"A lot of the other tenants didn't."

"I thought you agreed he was trying to cut back."

"He killed someone just the other night!"

"Technically, you killed her," Rebecca reminded me.

"Don't split hairs. He's a predator."

"He lapsed back into his addictive behaviour. It happens."

"Don't you do this."

"Do what?"

"You're casting yourself as his case worker. Some sort of half-assed counsellor. A blood-anonymous sponsor."

"I know what it's like trying to kick a bad habit."

"Did he admit what he did?"

"No, not as such," Rebecca confessed sheepishly. Admitting you have a problem was one of those big first steps in any step program. Marin had failed right out of the gate. "He just came up for a few minutes to see if you had found some rival necromancer yet. A necromancer who's after the two of you? Is this something I should be concerned about?"

"No. It's fine. I'm on top of it," I said. It didn't sound convincing. A string of poor lies rarely does. I tried to do better.

"What's a little professional competition in town compared to the whole staff at Eulogy Recoveries?"

When I'd first set up shop, and registered the appropriate paperwork, I had to pick a name to do business under. Eulogy Recoveries worked. It described the bulk of my cases, finding lost inheritances and dredging up financial information that had died with the person holding the account or combination numbers. At least the tax man was content with the moniker.

"Eulogy Undertakings," Rebecca corrected me.

"What? Why?"

I knew what and why before I even finished asking.

"Never mind," I said. "Rebranding. Gotcha."

"It's on all the new business cards. They're on rush order from the printers. We should be getting them in today, and starting tomorrow you're going to toss them around like confetti."

"Yeah, boss," I agreed.

"I'm not your boss. Your boss is in the other room sitting on a desk, watching funny cat videos on the web."

There was, in fact, the sound of hollow cackling laughter coming from the office. It was either cat videos or she was watching more terrible-accident compilations. Gladys was fond of dashboard-shot highway collisions and ship sinkings, but plane crashes were her favourite. It was her idea of slapstick comedy.

"Think of me more as your CEO," said Rebecca.

"What's my official position?" I asked.

"You're still working your way out of the mail room."

On my way out, I took a side trip to the basement to check the state of my casket. There were no occupants, just a lingering odour of garlic and decay. Confronting the vampire about his latest murder would have to wait while I was out confronting a vampire hunter about his.

As I expected, it took the whole c-note to get the woodworker at the shop to come across for me and let me have a look at the invoice for the stakes. I only hoped the hunter, who had come to the shop to pick up his order in person rather than have it delivered, had given a valid address. The description I got was better than the dead goths had managed, but it was still vague. The suspect was a young man—young to someone who would have already been retired if he weren't the place's proprietor—and pale. And he had prematurely white hair. Beyond that, there wasn't much to make him stand out. Medium build, medium height. If I came up empty, I'd get around to sharing that information with Frenz, but it wasn't the sort of description that would make a police sketch artist jump for joy.

When I arrived at the invoice address, I could see why the suspect had opted for pick-up rather than delivery. I was only visiting, and even I didn't want to be seen in such a dump. The place was a flophouse for transients, prostitutes, and junkies who wanted to have a roof over their head for their final over-dose. Most people who checked in checked out on a stretcher.

I found the manager stationed behind a sheet of reinforced Plexiglas. His cubicle office was in a tiny lobby that sported two chairs with torn upholstery and scant stuffing, bracketing a dead palm tree in a cracked pot of arid soil.

Approaching the counter, I tried to conduct a muffled conversation through the honeycomb of holes cut in the glass, situated above a narrow slot that would allow the passage of bills and coins but not bullets or blades. Once we established I wasn't any sort of cop, I brought the subject around to who was renting room number 27, which had been specified on the wooden-stake order.

"You mean the freak?"

"Why do you call him a freak?" I asked.

It was an honest question, but the manager thought I was calling him out for being insensitive.

"Fine. Not the proper term for it. The whatchamacall, albino."

"He's an albino?"

"Yeah, I guess. White hair, pink skin, pale eyes."

"Interesting," I commented, looking up the flight of stairs to the second floor, where the modest accommodations began.

"He's not up there," the manager told me.

"No?"

"Moved out yesterday. He came down with his one big duffle bag of stuff, paid out his week, and cabbed it. No forwarding address. I'm just as glad to be rid of him. He was always cooking something that stank to high heaven."

"Mind if I have a look?"

"Sure. If you rent the room."

"How much for five minutes?"

"Minimum one-night rentals."

"What's that run?"

"Eight dollars," said the manager, tapping the list of rates taped to the inside of the booth.

Between the bribe and the cab fare down, that was my ride back. I'd have to bus it home.

"Better be high-class for that kind of money," I said, forking over my remaining ten and waiting for change.

The manager listed the amenities I could expect.

"Bed, mattress, hot plate. Toilet and shower's down the hall. Don't block the fire exit waiting your turn."

He slid the key through the slot, followed by my two bucks change.

It was a couple of flights of stairs up to the rooms. I had to step over three drunks on the way, and turn down the half-hearted solicitations of a pair of hookers before I found the door I was looking for. The key got it open, but a swift enough kick would have managed just as well. The door hit the side of the single bed before I could swing it all the way in, and I had to squeeze to get inside and shut it behind me. The furnishings were meagre: a small table, a single chair, a coat hook screwed to the wall, and a low shelf with the promised hot plate. The lone electrical outlet was barely close enough to plug it in without tipping it off the edge of its perch.

There was a lingering scent in the air, but it wasn't from food or any attempt to cook. At first I thought it might be drugs, smoked or freebased, but the smell was neither skunky nor chemical. Remains at the bottom of the plastic-lined trash bin confirmed what my nose was trying to tell me. Incense had been burned recently. Lots of it, judging from how many spent tips had been dumped. The walls and ceiling of the room had been discoloured by all the smoke. Much of it may have been from previous renters, toking the night away, with the single window only a few feet from the brick wall next door offering minimal ventilation. But the newest layer of sooty residue was from the last transient. He had decorated the walls extensively during his stay, and although he'd taken his hangings away with him when he moved, their negative imprints from the permeating smoke remained distinct. All four walls were branded with outlines of crucifixes—at least a hundred of them, in all shapes and sizes, with holes in the plaster where the nails supporting them had once been.

The hunter could have been anywhere by now—may have even skipped town. My promising lead had gone cold, but there was still one more option at my disposal, if only I could swallow my pride and take it. Frenz's spoiled bit of evidence would come in handy once more, as soon as I could place it in the right hands. That is, if those hands and the psychic mind they were connected to were still up to the task and willing to cut a deal with me. I spent the city bus trip home ignoring the stares of commuters who were a little too fascinated or perturbed by my outfit, and calculating how I was going to manipulate Reynaldo the Fuckhead into doing my bidding.

Θ

Not owning a car, I hardly ever saw the inside of my building's modest parking garage except to dump trash or recycling in the bins there. The main door key worked in the lock at the bottom of the sloped driveway, and got the garage door to rise on its tracks. I cut through the ten narrow parking spots and took the shortcut to the storage locker area to check if Marin had returned to his nest. I was going to have it out with him and, if I had my way, have him out of the building entirely.

I didn't know if he was capable of shame or regret. His failure to stem his appetite had gone against his vow, and there seemed to be enough of an old-school human left in him to feel the sting of lost honour. Still, when confronted with it, the repressed vampire part could boil to the surface in an instant and turn him violent. One lapse could easily lead to another, and he might go digging for one of my arteries before I'd even finished accusing him of the crime he'd forced me to finish.

Once stationed in the locker, I gathered myself, took a deep breath, and threw open the lid of the casket, ready for anything. Even so, I still wasn't prepared for what I found.

Marin was inside, but was barely aware I'd even exposed him. His nose was stuck in a smartphone and he was playing a free-download video game, one clawed finger swiping his way through a competitive online match.

Θ

"I gave him my old phone to play with," Rebecca explained, after I described the disturbing scene downstairs. "The screen's cracked, but it works okay."

"You taught him how to use the internet?"

"He's been out of the loop for centuries. I thought he might like to catch up, reengage."

"Rebecca, he's an undead, bloodsucking parasite. He doesn't need to catch up, he just needs to feed."

"If that's all you expect of him, that's all he'll ever do. Maybe if we broaden his horizons, he'll develop new interests."

"Vampires have one interest, and one interest only. Blood."

"What's he doing online right now?"

"He's playing Cherry Bang."

"See? Nothing to do with stalking victims and feeding on them."

"He only likes it because the cherries look like drops of blood," I grumbled.

"How did the hunt for the hunter go?" asked Rebecca.

"I tracked him to his last known address. The trail ends there, but I have a backup plan to locate him."

"Okay, we'll assume you earned this."

Rebecca retrieved an envelope from her purse and handed it to me.

"What's this?"

"Your first week's pay, minus what you owe me," she explained. "Gladys transferred funds to my account and I hit an ATM. She'll transfer directly to you next time, but you need to reactivate your account at your own branch. It's been suspended due to disuse."

"Tell her I need to be reimbursed for business expenses. Payola and on-the-job transportation shouldn't come out of my pocket."

"You explain that to her."

"Not me," I said. "I'm just a salaried grunt. You're my HR department. That's on you."

Despite my reduced stature in my own business, I could see certain benefits to being demoted to the level of hired help. For one, I could use Rebecca as a buffer between me and Gladys's bullshit. Upper management could worry about the day-to-day logistics. My end was to clock hours and collect a salary now. It was strangely soothing.

"We need to talk about how we're going to expand Eulogy Undertakings now that it's back in operation."

"*We* don't have to do anything of the sort. I'm off the clock. This is *me* time," I said, kicking back and planting myself on the couch.

"Consider this board meeting overtime," Rebecca said, ignoring my attempt to relax.

"I'm sure I'll be compensated accordingly," I said, assuming I wouldn't be.

"I've been going through some of your old case files. I never realized how shit the police gigs pay."

"Yeah. They try to keep mediums and psychics and necromancers off the books so they won't have to explain what they're spending their money on to some bureaucrat. We get paid out of petty cash, which can be pretty damn petty."

"I see the real payouts come from the lost-inheritance jobs."

"True. But they're unreliable. The Higgins case Gladys fleeced me out of is an anomaly. More often than not, I only end up recovering somebody's piggybank."

"So isn't the solution obvious? Get richer clients."

"Easier said than done. Rich people turn to lawyers to recover missing wealth or contest inheritances. They only ever turn to weirdos like me if they're going behind the rest of the estate's back."

"I'm sure that happens often enough. We just need more face time with the wealthy jerks who want to screw over the rest of the family. We'll start with the Algonquin Tower opening."

"You get me invited yet?"

"Working on it. In the meantime, who else can you get in the room with? There must be other kooks out there who do creepy shit like you. Maybe they can recommend a gig, or sub-contract, or point you in the right direction."

"Well there *is* a convention coming up," I reluctantly mentioned. "It's out of town, which is why I hardly ever go, but if you can call this business an industry, then this is the biggest industry event of the year."

"Necromancers have their own convention? I guess the others are more social than you."

"It's not just for necromancers. All sorts of magicians—real or stage—show up to swap trade tips, buy and sell props, perform new tricks, and generally, you know..."

"Network?" Rebecca asked.

"Yeah," I admitted. "Network."

"You're going," she announced, like it had just been decided.

"It kind of sucks, really. There's always people I don't want to bump into again." There probably wouldn't be so many necromancers this year considering the recent cull, but I anticipated others. "Competitors and hangers-on and supernatural groupies. I hate all the schmoozing."

"You'll practise and get good at it," instructed Rebecca. "What's this shindig called?"

She poised her fingers over her laptop keyboard, ready to type in a search and, no doubt, book me a ticket and a room before I could object.

"It's called the Necronomi-Con."

"Cute," she noted as her fingers pecked out the name. I knew it would take more than a simple search engine to find it.

"Not so cute, and not so unique either," I said. "It's one of a dozen different conventions or gatherings with, more or less, the same name. People do like their Lovecraftian puns. Don't get me started about what goes down at the Hula-Cthulhu-Luau Dance Party, or the Jog-Sothoth Charity Marathon."

"This the one?" Rebecca asked, turning her screen so I could see the under-designed vanilla homepage that purposely did little to suggest the strange goings on that could be expected at each annual get-together. I told her it was.

"I know it," she said. "Tom has been before. Ask if he's going again this year. You two could share a room."

"I'm sure we'd both love that," I said, knowing I wouldn't, and expecting Tom would feel the same.

I hardly heard the door open as Marin crept in without even knocking. He probably didn't mean to creep, it just comes naturally to vampires. I was about to give him shit for letting himself in and assuming the initial mistaken invite stood as a permanent welcome, when he began what sounded like a heartfelt *mea culpa*.

"I am sincerely sorry, Mr. Eulogy," he said.

"You damn well should be!" I barked at him. If he thought he was going to apologize his way back into my good graces, he was dead wrong. Undead wrong. He was never in my good graces to begin with, and it was only a brief stint of bad judgement that had led me to treat him as anything more than bloodsucking filth.

"I barely noticed you had paid me a visit just now," he continued. "I find myself entranced by this magical device."

Marin held up his cracked smartphone. Even off, his eye was drawn to the screen, which reflected the room in its dark surface, but not its new owner.

"Fuck the phone!" I yelled. "What about that poor girl you sucked damn near dry and left for me to finish off?"

"Who?" he asked innocently.

"The one in the alley next to the bar we were drinking in!"

Vampires have so many victims, they can hardly keep track of them all. After enough time at it, they don't even bother.

One drained human two days or two hundred years ago is the same as the next.

"As I told you, I have not fed in days," he said.

"I saw you! You ran as soon as I tried to put a stop to it, but it was too late to save her. And rather than face me, you flew off like a coward!"

"I flew? How?"

"You turned into a bat and..." I held my hands together at the thumbs and flapped my fingers to demonstrate his method of retreat.

"I did no such thing!" For the first time, Marin sounded incensed, insulted. Even angered.

"I. Saw. You," I repeated.

"Bats are filthy, vile rodents! Leathery wings and coarse black hair! I hate them! Hate them!"

Marin's arms flailed as though he were trying to swat away a swarm of them. His lips were curled in disgust, his eyes clamped shut. Rebecca and I looked at each other.

"Marin?" Rebecca asked delicately. "Do you have a bat phobia?"

"I fear no creature of the night!" he insisted. "Lesser minions of the dark obey my commands, bend to my will! But bats I want no part of."

"You sure about that?" I wondered. "Because vampires are usually really into the bat motif."

"They are icky and they eat bugs," Marin concluded with a sickened frown. If it was an act, it was a convincing one.

"A vampire who loves garlic and hates bats," Rebecca shrugged. "Takes all kinds."

"Why do you think I spent so long learning to become mist?" said Marin. "The ability to fly is a great convenience, but to do so as a bat is repugnant."

"Assuming this isn't all bullshit," I said, "who or what did I see feeding on that girl?"

"By the time I caught up with your friend, Thomas, and his boisterous demon-fish, you were already gone," said Marin. "If you witnessed a vampire attack, then I would suggest it was the work of another vampire."

It would be easy enough to check Marin's alibi with Tom, provided he hadn't lost his memory of that night at the bottom of our seventh or eighth round. If true, that doubled the number of active vampires in my neighbourhood alone. The arrival of a vampire hunter was starting to seem less unusual. I decided to ask one of the flames drawing the moth.

"You don't know anything about a vampire hunter who's come to town recently, do you?"

"A what?" Marin asked.

The concept sounded foreign to him, of course. People don't hunt vampires as far as vampires are concerned. If you were a hunter who was at all successful, and you found yourself a vampire, from their perspective you were just some dumb human who was offering themselves as an easy meal. Like take-out food that delivers itself.

"Somebody is going around trying to slay vampires," I clarified.

"Preposterous!" Marin said. He knew perfectly well how unslayable he and his kind were.

"I didn't say he wasn't screwing it up. But something drew him here."

Marin thought about it, and his tone became much softer, as though pondering some half-remembered bit of arcane knowledge.

"There is a rumour amongst my ilk," he said. "A legend of one mortal man, capable of ending us. Always he is described in the same way, wearing the same armour, throughout the ages. Certainly it is a fallacy. No one man, least of all a mortal one, can account for centuries of lore. And though he is said to have slain dozens, if not hundreds of vampires, there are none I have ever encountered who can give a direct account of this seemingly impossible achievement."

"Not my guy," I said. "This one is a buffoon. A religious nut on a crusade who thinks he knows what he's doing but doesn't have the first clue."

"Then I know of no such hunter. Nor of any other vampire in the vicinity."

No help at all.

Θ

Reluctantly I agreed to let Marin keep freeloading in my casket in the basement. If he hadn't been the one to force my hand into ending a mortal human's life, I'd lost my best excuse to get rid of him.

As Rebecca and I let the television numb our troubled minds that evening, I took stock of all the balls I had in the air. It amounted to a juggling act that was headed for disaster.

"Two vampires, one on a diet, the other happy to leave his unfinished leftovers lying around to turn into more undead. Add a vampire hunter who's ringing up a bigger body count than both those vampires combined. Then there's Charlie Nocturne, still out there, moving pieces on his chess board, trying to bring about the apocalypse. I have a rival necromancer I've never even heard of bumping off the competition, and supposedly coming for me next. Plus, did I mention there's some gigantic head-eating hellhound that's followed me across an ocean and has probably made landfall somewhere along the waterfront?"

"I think you skipped that part," she said, at the end of my litany.

"Lost in the mix," I said.

"God, I need a drink," sighed Rebecca.

"I thought you gave that up."

"But now you're back. And the craving with you. Why do you think I started drinking in the first place?"

"You were a boozer when I met you," I reminded her.

"Not to excess. Excess only became necessary when you gave me things I needed hooch to cope with."

"I'll get on top of it," I assured her. "Go ahead and book the convention and get me into that grand opening at the tower. Meanwhile, I'll see about finding this vampire hunter before he goes on another killing spree."

"What about the rest of the mess?"

"I'll do my best to keep the supernatural bugaboos at bay so nobody else gets chewed up by denizens of the deep—the deep that exists just below the surface civilians are aware of."

"Does that mean I'm not considered one of the ignorant civilians anymore?"

"You never were," I told Rebecca. "Right from when we first met, I knew you could handle the truth, even if you needed the occasional belt to cope with it."

"I'll need to find a new addiction if I want to keep coping. Smoking alone doesn't cut it now that you're back."

"I'll see if I can score you a set of worry beads."

"I don't need a bunch of stones on a string. I need a rock. Just one solid rock to cling to."

Rebecca stared at me too long, waiting for a response.

"What? Me?"

"You be my rock," she said, "I'll be yours."

"Hasn't that always been the case?"

"I guess so," she agreed, and rested her head on my shoulder as the television kept filling the room with light and noise that meant nothing.

I knew I was Rebecca's rock from the start, years ago, but I never liked to play into that. I didn't want her to rely on me too heavily.

Because even rocks break.

Chapter Thirteen

Personal Stakes

SNIDE COMMENTS I EXPECTED. Maybe a cutting barb, an outright insult, or open mockery. Unbridled laughter, however, was above and beyond. In retrospect, I should have expected it. Reynaldo the Fuckhead could always be relied upon to select the rudest greeting possible and run with it.

Once again, Reynaldo had kept me standing at the door of his greystone for as long as he could, waiting for the precise moment when I was about to give up and walk away to respond to the doorbell and let me in. Before he could ask me what I wanted, or even invite me through his threshold, he doubled over in an uncontrollable fit of laughter. At least he made his response to my appearance seem out of control. I'm sure he was playing up his reaction, if not outright performing, like some bottom-of-the-bill stage thespian making the most of his walk-on role.

I let him have his laugh, patiently waiting for him to quit it and get serious. To react at all would only hand him a win. At last he gathered himself. Snorting and clearing his throat, he straightened up and regained his composure. He was just about to speak when he sputtered and doubled over again for a fresh round of hysterics. My patience ended there.

"All right, knock it off," I said.

Reynaldo, beyond speech, pointed repeatedly at his head, which made him laugh all the more. When he was finally able to form words, he sputtered, "The hat...the hat..."

"It was a final gift from Wilbur," I informed him testily. "It's what he left for me."

Reynaldo had to catch his breath as he spoke. His face had turned a ruddy red and the broad smile on his face had become a grimace of exertion. Still, it looked like I had made his day, if not his whole week.

"I'm sure he meant for you to keep it as a conversation piece. Not to actually wear. You look absolutely absurd!"

"Says the man who wears a turban to work," I countered.

"Don't be racist," Reynaldo scolded me.

"Oh, and you're secretly Sikh all of a sudden?"

"The turban isn't cultural appropriation. It's marketing."

"So's this," I said, pointing at the hat on my head. I removed it and hung it on a coatrack in the hall as I stepped inside without further invitation.

"What brings you here?" he asked. "And how soon will you leave?"

"A consult," I said. "And I'll go as soon as I've had it."

Reynaldo laughed again, but this one was curt and humourless.

"Make an appointment and pay like everyone else. I might have an opening for you in a month or two."

"I was more counting on some professional consideration," I said.

"I spare you as little consideration as possible."

"It will only take you a moment. I need to see if you can pick up on somebody's location if I provide you with a personal item."

I wasn't begging, or even asking politely. Reynaldo would do this for me, I was sure of it. He didn't know it yet, but I had the best card in the deck to play against him: ego.

"I haven't a moment to spare. Least of all for you. My time is limited and of far too great a value. Consider me fully booked, with no vacancies."

"Not what I've heard," I said. "Word is your gigs are drying up."

"Balderdash," Reynaldo declared, turning his head away from me, slighted.

"They say you're not hitting the mark like you used to."

"Poppycock," he said, with a dismissive wave of his hand.

"In fact, these days, you're wrong more often than not."

"Bullshit!" he shouted, too loud, before catching himself

That's when I knew I'd struck a nerve. I hit it again, hard.

"Pity, really. Frenz sounded so disappointed that you couldn't deliver anymore. Disappointed in you, but glad to have me back to pick up your slack."

Reynaldo's eye twitched at the mention of Frenz's name, like he'd been stung by an insect. If Frenz was sharing his negative client feedback with me of all people, then the word was out—and undeniable.

"Detective Frenz has had a lapse in faith," said Reynaldo flatly.

"Not in me, he hasn't. Or in anybody else in his collection of oddballs. You're the only one he said he's had a problem with."

"He may be a believer, but he's still a flatfoot policeman with the lacking imagination of a beat cop. He knows nothing of the ebb and flow of the ether or its whims. A few clouded pronouncements, and suddenly years of accurate forecasts and divinations are forgotten!"

I set down my medical valise, pulled it open, and produced the evidence bag with the wooden stake.

"Prove it," I said, holding the weapon out for him.

"I have nothing to prove to you," Reynaldo spat. "You think I lack work? Or clients? I have one in my parlour even now, while you waste my time with this rubbish."

A door down the hall swung open as we were joined by the aforementioned guest.

"Pfft!" Tracy Poole declared, blowing air out through her pursed lips. "You're *my* client, not the other way around."

Reynaldo said nothing, but rolled back his eyes and shut them. Seeing him embarrassed, publicly shamed, if only in front of me, was delicious.

"Tracy, sweetie, how nice to run into you again so soon," I said, playing up the unexpected reunion as grandly as I could, giving her a quick squeeze and light sociable kiss on the cheek. "Hustling your wares for the unlovable and unmournable, I see."

"Reynaldo has been a pre-need client of mine for years now," Tracy said. "We were just updating his policy."

"Planning on dying soon?" I asked him, hopefully.

"Hardly," he sniffed. "I intend to stick around for a great many years, if only to spite you."

"I suppose that will only make it all the sweeter when you finally kick off. Sad, though, that you have to turn to a moirologist to supply the grief."

"I intend my wake to be a splendid festival," Reynaldo informed me. "A party for friends and loved ones to celebrate my life. Still, as it will involve my parting, I think it only proper that there should be one present who will not join in the merriment, but instead will serve as a token mourner, shedding a few tasteful tears."

Reynaldo's shindigs were legendary. I, of course, had never been to one—had never been invited. But I understood there was plenty of debauchery and hedonism to go around. Throwing a final one of those, even if he wouldn't be around to partake, was very Reynaldo.

"I'm supposed to sit in the corner," Tracy explained, "in full mourning regalia, and weep softly and unintrusively, so as not to spoil anyone's fun."

"I will satisfy myself with a single, solitary cry," said Reynaldo. "A bit of performance art to remind everyone of the purpose of the gathering. Unselfishly, I wish no one else to be glum. One is enough."

"Oh, Reynaldo," I reassured him in all seriousness. "I'd cry at your funeral."

"Kind of you to say."

And it seemed, for a moment, as though he may have been genuinely touched. The sap.

"Tears of joy," I added, "but they'll be real tears."

Tracy helped herself to the top hat on the rack and twirled it around in her hands by the brim.

"New duds?" she asked, checking out the rest of my ensemble.

I nodded.

"Very sexy," she stated approvingly and, possibly, genuinely.

Tracy hung my hat up again and addressed Reynaldo.

"I'll have the revised contract for you to sign in a few days."

"Call when it's ready and I'll see where I can fit you in."

"Or don't," I suggested. "Drop by whenever you want. Reynaldo's schedule is wide open lately. Isn't that right, Reynaldo?"

He ignored me and instructed Tracy, "Call first. My regular clients often make appointments for readings on the day-of."

Reynaldo saw Tracy out and shut the front door behind her.

"I thought associating with my associates was beneath you," I said.

"Some are not wholly without talent. I sought Miss Poole out after seeing the display she put on at Wilbur's funeral," Reynaldo explained. "Very genuine, heartfelt."

"I'm sure it was. Tracy was fond of Wilbur."

"Yet I understand he was a client as well."

"Contractual obligation or not, I'm sure her tears were the real deal. Whatever she squeezes out for you will be all style, no substance."

"Isn't everything style over substance these days?" he asked, stroking the lapel of my pea coat between his thumb and index finger.

"Not everything," I reminded him, holding up the evidence bag. "There's keeping up appearances and there's delivering the goods. Which one are you offering these days?"

"Fine!" he said, snatching the bag out of my hand and leading me into the parlour. Through that room and beyond a set of sliding double doors was Reynaldo's reading room, where all the trappings of his profession, carefully arranged to impress the dubious and the devout alike, waited for the next customer who wanted a glimpse into the beyond for an inflated hourly rate.

Normally, Reynaldo would have outfitted himself majestically in order to make a grand entrance. That would have been followed by a scripted monologue about the mystery of psychic phenomenon and the supernatural forces that were about to be meddled with. Such a show cost money, and I wasn't paying, so I didn't get any of it. I was grateful Reynaldo skipped his usual spiel. I'm sure he would have subjected me to the entire song and dance if he knew how tortuous I would find it, but at the moment he was more in the mood to prove himself and be rid of me quickly.

Reynaldo sat at his round table, opened the evidence bag, and looked in at the stake.

"Really?" he asked, recognizing what it was supposed to be.

"Really," I nodded.

"Has this been dusted for prints?"

"No, but don't worry about it. There's plenty more where that came from. Most of them bloody."

Reynaldo grasped the stake between his palms and closed his eyes. He rolled it back and forth in his hands, like he was very slowing trying to start a fire, and wrinkled his brow in concentration.

"I sense a man of great determination," he said at last. "A man on a personal crusade. He grapples, not only with the evils of the world, but inner demons as well."

"Casting a wide net there, don't you think Reynaldo? You just described a few billion people."

"I see blood... So much blood."

"So I already mentioned."

"He is a man with many enemies."

"Thus all the stakes. Again, as mentioned. Give me a location."

Reynaldo's brow furrowed deeper as he reached for something tangible.

"He is close," he said. "Somewhere in the city."

"No shit. Frenz wouldn't have given me the case unless it was local."

"Perhaps some additional details about the suspect will help me focus on him."

"Uh-huh," I said skeptically. "So when I tell you he's an albino, you're going to miraculously deduce that he's been treated as an outcast his whole life."

"Well now that you mention it, I do sense a solitary existence."

"Quit fishing for details you can play off of. I know that mentalist trick as well as you do. You either sense something or you don't."

"Fine," Reynaldo said, opening his eyes and quitting the act. He tossed the stake onto the table with a wooden clatter, "I don't."

"Frenz wasn't kidding. You *are* slipping."

Pleasing as that news was to me, it wasn't what I wanted to hear. I was relying on Reynaldo to pull something useful out of the air, diminishing abilities or not. This was a wash.

"I came here hoping you still had some mojo left," I said, shaking my head.

"My mojo is just fine," Reynaldo insisted. "I keep a vast reserve of it. Lately, however, I have been having some difficulty connecting with the spirit world on short notice. It takes more time and concentration now, which makes it very difficult when I'm dealing with an impatient and unruly client."

"I hope this place is paid off," I said, looking around at the luxurious greystone. "Bullshit readings for gullible widows and widowers isn't going to pay the bills this sort of property must generate. You need real psychic powers to cash in on the wealth-recovery gigs."

"The state of my finances is none of your concern."

"What the hell happened to you?" I asked, genuinely interested if not-so-genuinely concerned.

"It's just a slump," he insisted, unconvincingly. "Even Reynaldo the Wise, Reynaldo the Magnificent, Reynaldo the Uncanny can have a dry spell. Something has been interfering with the psychic realm lately. It's been growing for years, causing ripples in the ether. And now..."

Reynaldo shook his head, defeated.

"Now," he continued, "those ripples have become vast rolling waves, cresting and frothing in a turbulent sea of the mind. I can't see through it anymore."

It seemed like there might be something bigger going on, something more important than Reynaldo being off-target lately. My connection with the endless void of consciousness that exists beyond the narrow restraints of life was not the same experience as what Reynaldo perceived. This turbulence he was talking about wasn't something I could feel, but the specifics of our talents were vastly different than what our often-overlapping fields might suggest. I couldn't do what he did any more than he could borrow from my own bag of tricks. Of course, Reynaldo was now running low on tricks of the psychic trade to such an extent, he seemed to be left holding an empty bag—or no bag at all.

"At least I still have the gift of salesmanship at my disposal," he consoled himself. "There's an upcoming event that promises many wealthy prospects. The rich can always be relied upon to have richer dead relatives they hope to squeeze more cash out of. Some charming conversation, a few rudimentary deductions, and my business cards should seal the deal for a whole new pool of clients I can serve. Or at least string along for a profitable series of sessions, as the case may be."

"This wouldn't be that grand-opening gala at the latest blight to disfigure our fair city's skyline, would it?"

"The same."

"I guess I'll see you there. I was thinking of swinging by."

Reynaldo snickered.

"It's *terribly* exclusive, I'm afraid," he said.

"I'm working on it."

"I hardly think you'll make the grade of the invite list."

"You better hope I don't. I might be the one poaching *your* clients for a change. Should be easy enough to demonstrate who can get the job done and who can't."

"You wouldn't!"

Reynaldo looked a little pale. It suited him. Suddenly he didn't seem so sure that I couldn't wrangle myself an invitation after all.

"Of course, if you kept banging away at my suspect, trying to get a read of something—anything—that might help me track him down..."

Reynaldo retrieved the stake and gripped it firmly with renewed determination.

"Give me a day with it. Twenty-four hours. I'll come up with your answers by then. This I guarantee."

I gave him the rundown of the whole massacre at The Craven Image as I knew it, and what little I'd been able to discover about the slayer. I didn't leave anything out, whether it could possibly be helpful or not. At the very least, I wanted to make sure Reynaldo didn't come back to me with redundant information that would be a waste of my time and his.

As he showed me to the door, there were footsteps upstairs. Someone had been roused by our conversation. One of Reynaldo's sleepovers, no doubt.

"That a new boy-toy clomping around, or did you reconcile with whatshisface?"

"The boys come and they go," sighed Reynaldo. "This is more of a relationship. We've been shacked up for some time now. Years, in fact."

"Reynaldo settling down?" I asked, genuinely surprised. "Things really have changed in my absence. Anybody I know?"

"Passingly at best."

"You should introduce us."

"I really shouldn't."

"Don't be shy."

"By 'shouldn't' I mean 'won't,'" Reynaldo clarified. "You've proven you can hardly be trusted to behave yourself socially. Doubly so in this case. You're certain to say something shameful or embarrassing."

"And you want to protect your special someone. How gallant!"

"Hardly. I want to spare myself an ugly scene."

"Well, maybe you can bring him over if I ever throw another party," I suggested, retrieving my hat.

"Normally I would avoid another such event like the plague, but I understand you have also recently become part of a couple."

Gossip travelled quickly. Or perhaps Reynaldo had gone probing into my thoughts without permission, using whatever traces of talent he still had left. His grin was one of smug superiority, probably because he knew I couldn't tell for sure.

"We're not a couple," I insisted. "We're just living together."

"Of course you are. In any case, I trust Ms. Stone would better know her way around a social engagement. At least enough to have edible food and imbibable drink on hand."

"Is that a criticism of my last party?"

"No," Reynaldo assured me. "A condemnation."

Some parties are remembered for all the wrong reasons. Nobody had had a good time that night, Reynaldo least of all. Reminding him that was his own fault would have been pointless.

"It's been swell as always, Reynaldo," I said, as I turned down the checker-floored hall towards the door. "It reminds me how I didn't miss you at all."

"And it reminds me how it's like you never left me in peace," he replied.

He shut the door behind me. I heard him lock it—assuring he got in the last word.

☉

Reynaldo had seemed certain he could come through for me, clouded psychic vision or not. At this point, I was counting on his desperation to prove himself, and not have me embarrass him at the tower opening as I threatened I might. I honestly couldn't see the path forward for him to make any headway in the mass-staker case, but I knew Reynaldo was resourceful enough to come up with something if he felt like his back was to the wall. With that last straw to grasp at, I felt more comfortable dropping Frenz a line and letting him know I was still on the job. At any rate, I was sure the cops hadn't made any better progress than I had. Sure enough, Frenz sounded satisfied when I assured him I was on top of things. He had another, newer problem to worry about.

"I need you to come in to identify a murder victim," he told me, before I could finish my thin report of how things stood.

"I've got my hands plenty full right now," I said.

"It won't take five minutes," he assured me. "And you can bill me for a whole extra day on the job. I've got enough bodies piled up, and I need at least a name on this one to get the investigation in gear."

"This better be a real five minutes. Not one of those five minutes that turns into five hours or five days."

"It's a simple one. No strings attached. Make contact, get me an ID, maybe an address or next of kin. Best-case scenario: the name of who did it. Basic stuff."

I had to admit, it sounded very standard. Easy money. The boss would be pleased, if she were capable of being pleased by anything. It might get me a day closer to making partner in my own firm that used to be a one-man operation.

☉

The Hillside General morgue just wasn't the same without Louie working the graveyard shift. Of course, Louie was now a partial brain, preserved in a jar of formaldehyde, and these weren't his regular hours. The daytime staffers were still on hand—mostly new faces I didn't know. Frenz was the only real acquaintance I had in the place. He'd met me in the lobby and escorted me down in the staff elevator, for which he'd signed out a key. I didn't bother to tell him I had an elevator key of my own in my medical bag. Some information is only to be doled out on a need-to-know basis, and the police didn't need to know I'd been up to anything illegal—like making my own copy of a hospital security key when no one was looking years earlier.

The autopsy of the murder victim was about to commence, but Frenz had made a personal appearance to put a hold on it until I'd had a chance to commune with the remains. He knew enough of my methods to understand I preferred an unsullied corpse, and coroners had a bad habit of sullying bodies in ways that made the art of necromancy less of an art and more of a pain in the ass.

"The victim is female," Frenz began, as soon as the elevator doors opened on level B8 and let us out into the cool basement corridor. "She was found with ID in her purse—a driver's licence we thought was a match. Turns out it's not her. She'd been drinking that night, so we figure it was borrowed or stolen in case she got carded. No luck getting in touch with the owner yet, but if the victim was underage you wouldn't guess it by looking at her. Hard living. Judging from the state of her teeth, she liked meth about as much as whatever she was having for her final bender."

The morgue itself was hopping with an unusual amount of activity. There were cops and technicians gathered around the slab, waiting for Frenz to give the go-ahead to the cutters. They parted for us as we entered, stepping back to reveal what I would have to work with.

The girl lay naked on the silver examination table. At least, most of her did. Her head was resting upright between her feet. Even without the dress she'd been wearing that evening, I recognized my mercy-killing victim immediately.

Awkward.

"Sick bastard tore her head off," Frenz explained needlessly. "There's evidence of cannibalism. I have to say though, compared to what went down at that goth nightclub, this is refreshingly normal."

I was not anticipating a pleasant conversation. Considering I was the last person she ever laid eyes on before I finished her off, I doubted she'd be terribly pleased to see me again.

"Do you need anything else?" Frenz asked.

"Just a moment to gather my thoughts," I said, and fell silent.

It wasn't my thoughts I needed to gather. It was my nerve. This could get embarrassing. It was certainly going to get ugly.

I cleared my throat and began, "Uh, hi. Anyone home?"

The other men in the room exchanged glances. They hadn't known what to expect from one of Frenz's Freaks. A casual introduction that, because of circumstances unbeknownst to them, came off as sheepish, even shy, was not what they had in mind. I suppose I could have put on more of a show—at least one that matched my new mortician-chic look—but I wasn't in the mood for meaningless but impressive-sounding Latin incantations, or waving a headless chicken carcass over the victim on the slab. Even if I had one handy, I've always found headless chickens do very little to improve reception, and better fit with witchdoctor shtick. My main concern was that the spirit of the departed hadn't had enough time on the other side to practise and improve its ability to emote. What I didn't need was a ghost who had discovered how to make her voice heard outside of my own attuned mind. I was already in for an earful, which would be unpleasant enough, but things would get nasty if the normals in the room could overhear both sides of our exchange. If they did, they'd get pointed at their murder suspect much sooner than they'd hoped.

"You!" came the immediate accusation, and I knew I'd been made.

I must have betrayed myself by wincing, because Frenz was leaning in at my side in an instant.

"You make contact?" Frenz asked, as he studied the look on my face.

"Oh yeah," I said, like it was a good thing. It wasn't.

"You murdered me, you fucker!" echoed an angry voice in my head.

I was the only one in the room who could hear what the dead had to say that day. She hadn't been gone long enough to exercise her new ethereal muscles. Judging from her tone, so far she'd spent her entire time deceased being pissed off and not coming to terms with it at all.

"Ask her who killed her," prompted Frenz.

"Tell him, you prick! Tell him how you killed me!"

The dead girl thought better of waiting for me to relate her message.

"Hey, officers! Officers! This prick killed me!"

"They can't hear you," I said aloud.

"What's she saying?" Frenz asked eagerly.

"It's a bit garbled," I claimed. "She's disoriented. Recently dead and all. She knows you're all in here and it's confusing her."

"The fuck it is!" the spirit screamed in my ear.

"I think it's probably a bit disconcerting for the deceased having a bunch of cops gathered around looking at her naked, decapitated body."

"Right," said Frenz sympathetically. "I guess that would make me pretty self-conscious, too."

"If I could have a few minutes alone with the body..." I began. "Or really, just the head would be fine. I can have a more private one-on-one and get the information you need that way."

"We'll wait outside," Frenz agreed, and turned to corral the rest of the team out of the room. Having heard nothing but my end of the conversation, most of them looked skeptical if not downright incredulous. But Frenz was in charge, and they knew his consultants—oddballs or not—had paid off for him in the past.

It took nearly two full minutes for them to gather their notes and files and shuffle outside. Throughout the duration of the relocation, I was subjected to an endless tirade of rage and insults. I kept my face blank, despite the abuse, until I confirmed the door had swung shut behind the last of Frenz's men. Only then did I dare show any reaction, albeit in a hushed tone.

"Listen to me, you dumb bitch!" I hissed, turning and pointing a finger in the severed head's face. "I didn't murder you!"

"You pulled my head right off my shoulders! What do you call that?"

"It was halfway off already. You were dying. I only put you out of your misery and finished you off in a way that would keep you from rising from the dead."

That only made things worse in her book.

"I could have come back from the dead and you stopped me? You bastard!"

"You wouldn't want to come back like that. You'd be more animal than human, feeding on other people, drinking blood."

I could have gone further into the necrotic incontinence and other downsides of vampirism, but I thought I was painting enough of a negative picture.

"Sounds better off than I am now!"

"Look, the cops need to know your name so they can inform your family about...what happened."

"You going to confess to murder while you're at it?"

"I'll probably skip that part, to be honest."

The police would be about as sympathetic to my motives as the victim.

"I'll get you for this, you fucker! I'm going to fucking fuck your fuck up!"

"Sounds like a plan," I agreed. "Good luck with that. Now are you going to give me a name?"

"My name is Denise Bennet. I want you to know that because you're going to regret ever hearing it, ever knowing it. I'm going to make you hate yourself for ever laying eyes on me, ever meeting me, ever killing me!"

She sounded serious. But I'd been threatened before, cursed before. And even the dead need a pastime to keep busy.

"You have a home address, or am I going to regret ever hearing that too?"

Θ

It took a good twenty minutes to pry the rudimentary information Frenz wanted out of the belligerent corpse. Denise was right about one thing. I already regretted ever crossing her path. That's what I get for being a good Samaritan and decapitating someone to save them from eternal damnation.

"We're done here," I said to Frenz, as I stepped out into the hall where he and his men were gathered. Someone had made a coffee run and turned the interruption of their investigation into a full-blown break.

"Don't you bet on it!" Denise the ghost screeched. "I'm not halfway done with you, you shit!"

I kept my poker face, not letting on that I was being aggressively, obnoxiously haunted.

"Did you find out who did it?" was the first thing Frenz wanted to know.

"Him! Him! He did it!" yelled the spirit into the police detective's face. He saw and heard nothing.

"You're not going to like it," I said.

"I never do, but do you have a suspect for me?"

I paused, letting Frenz brace himself for more bad news. "This was the work of a vampire."

"What? Like at the goth hangout?"

"No, those were a bunch of poser vampires who got killed by a poser vampire-slayer who didn't know what he was doing. This was a real vampire."

"Since when do vampires tear people's heads off?"

"Since they don't want their victims coming back as more vampires competing for blood."

A lie in this case. A small one. Often true, but not this time. I hoped Denise was listening and paying attention. She might learn something if she shut up for a minute and let a few facts penetrate her thick amputated skull.

"You think the cases are connected?"

"It's possible," I conceded. "Maybe our incompetent slayer knows just enough about the subject to realize we have a vampire problem in town. He's trying to do something about it, but he's got everything else wrong."

"What a fucking mess," said Frenz, shaking his head. "Any new leads on the mass murder?"

"I'm working on it."

"Any leads on this one?"

"Also working on it."

Just as I thought, this five-minute gig had blown up on me.

"I don't even know what sort of arrests I can make here. How do I lock up a vampire?"

"You can't," I told Frenz. That information didn't alleviate his stress any.

"Make the killings stop, Rip. You can do that much right? The caseload is stacking up way too high way too fast. That's twelve murders in a row. All of them a shitshow. This on top of the regular homicides and robberies."

"I'm going out of town for a couple days," I said, recalling my commitment to attend the Necronomi-Con trade show.

"You can't do this to me," Frenz protested. "Not right now."

"It's business," I said. "I'll be back. With a solution. I promise."

A long train trip would at least give me time to think, time to figure out how all the pieces connected, or if they connected at all.

"I wrote down all the pertinent details about the victim," I added, handing a page of hospital notepaper to Frenz. "There's not much in the way of family to inform. Nobody local, all of them estranged."

"Poor kid," commented Frenz.

"Yeah," I agreed, even as that poor kid continued pouring her tireless vitriol into my ear.

Θ

Home should have been my next stop, but I had to take care of something first.

Denise was buzzing in my ear like a thirsty mosquito, and I'd used up all my patience trying to keep my cool in front of Frenz and his men. As I rode the elevator back upstairs and walked through the hospital corridors, she kept on me, determined to haunt my every step. It was inevitable she would follow me home, and she said as much.

"Run!" she taunted, "Run to the ends of the earth and I'll be there, in your face, in your head. I'm never going to let you sleep again, fucker. Mark my words, I can keep this shit up forever!"

I didn't doubt it. Having a spiritual shade latch onto you like a barnacle is an occupational hazard. Eventually they get bored, drift away, move on, lose track of you. Denise, bitter and vindictive as she was, would probably be no different. But she was still a distraction, and I needed a way to turn down the volume until she'd had her fill and given up on this newfound career as my own personal banshee.

There was no other recourse but to have lunch.

Θ

The Hillside General cafeteria was about as drab and purely functional as a prison canteen, with the only real improvement being a lack of snitch shivvings between courses. I grabbed a tray from a stack and got in line in front of the sneeze guard until it was my turn to tell the servers behind the counter what I didn't particularly want to eat.

It was hard identifying what was in each of the fitted pans arranged under the glass. There was a selection of green mush, yellow mush, and orange mush. Nothing was labelled, but it all made claim to being edible. I was unconvinced, despite the number of people in the hall noshing dispassionately on their unappetizing meals.

"What are the non-vegetarian options?" I asked, when the line shuffled forward.

"We have fish sticks, chicken fingers, and spare ribs."

"Load me up with the ribs," I said, presenting my tray.

The fish and chicken would be useless processed meat to me, but the ribs promised enough bone to work with. To maintain the illusion of a balanced meal, I let the slop-server fill a few of the divots in the stainless steel tray with pulverized fruits and vegetables. Once I paid at the cash and collected cutlery, I selected an empty table that would give me privacy. My privacy didn't last, of course. My ghostly shadow sat—or at least went through the motions of sitting—opposite me, so she could have a front-row seat at my ongoing one-dead-woman roast.

I ignored her, and most of what was on my tray, and picked through the spareribs with a fork, trying to find a couple with the longest, most intact segments of bone. Finding a pair of candidates, I stripped the meat off with my teeth, chewed, and swallowed. They were pretty bad, even as hospital food went, with enough fat to drum up repeat business in the cardiac ward.

The blather from Denise was constant, relentless, merciless. I tuned it out long enough to concentrate on what had to be done next. Clearing a spot in the central divot, I arranged the two stripped ribs in a "X" configuration. The spell I had in mind was simple, and the reagents easy enough to come by. The bones put me halfway there. All I needed was some of the old special sauce liberally splashed around on the totem. To that end, I sawed at my finger with the serrated edge of a disposable plastic knife, reminding myself to go shopping and replace the rest of the missing tools I should have had in my bag. At least I didn't have to prick myself with a needle. Somehow opening a vein with a dull knife was more palatable, if infuriatingly slow.

Once I had a good flow of blood going, I stood over my barely touched meal and flicked my wounded hand above the crossed ribs, spattering them with blood.

"Spiritus tace!" I shouted at my dinner tray and slammed my open palm down on the stained ribs with great force.

Pea purée and semi-liquid mango salad splashed people at neighbouring tables, and the whole cafeteria fell silent including—mercifully—Denise.

"Mute button for ghosts," I explained to her, as she discovered she could no longer utter a peep.

It was a temporary fix, with substandard ingredients, but it would hold for a while. If need be, something longer could be arranged with a couple of intact human ribs and considerably more blood. I hoped Denise would see reason before it came to that. Either way, I knew I would be seeing a lot more of her. Getting a ghost to shut up was one thing, but she could still linger in the area, stay in my line of sight, and make a quiet nuisance of herself.

I wiped off my hands in some paper napkins and left before anyone could think to make some calls and have me transferred to a psychiatric hospital—preferably to a restraining room where they feed you through a tube so you can't play with your food.

☉

"Any luck reducing the supernatural bugaboo count?" Rebecca asked me after I let myself in and hung up my coat.

"Not as such, no," I reported. "In fact, the number has been upped by one."

"Oh shit," she said, dreading an update. "What is it this time? Some zombie-ghoul-wraith-monster thingamajig?"

"Nah, just a run of the mill ghost. The woman I sort of murdered. She's not pleased with me, so she's decided to give me a haunting."

On cue, Denise drifted through the closed door and into the apartment. She hadn't been able to utter a sound during the whole commute home, but her transparent essence kept milling about near me, irritating my peripheral vision like the waves of a scintillating scotoma announcing a pending migraine.

"So far she's pretty shit at it, but she knows I can see her, so she's being a real jerk about it."

"Can you blame her? I mean, reasons or not, you did kill her."

"Now that we're better acquainted," I said of my new companion, "I'm surprised no one thought to do it before me."

Denise's presence vibrated angrily but ineffectually. She made jabbing motions at me, like she still had a body and could land a physical blow. Other than a slight chill at each point of impact, I was unaffected, but the attempted assault was difficult to ignore. It was important to show no reaction whatsoever. Any hint of a wince or a waver or so much as a blink would only encourage her to keep it up.

"How long is this visitation going to last, do you think?"

My best estimate was a shrug. Between my return, plus Rebecca, Louie, Marin, and now Denise moving in, my old apartment was filling up fast. At this point, Gladys was the one with the best claim to the place. She'd been the only consistent occupant, and after her hostile takeover of my business, she pretty much ruled the roost. If push came to shove, I could always set her after Denise. Denise may have been an enthusiastic novice when it came to haunting, but Gladys was an experienced badgerer. If I put her in touch with this spiritual freeloader, Gladys could probably evict her with the power of her toxic personality alone. Failure to pay her fair share of rent would be a good excuse. Maybe that would work with Marin, too.

"I'm going to bed," I announced, which was a mistake. An hour later, I was still awake. Even with extra bedding, I couldn't seem to get warm and comfortable enough to drift off. I knew Denise was under the covers with me, intentionally or unintentionally putting a chill into me with her presence.

Stubbornly, I stonewalled her, determined to show no signs of discomfort. Rebecca, however, instantly blew my cover when she came to bed and curled up next to me. Her bare feet touched mine and she recoiled.

"Your feet are freezing!"

"There's probably a draft in here."

"You're cold all over," she noted, drawing closer.

"So warm me up," I complained.

Rebecca rubbed my arms and back, trying to heat me up with some friction. Eventually she settled into a spooning position, shivering with her flesh against mine, until we both got warm. At last, the body heat of two living humans overpowered the chilling effect of a single ghost, and I was able to fall asleep.

Chapter Fourteen

Faces of Death

THE ETHEREAL ESSENCE of a dead person needn't take any particular form, but more often than not, ghosts end up doing their best impression of what they used to look like when manifesting themselves. Denise was no exception. I recognized her visage from my memory of her severed head straight away—and it was making faces at me, not more than a few inches past my nose.

I tried to recoil, but I was lying on my back in bed, and the mattress kept me in place. What a way to wake up. It could have been worse, I guess. She could have woken me up screaming, but Denise was still incapable of making noise thanks to my rudimentary spell. It was holding, despite being composed mostly of cheap cafeteria food and bad Latin.

Now that she was reconfiguring her spirit to mimic what she looked like as a living person, I considered making a peace offering. Maybe Denise would better occupy herself if I explained she could twist and sculpt her intangible self into anyone or thing she could imagine and clearly envision. With a bit of practice, she could haunt me as any of her favourite celebrities, or even a startling and unexpected inanimate object of her choice. Much as I didn't care to be harassed by a transparent, incorporeal Hollywood above-the-title starlet or a vindictive-looking floating chesterfield, it might amuse Denise and make being dead a little more fun. Why it didn't occur to ghosts that the sky was the limit when it came to how they presented themselves mystified me, but I guess there was a certain comfort to be had from appearing, more or less, as they had when there was a physical body to accessorize.

Getting over the initial surprise of my morning awakening, I rose, passing right through Denise like she wasn't even there, bobbing over the bed. As far as most planes of existence were concerned, she wasn't. I was still the only one who could even see her, the only one who was aware she was there. Given a few decades or centuries, Denise, just like some of the more notable ghosts, could make other people see her too. But that required a real commitment. I was hoping Denise wasn't so determined. Or stubborn. If she was, I could be stuck with her for a very long time.

Having my morning pee was a challenge with Denise watching. Eventually physical need supplanted shy-bladder syndrome and I was able to let things flow freely. I was just flushing when I heard the apartment door open and close.

"Look what I have," said Rebecca on her return from the lobby.

I ignored Denise's ongoing efforts to bother me with needless visual noise and went to see what Rebecca sounded so pleased about.

There was an envelope in her hand, already torn open and inspected. She handed it to me and I pulled the single slip of expensive-weave paper out for a look. The edges were stylistically stressed, the type was a raised script in bronze. It was very fancy and my name was on it. A watermark logo set in the paper behind the writing itself was recognizable as the distinctive silhouette of the new Algonquin Tower.

"No shit? When did this get here?"

"Just now," Rebecca beamed.

"Hand delivered?" I asked, inspecting the envelope it came in. Rebecca's name had been written on it, and our address, but there was no stamp. "Since when am I such a VIP?"

"You're not."

"But I'm invited, right?" I asked suspiciously.

"According to that piece of paper you are."

I looked at it again. It seemed legit.

"Is this for real?"

"It's real enough. See?"

Rebecca pinched a corner of the invite and rubbed the delicate texture.

"Am I even on the guest list?" I asked more directly.

"Not...technically," Rebecca admitted. "But it doesn't matter. You come with an authentic invite in hand, they won't even check. Trust me."

"How authentic is this?"

"As authentic as they come. I tracked down the printing company that was making the invites and I might have asked someone I know to churn out one more with a name of my choosing."

"So it's a forgery."

"Can something truly be a forgery if it comes directly from the mint itself?"

I had to admit, Rebecca had done it. She'd cheated, but she came through.

"Did I do good?" she asked, fishing.

"If I don't get tossed out on my ear, you did good. If I get thrown out, we'll have words."

"And if I'm there with you, you won't even have to wait until you get home to give me shit."

It wasn't hard to see what she was sniffing around for.

"Want to be my plus-one?" I said.

"I thought you'd never ask."

Like I ever had a choice.

Θ

"False eyelashes?" I asked. "Really?"

I was still a while away from getting dressed for the soiree. Rebecca, however, had long been ensconced in the bathroom in her underwear working on her face. She would probably be at it for another hour before she was satisfied. The first hour had mostly been eaten up by shading and liner. Now she was adding full-blown plastic props for effect.

"What's wrong with making my eyes pop?"

"It looks like a bunch of spiders died on your eyeballs and got stuck there."

"Only to someone with your particular sensibilities," said Rebecca. "Everyone else will find them arresting."

"I don't know where women got the idea that men are checking out how big their eyelashes are."

"Even the cleavage-fixated need to make eye contact eventually."

"And that's when they realize you've got dead spiders trapped under your eyelids and run away in search of alternative cleavage."

I thought I could get away with a suit and tie when it came to be my time to get dressed, but Rebecca insisted I go outfitted in my new work clothes. Despite my misgivings, I put them on.

"I can't go dressed like this," I protested. "I'll look like a weirdo."

"You *are* a weirdo," Rebecca assured me.

"I'll stand out."

"That's the point, silly."

"Can I leave the hat at home?"

"Absolutely not. In fact," she added, "that might be the best place to keep your business cards. You can make a big show of taking off the hat and producing a card from inside for each prospective client."

"I'm going to look like a complete asshole if I do that."

"Yes," Rebecca agreed. "A memorable asshole. The new cards are still on order, so we'll have to go with the old ones for now.

"This is going to be humiliating," I moaned.

"Yup! And that's how new clients and contracts are landed."

"I go too," said a voice in the next room.

"What?" I asked, uncertain if it was a request, an order, or merely a terrible suggestion.

"I think Gladys wants to tag along," Rebecca translated.

"I keep an aye on my inveestmint. Make shur yoo breeng in da wurk."

Gladys had probably been reading about the biggest social event of the year online. I didn't know how she thought she would fit in. Now that she was a business owner and a multi-millionaire, she was getting airs.

"I don't need a talking skull looking over my shoulder and putting a rude word in for me when I'm trying to chat up potential clients."

Rebecca, as usual, came to her defence.

"Gladys will behave herself, I'm sure. It's not like she ever gets a night out," she said, and then added in a lower voice to me, "It might even improve her attitude."

It sounded like the worst idea I'd heard all day until I realized I could use it to undermine the second-worst idea of the day.

"I suppose I could stuff her into the false bottom of the hat and let her eavesdrop from there."

The top hat was enough of a stovepipe to house a fairly petite female skull a couple of inches above my own head if it went in at the right angle. Rebecca was immediately suspicious.

"You just want an excuse to not have to pull business cards out of your hat."

"I'll try to pull them out of my pocket with extra flourish," I promised her as I collected Gladys and started to position her under the hat's interior silk flap.

"I gooing for a ride!" she gushed with such joy, it would have been impossible to leave her behind at that point. Considering she'd been cooped up in the same few rooms since I'd first jump-started her skull, it was about time I took her for a walk.

I popped the hat on top of my head, to which Gladys shouted, "Yeehaw! Giddyap!"

"Just let me do the talking," I said.

Θ

Denise had done her best to molest me while I was getting dressed, pantomiming various attempts to kill me, even though she must have figured out by now that it was impossible for her to make physical contact. Whether it was the wispy tendrils of ghost fingers around my neck, or futile attempts to pick up a razor and introduce it to one of my arteries, she was certainly persistent. Or stupid. Or insane with grief at her own demise. The display was pathetic, and without her scolding voice in my ear, it was easier to feel sorry for her.

Once Rebecca and I were in a cab, working our way past a series of streetlights with good enough timing to make all the greens, Denise fell hopelessly behind. She'd tried sitting in the back seat with us, only to sink through the upholstery as the taxi pulled away without her. Ghosts can pass through anything physical, but even taking a direct path wherever they wanted to go didn't make them particular fast. She had no chance of keeping pace with a lead-foot cabbie. A few turns later and I was sure we'd lost her, hoping that meant a reprieve from her presence for the rest of the night—or at least until she latched back onto me at home.

Giving Gladys a piggyback ride wasn't as difficult as I thought it might be. With the hat pulled down slightly over my brow, the fit was firm enough to support a light bundle of bones without the burden becoming too top heavy and tipping over. She stayed quiet, despite her initial excited chatter about going for a car ride. Once we were on the road, she made an effort to keep her mouth shut and not distract the driver. I could hear her humming to herself softly, but I'm sure the sound didn't project outside of the hat where others might detect it.

If she had been excited to leave the apartment, and thrilled to take a car ride, she was absolutely past herself taking the elevator up from the Algonquin Tower lobby.

"Weeeeeeeee!" she exclaimed as we rode nine floors to the terrace level where the opening ceremony was to take place. I was glad we were alone for the trip up, but once we arrived at our destination, I thought it would be prudent to ditch Gladys before she had a chance to make a spectacle of herself in mixed company. She probably wouldn't be able to contain her delight once she was surrounded by people and conversation far beyond anything she had ever encountered at my own modest gatherings. At a cloakroom, a uniformed check-clerk was exchanging tickets for hats and coats, so I gently removed my hat and swapped it for a stub. Holding a finger up to my lips, I let the clerk know I was trying to get away silently. He didn't know what I was on about, but nodded dutifully as he filed the hat and its occupant away in a cubbyhole that matched the number I'd been issued. I tiptoed away before Gladys ever suspected she was no longer in our company.

Rebecca's prediction proved accurate. Her dodgy invitation saw us through the security staff, who didn't look us over more than two or three extra times. They wouldn't have looked at us twice, but given my apparel, they were probably trying to figure out what eccentric celebrity nutjob I might be, fresh off a movie set or concert tour.

The extra security wasn't just for the event that would christen the newest, highest point of the city vista, nor was it for the who's who of local money and power in attendance. It was all for the well-being of the guest of honour himself. Every tower needs its penthouse suite, and every penthouse suite needs its own rich asshole to fill the thousands of square feet of luxury space with wealth and ego. Nobody was going to be permitted that high up in the tower, but word was that Jeevak Menahem himself was going to attend the opening and say a few words. The Algonquin Tower was the latest piece of penis-extending real estate he'd had built as a monument to himself, and the first to grace the North American east coast. Supposedly, he was so enamoured with the onyx glass edifice—the largest yet to grace his empire—that he was planning to make it the new centre of operations for his corporate conglomerate. What exactly that international entrepreneurship did, other than make vast sums of money, seemed to elude everyone—including its own shareholders, who didn't question the vague annual prospectus so long as the dividends continued to pour in and their stock split at regular intervals.

The reception was on a balcony that crowned the wide base of the building, and was broad enough to easily host the ceremony that would see several hundred bigwigs from all corners of the city and beyond. The bank of elevators spat out investors, and those with a vested interest in the opening, at an increasingly rapid pace as the official start time passed. There were tuxedos and gowns aplenty. Most of the couples there hadn't dressed so fine since their wedding, and wouldn't dress so fine again until their funerals. Even in my new duds, I looked like a shabby interloper—or the undertaker who would be burying them at their next big social do. I'd only been on the premises for a few minutes and already I was longing for a drink to steady myself.

I looked forward to seeing the spread that would be laid out for such a lavish occasion right up until I actually saw it. There were some fairly uninspiring vegan hors d'oeuvres being trucked around the event by a spiffy waitstaff, and an open bar full of fruit and vegetable juices that looked like no fun at all. The closest thing to cocktails on offer were cans of iced beer being opened and served by a mixologist with nothing to mix. Even the beer managed to be an affront to the concept.

"Shit-brand lite or non-alcoholic shit-brand," I listed, after taking inventory of our sad options twice.

"I'll take a non-alcoholic," Rebecca told the white-suit black-tie behind the bar.

"Isn't that temptingly close to the real thing?" I asked.

"I like to pretend I've fallen off the wagon from time to time. It keeps me from really falling off."

I asked for a glass of the brand that could barely muster two percent alcohol and less than that in flavour.

"How is it?" I asked Rebecca after her first sip.

She nodded as she swallowed, like her drink was everything she hoped it would be.

"Awful. You?"

"I'd say it tastes like somebody pissed in my beer, but that would assume there was ever beer in here in the first place."

I took another sip anyway. At least it was wet and cold, unlike the rest of the gathering. Everyone was being kept un-seasonably dry and toasty despite the chilly night that lay just beyond the boundaries of the balcony ledge. Vents were blowing warm air across the exterior space at great expense and a greater waste of power, but it kept the money comfortable, so somebody thought it was worth it. It certainly prevented inclement weather from tempting anyone to punch their social card early and leave before the ribbon cutting.

I was just going to ask the staff for another pseudo beer when I noticed that the guy who had edged in next to Rebecca wasn't hired help looking to take our order. It was Tom. I barely recognized him. He was wearing a tuxedo, sure, but this wasn't his vintage stage costume with the tails and the moth holes. This one was crisp and new, and looked too tailored to be a rental.

"Hey Tom," I said. "Moonlighting as a waiter?"

"No," he said, sounding insulted. "I'm on the list."

"Bullshit," I challenged him. "Show me your invitation."

"You show me yours," he retorted.

"There's no point me showing you mine. Mine's fake. Obviously."

He couldn't argue that and reached into his inside jacket pocket for an envelope. I was looking over the embossed lettering a moment later. Even as I read it aloud, I couldn't believe it.

"Thomas Kincaid," I said, and flashed it to Rebecca for confirmation.

"Well it's not going to say The Amazing Barfo, is it?" Tom said.

"The question is, how does The Amazing Barfo get an invite to an event like this, with or without the stage name?"

"It wasn't my idea," Tom moaned. "My parents insisted I make an appearance since they're off on a Danube river cruise."

"Your parents...?" I began.

"Are rich. Yeah," confirmed Tom.

"Did you know this?" I asked Rebecca.

"It came up," she confirmed.

"And you never thought to share?"

"We saw each other for nearly three years. It was old news. I didn't think it was relevant."

"So you're a trust-fund kid," I said, relieved. I'd wondered ever since I'd first met him. It was like having a persistent itch scratched at long last. "Now I get the whole performance-art routine. Someone else needs to be paying your bills to go chasing that impractical dream. It was very nice of your parents not to disown you outright."

"They don't know about my stage career," Tom said, like that much should be obvious. "They don't even know I dropped out of school. As far as they're concerned, I'm working on my third post-grad thesis."

"What happens when they expect you to turn all those degrees into a paying career and the cheques from home stop?"

"The plan is to be a rich and famous regurgitator by the time that happens."

"How's that working out?" I asked, expecting not well.

"I really think I'm making headway now that I've got a solid team act."

"Team act, huh?" I repeated aloud, and immediately regretted it.

"This is no simple pairing as equals!" roared Tom's pocket partner. "Our relationship is purely one of master and slave, for I am Qixxiqottltoq!"

People turned to stare at the outburst in the midst of a sea of otherwise courteous discourse.

"Shhhhh!" Tom said, holding a hand over the vest pocket where his watch chain disappeared. He looked uncomfortably over his shoulder at the many eyes on him.

"I shall not be shushed, hu-man minion!"

"Dammit Tom, would you shut your pet demon-fish up while we're in public!" hissed Rebecca. "You may be on the list, but we're not. If anyone checks, they're going to bounce us."

"Silence your female meat-mount, or I shall chew her tongue out of her speech orifice myself!" threatened Moby-Dick.

"She's not my female anymore," Tom corrected the fish.

"I was never *your female*," Rebecca corrected Tom.

"I'm guessing the third wheel in this relationship wasn't so conducive to long-term success," I observed.

"Shouldn't you be out there selling your wares?" Rebecca reminded me.

"After that scene?" I said, looking at the other guests who had only just started to return their attention back to their own conversations. "I think I'll hide out here a bit longer, let everyone get a few drinks in. Myself included."

"Go!" she insisted, mouthing the word at me more than actually saying it. She might as well have screamed it at me for as much energy she put into it.

"Was she like this with you?" I asked Tom.

"No. Rebecca never really believed in *my* talents," he said. "Isn't that right?" he added pointedly.

Rebecca started to sputter a response, trying for indignant and only coming up with guilty-as-charged.

"Confess wo-man receptacle!" prompted Moby-Dick, like the inquisition was a go.

That did the trick. Rebecca managed to nail indignant in a split instant. I took the opportunity to back away from the fireworks.

"Receptacle?" she began.

"...Yeah. I'm gonna go now," I muttered, trying not to interrupt. "Sell those wares. Like you said."

Spinning on my heel, I walked away into the more civil fray ahead of me and scanned the faces of the milling crowd. They nattered back and forth the way those who recognize each other as being from the same elite stratosphere do when the only little people around are the hired help who are paid to serve them and hear nothing. There was only one face among them I knew from real life—instead of from news media or bookstore memoirs. He was another fat cat in his own way. Mostly he was just fat, but catty when the mood struck. I decided to hit him up first.

"Find anything?" I asked, rather than offer any sort of small talk or social greeting.

I hadn't noticed when he'd arrived, but I was almost glad to see the familiar jowls in front of me.

"I'm mingling," Reynaldo told me. "Come talk later."

Cutting the exchange there, he left me staring at his back, disinclined to invite me into the conversation he was having with three prospective clients. So much for my wares. I started to head back to Rebecca's side, but she stared me down at range and made a shooing gesture with her drink so sharply, she spilled a few drops. The sneer on her lips and the glare in her eyes made it clear I wasn't welcome back. I was there to hustle, not hang out under her wing all night. Besides, she was still having it out with Tom and his fish in harsh, hushed tones. Best, I agreed, to leave them to it.

Alone and adrift, I picked a high roller at random to accost with my sales pitch, suspecting it would go every bit as poorly as the worst expectations I'd been having since I first laid eyes on Rebecca's forged invite.

"Any idea when they're going to get around to christening this phallic eyesore?" I asked, casually tapping him on the back.

It wasn't my best opening line, but I was banking on the likelihood that most of the attendees were there out of obligation and were growing impatient, waiting for the show to get on the road.

The man turned to look at me with piercing eyes, and everyone in his group fell instantly silent. I'd thought he was just one of a collected cluster in the middle of the function. Too late, I realized he was the centre of everyone else's attention. The man—not just any man—had been holding court, and I was interrupting.

"Oh, uh, sorry," I said, recognizing the face from snippets of televised file footage I'd been seeing for days. "You must be Jeevak Menahem. I didn't mean to intrude."

I was about to retreat and try my luck elsewhere when he stopped me, placing a hand firmly on my shoulder.

"Not at all," he said. "You are precisely who I should be talking to at precisely this moment."

"I don't want to take you away from your friends."

"These are not my friends," he said, indifferent that all this non-friends could hear him. "They are of no particular concern to me. You, however, I have been most intrigued to meet."

"Wait," I said, imagining Rebecca's coaching in my ear, "I'll give you my card."

"No need," he replied, stopping me from rummaging through my coat. "I know precisely who you are, Rip Eulogy. I know what you do, I know what you've done, and I know what you have yet to do. At least, up to a point."

"You do?"

"More so than yourself, even. Come!" he invited me—commanded me—and left the other crème de la crème in his group behind without so much as excusing himself.

As Jeevak Menahem led me away from the rest of the party, I dared hope that Rebecca was right—that some of the wealthy elite would need the sort of service I could provide, and would be willing to pay an inflated price above and beyond my usual rates. Menahem had become a self-made multimillionaire while he was still in his twenties. He was a multibillionaire by the time he hit his mid-thirties. Now he was in his forties, and there was no telling how swollen his pocketbook had become. He collected landmarks, and when he couldn't find one for sale, he built it himself. Whatever he wanted from me, I hoped I could charge him even a tiny percentile finder's fee.

There was another door off the terrace—not the one facing the elevators. This one was marked private only. Menahem invited me through it and into a lounge that looked like it had yet to seat or host a single person, it was so new. We had the place to ourselves.

"So how do you know me?" I asked.

"I can recognize a kindred spirit when I encounter one. As can you. I was forewarned of your ties to this city. It is fitting you would return to it eventually."

It was obvious to me then that this wasn't some entrepreneur interested in digging up family history, or a captain of industry looking for assurance of an afterlife now that he'd accomplished everything he could in regular life and had become bored. This was an insider.

"You're in The World?" I asked hesitantly. I didn't have to elaborate on what I meant by "The World." It wasn't a term I cared for, but it was often, undeniably, a world unto itself. An underworld.

"I am intimately intertwined with it," he confirmed.

I was so busy trying to figure out what type of practitioner he might be, I felt stupid when I finally figured out what sort he had to be.

"Necromancer," I said aloud.

I knew then that I hadn't picked him out of the crowd at random. I'd been drawn to him, like I sensed what he was before I had any idea who he was.

"A lucrative trade," he commented. "How do you think I paid for all this? This and other properties all over the world."

"Necromancy?" I asked, trying not to sound surprised.

"Of course. The gift to probe past the limited confines of life is a power beyond measure. And, it must be confessed, an easily exploited generator of immense wealth. You know this. You practise the craft as a businessman yourself, do you not?"

"Right. Yeah," I noted casually. "I make a buck here and there."

Menahem stared into one of the floor-to-ceiling tinted panes of his skyline gem. Where we stood was beyond the limits of the ninth-floor terrace, and it was a sheer drop to street level only inches past the glass barricade. His faint reflection stared back at me, transparent and indistinct compared to the rest of the room. I felt dizzy, and it wasn't the height.

"My first million came so easily, it felt accidental," he told me. "As though I'd tripped over it like a stone in the road. From there, my fortune multiplied as if it had a mind of its own. All I did was what came naturally. And for this, I was compensated beyond the dreams of kings. I'm sure you're no stranger to being overpaid for the simplest of necrotic tasks."

"Oh sure, sure," I nodded. "The last major gig I had netted me eight figures for ten minutes of work. I took some time off after that one."

"I do not take time off," he stated at my off-handed mention of a vacation.

"No rest for the wicked, huh?"

"None whatsoever."

He'd been busy all right. He was a man with a plan. While I'd been picking up the pieces in the middle of the ocean, one grain of ash at a time, Jeevak Menahem was trying to fill the vacancy I'd left. The difference was he was willing and eager to do so.

"I've heard about you, too," I said. "Advance warning, more like. Not the public figure, I mean. Everyone knows about your front. I mean you, the necromancer. I just didn't know you were one and the same until now."

His back to me, his reflection smiled smugly.

"Your replacement in the grand scheme," he said.

"I was going to say 'understudy.'"

Menahem didn't look insulted as I hoped he would. And he already knew who had tipped me off about him.

"Marin's opinion of anything or anyone is not to be taken to heart," he told me. "Centuries on, he's still in horror of what he has become. Why not embrace it? As you and I have. Are we not also terrors of the underworld? Necromancers raising the dead, desecrating graves, robbing the departed of their dignity in repose? Denying them the simple mercy of eternal rest whenever we task them with our self-serving errands or duties? Vampires merely hunt and feed, as any creature might. We contrive the true cruelty that is to be delivered in death. But that is only in our nature. Who has any right to condemn our calling? Typically it is those who hear no calling of their own—never learn who they really are, never find purpose in life, or in death. Their impressions of us are not worth a moment's consideration."

"Charlie Nocturne must think you've got game if he went after you once I turned him down."

"It's not like I left him many options."

"No," I agreed, "you didn't."

"I should have been his first choice, of course. Once I forced his hand, he recognized what an asset I was. I have a unique talent, which told him all he needed to know."

"Yeah? What's that?"

"I know how everybody dies."

He turned around and faced me to tell me that part. He wanted me to see his eyes, to know he was being absolutely serious, and worse, completely truthful.

"Everybody?"

"Everybody."

"So that means..." I stopped myself. I didn't even want to say it.

"Charlie Nocturne's plan, the prophecy, the apocalypse—it all comes to pass. I was able to confirm this for him. He seemed pleased. Or at least as pleased as a void such as him can be."

"The grand finale," I echoed. "That's how everybody dies."

"Oh, not everybody. There's time enough left for plenty of mundane deaths. I can see them all."

Menahem gazed out the window again, surveying the gathering thick with his guests, all of them socializing and chattering away like they had an endless supply of tomorrows.

Yet everywhere he looked, Menahem saw death—pending or plotting, sooner or later. They were all dead men and women walking, with expiry dates ticking away faster than any of them knew.

"Bowel cancer, a year from now," Menahem said of one man. "Brain tumour in ten months," he said of another.

From one to the next, his gaze shifting to each face in turn, a death sentence was declared.

"Plane crash in sixteen days. Septicemia in eleven months. Internal hemorrhaging during childbirth in six months. Likewise the fetus she carries. Accidental drowning next summer vacation. Suicide by overdose in three weeks. Double pneumonia at the age of ninety-one."

He added, "Good for him. That's a long full life. Not so much his wife next to him who dies of a blood clot in her left lung next year. Nor his business partner who is so busy right now, chatting up that blue-chip CFO, trying to seal the deal, thinking big, planning for the future. He doesn't suspect there isn't one for him, or that he will suffer of a massive heart attack three and a half hours from now. Dead before he hits the floor. Dead before he suspects anything more serious than indigestion."

"Given the shitty catering, it's no wonder he goes out suspecting indigestion."

"Can I offer you a stronger drink?" Menahem said, stepping behind the lounge bar. "You may need something bracing."

"I wouldn't want to mix anything with this beer-flavoured soda pop," I replied, holding up my beverage.

Menahem poured himself a drink from a bottle in a cabinet under the bar.

"I do not serve hard alcohol at events such as these," he explained. "There are powerful people in attendance, with secrets worth protecting. A few too many drinks and information begins to slip out. One closely guarded secret gets traded for another, and the best-laid plans of gods and monsters are brought to naught."

"What do you care about insider trading between members of the high-society stratosphere?"

"Nothing," he said, topping off his glass flute. "But they all have their roles to play in the times ahead. Each of them is an unknowing piece of a puzzle far too vast and complex for them to understand. The actions of those at the pinnacle of the social order work to tear it all down unknowingly. Short-term gain is bought with long-term consequences they all think they'll never live to see. Many of them are right. But most are wrong. The day of reckoning is coming fast, and the majority of them will get to taste the spoiled fruit of their selfish, destructive labour. Don't pity the ones with growing tumours or heart disease— the depressed, the suicidal, the accidents waiting to happen. Their deaths will have the benefit of being ordinary. Reserve pity for those who will still be around for the final act."

"What are you drinking?" I had to ask when I saw him take his first sip. Even in the dim lighting of the lounge, it didn't look appealing.

"Something you would not care for," he said. "An acquired taste."

I thought it might be ouzo until I saw how dark it was. It looked like fish sauce and smelled worse. Thick and syrupy—it was as black as the tower he'd build for himself.

"Stronger stuff than what I'm having?"

"Most certainly."

He looked at me like he was daring me to probe deeper. I didn't get the chance.

"Hide me," said another voice in the room, intruding on our conversation.

It was Tom, who had just slipped in through the terrace door, looking for me.

"Rebecca's on the war path," he elaborated. "I can't say or do anything right."

"Tom, I'm in a meeting right now," I told him. He didn't take the hint.

"You going to introduce us?"

"No introduction necessary, really," I said. "This is our host, Jeevak Menahem."

"No shit? Real-estate tycoon, entrepreneur, famous rich guy?"

Tom sounded suitably impressed. I rounded out the résumé, never taking my eyes off of Menahem.

"Necromancer."

"Like you?" Tom asked.

"No, not like me."

"We have differing skill sets," Menahem said.

"And ethics," I added.

Tom ignored my comment and blurted an introduction.

"I'm Tom Kincaid. It's probably my parents you know. George and Angela. They couldn't make it."

"I know who you are," Menahem said, not even bothering to shift his gaze to Tom. "I know who everyone here is. Even that lesser demon you have burdened yourself with."

I anticipated an outburst, but the ensuing silence was deafening.

"What's the matter, Moby?" I asked, "No objection to being called a lesser demon?"

"The necromancer speaks accurately," I heard from Tom's pocket. Moby-Dick's tone within his enclosure wasn't simply muffled. He sounded hushed, respectful. It was utterly out of character and worrying to me. But Tom didn't catch on.

"So you have a different set of tricks up your sleeve than Rip here? Anything cool I should know about?"

"You'll find out in due course," Menahem said.

I knew that wouldn't satisfy Tom. He'd goad Menahem into casting some spell, or performing some ritual, just as he had when he'd first met me. And I expected whatever Menahem came up with would pan out even worse than the aquatic curse I'd inadvertently stuck him with years earlier. So I threw him a bone.

"He can see how people will die," I said.

That seemed to impress Tom plenty. His next question was obvious.

"How do I die?" asked Tom.

"You don't want to know that," I interrupted.

"Sure I do," Tom insisted. "So how about it? How do I check out?"

"You die on the toilet," Menahem informed him, so matter-of-factly, it seemed beneath him to illuminate such a drab detail.

"Like Elvis?" said Tom, taking it in stride.

"An inglorious end," nodded Menahem.

"You hear that?" Tom asked me, brightly. "I'm going to die just like Elvis Presley!"

"Congratulations," I said. "We'll be sure to put that in your obituary."

"Hey," said Tom, "Speaking of toilets, I really gotta take a leak. This non-alcoholic beer is going right through me."

"There's a washroom by the elevators, straight through that door," Menahem instructed.

"Don't sit on the toilet," I cautioned Tom, as he followed directions.

"Right, of course," he laughed. "Urinal and sink only, promise."

Once Tom was gone, I made excuses for him.

"He still thinks it's all games and party tricks."

"He'll know better soon enough."

"The end times can't be that close," I surmised. "What about that guy you said makes it to ninety-one?"

"He's already ninety."

"Oh. Really?" I asked, gazing out the window and finding the man in the crowd again. "He looks fantastic for his age."

"He'll deteriorate rapidly. You, on the other hand, look fit and well for someone who has been dead as many times as you have been."

"You been keeping score?"

"I have been monitoring your career for a long time now. And I have predicted each of your deaths in turn. Some have been most amusing."

"Ever think to give me a heads up?"

"I can only ever see the next one pending. Anything beyond that is shrouded. I wonder, can one such as you face a death you cannot return from?"

"So far, nothing's stuck."

"I enjoy a challenge," he said, and sipped his drink.

"So how do I drop dead next?" I asked, not too worried about the answer.

"You die at the end of this conversation."

"Oh yeah? How's that?"

"I strangle you for your insolence."

"I'll just come back," I shrugged.

"No matter. I foresee it. I also foresee it being most satisfying."

"I guess that makes me the one necromancer who won't stay down for the count for you."

"Why should these petty practitioners go about their business unchallenged, untouched, as they discredit our discipline with mediocrity at best and charlatanism at worse?"

"Did you kill Oliver Franck?" I asked pointedly.

"Did I?" he wondered aloud. "I've eliminated so many competitors at this point, I've lost track. Friend of yours?"

"Yeah," I said coldly. "Oliver was a friend."

"My condolences. Did he die well?"

"He had his head chewed off by a giant hound. Your do-ing?"

"You're wondering if I held its leash?"

"Something like that."

"What would you do if I said yes? Avenge your friend?"

"Something like that."

"Here? Now? At my own dedication ceremony?"

"Maybe."

"That's not how I die," Menahem said, and downed the last of his smelly drink.

"Are you so sure?"

"Positive."

"Care to tell me how you die, so I can figure out my role in it?"

"I don't die."

"Ever?"

"Details grow faint the farther away a death lies, but I don't foresee any end for myself."

"So you're immortal?"

"Not yet. It's an ongoing project. I know, at the very least, that I don't die before I succeed in achieving immortality. And once that is in my grasp, I can never be stopped."

"I'll have to see about that," I stated, putting on my best threatening voice. Menahem only chuckled in my face.

"As you've just said, Mr. Eulogy, we are not playing games and tricks here. Death brings real consequences. And life, it should be noted, is no game either."

I shored myself up for a lecture about the sins of frivolity.

"Life is a sandbox," he said, which was a new one I hadn't heard before, so I listened. "We're all in this sandbox together, we children. How we spend our time in it is entirely up to us, whether we realize it or not. Some of us make castles, some of us make mud pies. Some toil and plan, others fiddle about with no aim or end goals. Whatever we're up to, we're all doing two things. Building and passing time. There's no right way to do either of these things, just your own way. But you must be careful. There are other children in the sandbox who aren't content moulding their own allotment of sand. Naughty, nasty children. Their idea of time well spent is to kick over the castles the others are trying to build, or worse, bury their playmates in the sand. They're horrible, brutish little bullies, but they're not the worst of the worst."

"I got buried in the sand by one of the bullies once," I recalled.

Okay, it wasn't sand, it was mud, and it wasn't playground bullies, it was an Axis death squad, but close enough.

"I can't imagine much worse," I added, because I couldn't. As my various deaths went, that one was pretty horrible. Certainly in the top two or three.

"Ah, but there is," he countered. "The ones you really have to look out for are the children who make up the rules. You know who I'm talking about. The ones who don't want anyone to play unless it's by arbitrary rules invented on the spot to suit their own selfish needs. Too many children fall into their trap, and that is the moment when play becomes work, and time goes wasted."

"I bet I can guess which kind of kid you are," I said.

"Are you so sure?"

"Sounds to me like you're planning on kicking over a whole lot of sand castles following Charlie Nocturne's plans for you. Every sand castle there is, in fact."

"Destruction is itself an act of creation. Uncreation if you will. Just as death is not the antithesis of being alive. Destruction can be a force for renewal, and the end of everything will bring a fresh start to a world unblemished by futile, struggling, desperate life."

It sounded like he'd given this a lot of careful thought over many years. I dismissed it out of hand just the same.

"You're out of your fucking mind."

"Submit to a higher power and kneel before me," he said.

"You have power all right. Maybe greater than my own," I conceded. "But you're no higher power. You're about as low as they come."

Menahem nodded knowingly and set his glass down delicately on a coaster waiting on an end table next to a plush settee. He did so with such calm and dignity, I didn't expect him to come at me so fast and with such rage. In a split instant, his hands were around my throat, squeezing the life out of me. He was much stronger than I anticipated, and I was unbalanced and unable to fend him off on such short notice. The pressure throbbed in my skull and I felt a blood vessel burst in one of my eyes. I tipped backwards as he throttled me and lowered my flailing body to the floor. Briefly, I felt carpet at my fingertips, but I blacked out before I was laid down and finished off.

$$\Theta$$

As soon as I felt my spirit and body separate, I hurried to wriggle back in and revive. I didn't want to leave my body alone with that psychopath for long. Who knew what condition he'd have it in if I gave him time to get creative.

With a deep choking breath, I sputtered back to life and sat up, holding my sore throat. The world had gone dark, and remained dark even as I returned to the land of the living. As if in response to my revival, the lights snapped back on and I saw I was still in the tower lounge. Jeevak Menahem was there, standing over me. Calm civility had returned, and no one would ever have suspected him of having just committed murder with his bare hands.

"Four minutes," he announced, consulting his watch. "Most impressive."

"Fuck you," I croaked.

"I trust your crushed trachea will spring back in short order as well. Pardon my lingering, but I had to see one of your miraculous recoveries for myself. I may not get another opportunity."

I hacked a few times, but stopped myself short of having a full-on coughing fit. I didn't want to show any more weakness in front of this asshole than I had already.

"You know how I go out next?"

"Of course. It is clear to me now."

"What'll it be? You want to try shooting or stabbing me next?"

"Your next death is of no consequence to me. It's not of my doing and I take no part in it. The one after that, however... That one will be special. That is the one I have planned for you."

"You can see that next one, too?" I asked, trying to get the limits of his power straight.

"Only in my own machinations," he said. "My plots and schemes. It will become clearer to me as soon as you get your next demise out of the way."

Menahem turned and walked to the terrace door, returning to his guests and the ritual of officially opening his shiny new tower for business.

"There are no rules in the sandbox, Mr. Eulogy," he reminded me as he left me alone to recover from his assault. "Only time and sand and those with the resolve to make of it what they will."

"Charlie Nocturne know what a freak you are?" I asked him as he let himself out.

"Ask him yourself," said Menahem, as the door swung shut behind him.

I picked myself up and scanned the lounge, searching it more thoroughly than I had thought to when I first entered.

The low lighting cast many shadows, but I was looking for the one that was sentient.

"You're awfully conspicuous, standing there in a corner like a wallflower at the prom," I told the darkest spot in the room. "What if some of Menahem's guests spotted you?"

"I am seen by those who are meant to see me," said Charlie Nocturne. "I elude the notice of those who are not—either because I do not wish to be seen, or because they are not mentally equipped to deal with the sight of me. I am an existential blind spot for dull-witted mortals who cannot comprehend a world more complex than the insular one they travel in daily."

I didn't know if Charlie had been there the whole time, or had only come in while I was dead. Asking him didn't sound productive. He'd probably only answer in riddles and vagaries.

"I'm back, by the way," I informed him. "Though, I heard you predicted as much, so don't fake looking surprised."

"Of course you have met Marin Venerio Grissoni. No doubt he fled to you, looking for your counsel on how best to avoid his fate."

"You don't like to take no for an answer, do you?"

"Fate, destiny, inevitability. These are the things that do not take no for an answer. I merely facilitate. Marin is not yet prepared to join us, but he will once he receives the mark."

"What about the rest of Team End Times? Has your War recovered from our last tangle?"

"Csaba Szabo persists. You cannot destroy War as an entity any more than you can destroy it as a concept."

I was afraid of that. My encounter with Szabo had ultimately put me out of commission for years, but I figured a trocar to the eye and an imploding arthouse wasn't going to slow him down for long. When the authorities failed to dig his remains out of the rubble, I knew he must have escaped somewhere. War always lives to fight another day.

"So you've still got Szabo in your back pocket. You're working on Marin. And Menahem seems like an enthusiastic zealot. Your horsemen-of-the-apocalypse cavalry charge is shaping up nicely. But I don't get Menahem's angle. The guy is chasing after immortality, but he wants in on a plan that's just going to end all life anyway?"

"He wishes to become Death Incarnate because he knows Death is the slayer of all things," Nocturne explained. "Death itself will never die, and once all life is snuffed out, he alone shall remain."

"Just him, by himself, for eternity?"

"A happy outcome for a misanthrope."

"Well, he seems to have the goods, I'll give you that. Pretty impressive talent for predicting death, if he's not bullshitting."

The pain in my neck suggested he wasn't. But it's not a great leap of deduction to predict your own actions.

"His talent is genuine, yet he, too, is lacking."

"Picky, picky."

"Unlike you, unlike the others I must select for my task, he is not yet immortal. Nor has he received The Mark of the Sighted One."

"Bummer," I said with no sympathy at all.

"Not yet. But soon. Very soon."

"Rip, have you seen Tom?"

Someone else had ignored the private sign on the lounge door and come in looking for me. It was Rebecca now, carrying a refill of non-beer and an attitude as irritable as if she'd been drinking the real thing all evening.

"He's hiding from you in the bathroom," I said, pointing out the opposite lounge door. "If you find him sitting on the toilet, leave him be, he might already be dead."

She ignored my comment, content not to know what I was talking about.

"I saw you come in here with Jeevak Menahem. You're swinging for the fences tonight. How'd it go?"

"We didn't exactly hit it off."

"What did you do?" she asked, unable to narrow it down to a more specific accusation.

"Me? How is it always on me? It didn't occur to you that he's the one who might have done something rude? Like murder me?"

"As if," she said.

I took off my glasses to reveal the shaded milky one with the burst blood vessel. Even without checking in a mirror, I knew it probably looked awful. Rebecca's reaction confirmed it.

"Ew," was her assessment. "How did that happen?"

"I just told you."

"Right," she said, still not convinced. "One of the world's foremost real-estate moguls takes you aside in the middle of his own party and clubs you over the head."

"Strangles me, actually. It seems this eye reacts poorly every time I get murdered," I added, hoping she would feel the personal dig. She did.

"I know why I killed you. You give me good reasons all the time. What possible reason would Jeevak Menahem have?"

"He's another necromancer. And a highly competitive one who's set to replace me in Charlie Nocturne's scheme."

"Feeling rejected? Is that why you're sulking alone in here?"

"I'm not alone," I informed her.

Give him some faint lighting or a few shadows, and Charlie Nocturne can fade into the background very easily. Rebecca only noticed he was standing right there with us when he spoke.

"Good evening, Ms. Stone," said the monotone.

Rebecca looked around, unsure where the voice came from. Even when she narrowed it down, it took her a moment to make out the contour of Nocturne's humanoid silhouette.

"You," she said with a sneer.

"I trust you are well," said Nocturne.

"I'm super, considering the last time I saw you, you were perfectly happy to let a complete maniac cut me up into little pieces for shits and giggles."

"I do not intervene in such matters, either to encourage or discourage them. So long as things proceed as planned, towards my ends, I am content. As Szabo was denied his amusement, you too must be content."

"Yeah, great," fumed Rebecca. "I didn't get murdered that night. I'm lucky enough to hang around for that end of the world you're planning. Thanks!"

"You are quite welcome," said Nocturne unironically, which infuriated Rebecca. She took it out on me.

"Don't any of your supernatural buddies understand sarcasm?"

"Not a lot, no," I admitted.

"It is a difficult trait to comprehend," agreed Nocturne.

"Comprehend this, asshole!" growled Rebecca, and threw the rest of her drink in Charlie Nocturne's face. There was no face to stop it, nor absorb it, so the liquid merely flew into the void, lost in time and space.

Rebecca launched her glass at the floor, hard enough to break it on the plush carpeting, and stormed out. I simply shrugged at the affronted entity who felt no shame or insult.

"Winning hearts and minds as always, Charlie," I said. "It was crap seeing you again. Be a stranger."

I caught up with Rebecca outside.

"I'd commend your aim, but there was nothing there to hit. Who even knows where or when that went?"

"I don't care," she said. "It felt good anyway."

"Can we leave yet?"

"Yeah," Rebecca conceded. "I've had a shitty enough time for one night."

"At least you didn't get murdered."

"Do you always have to one-up me? Can't you let me be miserable without always trying to top it?"

"You're an angry non-drunk," I told her, as we returned to the cloakroom.

I had to ring the bell for service a few times before the hat-and-coat-check guy came to the counter.

"Oh it's you!" he said, relieved to let me swap my stub for my hat. "Thank God! Please take this thing away."

I took it, turning it over in my hands to see if anything was amiss. Reaching in, I parted the flap in the false bottom to make sure Gladys remained at her station.

"We go now?" she asked through the slit. "Thees fakker loose hees sheet eevary time I say sumting."

"I've had to take three coffee breaks since you checked it," said the checker, backing away into the relative safety of his cloakroom. "It won't stop gibbering! What the hell is it?"

I popped my bonnet back on my head and told him, "You know what a top hat is, right? Well this is a talk hat."

"Dats rite, fakker!" came the muffled voice from inside.

"It keeps calling me a fakker. What's a 'fakker'?"

"Nothing nice."

I threw a buck into his tip jar. Just a buck. Maybe I'm cheap, but he'd already been overcompensated with an anecdote he'd be telling his skeptical friends for years.

As I walked away, I flicked the brim of the hat and told Gladys, "Sorry if you got lonely after you drove the staff away, but it's your own fault."

"I nat git loonly. I had coompinny."

"You hit it off with a fedora and derby?"

She ignored the hat humour and got straight to business.

"Yoo git jabs? Lotsa jabs?"

"Yeah, I got a jab all right."

"Nat jab! Jab!"

The subtle difference in pronunciation was too subtle for me to detect.

"No, no jobs. Just a task," I mused. "Something that needs doing. A quest."

It was a quest to deal with Menahem before he had a chance to kill me too many more times. Once was bad enough. Twice would be humiliating. I was hoping to keep the number of personal fatalities to under a dozen.

"A queest? How mach dat pay?"

"You guys leaving?" Tom called after us, spotting Rebecca waiting by the elevators.

"It's more of a tactical retreat, really," I said.

"Mind if I come with?"

"You don't want to stay for the ribbon cutting?"

"I've done my duty, made an appearance, said my hellos. I'll skip the goodbyes and just ghost this place."

"Bad choice of words," I muttered.

"I don't want to fight with you anymore," Tom told Rebecca.

"We're not fighting," she replied sternly.

"Good, because I don't want to."

"Okay then!"

"Fine!"

It still sounded like a fight to me, but Tom was content to leave it at that. All the way down in the elevator, he had a dumb smile on his face, despite Rebecca's continued foul mood. It took me a while to realize he was still glowing about the news concerning his eventual demise.

"You're a tad too pleased about having your fortune told," I said.

"What's not to like?" said Tom. "We all have to go some-time. Dying on the toilet sounds like an old man's death."

"Old like Elvis?" I asked.

I'm sure forty-three sounded ancient to him.

"Older than that, probably. Ripe-old-age old."

"You know that's not how it's going to go down, right? Just by saying it, you've pretty much assured it won't play out like that. Death always likes a good surprise."

Once we were out of the building, we found Reynaldo was already ahead of us, waiting by the curb where the slow trickle of early departures were exchanging tickets for their valet-parked cars.

"Forgetting our appointment?" he asked upon seeing us exit.

I had, but I didn't let on.

"No," I said. "Did you? Looks like you're leaving."

"I knew you would be down shortly," Reynaldo said, touching his fingers to his temple.

"No you didn't," I corrected him, aware of his psychic troubles.

"No, I didn't," he admitted. "I didn't really care one way or the other. But now that you're here..."

At that moment, Tom's car was pulling up to the curb. The valet left it running for him as he got out. The engine purred so smoothly, I would have felt the sticker shock without ever laying eyes on the machine that housed it. I couldn't place the make and model. It was too new, too sporty, too expensive.

"Nice wheels, Trust Fund," I commented.

"This new?" Rebecca asked, unimpressed.

"Newish," Tom said, walking around the hood to the driver's side. "I've had it a couple of months."

"How often does he trade in?" I asked Rebecca.

"Cars or women?"

"I'd offer you both a lift," said Tom, "but, uh, y'know. Two seats."

What might have been a back-seat area in some early schematic for a more practical car seemed to be occupied by a sound system that was more pricy than the average no-frills commuter compact on the road.

"Let him drive you home," I told Rebecca. "You can continue your non-fight on the road."

"Arguing in a moving vehicle is always a bad idea," she said.

"Don't worry. Tom doesn't die in a car crash."

"Maybe *I* do."

"Or you can stay here and hang out with Reynaldo."

"Angry car ride with my ex it is," announced Rebecca, pulling open the passenger door and getting in next to Tom.

They were away a moment later, beating the traffic light at the end of the block even though it had turned yellow before Tom even hit the gas. I returned to Reynaldo, who stood impatiently in the cold, reluctantly upholding his end of our arrangement.

"I would have attended to this exchange earlier," he said, "but you were too busy monopolizing the biggest catch of the night."

"Menahem? Believe me, he's no catch. Steer clear."

"Another cagey client?"

"More of an outright psychopathic monster."

"Certain allowances can be made for an extremely wealthy psychopathic monster," Reynaldo suggested.

"You think you can squeeze some work out of him, that's your choice," I said. "But if he gets his way, you better spend whatever you earn fast. There might not be any world left to enjoy your wealth in once he's done."

"Ah," he said knowingly, "another one of *those* monsters. I'll leave you to it in that case."

"What about my other case?"

"I have communed with the beyond and all has been revealed," Reynaldo announced, handing me back the wooden stake once he retrieved it from his coat pocket.

"You couldn't do it, could you?" I said, cutting through the bullshit.

"No," Reynaldo admitted, hanging his head in shame. "The ether is muddled, confused. Normally it's like looking through a veil of silk. Lately, it's been like trying to see through a bowl of thick, lumpy porridge. Tonight was the worst it's been yet. Chatting up prospects at the opening, I had to resort to simple observation, rudimentary deductions and, when they weren't looking, covert bouts of Google searches in order to impress them with my insights into their personal lives."

Reynaldo being this candid with me was so unlike him, I couldn't even come up with a suitably vicious remark to cut him off at the knees. He looked so vulnerable, whatever quip I chose wouldn't be mean, it would be gratuitously cruel. I didn't know what I'd done to put him so much at ease that he was capable of showing vulnerability to me. Maybe the last few years apart made him forget how much we hated each other.

"Don't sweat it," I said. "I can't expect miracles when you're going through such a rough spot."

Reynaldo nodded sadly. I was about to leave him alone when he interrupted my departure.

"However...I did manage to find your vampire hunter just the same."

He got me. Of course Reynaldo was going to sit on that bit of information, waiting for the big reveal. Diminished talent or not, it was still about the showmanship.

"How?" I asked, genuinely curious.

"Simple old-fashioned detective work. Where would a religious man, a devout Christian of limited means, paranoid and delusional, expecting vampiric retribution after having slain what he thought was an entire den of undead, go to seek shelter?"

I felt stupid for not having jumped to the same conclusion.

"A church."

"Not just any church," Reynaldo continued. "Churches have business hours. He would want a defunct church, shut and shuttered to the public, where he could set up shop and prepare to stand his ground if need be. What matters was that it remained sanctified ground, capable of fending off what he sees as an unholy threat."

"There are a lot of closed churches in town," I said.

The faith fad had played itself out in a lot of urban areas. God was passé, and everyone had a host of new deities to worship. Polytheism was back in style. Now it was all about the cult of personality, political-ideology purity tests, and unconditional love for The Almighty Buck. You didn't need churches for that. All you needed was a TV, an internet connection, and a bank card.

"Which is why I narrowed it down for you," said Reynaldo. "If he went through so many stakes at the club, he'd need more. Not from the same shop, but another woodworker closer to his base. I made some calls to see if there had been any new orders for more of those 'wooden nails' and indeed there had been. Another carpenter, a few miles north of your suspect's last known whereabouts. After that, it was a simple matter of checking where the nearest boarded up church lay. An insolvent Presbyterian on Weatherly Street was the obvious choice."

"Okay, you've got a best guess," I admitted.

"Confirmed sighting, in fact. I parked across the street for a few hours this afternoon—to stake out your staker, so to speak. I just happened to spot a young man with snow-white hair lurking around a side entrance with a bag of groceries. No doubt he's camping inside. You may now be impressed."

"Very clever, Reynaldo," I reluctantly commended him.

"No," he corrected me, "only mildly clever. You might consider being ashamed for not thinking of it yourself."

The valet pulled up with Reynaldo's vintage Citroën DS. By night, it was dark enough to look like it was a tasteful shade of black. I knew from past encounters that it was actually a garish deep purple. Typical medium. I was surprised Reynaldo had restrained himself from having his profession and contact information stencilled onto the doors. Maybe he'd have to if his business and powers remained in decline.

"Do be careful, old boy," he said, walking around to the driver's side. "This is, after all, a mass-murdering lunatic you're pursuing."

Reynaldo's concern was slight, but genuine.

"I'll watch my step. But the guy would have to be a complete idiot to mistake a normal-looking human being walking into a church in broad daylight for a vampire."

Reynaldo shook his head at me sadly.

"What terrible liar ever told you you were normal looking?"

I watched Reynaldo pull away from the curb and disappear down the boulevard. As I stood there, I heard a distant noise over the din of late-night traffic, familiar and haunting. It took me a few moments to recognize the protracted howl of a great hound.

Glancing up at the skyline, I caught a distinct canine outline, perched atop one of the peaked rooftops of a nearby building. It was dwarfed by the Algonquin Tower, but that still put the animal a good thirty storeys off the ground as it bayed at the moon.

I decided not to linger, and immediately began scanning the oncoming vehicles for a vacant cab I could hail. Another long howl rose over the urban jungle.

"Doogie!" Gladys cooed from inside my hat. And she sounded tickled pink.

Chapter Fifteen

Divine Intervention

"**D**ID YOU HEAR A DOG barking late last night after you got home?" Rebecca asked me at the crack of noon, once I'd finally rolled out of bed.

"Yeah," I admitted.

"Like a really big dog."

"The biggest."

"Wait, is that...?" she began, making the connection to my recent tales of woe.

"The hellhound, yeah," I confirmed.

Leaving town for a convention was seeming like a better and better idea all the time. If that ravenous creature had tracked me to my neighbourhood, perhaps even to my specific apartment building, how long would it be before it came barrelling through the door as it had done at Oliver's?

"Doogie!" enthused Gladys from her desk in the office, reiterating her sentiment from the previous night.

"What's it after?" Rebecca asked.

"My head," I said. "He wants to eat it."

"Good boy!" Gladys praised.

"Me or the hellhound?" Like I had to ask.

"Heel-hund, duh! He good doogie."

"I thought Gladys was a cat person," Rebecca commented.

"Apparently she swings both ways."

"I meet heem in da clookroom."

"You *met* him?" I asked Gladys. "Like socially?"

The idea that the hellhound had been in the Algonquin Tower with us, just a short distance away from the opening, prowling though the cloakroom, while the city's elite obliviously choked down party snacks as easily as the beast might have choked them down, seemed unlikely.

"All da lites go oot an I heer beeg doogie cam sneeffin arund," Gladys elaborated. "I leek doogies. He good doogie. I tell heem dat an he jast sneef me an go awee."

"What does it mean, Rip?"

Rebecca had understood Gladys's fractured account as well as I had. It was the significance of this tidbit that was elusive.

"Nothing good, I'm sure," I said, which was the best guess I had to offer.

Θ

Rebecca wasn't wild about me leaving her behind with a man-eating dog hanging around the hood, but she felt better about it when I assured her it was only after me, and would probably hunt me wherever I went. Suddenly the farther away I was going, the better.

The church on Weatherly was clear across town on a block that was full of pawn shops, cheque-cashing services, and liquor stores. They all seemed to be doing well. The Presbyterian, however, had only been selling salvation, and there were no buyers. The place had been shuttered for ages, with no offers to develop the property, and not even enough interest to demolish it to make way for another pawn shop or three. I could see the holes in the roof from the subway exit across the street. The masonry at street level had become a canvas for spray-can artistes, and half the district seemed to have stopped to carve their initials into the heavy wooden door. Whatever stained glass hadn't had rocks thrown through it by vandals was preserved by the pressboard panels that had been nailed over every window. They, in turn, had been carved up and painted over as well.

I wasn't going to be so brazen as to kick in the front door, though no one passing on the street would have cared, I'm sure. Instead, I climbed over a low wall into the small churchyard and looked for another entrance my slayer-squatter must have already forced open. A simple featureless door at the top of two low steps allowed entrance to what had once been the minister's quarters. That was my best bet, and I found it unlocked to any human infiltration. Steps had been taken to keep out inhuman visitations, however, as evidenced by all the braids of garlic slung around a phalanx of large crucifixes stationed throughout the entry passage. They all pointed at the doorway, as though their combined might would act as a force field against malevolent intrusion. Everything in the room was slightly wet with water droplets yet to evaporate. I looked up, thinking there must be a leak dripping through the ceiling, but the aspergillum resting in a plastic bucket that served as a makeshift aspersorium suggested the place was routinely splashed with holy water as an added line of defence. It was uselessly symbolic, but showed a determined effort to be thorough.

Slipping between the moistened guard-crosses, I made my way into the church proper. The place was a mess after years of neglect and break-ins. All the brass pipes of the massive organ at the head of the hall had been looted for scrap metal long ago. Debris from broken glass, melted wax, and nesting pigeons littered the floor, but there also seemed to have been a recent attempt to arrange and redecorate. The pews were all properly aligned, as if anticipating a future service; potted candles had been replaced and left burning; and the original cross of the resurrection had been supplemented by at least a hundred other crosses and crucifixes of any and every Christian sect, affixed to the walls or suspended from the beams above on string.

The additions weren't solely religious. The choir stalls had been zoned for what could only be called an ammo dump. The equipment collected there was a fanciful mix of army surplus and hardware store by way of sports-equipment outlet. Everything from deadly combat knives to mundane home-and-garden tools were represented, along with a selection of knotted ropes, bungee cords, and what looked like an attempt to weld together a homemade grappling hook. And, of course, there was the expected stack of freshly carved wooden stakes. Much like those scattered around The Craven Image massacre—but of a subtly different style indicative of a new manufacturer working from an imprecise design—they awaited use in ineffectual combat with the undead. Or much more effective murder against vastly softer human targets.

It all looked like a little boy's idea of what a mercenary comic-book hero would arm himself with before taking on the forces of evil—or, if circumstances permitted, a small army of anonymous bad-guy cannon fodder on his way to the final boss. Accessories for an action figure, sold separately.

"Knock knock," I called out.

Creeping around unannounced seemed impolite, even though the derelict church's current occupant was also an intruder, guilty of breaking and entering. Or at least trespassing and unlawful tidying up.

"I know you're in here," I added, knowing no such thing. It was a lie, but if I was wrong, only the pigeons in the rafters would hear it.

Creaking floorboards was the response. Where exactly the sound had come from, I couldn't determine. The building was in such poor condition, I'm sure there wasn't a single floorboard or stick of furniture that wouldn't creak if leaned on.

"I'm not here to fight you or arrest you or loot this fine collection of monster-hunter gear you've assembled. I just want to talk."

"About what?" said a voice.

I whipped around, trying to find the source. Church acoustics are great for projecting to a congregation, not so good for pinpointing small noises. And these words sounded very small in so large a space. It was a whisper from a voice that had only recently finished cracking its way through puberty and into young adulthood.

"You've been busy around town lately," I said to the empty space across the pews. "It's been drawing attention, this thing you do."

"The Lord's work."

Again a whisper from nowhere distinct.

"That's debatable," I said.

"That I'm doing the Lord's work?"

It was closer now.

"That there's a Lord at all, holding out a job-jar or otherwise."

A bit of apostasy did the trick. The next thing I saw was a shock of white hair perched atop a face red with rage.

"Unclean!" was the sole word hollered as the figure ran at me from out of some nook or from behind one of the columns.

The accusation certainly sounded like my man. Or manchild, as the case may be. He was a wisp of a kid, stringy but quick on his feet.

"You talking to me?" was as much as I was able to ask as I turned and caught the full force of him straight in the ribs.

I thought he was trying to tackle me as we both hit the deck, but then I realized I was outside my body, looking down at the one-man pile-on happening on the floor below. If my spirit was out and about, that meant my body was dead—instantly so. Once I drifted in for a closer look, I saw that the little prick had stabbed one of his stupid stakes through my heart with all the force a two-handed blow and a running start could muster.

Not pleased at all, I waited a moment, hoping he would yank the stake out again and make it easier for me to revive. Once I was up and about again, I'd give him what for. But the slayer seemed to be in no hurry to pull out that thorn. Instead, he left the room for a moment and came back with the aspergillum to lightly spritz my body with holy water. He then went to his stash of supplies, returning with a handful of sacramental bread, and began crumbling the wafers over my corpse. I didn't know how many cleansing rituals he was going to subject me to, but I was already bored watching him.

There was another spirit close by who was also observing the show. Denise was more amused by it than I was. She still couldn't utter a sound, but she went through the motions of laughing at me anyway.

"You think this is funny?" I asked her.

Denise nodded enthusiastically.

"Well pardon me if I don't stick around to share in your giggle-fest."

Coming back with that hunk of wood stuck through me was going to hurt like hell, but the option of hanging out in the afterlife with Denise's snickering ghost was equally unappealing. I decided to force myself back into my body and get my resurrection underway, regardless of the less-than-ideal circumstances.

The moment the murderous kid's back was to me, I dove in and concentrated on raising a single hand to grip the exposed end of the stake. With a mighty tug, I pulled it out of my chest and sucked in a lungful of air. Despite the massive perforation, my heart fluttered to life and began the long process of resealing itself. This didn't go unnoticed, and the kid was on me again in an instant, another stake in hand, struggling to stuff a fresh one into the vacant bloody hole.

"Nosferatu!" he screamed, panicking.

"It's daylight, idiot," I grunted, pointing out the obvious and pushing him off of me.

He landed on his ass a few feet away as I sat up, and we spent the next several moments staring at each other awkwardly.

"Do I look like a vampire to you?" I asked him.

"Kinda," he said, not sure if he still needed to be terrified or not.

"I don't look anything like a vampire. You'd know that if you'd ever seen one."

"I've seen plenty."

"No you haven't."

"Of course I have! I am a vampire slayer," he announced proudly, like I should be impressed.

"There's no such thing," I told him.

"As a vampire?" he scoffed, thinking he knew so much more than he did.

"As a vampire slayer," I specified. "Vampires can't be slain. They don't die. Ever."

"Is that why you're still alive?" he asked, his world view—or at least his underworld view—shaken.

"No, I'm human. I'm just not a regular mortal human."

"Are you in league with... them?"

With my breathing steadied and my battered heart doing an adequate job of pumping at least half the blood passing through it in the right direction, I slowly rose to my feet. The kid mirrored my move, keeping a suspicious eye on me.

"I'm not in league with anybody," I said.

"You could be one of their pet humans."

"Well, I'm not."

Such a thing was possible, but rare. If a vampire kept a human servant to attend to its business in the living world, it wasn't a relationship that lasted long. Inevitably, the vampire host gets the munchies at an inopportune moment, and they can't keep their claws off the hired help.

"Prove it!" demanded the would-be hunter.

"How?"

"Think of something," he said, laying down a challenge.

I thought of something and punched him squarely in the face. It put him back on his ass on the floor, and it was another minute or so before he could gather his senses and stand up again.

"Happy?" I asked.

"What was that?" he said, pinching his nostrils and trying to stop the nosebleed.

"Proof. You were at my mercy for a long time there. I could have killed you, but I didn't. ...So?"

I let him draw the obvious conclusion.

"Okay, I guess I see your point," he admitted.

"How's the nose? Did I break it?"

"No, it's just a little bloody."

I'd done battle was all sorts of ageless, evil entities and come out on top. But I still couldn't throw a decent punch. It was embarrassing.

I sat down heavily in a pew and reached into one of my pockets. The kid must have thought I was going for a weapon because he dove for his stash and came up with a crossbow, firing a single bolt at me. It missed by a foot and splintered through the back of the pew right next to me. I ignored it and flung my business card at him. It fluttered to his feet where he retrieved it and read the exact words I said next.

"Rip Eulogy, Necromancer."

It was like he'd been thunderstruck by a great revelation.

"You do battle with the dead, like me?" he said.

"Sometimes. When they misbehave."

"Sunder Lone," he said by way of introduction, crossing the distance between us and offering his hand to shake. I took it and accepted it as a truce.

"We must be hunting the same quarry," he said.

"Good guess, but no. I'm hunting you because the quarry you're hunting isn't the quarry you think it is."

"What do you mean?"

"I mean this killing spree you're on is only killing regular human beings. Not vampires."

"No, no, I'm quite certain they're vampires."

"And I'm telling you they're not. The cops are looking for you, and they'll back me up on this point."

"The police? Are they here with you?"

"No," I said, "I came alone."

But it didn't sound like I was alone. There was a thud on the roof of the church, the sound of heavy steps.

"Is that a SWAT team?" asked Sunder, expecting heavily armed and armoured cops to come rappelling through the boards and stained glass at any moment. I couldn't help but wonder if he was right. Maybe Frenz had me tailed and called in a tactical squad to deal with the mass murderer I'd led them to. But no one came busting through the windows. Instead, a heavy fog descended from the holes in the roof, dropping to the floor and drawing in on itself until it became a towering form, eerily stiff and still, humanoid but inhuman. Pale unblinking eyes looked down upon us as a maw of mangled teeth gnawed at its lower lip.

"What the hell's that?" Sunder Lone sputtered shrilly, like he'd just shat his pants in fear.

"You're not serious are you?" I asked.

"No, what is it?"

"*That* is a real vampire," I enlightened him. "Not a pretend vampire or a goth kid like all those people you've been running around staking, but the real deal."

Sunder began to fumble through his arsenal of stakes, knocking half of them over and sending them clattering to the floor until he was able to grip a single one.

"Ug, this again," I groaned.

"Die, unclean!" he hollered, and brought the stake down with both hands into Marin Venerio Grissoni's chest with as much strength as a single mortal man could bring to bear.

Marin remained standing. Didn't so much as budge an inch. Sunder would have had better luck trying to move a brick wall. The wooden stake penetrated Marin's chest well enough, fixed there as firmly as a stick stuck in clay. And it had about as much effect. Marin sprung a leak, but what trickled out wasn't his blood. Not really. It was the stale leftovers from his last meal, however long ago that had been.

The vampire stared down at the wound that would have been fatal to any living creature, then into the eyes of his would-be slayer. Sunder dared to look up into the face of the tall figure he'd ineffectually tried to end. Marin offered the puny pale human a chipped-tooth grin. It might have been an attempt to be personable, but its effect was chilling. Sunder let go of his stake and recoiled in terror.

"That's not how you kill a vampire," I flatly informed him.

"It's not?" Sunder asked, backed into a wall.

"Nope."

"So how to you kill a vampire?" he whispered at me, his eyes searching the hideout for any other tool or weapon that might be employed to gain the upper hand.

"You don't," I said. "I think I already mentioned that part. You weren't listening."

"What's it doing here in daylight?" he asked. Good question.

"Subway?" I asked Marin. He gave me a slight nod. Same route I'd taken, possibly the very same train, gripping the roof or undercarriage. The final leg across the sunlit street would have been uncomfortable but brief. Sunder might not have even broken his skin if he hadn't been recovering from the short exposure.

The sight of the inky necrotic blood seeping out of Marin's stake wound struck me as oddly familiar, but it was the sickly stink of it that really rang a bell. I dipped a finger into the flow that was running down the front of his coat and brought it to my nose. The smell of blood that had been lapped up fresh days or weeks earlier, and then left to spoil and putrefy inside a vampire's unliving organs, was appalling. But then, I'm subjected to all sorts of awful odours on the job. Occupational hazard. I ignored my natural revulsion and focused on identifying the scent. Why was this so familiar to me, I wondered. It's not like anyone gets much opportunity to smell vampire blood—or rather the blood they steal from victims and contain inside their bodies until its done working its way out. It's beyond most mere humans to subject them to so much as a paper cut, never mind make them bleed profusely. The only reason Sunder had been able to land a blow on Marin at all was due to his trying so hard to be a reformed, pacifist vampire. Normally, instinct would have resulted in Sunder being split open and sucked dry in moments.

Then it struck me. I had smelled something just like this before. Recently. I'd been a few paces away, but I'd caught a whiff of it rising out of a slender glass, being raised to a man's lips. I'd smelled it last on Jeevak Menahem's breath as he'd strangled me to death. Perhaps it would have better registered in the moment, but I'd had other things on my mind as he'd cut off the oxygen supply to my brain.

So that was my rival necromancer's acquired taste: vampire blood. And I had thought it was just some obscure fermented full-bodied port for the obscenely wealthy. I might have taste-tested it off the tip of my finger, just to see what the appeal was, but the idea repulsed me. Plus there was the fact that I didn't know what effect it would have. Menahem had seemed spry enough. He was certainly no weakling. But I knew better than to indiscriminately sample decaying blood from an unknown source that had been filtered through the undead organs of a supernatural entity. I didn't need a warning label to dissuade me, and I wiped my finger clean on Marin's lapel. He didn't seem to mind.

"What are you doing here?" I asked the interloper.

"Ms. Stone dispatched me to assist you. She was concerned about you facing what she called 'a delusional maniac' on your own."

"You're after a delusional maniac?" Sunder Lone asked, glancing around, paranoid about what other horrible creature might jump out at him next.

"You're the delusional maniac, dumbass," I told him. He was also a moron, it would seem.

"I don't need backup," I said to Marin, who was staring at the open wound in my chest that was a close match for the one in his. Mine, at least, was starting to close up following my revival. Marin's still had a big hunk of wood stuck in it. It appeared to cause him no discomfort. In fact, he seemed to have forgotten it was even there.

"You have been gravely wounded," he stated. "Perhaps Ms. Stone's concern is justified."

He caught himself licking his lips at the sight of my blood and turned away guiltily. I buttoned up my coat so he wouldn't have to face temptation.

"I'm fine. I've had worse. She would know. Heck, she's given me worse herself."

"Wait," said Sunder, who had been listening and was starting to absorb the flood of new information, "if that thing's a vampire, what have I been slaying?"

"That's what I've been trying to tell you," I said. "You're not a vampire slayer, you're a serial killer."

It was like watching the rusty engine of an old jalopy sputter to life after many long hours of repair and tender loving care. As last the combustion chamber was firing and the pistons were starting to pump, but it was a slow, grinding process and you could smell the burning.

"Oh, shiiiiiiiiiiiiit," he announced, squinting with regret and shame.

"Just out of curiosity, how many perfectly innocent, regular human beings have you staked for being suspected vampires?"

Sunder Lone winced. His pink face flushed red.

"Kind of a lot."

"Oops," I said on his behalf.

"I was always expecting them to burst into flames, or turn to ashes or something. But they always just, basically, died."

"Most living things do that when you stab them in the heart."

"Except you," he noted, catching on.

"Right. I come back."

"And him," he added.

"Yeah. Because he's already dead and stabbing him isn't going to make him any worse off."

"This is really embarrassing."

I was expecting him to fall apart in a moral panic about what he'd done any moment now. But he didn't. Sunder Lone—vampire slayer, bane of the undead, devout albino fuckwit—was more troubled by time and effort wasted.

"What am I supposed to do with all these stupid stakes I've had made?"

"Use them as oversized novelty toothpicks," I suggested.

"I have to get to a church."

"You're in one," I reminded him.

"I mean a real Catholic church. I need to confess my sins."

"Why don't you try confessing to me first?"

"Are you ordained?" he asked, hopefully.

"I've been around. Try me."

Sunder cautiously sat down in the pew behind me, keeping an eye on Marin, who remained as still and monumental as one of the church's columns.

"Is he going to eat us?" Sunder whispered at me.

"Nah," I said. "He's on a diet."

I half-turned in my seat so I could better hear the kid's soft, low voice. The chest wound complained about the move, but a quiet conversation for a few minutes would give my body time to stabilize itself.

"What got you started on this whole anti-vampire jag anyway?" I asked. "Was it too much TV, too many old horror movies?"

"My entire family was wiped out by a vampire."

"Are you sure it was a real vampire and not another regular human with black clothes and a bad dye job?"

"I never saw the thing that did it. I only saw what it left behind. My parents, my brother, my sister. It was horrible. Their throats had been ripped wide open. There should have been blood everywhere, but there was hardly any to be seen. It's like they had all been drained."

It sounded like a genuine-enough vampire attack. But there were a lot of things it could have been. All-too human monsters leave bizarre crime scenes behind them as well.

"They weren't bleeding anymore," Sunder continued, "even with those terrible wounds. They were dead, they had to have been. But then they started to wake up and move again. They all looked like corpses—grey, bloodless—but moving. I ran to get help. Ambulances and police were there in a matter of minutes. It was no good. When I led them back inside, they were gone. My whole family, just gone. There were bloodstains and enough damage to suggest something bad had happened. I was questioned as a witness—probably as a suspect—for hours and hours. The police finally decided they were missing.

Abducted certainly, maybe killed. But with no bodies, they refused to classify it as a murder case. I'm sure they didn't believe much of what I told them, but I knew what I saw. I knew what sort of creature does that to a person. And I knew what made their victims rise from the dead."

There were tears in his eyes. The grief was still fresh.

"When did this happen?" I asked.

"It's been nearly a year," he said. "I've been on my own since. Training myself, arming myself, getting ready. I only started my hunt a couple of weeks ago."

"You just ran off on your own, with this crazy plan?"

"We were God-fearing people, Mr. Eulogy. Devout and devoted to the church. My family didn't deserve this. Neither did I. When the police didn't help, I turned to the community. I spoke to priests and deacons—more than I ever knew lived in this city. I got as far as the bishop of our diocese before they shut the door on me as a nuisance. After all we had given the faith, the time and the tithes, no one was willing to help, and their patience for listening to my story was short. That's when I took the battle as my own and began my research on how to fight such evil."

"Ah, so *this* is where too much TV and old horror movies come into play."

"I read many texts as well," Sunder claimed in his defence.

"*Dracula* is a good read," I said, "but it's not an instruction manual."

"Older than that," he said, as though I'd insulted him.

"*Varney the Vampire* either," I noted. The infamous penny dreadful was mostly dreadful continuity, with unhelpful inconsistencies throughout. Anything much earlier than that was all mythology or oral tradition, never printed.

"I've learned all I can, and I've acted on that knowledge to the best of my ability. What else can I do?"

"You? Nothing. The less the better."

"I have to do something!"

"What happened to your family is unusual but not unique," I said. "Occasionally vampires fuck up. They don't finish their meal properly and their condition gets passed on. It's how new vampires are made. They never do it on purpose though. Even vampires don't want more vampires running around. But between your parents and another recent case I'm aware of..."

Denise manifested in front of me and pointed at herself. An implied question the others couldn't witness.

"Yeah, you," I told her.

"You who?" asked Sunder.

"Not you. I was talking to someone else."

"Jesus?" he guessed after a moment's contemplation.

"Different invisible friend."

I continued, "As I was saying, it looks like there's another vampire out there who's been leaving leftovers on his plate."

Marin caught Sunder and I both looking at him. Denise was looking as well, though he couldn't see her.

"I have not fed since before we first met," he claimed. "And even then, for centuries stretching back into the shadows of memory, I was careful to never inflict this curse upon another soul."

"Have you had any contact with the underworld since you rolled into town?" I asked.

"None," he replied. "Nor am I even aware of where other active vampires might be found in this city."

"But *you* know, don't you?" Sunder asked me.

I did. And I always gave the spot a wide berth. So long as they kept their numbers down and their body count modest, I let them be. There was nothing to be done to stem their eating habits, and trying to run them out of my jurisdiction was only going to set them to feeding on derelicts and junkies someplace else.

"I better swing by and see what's changed. One of their kind had Denise as a midnight snack only a couple of blocks from my home."

"Who is this Denise?" asked Marin. Sunder looked like he was wondering as well.

In response, Denise started doing what looked like ghostly jumping jacks in front of them. A useless gesture.

"Denise is a ghost," I explained. "A vampire's victim."

She pointed at me vigorously with both hands.

"And mine," I admitted. "I had to finish her off before she turned. She's been haunting me ever since. She's here now if you want to say hello."

"Hello," said Marin to no one in particular.

"Hi," Sunder waved, facing the wrong direction.

"Okay, let's go," I said. "Marin, you're with me. You're my in, and I expect you to stand between me and any attempts to use me as a blood-bank-ATM open for withdrawals. Denise, you can tag along too since there's no stopping you."

"What about me?" asked Sunder. "If we're going to hunt vampires, I have to come!"

"We're only hunting them for conversation purposes. I need information."

"But there's so much you can teach me about dealing with the undead!"

"I'm no mentor," I said.

"I'll be a faithful student!" Sunder insisted.

"Okay, lesson one: avoid them at all costs. That one was free. Write a thousand-word essay about that and have it on my desk next week."

I turned to go. Marin and Denise followed.

"I can help!" Sunder protested. "I have so much useful equipment!"

"Nah," I said, "all this shit's useless. I have everything we need here."

I gave my medical bag a slap on its leather side for emphasis.

"I also have a car," he added.

That gave me pause. It was a long trip that ended nowhere near a subway station, in a part of town bus lines feared to tread.

"Do we have to chip in for gas?" I asked.

"I filled the tank yesterday."

I carefully weighed bringing an overenthusiastic rank-amateur zealot, with poor instincts and worse impulse control, bent on holy retribution, into a den of murderous bloodsucking monsters, against the convenience of a lift.

"Where are you parked?" I asked.

Chapter Sixteen

End of the Line

DOWN BY THE TURLINGTON EXCHANGE, there was no right side or wrong side of the tracks. It was just tracks—layers upon layers, parallel and intertwined, crissed and crossed. This was the final destination for freight trains coming into town by rail. After being unburdened of their loads, the cars were sent a few more miles along the line to the exchange where they would be broken down into their individual wagons, tankers, hoppers, and engines, and reassembled for a new run, with a new manifest, destined for another city somewhere on the continent. Compared to the hive of activity where the loading and unloading happened, the train yard at the end of the line was a sparse, lifeless ghost town. Filled with thousands of empty vessels parked in seemingly scattershot disorder, every door and cap yawned open for the air currents to whistle through, emitting a haunting drone like the world's largest wind instrument. Even at peak hours, the place was populated with a skeleton crew, who mostly occupied control towers at the outer edges of the vast yard, remotely switching tracks as segments were coupled and uncoupled by lone engineers piloting diesel-spewing behemoths capable of pushing around so much tonnage.

By night, there was little activity. Worker unions and insurance companies had long since won the argument that smashing boxcars into each other in the dark was too dangerous for anyone on the ground, so the blackest hours saw the skeleton crew reduced to a few straggling bones—mostly security with nothing much to secure, sitting behind monitors indoors. With all the cars standing empty, there was nothing to steal. Vandals and urban explorers were the only real concern, but they had become extremely rare. Everyone knew to avoid the Turlington Exchange, even if they didn't know why. Word was it was too dangerous, which is true of any rail yard. But the danger wasn't about reckless intruders having their limbs clipped off under steel wheels, or getting crushed between flatbeds. People went missing at the exchange, gone forever without a trace. Or, on rare occasions when remains were found, what was left of them was rumoured to be more dried parchment than identifiable human corpse.

Sunder Lone's car was a rusted compact I suspected was rescued from the crusher for three figures or less. It ran—barely—but was in such poor shape I would have recommended tossing it the moment it ran out of gas or oil or wiper fluid. It just wasn't worth the effort. There was a backseat, technically. To allow for any amount of acceptable legroom, the front bucket seats were set back to the point of eliminating all legroom in the rear. It didn't matter. The third occupant of the car wasn't sitting there. With the sun yet to set, Sunder had brought the car around to the rear of the church and we'd loaded Marin in the trunk. He immediately assumed a corpse-in-coffin stance, with his arms crossed over his chest. Admittedly, he had to tuck his legs in, bending at the knees and twisting his hips to one side, but otherwise he was snug as a bug.

"You sure you don't want to transform into something smaller?" I'd suggested. "Like a bat or some rats or maybe a wolf that was the runt of the litter?"

"I do not transform into beasts," he said, betraying offense at the notion. "Never again. It is degrading."

"Okay," I said, slamming the trunk shut. "Don't bitch at me if you throw your back out."

I suppose he could have squeezed in as a cloud of mist, but he'd have probably ended up leaking out one of the rust holes during the trip, only to get lost in the toxic exhaust the shitbox spewed as we wove our way through rush-hour traffic. Even though I knew all about the awful place we were going, and the terrible danger we were about to face, I was mostly afraid of being pulled over by the cops for an emissions violation.

It was dark by the time we were on the empty service road that ran parallel to the Turlington tracks. I instructed Sunder to pull over about a quarter of a mile past the employee parking lot that had almost completely cleared out for the night shift. We stopped under a broken streetlight that offered us near complete cover once the engine was off and the remaining functional tail light was extinguished.

"What do we do now?" Sunder asked.

"We wait and we watch," I said.

"I don't see any signs of life," he observed of the long shadows in the yard cast by tall overhead floods.

"We're more keeping an eye out for signs of death."

Sunder nodded knowingly and dug under his seat where he had a bag of crisps. After noisily tearing his way through some crinkly cellophane, be began noshing on what I, at first, thought were potato chips. I only took a closer look when I noticed they were white and not particularly crunchy.

"Wafer?" Sunder asked, offering me the bag of Communion bread.

"Thanks, no," I said. "I had body-of-Christ for lunch."

"Silly, I know," he admitted, "but I developed a real taste for them when I was trying to make myself immune to evil."

Sunder popped another one in his mouth and chewed.

"After we're done here, we can stop by a liquor store and I'll help you polish off a bottle of blood-of-Christ," I offered.

As the car filled up with smoke, I thought something was burning in the ashtray. Or that maybe the engine had caught on fire. But the smell wasn't of ash or soot. It was more of a cold-soil smell. Once it finished manifesting, the distinct stench of corpse and spoiled blood took over and became overpowering.

"Are we there yet?" asked Marin, once he'd finished seeping through the upholstery and composing himself in the back seat. It would have been a tight fit for him had he been able to sit normally. With our seats back, he was crouched on the torn, exposed stuffing, with his legs up and his hands on his knees, looking like a gargoyle that should have been perched atop some Gothic Revival masonry high above street level.

"This is the spot," I confirmed.

Marin looked around the interior of the compact. It was a drab and uninspiring view, but apparently more fascinating than the inside of the trunk.

"I long thought these horseless carriages were a passing fancy," he said. "Now that they seem to have caught on, I might procure one for myself."

"Good luck getting your licence. Vampires don't photograph well. Or at all."

My words of discouragement didn't sway him. Marin was trying to become a modern vampire. First a smartphone, now a car. Rebecca had inspired him to drag himself into the 21st century. Or at least the 20th.

"One with a larger trunk," he decided.

Unsurprisingly, the draw was less about mobility and more about a novel new place to sleep away the day. I was about to direct him to the nearest auto-parts dealer where he could have his pick from stacks of third-hand heaps—any one of them likely nicer than what Sunder was driving—when our chauffeur suddenly grunted in distress and went digging into his pocket for a tissue.

"What's wrong?" I asked.

"My nose is bleeding again," he said.

No sooner had the words crossed his lips than Sunder froze, aware of the implications. He glanced in the rear-view mirror, but the backseat vampire cast no reflection. Marin, however, could see the trickle of blood flowing from Sunder's right nostril perfectly clearly in the mirror.

"Behave yourself!" I insisted, turning in my seat to issue the command at Marin for all the good it might do. I expected him to lose control and turn the inside of the car into a battleground at any moment.

"I assure you, I feel no temptation whatsoever," claimed Marin, with what looked like genuine disinterest in the blood flow before him.

"Bullshit," I said. "I saw you eyeing my chest wound back at the church."

"You bleed well," he replied, like it was a compliment, "but this one is not to my taste."

"Too devout?" I wondered.

"Too sickly," said Marin.

"I'm a hemophiliac," said Sunder, plugging his nose.

"Type B?" asked Marin.

"How did you know?"

"I can sense it on you, taste it in the air.

"So he's a bleeder," I said. "Why pass up an easy meal?"

"You drink alcohol, do you not?" Marin asked me. "Beer?"

"You know I do."

"Do you enjoy it?"

"Yeah," I said. "It gives me a buzz."

"Do you enjoy light beer? Non-alcoholic beer? Beer with no such buzz?"

I thought about the piss served at Menahem's opening.

"No," I said. "What's the point?"

"Precisely," he replied.

Sunder's low-quality blood might explain why he was spared while the rest of his family was slaughtered. He'd been the least appetizing morsel at an all-you-can-eat buffet. Marin elaborated for Sunder.

"You have a mutation of the factor-nine gene, which gives you a deficiency of a serine protease in your coagulation system. Pity. I find such proteins in the S1 peptidase family to be quite delectable. A meal without is nothing more than an unsatisfying tease."

Hearing Marin talk about Sunder's blood like a sommelier might talk about a disappointing vintage was weird enough. The precise degree of his knowledge was stranger still.

"That's pretty current technical talk for an old-fashioned guy who's never even been in an automobile before," I noted.

"I like to keep up to date with medical texts. At least as far as they apply to my condition."

"Hey, hey, hey," said Sunder, excited, slapping my shoulder repeatedly.

"What now?" I asked.

I looked at Sunder with the reddened corner of tissue sticking out of his nose, but he didn't return my stare. He was looking out at the rail yard, pointing at movement between the cars.

"Is that a vampire?" he asked.

The figure lurking in the shadows was shabby and dishevelled enough to be one. The way he moved was cautious, feral, like a nocturnal scavenger from the ranks of urban wildlife. And he certainly looked like he stank, even from a great distance.

"No," I concluded, "that's a hobo."

In the next moment, something snatched him off his feet from behind so quickly, the abrupt movement seemed to defy physics. He had no time to struggle or cry out. He was gone in an instant.

"Was a hobo," I revised my statement.

"What happened to him?" said Sunder, baffled by what he'd just seen.

The depression-era heyday of hard-luck cases hopping around the country, seeking scarce work and odd jobs, was long in the past, but there were still plenty of transients out there with their own reasons for needing to get from city to city. Bus fare was often out of reach; plane tickets were a fantasy. There was always hitchhiking, but exploitational true-crime shows on specialty channels had made most roadsters too paranoid to pick up anybody trying to thumb a ride. In bad weather, you could die of exposure before anyone offered you a lift. Freight trains remained a viable option, even in this brave new age.

Exchanges were the safest spot to sneak on and off boxcars as they were reconnected. Discovery was possible during loading or unloading, requiring modern-day hobos to play a shell game with watchful workers. The trick was to hide in an empty car and then switch over to a newly loaded neighbouring car as soon as one with a bit of spare space presented itself. This was a system that worked in other cities, at least. Locally, the exchange at Turlington was far more dangerous than the possibility of capture farther up the line. At the cargo hub, all you had to worry about were yard bulls, guard dogs, and ten times the number of security cameras. Sudden death only came from the calculated risk of jumping on and off moving trains. Child's play.

"Okay," I said, "that's our cue. We've got a hot one who's going to be distracted and well-fed. We'll approach while it's safe—*safer*—and see if we can make him talk."

"I get it," said Sunder, who didn't. "As a necromancer, you have power over vampires!"

"Not as such, no," I said, opening the door and letting myself out. Sunder followed my example. "They're not all-the-way dead. Only undead. Which isn't dead enough to give me any sort of control over them."

We shut the car doors, leaving Marin locked inside. I was going to go back and tip the passenger seat forward for him, but a window in the back was cracked, allowing him to easily come puffing out as mist. The interior of the car quickly turned from a dense fog to a light haze that lingered even after Marin was out. I assumed the lingering haze was an exhaust leak that had unsuccessfully tried to asphyxiate us during the commute.

"So if you get a vampire to talk, what are you going to talk about?" asked Sunder.

"We'll enter negotiations. He has information he won't want to give, I have blood I don't want to share. One of us is going to end up very disappointed."

"Vampires are not ones for negotiation," noted Marin, as he reformed into something capable of speech. "Particularly the young, ravenous ones. They barely speak at all, let alone negotiate."

"I have my techniques, tried and true. I've always found the best tactic for negotiation is to make myself so annoying that I can get what I want if I just agree to go away."

We arrived at the yard fence that blocked off the grounds from the edge of the curb and stretched a good mile in either direction. It was a stainless steel chain-link, seven feet high, topped with spools of angry razor wire. It wasn't likely to thwart determined intruders like us, but it could be relied on to keep vagrants out—particularly ones who were drunk or high and therefore more likely to get themselves killed during normal rail-yard operations. If they weren't sober enough to climb a fence and circumvent razor wire, then they weren't fit to train hop with the more motivated transients.

"I got this," said Sunder, shrugging off the backpack he'd insisted on bringing.

Eager to help, he rummaged through his collection and came up with a cheap pair of wire cutters.

"No no no," I said, digging into my own kit and coming up with a better pair. "The right tool for the right job."

"Those are just a fancier pair of cutters. They're no sharper than mine."

"These are heavy duty," I told him. "Yours are flimsy shit."

"Just because I was sensible enough to buy them on sale..."

"They're junk."

"They're discounted. That doesn't make them junk. Besides, I'm on a budget. Slaying vampires doesn't pay well."

"No one's going to pay you to do a job that can't ever be done," I said. "It's a bad business model. That's lesson number two for you."

In the time we'd wasted arguing about the tools of the trade, Marin had dissolved and flowed his way through the chain-link. He rematerialized on the other side of the fence directly opposite us, intertwined his fingers with half a dozen links, and tore a long vertical gash in the wire grid like it was made of two-ply tissue paper.

"Gentlemen," he said, "the sun will be upon us again in six hours. Let us not spend this entire window of opportunity debating the irrelevant."

"Fine," I said, tossing the cutters back in my bag and slipping through the gap Marin held open for us. Sunder followed suit.

"Show off," I muttered at Marin as we passed.

We weren't more than a dozen feet past the fence before Sunder was digging in his pack again. By the time he had it hooked back over his shoulders, he had a crucifix in each hand, looking like he was ready to lash out at the first shadow he saw move. For good measure, he pulled a third out from under his shirt. It dangled from a loop around his neck.

"What are you doing?" I asked him. "I told you to leave that crap behind."

"You never know," he said.

"Yes, I do."

"It makes me feel better."

I let him keep his useless security blankets, but assured him, "I have us covered."

"What else did you bring? Other than overpriced wire cutters?"

I opened my bag so he could peer into my kit. Curious and confused, he concluded, "You have an even stranger idea of lunch than I do."

"I'm not out on a picnic. These are all tools of the trade."

"Garlic I understand," Sunder said. "That still wards off vampires, right?"

I'd brought some along just in case. There wasn't much hope of using it offensively in the heat of the moment, but the apartment was still ripe from my having bought so much of it.

"Some vampires," I said, tossing an entire bulb to Marin. "Other vampires, not so much."

Marin held the garlic in his palms and breathed it in like a junkie huffing glue.

"Chew a clove or two," I suggested to him. "It can only improve your breath."

"I would if only mortal food did not make me ill," Marin lamented.

"So if we can't rely on garlic, what do we do?" said Sunder, as he watched our vampire associate revel in his favourite scent.

"That's what the sack is for," I said, referring to the plain brown bag in my kit.

"You serious? It's not even cooked."

"Best kind," I said. "You'll thank me for it when it saves our lives. You want to know how to square off against vampires? Consider this on-the-job training."

"So where exactly are we going?" Sunder asked, as we hustled from one boxcar to the next. I wasn't hiding from vampires so much as security cameras.

"There," I said, motioning at the big black space that yawned out before us another fifty yards down the track. It was a tunnel that ran under the highway—relatively short, but deadly. Locally, it was vampire central, with endless crevasses for the undead to bunk down in, and a steady supply of hobos, drifters, and vagrants-on-the-move who probably thought they were only passing through on their way to greener pastures. Few ever suspected they would never make it out the other end of the tunnel alive.

Sunder and I approached, hustling from car to car, but Marin was free to walk out in the open. Like the vampires who hung out in the yard, he was immune to the security cameras. Nothing seemed capable of capturing a vampire's image. The silver in mirrors refused to reflect them, as though the purity of the metal rejected their very presence. And they seemed to get lost between lens exposures, film frames, and video scans whenever any sort of camera was pointed their way. It made hunting the supposedly secure grounds unsportsmanlike, but the thrill felt by a newborn vampire didn't last much beyond the first couple of feedings. After years, decades, centuries, all they wanted was an easy meal and a private dark place to sleep.

We stopped at the mouth of the tunnel. The crumbling walls were filthy from diesel smoke and graffiti. I saw Sunder checking out the spray-painted designs. Subconsciously, he knew something was wrong with them, but he hadn't put his finger on it yet.

"Taggers still come here?" he asked.

"Look again," I said, testing him.

"The style is weird," he said. "Retro."

"Anything else?" I prompted.

"None of them are finished."

"A-plus," I graded him. "No one's so much as squirted a single can down here in decades."

If you knew enough about graffiti trends and fashions, you'd be able to pinpoint the decade, if not the exact year the vampires started moving in and feasting on anybody who wandered into their territory. It didn't take long for the community of street artists to figure out something was very wrong, very dangerous about the Turlington Exchange. The ones who didn't get the message got picked off before they were able to finish immortalizing their alias in giant flashy letters. The only contemporary pieces of graffiti in the yard came from out of town, on the sides of boxcars that had been tagged in safer depots in distant cities.

I got out my new flashlight and checked our party before heading inside. Denise was absent, which suited me. She'd kept pace with Sunder's ride through bumper-to-bumper traffic, but had failed to keep up once we were off the beaten track and driving at quicker speeds. It's not like she could have offered any useful assistance anyway. If anything, she probably would have been happy to distract me at a crucial moment, just to see me get killed again.

"Marin," I said to our emissary, "after you."

We began our march, three abreast, with me waving my flashlight around at shadows on one flank, and Sunder Lone waving his novelty Jesus memorabilia around on the other. Together we made our way down the tracks one cautious step after the next, listening carefully for any hints of danger in the dark. My beam of light searched every corner, including the highest points of the tunnel which served as the underbelly of an eight-lane highway. You can never tell when you might find a vampire dangling from the ceiling, like it's only remotely acquainted with gravity and isn't subject to the same rules governing the concept as the rest of us.

When we were well inside the tunnel, an unsettling distance away from the mouth, my light found our target. It made no attempt to hide, had no notion to conceal itself, never considered interrupting its meal for even a moment to acknowledge those who were intruding on its lair. We could have taken its seeming indifference as a cue to turn and sprint for safety, back to the yard, the fence, the car. Nobody human would have made it more than two strides. Not if the vampire chose to cut us down, and leave us floundering helplessly like a wounded deer waiting for the wolf to build up its hunger again.

The yard vampire was crouched in the middle of one of the lines, between the glinting rails, huddled over the hobo it had helped itself to so recently. It slavered and suckled at its prey, biting at new extremities when the one it had been working on became less fruitful. As it milked the arteries and veins dry, a sickening ambient sound echoed off the tunnel walls—a slobbering, slurping noise that would have competed with the guttural utterances of the biggest, ugliest wildebeest at the watering hole. Just the din of it savouring its meal made me want to upchuck the last thing I had to eat. I thought Sunder was likely to start blowing Communion chunks all over the tracks but, to his credit, he kept his lunch down and his wits about him. He hadn't witnessed the attack on his family, only the aftermath. Even then, he never saw the final results of a vampire fully gorging itself.

"Let it finish," I cautioned him, "or it's only going to get worse for the poor bastard."

Watching a vampire eat is something nobody should have to witness, but interrupting the meal would be nothing but trouble. Not only would it lead to a new vampire rising from the dead in a day or so, it would leave us to deal with an unsatisfied bloodsucker looking at us as a second course.

Seemingly oblivious to our presence, the vampire continued sucking his victim empty of not only blood, but of all the
moisture in his body down to a cellular level. The end result
resembled an inflatable mattress with the air let out, and it was
hard to imagine that the crinkled, dehydrated flesh clinging to a
base of brittle bone was a living, breathing person only minutes
earlier.

Once the man's essence was running on empty, the vampire threw its blood-drenched face back and filled its dead lungs
like an oyster diver who had finally come up for air. It didn't
need oxygen, it didn't need to breathe. It only needed blood.
Taking a breath was residual muscle memory at best. It meant
this thing that used to be human hadn't been a vampire that
long. Older ones gave up on going through the motions of their
old humanity. Things like breathing and blinking were just
forgotten about eventually—old habits that stopped being
habitual. In the time I'd known him, I hadn't seen Marin do
either.

"Did that hit the spot?" I asked.

For the first time, the yard vampire reacted to us. He
laughed. Our being there delighted him, but not in a humorous
way.

"Have you come to offer yourselves to me?"

Not unheard of. There were mortals who, on occasion, got
to learn that vampires were a real thing the easy way—outside
of the context of being made a meal of. Most spent the rest of
their days trying to forget that truth. Rarely, you'd get a brave
and foolish idealist like Sunder who thought it was their duty to
rid the world of such creatures. More commonly, you'd get
idiot romanticists who saw an opportunity that didn't exist.

As deadly dumb ideas went, trying to find a vampire in the
hopes of joining their ranks was up near the top of the list. I can
only imagine their disappointment when they first set eyes on
one. The genuine article wouldn't live up to their pop-culture

fantasies. They weren't seductive, didn't sparkle, and, on the looks front, made Max Schreck look like Clark Gable.

Dreams of immortality, or an eternal nightlife, gave way to quick, miserable, permanent deaths. If the vampire they approached even took a moment to assure a groupie it would fulfill their wish, any promises went out the window with the first taste at an open vein. Once they got going, they wouldn't stop. Not until their victim was squeezed dry. Even if they wanted to show restraint—and they never did—few had the willpower to leave so much as a drop untapped.

"No, this is more of a social call," I replied. "We came to talk."

And the yard vampire laughed harder, and with even less good humour.

As deadly dumb ideas went, trying to find a vampire in the hopes of a civil chat was also near the top of the list, right below any of the other stupid reasons you might have for seeking one out.

"Do you know of me, young one?" said Marin, staring down his compatriot blood-drinker.

The yard vampire switched off his derisive snickering and assumed due reverence.

"You are one of the ancients," he said. "You are Grissoni. And you have been chosen."

"I have been targeted," Marin corrected him.

"Chosen, selected, set aside, ear-marked. It matters not. He seeks you out. They both do. The one who will give you The Mark of the Sighted One, and the one who shall give you your place among the four."

"I reject this mark, as I do my place among the riders. I will not help bring about the End Times."

"Do you know what they're talking about?" I heard Sunder whisper at me.

"Unfortunately, yes," I said.

"You must, Master Grissoni," said the yard vampire like he was pleading. "Only the apocalypse can bring about an end to our torment, the demise of this interminable undeath."

"And the end of all life on earth," Marin reminded him.

"A small consequence for a blessing so great."

I wondered how many other vampires shared his opinion. I would have asked, but none of the others had come out to scout a meal.

"Where are all the other leeches?" I asked. "This tunnel is supposed to be a hive of vampirism."

"I am the only one who lingers. Me, alone, Yarwick the Lean. The rest clambered aboard boxcars and tankers, squeezing into the dark corners, or wedging themselves within the workings of the wheels. All gone, to destinations random and unknown. Their fates are uncertain, but better than what would have befallen them had they remained in this cursed city. Death Incarnate has come for the vampires."

"What does he want from you?" I asked.

"To feed," answered Yarwick, simply. "We are being rounded up like cattle for the slaughter."

"The way you feed on humans?" said Sunder, more an accusation than a question.

"What he has planned for our kind is a fate much worse. I can drain a human but once. Death Incarnate seeks to fill and drain us over and over, without end, making him ever stronger as we grow weaker and weaker."

"You're vampires," I said. "You can't be killed."

"There are worse things than being destroyed. Being fed upon, drained in perpetuity, is one."

"Yet you have not fled from this place with the rest of your kin," said Marin.

"I, too, would be long gone. But I remain weak and must feed before I dare journey. When I lived in this city, I did so in its early days, generations past. I fell to the curse and was buried deep before I awoke again as the undead. Trapped and starved, I existed with my insatiable hunger for more days and nights than I could count."

"You were buried in Algonquin Fields, weren't you?" I said.

Yarwick nodded.

"I was only set free when those grounds were upturned, desecrated, made foundation to the necromancer's tower."

"Urban gentrification has its downside," I agreed.

"The site of his choosing was no accident. He knew there would be entombed vampires such as myself under the soil. As the fields were plowed and the graves torn open, he was at the ready to capture and secure any of my kind who were unearthed. I alone escaped. The others..."

Yarwick visibly shuddered at the thought.

"The others formed the basis of his collection."

The idea that Menahem was capturing and draining vampires of their necrotic blood, drinking it as some sort of ill-conceived liquid diet, was bad enough. I didn't like the implications of a collection. The problem with a lot of collectors is that they can't stop collecting.

"What do you mean 'basis' of his collection?" I asked.

"The vampires trapped in their cemetery graves were not enough for him. They only served to develop his taste. He seeks more for his collection—a steady supply to be tapped and devoured. Once his intentions were known, the migration began, and our haven emptied out as the rest retreated. But the absence of old stock has not thwarted him. If the supply cannot meet his demand, he merely creates new supply."

"Menahem is making more vampires," I said to no one in particular. My words hung heavily on everyone who heard me state the obvious. Both vampire and human alike understood the dread of it, the reckless irresponsibility of swelling the ranks of the nosferatu on purpose. Accidents happened from time to time, and they were always regretted. It was a regret, a guilt, that cut deep, even through the moral degeneracy of the vampire community. To forge new bloodsuckers with intent, for some unclear personal gain, was a sin beyond redemption.

"Fed or not, satisfied or not, you must depart this place," Marin told Yarwick. "Your falling victim to the necromancer, Menahem, will only serve his purpose and strengthen him."

"I know I must go, yet I feel tethered by my desire," Yarwick keened. "So many years underground, with only my mad hunger to keep me company. I have been free of the grave for many months, yet no matter how many humans I feed upon, I have yet to feel sated. Even now, this trifle has only whetted my appetite."

He turned to Marin, gratitude in his dead eyes.

"Thank you," he said. "Thank you, Master Grissoni, for delivering to me two more morsels. By your leave..."

Yarwick tossed aside the hobo husk he'd been cradling in his lap and leapt to his feet. Although he'd asked Marin permission to indulge himself, he didn't wait for confirmation. Sunder, looking like the fresher, tastier treat, was selected as first blood, and the vampire went for him in long decisive strides that closed the distance in moments.

Sunder, foolish and brave, stood his ground until Yarwick was within arm's reach. He then stuck one of his crucifixes directly in his face. It was such a sad attempt to protect himself, it made Yarwick halt, and he stopped to stare down the holy icon.

"It worked!" Sunder exclaimed, palpably excited.

With his confidence bolstered, Sunder leaned in, pressing what he thought was an advantage.

"Back, unclean! The power of Christ compels you!"

"Compels me to what?" answered the creature in the face of the trinket being flashed at him.

Yarwick was on Sunder so fast, you didn't even need to blink to miss it. Faster than any human eye could follow, he had a hand around his neck, and another gripping him by a fistful of hair at the back of his skull. Poised to feed, he only hesitated at the sound of Marin's booming command.

"Cease!"

The sound reverberated through the cement arches and supports like a cannon had gone off. Yarwick stopped, but did not withdraw.

"You are ancient, but you are not my master!"

"Leave the boy alone!" Marin bellowed, his voice so imposing, even I felt compelled to obey.

"Why should I?" the lesser vampire hissed back at him.

"Hemophiliac," replied Marin, more civilly.

The vampire sniffed at Sunder's neck, then ran his sickly purple tongue up the length of his throat, assessing the artery he had been about to open.

Repelled, offended, he shoved the kid away like he'd been served a plate of bad cheese.

"A spoiled offering," he hissed. "Nevertheless a promising alternative remains."

I knew who that promising alternative was, and I didn't expect another one of Marin's commands was going to deter Yarwick from splitting me open. The moment he turned towards me, I launched into my counter measures.

"Question!" I shouted. "How many pieces of gravel are in this tunnel?"

My query caught Yarwick off guard, but there was only the slightest hesitation before I had my answer.

"Three million, nine hundred and fifty-six thousand, eight hundred and eleven," he said, like the number was at the forefront of his mind at all times. He'd probably counted every stone a dozen times over, just to be sure. The need to obsess over minutiae like that would have kept him occupied for days, weeks, months after he'd first arrived and made the tunnel his home—a way to pass the time between feedings. Vampires don't have to get obsessive-compulsive over every little thing in their path. Usually it has to be an unexpected anomaly in their environment or territory in order for it to grab their attention. But if it's something that stands to be counted in a place they claim as home, you can be sure they know every precise number involved.

Before he could close the distance more than a few feet, I tried another.

"Question! How many rail ties are in this tunnel?"

"Three thousand and eight," he said without any hesitation at all and took a few more steps towards me.

He was almost on top of me before I could try one more.

"Question! How many grains of rice are in this tunnel?"

That one gave him pause, like it was a trick question. It was.

"Zero," he said, only inches away.

"Wrong," I replied. He was too close to see me fishing in my kit, working my fingers through the fabric of the sack inside—a sack of plain, ordinary basmati rice. I came up with a pinch of grains and flicked them at him. The tiny projectiles bounced off his forehead and cheek bones and fell to the earth. At first he seemed confused, then alarmed. The vampire backed off so he could better see the small number of grains that had landed on the stones at our feet.

After being caught without any rice on hand when Marin had first shown up in my basement, I'd made a point of keeping a small sack within reach in case he ever got out of hand. It had weighed my valise down for days, but it was worth the extra burden. Rice was always enough of an anomaly in just about every environment to force a vampire to take a minute or two to tally any spilled amount.

"Forty-nine!" the yard vampire and Marin both said at once, after letting their eyes dart from grain to grain for a few moments.

"Marin, cover your eyes. This is going to get ugly," I said,

Suspecting what was coming, he did as he was told. The instant Marin clapped his palm over his sunken sockets, I came out of my kit with a handful of rice and held it high.

"Don't you d..." was as far as my would-be siphon got before I cast it down on the rails, sending grains bouncing everywhere.

Yarwick screeched in anger and frustration. His vampiric OCD kicked in hard and locked his eyes to the ground, tallying the spilled grains as fast as his brain could go.

I could hear him muttering gibberish under his breath. It sounded like an incantation, but if you listened closely you could make out numbers. He was counting, and fast enough to be well-practised at it. In mere moments he'd summed up well in excess of a thousand grains. His eyes darted all around for clumps, clusters, and individual specs of rice. Given a minute or two max and he'd have an accurate total for all I had spilled. Then the attack would resume.

"Twelve! One hundred and eighty-two! Ninety-six! Three thousand eight hundred and forty!" I shouted.

"Stop it! You're making me lose count!"

He resumed his rapid muttering, starting over in the single digits.

"That's the idea. I'll keep doing it until you answer one more question."

"What?" Yarwick asked irritably.

"How many vampires does Menahem have in his collection so far?"

"That," said Yarwick grimly, "is one number I dread ever having the opportunity to count."

His eyes were back on the spilled rice, picking up his sum where he'd left off.

"Come on!" I said, helping Sunder to his feet. "We're leaving!"

I pushed him hard towards the mouth of the tunnel, shouting over my shoulder, "Seventeen! Three! Eight hundred million, six hundred and twenty-one thousand, four hundred and eleven!"

Yarwick roared, as if screaming could drown out the random numbers I was putting in his head.

"I can keep this up all night," I promised. "There are plenty more I can throw at you. I have an infinity of them!"

"Mr. Eulogy," Marin complained, his hand still fixed over his eyes, "you should have warned me that there would be math involved!"

"Play your phone game or something!"

Apparently Marin thought that was a good idea to keep his mind occupied and his compulsion to count in check. The last thing I saw in the pitch back tunnel was his face lit up red by the light of his phone screen running his Cherry Bang app.

Sunder and I were out in the rail yard a moment later, leaving the two vampires behind to their respective diversions. Marin was happily occupied for the foreseeable future and would rejoin us at his convenience. Yarwick, however, would be on our heels at the earliest opportunity.

"What do we...?" Sunder began, but I knew there was no time to waste on obvious questions.

"Run!" I said, "Run fast!"

And we did. When we'd parked the car on the edge of the yard, it seemed dangerously close to the tunnel hive. Now that we were out, it seemed impossibly far. And it was too much to hope that Sunder had a key fob that could start it remotely to save time.

"How long do we have until...?" he panted as we pumped our legs, hopping tracks and sliding in gravel.

Yarwick landed right in front of us with a powerful impact we could feel from thirty feet away. Apparently he'd leapt to the spot all the way from the mouth of the tunnel.

"Six thousand, one hundred and two!" he snarled at me.

"You positive?" I asked.

"Every grain accounted for. Twice," he said, and took his first step towards us.

That's as far as I let him get before digging into my bag and chucking another fistful of rice between us and the vampire.

Yarwick groaned and cast his eyes down again, flittering across the diverting anomaly as quick as he could.

"Go!" I told Sunder, and we resumed our dash for the car, passing Yarwick on either side by no more than a few feet. Distracted, he made no move to grab us.

"One hundred and fifty-five! Eleven thousand nineteen! Twenty-four!" I shouted, rattling off more numbers until we were too far out of earshot for it to do any good.

I could see the car through the fence, but it was still a long way off. And there was another obstacle in our way. Denise had finally arrived on the scene and was hovering in my path, with an annoyed so-there-you-are face to greet me. I ignored it and ran straight through her.

Sunder and I attempted a shortcut through an open boxcar, only to be greeted by Yarwick and another total on the other side.

"Four thousand, seven hundred and twelve!" he announced. "Considerably less than before. Are you running low?"

Yarwick smirked, confident I'd be out of rice, out of space, out of time before long. And he wasn't wrong. It was a small sack. I threw another generous handful anyway.

"Prick!" hissed the vampire, and started a new count.

I saw Denise approach, observing the grotesque, blood-soaked vision glancing from point to point on the ground like a bestial tracker trying to pick up the trail of its prey. Even from her vantage point, filtered through the afterlife haze, it was an unnerving, ugly sight. Her brief introduction to Marin had been one thing, but this was a whole new degree of vile, with all civility and dignity stripped away.

It's hard to read transparent lips, but the sentiment was clear: *what the hell's that?*

"That," I said to her, "is nearly what you became."

Her face said it all: *ew!*

I gave Sunder an encouraging shove and assured him, "Not far."

Even as I said it, I knew we'd never make it. I dug my hand into the sack, trying to arm myself with another volley of rice, and only found disappointing remnants that would hardly make for a sufficient single serving.

"Get the car started," I instructed Sunder. "He'll probably kill you too, but he wants to eat me more!"

Sunder nodded and made for the split in the fence. I stopped on the last parallel track, behind one of the lengths of train, and got ready to make a final stand. I glanced around the yard, trying to spot where I'd left Yarwick behind, but he had probably already finished counting and moved on. Looking up, I made sure he wasn't above me, ready to leap down from the nearest freight unit. That's when I heard the whisper.

"Three thousand and six."

Too late, I realized the voice had come from under the boxcar to my left. Yarwick clung to the undercarriage like a fly, and came skittering out faster than I could react. Twisting unnaturally, limbs bending at angles that would have snapped any mortal's bones, he landed on his feet between the rails, mere inches away from me. Reflexively, I reeled backwards, my heels tripping over the iron bar. I landed heavily in the gravel base. Yarwick could have had my throat open in an instant. The only thing that thwarted him was my final handful of rice. I didn't throw it so much as let it go on impact. The grains scattered all over the tracks, all over the ground, all over my coat, and Yarwick froze to the spot while he counted them all.

I rattled off more random numbers as fast as I could, trying to delay him. That's when Denise drifted over and resumed her study of the vampire. Fascinated, horrified, and repulsed—yet compelled to take a closer look—she could hardly tear her eyes away.

"One hundred and six thousand! Seven hundred and sixteen! Two! Four! Three! Eleven!" I desperately spouted.

Denise turned and mouthed another question at me I couldn't make out, trying to get me to explain what was going on and what she was looking at.

"Don't distract me while I'm trying to distract a vampire!" I yelled at her.

The momentary pause was enough to allow Yarwick to catch up. His eyes shifted from the rice on my clothes to the flesh on my bones, and the bounty of blood that lay beneath.

"Ninety-nine!" I shouted, but I was a beat too late.

Yarwick smiled and replied with the final total, "Two thousand, two hundred and eighty."

I yanked the nearly empty rice sack out of my bag and shook out the straggling remains, but it wasn't nearly enough to even make Yarwick pause. At a glance, he announced, "One hundred and forty-three," and took a stride towards me.

The loud clack of metal wheels passing over a joint in the tracks reverberated through the silent yard. It was a sound that would have been common on the site during operating hours. In the middle of the night, it rang out like a sudden peel of thunder. I looked for the source and saw a lone boxcar rolling down the track, on the same line where Yarwick now stood. And it was gaining momentum fast.

Yarwick was too focused on his next meal to pay any attention to what was bearing down on him. The first he knew anything was amiss was when the rolling boxcar's coupling caught him mid-hip and crushed him against the opposing coupling of the car right next to him, pulverizing his pelvis.

Yarwick wailed and screeched, pinned to the spot. There was no pain or mortal danger to his predicament, only frustration and anger at being denied his prey by only a few short feet. His arms windmilled wildly, his claw-like hands grasping at nothing but air, but he remained fixed. I doubt anyone had ever found safety so close to a ravenous vampire intent on the kill, but I did indeed appear to be perfectly safe. Yarwick, not long out of the ground, wasn't experienced enough to transform into anything that might extract him from the trap.

I looked to my right, to the other end of the boxcar that had been my salvation, and saw Marin standing there, still holding the metal rung he had grasped to push the tonnage down the line. It had only taken one hand to accomplish the Herculean deed. With the other, he continued to thumb through his phone app, paying the outcome of my near-deadly encounter no more than its due.

"New high score!" he announced proudly, turning the phone so I could see.

Θ

"Marin, put on your seatbelt," I demanded.

"Wouldst that I could perish in a mere automobile collision," he said.

We were several miles out from the Turlington Exchange, crossing the boundary of the industrial park, and heading into downtown traffic. With a few hours of darkness left in the night, Marin had chosen to ride with us instead of tucked in the trunk. Perched on the backseat, he was an obvious moving violation to any cop we might pass.

"I don't care if you put your head through the windshield in a fender bender. I just don't want to get ticketed. If we get pulled over, they're likely to impound this pile of junk and arrest the lot of us for ever taking it out on the road."

Sunder had nothing to say in defence of his wheels. He hadn't spoken a word since the rail yard. Only when I leaned forward to see his face, and judge how he was handling a long day of having his understanding of reality revised from the ground up, did I notice him shaking his head in disbelief.

"Counting..." he muttered.

"Obsessive counting," I elaborated.

"All the books I read. All the movies I watched. All that research, and it turns out *Sesame Street* offered the most accurate depiction of vampirism."

"The most profound insights into the fabric of the universe come from strange places sometimes," I agreed.

"Just tell me there's no such thing as a Snuffleupagus."

"I make no guarantees."

Denise had stayed behind, compulsively examining the wild creature we'd left pinned in the yard. I didn't try to talk her out of it. Seeing what she might have become could have been just the wake-up call she needed. Plus I didn't want to linger to see if Yarwick was ever going to be able to free himself. He'd probably figure it out once his rage had subsided. If not, he was due for an unpleasant dawn. Sun was in the forecast.

I had Sunder drop me off outside my building.

"I still have so much to learn, don't I, Mr. Eulogy?" he said with a mix of disappointment and anticipation.

"I'll be back in a couple of days," I assured him. "Try not to kill anyone while I'm gone."

Sunder nodded.

"Same goes for you," I instructed Marin, as he fogged the interior of the car and reformed himself outside, next to me.

"I will continue to practise restraint," he promised.

As Sunder pulled away, I noticed Marin wasn't following me.

"You coming?" I asked.

"The night is not yet ended, and I have a different destination in mind."

Marin drifted away, receding into the shadows.

"I thank you for your hospitality," were the final words I heard echo between the bricks and concrete of the vacant street.

Chapter Seventeen

Unconventional

MY EMAIL INBOX WAITED FOR ME, as it always did, in ambush. It was why I avoided it most days, and let Gladys sort through all the offers from prospective Russian brides, erectile dysfunction pharmaceutical companies, and sure-win stock pumpers. My years spent dead had done nothing to stem the flow of gunk raining down from the cloud, and the backlog begged to be mass deleted. Only the notion that there might possibly be something of value buried deep in the digital sewage kept me from trashing the lot. I kept promising myself I would take a day out to sort through it all, but mostly I just looked at new arrivals from the past week. Since my miraculous return, emails from real people had resumed at a slow trickle. One automated notification in particular caught my eye.

"Why is the ancient vampire in the basement trying to friend me?"

I avoid social media like the blight on human civilization it is, but with the convention pending, I wanted to do a preliminary head count of who might be in attendance and who might be worth networking with. As soon as I closed my email and logged onto the platform, there was a lengthy list of old messages to ignore—mostly asking if I was alive or dead, based on unsubstantiated rumours that had filtered through the community. Among them were a few connection requests from associates who apparently presumed I wasn't quite so dead after all. The one on top was familiar. Marin had made a quick study of Rebecca's hand-me-down phone, and was moving past pay-to-win app games.

"I showed him how Facebook works," said Rebecca. "He likes it."

"Of course he likes it. It's an online restaurant menu of gullible idiots looking to get bled dry."

"This is all part of him reengaging with society. It's safely anonymous. No one will judge him by the way he looks."

"Or smells."

"Exactly."

"Stop it," I said.

"Stop what?"

"That thing you do."

"Which thing?"

"You're trying to make him a project. A fix-er-up. You can't fix him," I told her, "he's a soulless monster."

"If my last makeover project panned out, I can fix anybody."

"Which makeover project?" I asked.

"You, silly."

Walked right into it.

"Have you heard anything more from your new psychomaniac pal?" said Rebecca.

I'd given her the rundown on how my evening had gone, and how I'd left things. Rebecca had made her disapproval known then, and she was reiterating it now.

"I don't know what to do with him," I admitted. "He's not a homicidal lunatic. He's a confused teenager, full of bad ideas, like grief, faith, and the notion he's some sort of avenging angel."

"Let the system deal with him. Easy solution."

"If I hand him over to Frenz, he's going to spend the rest of his life in prison getting passed around like a blunt at a frat party."

"You don't know that."

"Some baby-faced albino mixed in with all the maximum-security lifers? Don't tell me he won't be the most popular debutante in Cellblock A."

"Short of putting him down like a rabid dog, what else is there to do?"

"He's trying to do the right thing for the right reason, he's just been going about it in the worst possible way. What he needs is someone to set him straight, put him on the correct path, give him a clue."

"Someone like you?"

"Maybe," I said.

"Like a fixer-upper? Are you going to make him a project?" she taunted.

"Maybe."

"He's a mass murderer."

"So's yours," I said. "At least mine's human."

☉

I had an overnight bag packed for the trip by the time Tom showed up with his own modest bag slung over his back. He had already been booked to appear at this year's Necronomi-Con before my return. Rebecca badgered him into taking the train down with me but, as I expected, he'd drawn the line at sharing a hotel room to help me save a buck. Adjoining singles kept us at a more comfortable arm's length.

"Travelling light," I commented.

"This is just my stage tux. Plus a change of underwear and socks. I have another piece of luggage in the car."

"I printed out your tickets online," Rebecca said, handing out a couple of sheets of paper to us, each with a bar code. You'll be there bright and early tomorrow. Try to get some sleep on the train."

"Can't we just fly?" Tom asked, not for the first time. "Let's fly."

"Some of us are on a budget, Trust Fund," I said. "Plane tickets this late will break the bank."

Rebecca was already spotting me for the train ticket. My first cheque from Frenz would be weeks in processing down at the cop shop, and my advance from Eulogy Undertakings was dwindling fast. I still had my eighteen cents in Switzerland, but I was saving that for a rainy day.

"It's a fourteen-hour trip," Tom groaned. "So long!"

It was supersonic speed compared to my last couple of long-distance jaunts. I looked forward to a brief break, with nothing better to do than sit on my ass and watch the world go by.

"You coming to my house party after we get back?" Tom asked us both.

"There's a party?" I said.

"I got your invite," Rebecca confirmed, without committing. The mood between her and Tom was still wallowing in its awkward-ex phase.

"Are you sure you invited me?" I asked, dipping into the office to check my email again.

"I invited everybody," Tom assured me.

Leaning over Gladys, I took control of the computer mouse and switched windows. She didn't take well to me interrupting her perusing the Saks Fifth Avenue catalogue for accessories that would complement the bleached bone of a skull-about-town. I ignored the barrage of filth she directed at me and checked the bottom-most recesses of my inbox. Tom's recent message had been overlooked, sandwiched between benign spam and malicious phishing.

"You dumb shit," I said, finding the party page and scrolling through the list of attendees. One with no profile picture stuck out. "You just friended Count Toothy, didn't you?"

"Yeah, a couple of days ago."

"You mass-invited everyone you know on social media to your home?"

"Yeah."

"Including a vampire."

"It's not like everybody's going to show up," said Tom. "Most of them ticked 'maybe' which always means 'no.'"

"Any invite to a vampire is a big 'yes.' Always and forever. Now he can pop by for a visit and a bite any time he wants."

I turned to Rebecca and added, "You see why I didn't want him tooling around on the web?"

"What's the big deal?" said Tom. "I've crossed paths with him before. I went out drinking with the guy. Nothing bad happened that night."

"Not to you," I muttered.

"He doesn't seem to want to hurt anybody."

"Which is something that can change in a split instant if his instinct to feed kicks in. He can't keep that at bay forever. One day soon, he's going to crack, and you don't want to be around when that happens."

"I'm sure you know what you're talking about," Tom reluctantly admitted. He'd seen enough to know that much at least.

"You have to be more careful with the supernatural elements out there," I warned him.

"You play with fire, you get burned, right?"

"It's a little more serious than that. Eternal damnation isn't a boo-boo you can put ointment on."

"You know, everything was perfectly normal until you came back," Tom said. "We only have to worry about vampires and supernatural stuff when you're around."

"Says the guy with a demon in his pocket."

"And who put him there?"

"I told you not to adopt him. You wouldn't listen."

"Well I'm not adopting Marin. I'm just being...polite."

"The world is full of polite corpses. People who were too nice, too worried about keeping up appearances, to run away from a clear and obvious threat."

"Boys, don't miss your train," Rebecca cautioned us.

I consulted my watch.

"We're still early."

"But it's never too soon for you to get out of my hair," she said, beaming an insincere smile at us. "Run along now."

Θ

Tom was parked by the curb right in front of my building. I went to toss my bag in the back, but there was no room. A hefty chest, painted red and decorated with dozens of stickers and decals from all the towns and venues The Amazing Barfo had played, was poking out of the trunk. It looked fit for a sea voyage around the world, less so for a quick trip out of town, with only a single night's stay booked in a hotel that would provide all the usual amenities.

"You're bringing that on the train?" I said. "I don't think it's going to fit under your seat."

"There's a baggage car for checked luggage," Tom said.

"What did you pack in there? Your refrigerator?"

"My act has a lot of props. I've been expanding the reper-toire. You're lucky. You only have to bring business cards and a dumb hat."

Rebecca had accepted delivery of my new business cards just in time for a stack to join me on my trip. The redesign had amounted to little more than a new font and finish, but I had to admit, looking at them for the first time, they made me come across as more professional. Even I would have to take myself seriously handing these out.

The ride to the station was mercifully short, with me sitting on the passenger side of the sports car, our two bags stacked awkwardly in my lap. A porter was able to help Tom with his ridiculous trunk, while I slipped aboard ahead of him and took the window seat.

"How's your new living arrangement going?" Tom asked, before all eight cars had even cleared the platform.

"Oh, you know," I said vaguely. "Everything is an adjustment."

"Who gets to sleep on the couch?"

"Nobody," I replied honestly, and realized my one-word reply was too much information.

"Oh?"

"It's not like that," I was quick to elaborate. "It's a big bed, and I keep odd hours. We're hardly ever using it at the same time."

"None of my business," Tom said, and looked away like there was something far more intriguing happening in the aisle. I felt like agreeing with him, but that would only make it worse.

By the time urban blight gave way to suburban blight and finally rural blight, the sun was set, and there was barely any light to be seen out in the wilderness between cities. After an uneasy start, I was glad when Tom nodded off in his seat, making the best of the overnight red-eye. I tried to catch a few winks, but the constant clatter of train tracks and the swaying of the carriage as it barrelled through the blackness kept me awake rather than rocking me to sleep. Instead, I found myself staring out the window at nothing. The overheads in the car reflected back at me off the glass, and let me see more of what was inside the train than outside.

The steel wheels screeched as we rounded a bend, and all the lights in the train flickered a moment before going out. I waited for them to snap back on, but they stayed dead. With nothing reflecting off the glass, I was offered a better view of the landscape. My eye was drawn by movement at the tree line—an anomaly amidst the twisted overlapping silhouettes of branches and trunks.

There was something out in the dark, parallel to the tracks, keeping pace with the train. Twin spots of glowing red blinked in and out from between trees, racing through the woods at breakneck speed. At first I thought it must be the tail lights of a car or truck, flooring it along a dirt road I couldn't discern. But then I realized it wasn't the back of a vehicle I was looking at, but the front of an animal. Fiery eyes burned with the effort of a full sprint—with the excitement of the hunt. My hellhound had caught up with me again, out in the barrens between dots on the map, far from any sanctuary or assistance.

I looked back at the rest of the passengers in the car with me. The train had been underbooked, and the people in our section numbered about a dozen. Most, like Tom, were fast asleep. One or two were lost in their headphone music selections. Nobody was put out by the abrupt loss of light. Everything was as peaceful as could be, but that would change in an instant if the beast blew in through one of the windows and started a fight at cruising speed. There would be panic, casualties, deaths. Probably all three, and me among them.

My eyes searched the dark for the dog again, and I wondered how long it could keep up with a hurtling train. Would it grow tired? Could it even get tired? Was it merely giving chase, or was it moving to intercept?

That last question was answered moments later when we cut through a straightaway that had been excavated through a ridge of rock when the line was first built. Walls of stone rose up on either side of the train, and I saw the blazing eyes of the hound dart up the crest and out of sight. I heard another screech, but this one wasn't a metal-on-metal squeal. It was the bray of an animal as it pounced on its prey.

There was a tremendous thud on the roof of the car. I looked up and could see a concave dent in the ceiling. Claws scraped and tore at the damaged sheeting as the dog tried to dig its way in. I had no doubt it would crack open the fragile aluminum shell in moments, and make a hole big enough to let itself through. Desperate, I looked around for a weapon I could use to fend it off. Any weapon. The best I could come up with was a railway magazine advertising scenic tours of mountain ranges in glass-domed cars that would have offered even less protection against invading supernatural canines. I considered rolling it up and giving my hellhound a good whack on the nose. That was supposed to work as a disciplinary measure for most dogs, but I was dealing with something rather more threatening than a surly cocker spaniel.

Before I could consider all my options, which were amounting to none at all, I heard a long blast of the train's horn that abruptly switched from piercing and clear, to hollow and echoing. The car, already dark from the blackout, was plunged into complete pitch a second later.

We were, I realized, entering a tunnel.

With a sharp yelp, the giant beast directly above us was punted off the roof by the low overhang that offered no more than a foot or two of clearance. Those still awake continued to enjoy their music through the interruption that had only shut out the lights, none the wiser as to what had just happened. By the time we were halfway down the passage, the overheads flickered back on. Tom, closest to the point of impact, stirred.

"What time is it?"

"We're still a few hours away," I said. "Go back to sleep."

Tom shut his eyes and lowered his chin again. He was out a few seconds later, and probably wouldn't even remember waking at all by the time we arrived at our destination. But there was someone else in the car who was less oblivious to what had just happened.

"Necromancer!" I heard a voice whisper sharply. "Hear me!"

I knew who it had to be. I didn't fancy a conversation, but he'd keep at it until he was at a full shout and woke up everybody. The end of Tom's pocket-watch chain was hooked to a belt loop on his pants. Giving it a tug, I pulled it free without disturbing my travel buddy.

Moby-Dick peered out of his fish-eyed aquarium in profile and burbled, "I sensed a powerful presence."

"It's gone now," I told him.

"I have not felt such a sensation in many centuries."

"Do you know what it is?" I asked, still unsure of what exactly was after me and why.

"It is doom!" he said, and refused to elaborate. Given his past history as a harbinger, I didn't doubt him. Moby-Dick could still sense impending demises, particularly if they were related to any of his morbid fetishes. The best I could hope for was that I was the only one on the chopping block. And that I could still come back after losing my head down a monster's gullet.

Doom or not, the beast had been taken out by a piece of slapstick fit for a vintage cartoon short. That reassured me somewhat. It may have been a vicious otherworldly hound, immensely strong and tenacious, but at least it shared some common traits with regular dogs. Like stupidity.

Θ

I was able to get a couple of hours of sleep on the train after my canine companion got scraped off the roof. It was about as good as I could expect from a travel day. A shower and a change of clothes at the hotel was all that was keeping me from the convention floor, and I got to it as soon as we checked in.

I was drying off when I heard a sharp cry from the next room. Tom sounded caught somewhere between dismay and fright. I considered it worth responding to, but not so quickly that I didn't make sure my hotel towel was tied firmly around my waist.

We had left the adjoining door between rooms unlocked. When I threw it open, I found Tom standing over his colourful travel trunk. The lid was hinged back and Marin was sitting upright inside. Apparently, Tom inadvertently packed a stowaway.

Having gotten over the initial shock of discovery, Tom had already moved on to being cross at the undead freeloader. It seemed he was up one vampire, but down a whole inventory of stage essentials.

"Where's all my stuff?" Tom demanded.

"I had to move some of your possessions so I could fit inside," Marin explained.

"I'm on stage tomorrow and I've got no props to work with!"

"I apologize," said Marin. "I assumed the trunk contained nothing more than a collection of rubbish saved for sentimental reasons."

"That trash collection was my whole act!" Tom fumed. "How'd you get into my apartment?"

"I was invited," Marin stated simply.

"You see?" I said, but Tom wasn't interested in hearing me proved right again.

"Why is he even here?"

"Good question," I nodded. "What are you doing here, Marin?"

"It has been pointed out to me that if I am to reconnect with my humanity, I must socialize with humans."

"Pointed out by who?" Tom asked.

"Do you need to ask?" I said.

Tom shut his eyes and muttered, "Rebecca."

Marin took her gifted phone out of his pocket.

"This device offers a superficial social connection, but I am a traditionalist, and prefer to engage with others in person."

"You can't draw blood from an emoji," I agreed.

"Is this another one of Rebecca's makeovers?" Tom wanted to know.

"The latest one," I said. "I was a challenge. But Marin, here, would be her magnum opus."

"She should stick to self-improvement," Tom said. "Maybe sort her own shit out before she tries to fix everyone else."

"Quitting the bottle seems to have stuck. That only leaves her with another fifty bad habits to kick."

"When am I to be introduced to the humans attending this convention?" Marin interjected. "I am informed they are of the 'freak' and 'weirdo' variety who may be more accepting of my affliction than most."

"Let's take this one step at a time," I cautioned. "There are some attendees who understand vampires exist, sure. But most of them know to steer clear. There might be some wiggle room with the less-informed, but if you want to engage, maybe Tom and I should scout out the crowd today. We'll see who's here, and who might be open to a meet and greet. The after-party starts tomorrow night. That would be the best time to roll you out and make introductions. The sun will be down, so you can avoid the stigma of trying to make a good first impression with third-degree burns all over your face."

"That will only leave the stigma of the rest of his appearance," said Tom.

"You've been to convention after-parties," I reminded him. "Everyone should be drunk enough to look past some of Marin's more obvious flaws."

"I do so look forward to re-engaging in festive human exchanges," said Marin. "It has been centuries, and I have forgotten much."

"Just remember party rule number one," I said. "You remember party rule number one?"

Marin's eyes swung back and forth like a pendulum as he pondered the rules of social interaction he hadn't needed to consider since the Middle Ages.

"No..." I prompted.

"No..." he repeated.

"...killing people."

"No killing," he agreed. "Only conversation."

"Good boy," I said. "Now get the hell out of Tom's box. The humans need to talk."

Marin stiffened his legs and rose erect in a way that would have snapped a mortal's kneecaps. He stepped out of the trunk and walked to the open door between rooms, stopping in the frame as though a solid wall stood in his way.

"May I repose in your room, Mr. Eulogy?" he asked.

"Yeah, yeah," I said dismissively.

"You must invite me," he said.

"It's a hotel room, Marin. Nobody owns it. You don't need an invite."

"You are the rightful master of the room each day you pay for it."

"Just get in the fucking room!"

Marin took that as invitation enough and gave Tom and I our privacy.

"Who travels around in a box?" Tom wondered as he looked at his trunk. It was large, but would have been cramped for a whole person. Especially on a long train ride.

"I know," I agreed from experience. "Sounds awfully uncomfortable."

"What the hell am I going to do now?"

I walked over and took inventory of the remaining scraps that had made the journey.

"There are still a few doohickeys left in here," I noted. "You've got your numbered balls, some knotted twine, and um...finger puppets? I don't even want to know what you do with those."

Tom leaned over to peer inside the vacated box.

"Yuck," he said. "Everything in there stinks of vampire. I'm getting sick just thinking about what they'll taste like."

"Won't that make it easier to barf them back up for the show?"

"I'm going to have to do this old school," Tom decided "I'll hit a few shops around here. Dollar stores and stationery outlets. Grab some essentials, fall back on the standards, like when I was starting out. I just hope my fans will be happy with an all-classics set."

"You still have me to subjugate your simpering sycophants!" boomed a tiny voice from inside Tom's pants. He retrieved his pocket demon for a creative consult.

"Are you going to stick to the script this time, or do I need to stop by a pet store and shop for an understudy?"

"I will not attempt to rewrite your asinine act," Moby-Dick agreed.

"Help me get through this performance and I'll let you improv at the next comedy club we play," promised Tom.

"May I degrade and humiliate the simpering cretins in the audience? Shatter their illusions, and sap their wills to continue the struggle to sustain their worthless existences?" the fish asked hopefully.

Tom considered the request.

"Just the hecklers," he said. "Wait until one of them starts calling out stupid shit and then have at it."

"I look forward to robbing another such heckler's life of all hope and meaning. I can already taste his sad, lonely suicide in the parking lot of Guffaw's Chuckle-Shack!"

"Another?" I asked.

"There's no evidence the last one had anything to do with us," Tom claimed.

"Okay then," I said, "I'll let you two sort your next gig out. I'm going to get dressed. I'll meet you in the lobby in ten minutes."

I returned to my own room and closed the door behind me. There was no sign of Marin, but there were few places he could be hiding. It was probably too bright for his taste. There were already curtains over the window, but I pulled the heavier blackout drapes shut as well before knocking on the wardrobe.

"It's nice and shady," I said. "You can come on out."

Marin opened the door and his stink came spilling out first. In just a few minutes, he'd turned the inside of the wardrobe into a morgue drawer. I was glad I hadn't hung up my clothes. The vampire poked his head out to confirm the room was dark and to his liking.

"How long do you expect to be gone, Mr. Eulogy?"

"Tom and I will work the room until closing at six. I'll check in on you then."

"How shall I occupy myself until then?" he wondered. "I grow weary of the repetitive nature of Cherry Bang since I last beat my personal best score."

"Watch some TV," I suggested, handing him the remote. "Use this. Push the buttons until you find something you like. No porn. I'm not paying for unlocked video-on-demand. You need anything, call room service. Just don't eat whoever brings it up."

"How do I summon this service?"

"Use the phone."

Marin turned his cracked smartphone over in his hand and gave it a slight shake, as though it might ring like a bell that would summon the help.

"Not that phone, this phone," I said, pointing to the one on the end table.

"These devices bear no resemblance to each other," Marin said, as he picked up the receiver and stared at it. "How do I make this machine play games of amusement?"

"You don't. Just stick to the TV, like so."

I took the remote and switched on the LCD that was mounted on the wall, demonstrating which buttons would change channels. The hotel hook-up offered all the usual cable crap, including various twenty-four-hour news networks, national and international. Something caught my eye as I flipped past the BBC. There was a familiar face on what looked like a police mug shot. Apparently a suspect had been apprehended in the Canning Town Charnel House case. As mug shots went, this was more flattering than most celebrity DWI pictures, but not by much. Zombies don't have a good side for cameras to capture.

"Oh no," I moaned.

"Friend of yours?" Marin asked.

Poor Shambler. His freedom from indentured servitude hadn't lasted long. I could only wonder what Scotland Yard was making of the vagrant they had picked up wandering the streets of Canning Town, acting suspicious and unlike any living person. He would doubtless exercise his right to remain silent by virtue of being unable to speak, but I was sure his medical exam wouldn't go so well. A breathalyzer test would find no alcohol or breath. A blood test would only reveal barren, uncooperative veins. How they managed to connect him to the scene at Oliver's house was a mystery, but forensics would probably come up with fibres or hair follicles or skin samples that would hold up in court. Shambler would get upgraded from a holding cell to a prison in short order, if he didn't find himself on a medical examiner's table for an autopsy along the way.

"It's an overseas case I'm following," I told Marin. "Flip back to this channel from time to time and keep an eye on the breaking news. Let me know if there are any developments."

I left the technology neophyte behind to rot his mind on morning game shows, afternoon soap operas, and around-the-clock infotainment passing itself off as journalism. Nothing from his medieval-world heyday could have prepared him for the mental assault of modern television as it struggled to remain relevant in a new-media age. App games had proved addictive. This, I speculated, might break him. If anything could destroy a vampire, the boob tube was a solid bet. It was worth a try. I was interested to see what I would come back to at the end of the day.

Θ

The ticket kiosk was thick with regulars, plus a disturbing number of normies. They had started to infiltrate the event last time I'd been out to it, and had made for a good excuse to never return. I didn't care for the mix of gawkers and casuals who had started to seep in from the suburbs and beyond. The Necronomi-Con had become less an exchange between professionals, and more a safe space for the curious to get an eyeful of a world they didn't understand or even believe in.

The floor of the show was no better, and I had no love for the airplane-hangar size of the new venue that was more interested in packing in death-metal t-shirt vendors and sullen artisans of occultism over proper practitioners. The lighting, for one, was just too bright. The floods were shining like they were trying to illuminate an indoor World Cup final. No mood at all. Given the gallows collection of morbids obsessed with everything in the paranormal spectrum, a more suitable venue might have been a haunted house, a defunct lunatic asylum, or a nice spacious abandoned factory full of rust and safety hazards.

Instead, we were housed in a terribly conventional convention centre that had, in recent weeks, hosted a vintage car collection, a coin-and-bullion bourse, a gun show, and an awards ceremony for strippers and burlesque dancers. The Necronomi-Con had gone mainstream. Death had come out of the closet; the supernatural was seeming a lot less super, and a lot more natural. I already missed the days of only a few dozen of us getting together in a cheap hotel's conference room and hoping the management wouldn't find out what our meeting was about and chase us off.

Tom and I did the tour, making a quick recon of the various alleys of booths and tables, just to see who was there and what we could expect to get out of our short stay. We made a few stops at the ones that had direct bearing on our respective professions, scouting out goods for sale that might be worth stuffing into our already over-packed luggage for the return trip. I made a note to stock up on some modern editions of grimoires that were being peddled by a lanky fellow in a leather jacket and no shirt. I had reprints of a few colonial-era texts at home, but the tongue-twister English was a headache at the best of times, and potentially deadly when trying to recite an incantation under duress. You don't want to trip over your vocabulary when some extra-dimensional terror is trying to tear a hole in the fabric of reality, eager to flay your soul to ribbons with the power of its malevolent rage. In such an event, time could be a factor. And I always found magic words work just was well when translated into common modern vernacular. It's the intent that matters, not the syntax.

Skipping the first day of the convention had been a sound choice. Although there was networking and glad-handing to be done in those early hours, the exhibitors were always too busy setting up their shops to pay proper attention to what was being said to them, and few would be able to remember where they stashed any business cards handed out during that chaotic scrum. It was better to make my presence known later, and then concentrate on swapping contact info during the wrap-up when everyone was more relaxed and receptive.

"Back from the dead?" said one past acquaintance upon recognizing me at his table of homemade scented candles. All the homebrewed wax purported to be made from the tallow of human fat. The scents were grouped under headings like "cozy corpse bile," "delicious decay," and "maggoty moments," but I thought they all smelled vaguely of apples.

The proprietor was a necromancing semi-pro named Paul Berrer. I kidded myself that he was the only practitioner on my end of the business with a cheesier name than mine. But that wasn't accurate. Most people didn't recognize his *nom de guerre* for the bad pun it was.

"Is that back literally or figuratively?" he added.

"I took some time off," I said, not wanting to get into it.

"I thought you might have joined the body count. We're in a rarified profession these days, it would seem. You hear about Oliver?"

"Yeah."

"So weird. You two were close, weren't you?"

"Kinda."

"I wish I could have met him," said Paul. "That guy was a legend."

Oliver would never have dreamed of flying overseas for a convention. Or flying anywhere for that matter. And Paul was barely scraping by on candle sales and a credit line. Poverty and indifference had conspired to keep their paths from ever crossing.

"I heard a bunch of other necros got their ticket punched lately. Xun Ji in Beijing, Yamajit in Mumbai, Dabria in Seville..."

I'd heard all those names before, but hadn't met any of them in person. None of these victims had been on the list of kills Marin mentioned. Jeevak Menahem had been busy. And thorough.

"Where did you hear about them?" I asked.

"Everything's on the Web now," said Paul. "I'll send you an invite to our chat room. Not that there are many left in it."

The list of carnage hadn't gone public, and the convention was the first chance the news had had to get whispered about in earnest by the gossips of the trade.

"Anybody else survive to make the show?"

"I think Khalida is here," he said. "She hasn't been by to schmooze me yet, but then I'm not a potential client."

"Isn't she one of your regulars?"

"I made a Hand of Glory for her last year, but nothing since."

"You sell those things at a convention?"

"Are you kidding me?" Paul said, lowering his voice. "They're super illegal, and there are eyes everywhere in a big hall like this. I get busted for selling real body parts, they'll shut me down. We're talking fines and jail time."

That made me sad. What good was a trade show for wielders of the dark arts if you couldn't buy basic reagents and human remains? I could see the law cracking down on certain health hazards, but didn't understand what objection they might have to us dealing staples like the pickled hand of an executed prisoner, grasping a candle made of his own fat, entwined with a wick of human hair. As far as I was concerned, that sort of thing should be available in any well-stocked flea market or hardware store.

"I see the identity-politics crowd sprang for their own booth this year," I said of the table next to Paul's. Nobody liked to see socio-political agendas worm their way into our gathering, but it had been brewing on the periphery for a long time and was starting to bubble over.

"Oh, they've had a space on the floor for the last few years," Paul informed me. "No more handing out awareness fliers in the lobby for them anymore. They're getting bigger and bigger."

"So's their name," I noted.

The LDDURR&R community was always adding letters to its alphabet soup. This year it stood for the Living-Dead-Dying-Undead-Reanimated-Revived and Resurrected community. By the time the Necronomi-Con rolled around again, there could be half a dozen other states of being added to the increasingly unwieldy list.

"Breathe deeply," said Paul, "before they suck all the oxygen out of the room."

"I should go say hello. See you at the closing?"

Paul nodded. "I'll keep a candle lit," he said, paraphrasing what was written on all his shop's literature.

Stepping through the milling masses clustered in front of the next table, I gave the booklets and pamphlets a quick once-over. Most of the material was free, and their cash box was looking light, but someone must have been subsidizing them. Last I'd seen, they could barely afford photocopies folded and stapled by hand. The current batch of books was properly printed, with glossy covers and a professional design. The presentation was slick enough to at least draw the curious casuals, looking for a window into a new and novel subculture.

"Coming up in the world," I commented to one of the activists who was standing vigil in front of their logo-laden backdrop. "Real lively."

I remembered him from the early days of the movement. His name was Rufus. Rufus something or other.

"Don't assume my state of being," he said, sounding offended.

I can sense death about as keenly as your average fly—the smell, the taste in the air, the vibe. This guy was firmly in the land of the living, pulse and all, but I refrained from pointing out what would have been obvious to even someone less attuned.

"Well, you certainly seem to be on the right side of the grass at any rate."

"I'm trans," he said, making me wonder if I'd already committed some pronoun faux pas.

"Boy, girl, other?" I asked.

"I'm trans-living," Rufus clarified. "I'm alive, but I identify as dead."

"It's easy to make the leap, you know," I said. "Literally. Leap in front of a bus. Leap off a tall building. Poof, you're dead, just like that."

I knew very well from experience. My problem was my body wouldn't commit to staying dead.

"I don't want to *literally* be dead," he huffed at me impatiently. "I'm alive and I want to stay that way. But I'm dead inside. And it's what's inside that counts."

"It's kind of a binary state of being," I cautioned, reluctant to open the whole undead can of worms.

"Don't you try to file me away in any one box!"

"Even if it's a coffin?"

I was worried this was going to escalate into a public debate I wasn't interested in having, so I was relieved when Tom caught up with me after his brief side trip to a vendor pushing loaded dice and unloaded bullets. It was a niche market for cheats and magicians looking to win at games of chance, or bolster their odds of not getting killed doing a bullet-catch trick.

"Hey, Tom," I said. "Find anything worth making yourself sick over?"

But Rufus, the advocate, wouldn't be thrown off his argument.

"How does he identify?" he asked of the new arrival at his table, who looked like he might be dressed for his own funeral.

Tom didn't understand what we were talking about and introduced himself accordingly.

"I'm a professional regurgitator," he said.

I came up with an answer more suited to the agenda in question.

"He's in a state of pre-death."

"Pre-death?" Rufus pondered. After spot-checking the booklets in front of him, he consulted his fellow activist, who was busy proselytizing to a clueless civilian at the other end of the table. "Anita, do we have pre-death on the list?"

"I don't think so," she said, after careful consideration.

"We should add it. More inclusive that way."

"Sure," I agreed. "It kind of includes everybody else in the world. The more the merrier."

"How about you?" Rufus asked me. "Are you pre-death?"

"I've always got one pending. I'd say I identify more as multi-post mortem."

"Add that one, too?" asked his companion, who had produced a notepad.

"I've never heard of it, but yeah," he said. "We better stick it on the end, just to be safe."

"So it's the LDDURRRPD&MPM community now?" she confirmed.

"I guess so."

"I'll call the printer for an estimate first thing tomorrow."

"What do we do with all the material we already have?" said Rufus, surveying the spread of literature that covered every inch of table.

"Better shred it," she said. "It's all hopelessly out of date now."

"I guess we're closing shop early this year."

"Well yeah, obviously," she confirmed. "We don't want to be distributing disinformation."

I took the opportunity to vacate the area before the monster acronym broke free of its moorings and went rampaging through the hall. Guiding Tom down the nearest intersection, I wasn't watching where I was going and instantly regretted my escape route.

The Wiccan quarter was the one area I'd been trying to avoid during my systematic coverage of the convention floor. Not more than three paces into the realm of broomsticks, mixing cauldrons, and feminist manifestos passed off as paganism was I spotted, cornered, and forced into a reunion I'd hoped to avoid for the rest of my many lives. I never saw her coming, but then how could I?

"Well well well. Rip Eulogy, as I live and breathe."

The voice was known to me, the face not at all. Perhaps around the eyes—not so much because they're a window into the soul, though. I remain unconvinced Magna Aslaug Holgersson ever had a soul. But the eyes are where a lot of basic human personality is expressed. The look in them, situated on a complete stranger's face, exuded an instantly familiar attitude—a mix of flirtatious and disdainful, with a certain hint of hunger. She looked like a cat that was wondering how long it should play with the bird it caught before pulling off its head and clawing out its guts.

"Look at you," she said, taking me in for the first time in years, "living and breathing as well. There's a switch. Last I saw you, you were dead as a doornail, stiff as a plank."

"I got better," I said.

"I figured you couldn't survive without me."

"Couldn't survive with you, more like."

Her laugh was like a tiny ringing bell, the brass tongue clapping furiously, metal on metal. It managed to be adorable and creepy as hell at the same time. I'd come to hate it. In our time together, I had started to make a point of not being amusing for fear of having to hear it again.

"Who's your delicious friend?" she asked, looking Tom up and down in a probing way that would be rude and intrusive from a normal person. Attractive people were given a pass.

"That's Tom," I said, and tried to keep the introductions brief enough to be quickly forgotten. "Tom, this is Magna."

I could see Magna was already burning herself into Tom's brain.

"The Amazing Barfo," Tom was quick to add, apparently hoping his stage persona would make some additional positive impression.

He offered his hand for a cordial shake. Magna didn't shake back. She placed her hand in his, like she expected him to kiss it as some continental fop might have, back when that sort of thing passed as manners.

"Enchantée," she flirted, with a faux French accent that made me want to gag. Over the years, Magna had probably logged a century or more of her time within the borders of France—Paris mostly—but she was about as French as French fries.

"Such well-dressed gentlemen," she added, taking us in— Tom in his tux, me in my mortician getup. "Is this what necromancers are wearing today?"

"The outfit is new. Retro but new."

"So's the facial hair. Is that a *goatee*?"

She said "goatee" like she was trying to push a button she knew was there. Of course she knew it was there. She was the one who installed it.

"Otherwise, you haven't changed," she concluded, making an effort to sound disappointed.

"You have," I said. "But, of course, you always do."

I wondered where she had stolen her current look. Who had been her donor, her victim? It was better not to ask, and to never know what had become of the poor girl.

"The convention has been an absolute gas so far. Pity you missed day one, but you're here now. The both of you," Magna added, careful to include Tom with another smouldering gaze. "You'll stay for the closing ceremony tomorrow?"

"Not late," I said. "We have a return ticket."

"We could always refund it, stay another night," suggested Tom.

"No we can't," I insisted. "Some of us need to get back to business."

"Maybe you do, but..."

"You do, too," I said, cutting Tom short as firmly as I could.

"Ah well," sighed Magna, in mock disappointment. "I guess that just means we'll have to make the best of tonight then, won't we?"

She left the suggestiveness of her notion hanging heavily in the air and drifted away to make a few more social rounds. But she made sure to swing Tom and myself a naughty smile over her shoulder as she departed. It hooked Tom, but I did my best to cut the line.

"Don't," I told him. "Trust me. Don't."

"Don't what?"

"Whatever is in your head right now. Don't act on it. Don't think about it."

"So that's who screwed you over," Tom said knowingly, like a wisdom of the ages had been revealed to him at last. "Now it makes sense. I don't blame you for being hung up on her, she's hot."

"She's a witch," I said.

"Did she break your heart?" Tom replied, tauntingly.

"That's beside the point. She's literally a witch. Stay far far away."

"You mean like wands and gingerbread houses and twitching noses?"

"Don't be an idiot. That stuff is from old fairy tales and bad sitcoms. She's the real deal. Real hexes, real curses, real magic. And no silly hats."

"Speaking of which..." Tom said, looking up at the towering prop on my head.

"This," I said, taking it off and shaking it at him, "is marketing."

"Can I borrow it?"

"You said it was dumb."

"That was before my trunk of props got dumped to make room for a vampire. I need all the stage pizazz I can lay my hands on."

"Fine," I said, handing it over. "See if you can workshop a new shtick with this."

"Thanks," Tom said, accepting the hat. With his tux and tails, it was a natural fit.

"*Do not* barf it in," I said, firmly.

"Promise," Tom swore. "Now I just have to go find a bunch of weird and interesting doodads I can swallow and spit back up."

"And don't go storing anything you've had in your stomach inside that hat either," I called after him as he started his treasure hunt. "Clean items only!"

☉

I lost track of how many introductions and reacquaintances I subjected myself to over a gruelling eight hours of forced socialization. With Tom having peeled off early to score a few more props and practise his pared-down act in his room, I grabbed a quick bite alone and retired to my own quarters. Stripped down in the dark for bed, I noticed there was no light visible under the adjoining door. Tom had probably already fallen asleep by the time I got in. Marin was up of course, but he'd shut himself into the wardrobe to play with his phone. Only a tiny sliver of illumination filtering between the hinges let me know he was there at all.

Standing at the window in my underwear, I admired the view of the city that stretched out to the horizon. With the sun down, the blanket of pinpoint lights went all the way to the distant mountain range before tapering off as they climbed the lowest hills. The peaks themselves were shrouded in black, blocking out the stars that hung low in the sky behind them.

Even as I took in the view, the dark mass of the mountains seemed to be bleeding into the outer city limits. Perhaps it was a trick of the light, or a rolling blackout caused by a dodgy power grid out in the remote districts, but entire neighbourhoods seemed to be winking off and on in sequence. Watching the light show was relaxing. Alcohol would make unwinding after a long day even easier. There was no way I was going to get dressed again just to hit a liquor store, but the hotel offered temptation at arm's length.

The window reflected the room back at me as I opened the minibar and the blinding white light of the refrigerator switched on. I took my time choosing between a tiny bottle of vodka or a miniature flask of gin. Either way, I'd regret the choice once I saw the overpriced impulse drink added to my bill. The vodka won and I twisted the cap off, kicking the cooler door closed with my bare foot and plunging the room back into darkness.

As soon as the light was out again, I saw someone staring back at me through the window. There was a gentle tapping noise on the glass, like the person outside wanted to draw my attention without freaking me out. A tall order, considering we were twenty-three stories up with no balcony. I promptly dropped my beverage with a yelp, and the thick carpet ended up drinking my vodka for me in several burbling gulps.

Closing my eyes and inhaling deeply, I composed myself before switching on the bedside lamp and going to the window to crank it open.

"You look naked without your broom," I commented to the witch, suspended in the night air with nothing holding her up beyond a discipline of magic outside my purview.

"Brooms went out with the burning times. I'm a modern girl," Magna said, and stepped onto the ledge, letting herself into the hotel room.

"Your Hoover vacuum cleaner, then."

"Pocket totem," she said, holding up an unsightly craftwork of sticks and bird bones she grasped in her hand.

"What do you want, Magna?" I said, knowing that her multi-layered motivations for everything she did would not be forthcoming.

"Can't I pay a visit to an old pal without having my intentions being suspect?"

"No."

"That hurts," she said, sounding delighted rather than injured.

"You had your reunion this afternoon on the convention floor."

"But it was so crowded! All those people crammed together! And your yummy friend. Tom, was his name? I understand he swallows."

"And regurgitates."

"Pitching and catching. He's a man of many talents."

My patience with Magna's flirtations and innuendo had run out years ago. It used to work. It still did with most people. But I'd been made immune. She was the one who had inoculated me.

"If you have something to say, get to it," I said. "Then go."

"Oh Rip, darling, we haven't seen each other in ages. I was hoping for something a touch more substantial than a passing nod at a trade show. Something more intimate."

She stepped right up to me until there was nothing between us—not time, or history, or any sense of propriety. It gave me chills. Not the fun, arousing kind. The crawling-skin kind, borne of bad memories and post-traumatic stress disorder.

I was so busy holding my ground, playing it cool, pretending to be indifferent, I failed to anticipate an abrupt change of subject.

"Are you going to introduce me to your ghost?" she asked.

The non-sequitur caught me off guard, and I had to look around to remind myself what she could be referring to. Sure enough, Denise was there in the room with us. I don't know when she caught up with me, or even how she found me hundreds of miles from home. She'd dropped so far down my list of priorities, I'd forgotten to enjoy my time without her.

"You can see me?" Denise asked Magna hopefully.

"Of course."

"You can hear me!" she squealed from the other side of eternity.

"Loud and clear."

"I have my voice back!" Denise gushed. Her joy was short-lived. Vindictiveness swept back in almost instantly as she turned to me and snarled, "You are so screwed."

The silencing spell I had cast on her had probably worn off hours, if not days ago. If it hadn't been for goddamn Magna, she might never have thought to try to speak again.

"What did you do to bring on this haunting, I wonder," Magna teased.

"He murdered me!" Denise barked in response.

"Did he really?" said Magna, making eyes at me. The possibility that I had switched from dealing in death to being openly homicidal aroused her.

"No," I said, adding, "And yes. It's complicated."

"I love complicated," cooed Magna.

The hotel management would be quick to double charge me if they found out how many different entities I had squeezed into my single room with me. Any more and we'd probably be breaking fire department regulations for exceeding occupancy.

Magna abruptly dove onto the double bed and bounced up and down on her back, testing the springs.

"We should fuck," she casually said. "For old time's sake, if nothing else."

I wasn't taking the bait.

"Asmodeus's sloppy seconds? Pass."

I remembered Magna's patron demon all too well from our time together. I still thought of him as the other man.

"I'll have you know, I've been a good girl since I acquired this body," she said. "I'm practically a virgin. I can't speak for what the previous owner got up to with it, but I haven't noticed any unsightly blemishes. Come on, let's get laid!"

"In front of the ghost?"

"Especially in front of the ghost!" she smiled, leaping back off the bed on her last bounce. She was in my space again an instant later, picking at the neckline of my undershirt with one of her ink-black nails. "It'll be kinky. Like a threesome."

Magna leaned in, her lips nearly on mine. I could taste her breath and it smelled sweet.

"I also have a vampire in my wardrobe," I mentioned, hoping it would be a mood killer.

"I'm more interested in the monster in your pants."

But I didn't even have pants as a protective layer. Just a pair of boxers, and I could already feel her razor-sharp manicure worming its way past the elastic waistband. I was hoping Denise would interject with something distracting or inappropriate, but she was watching the scene unfold like I had paid to unscramble the adult channel. A bowl of popcorn would have suited her perfectly.

I grabbed Magna firmly by the wrist and extracted her hand before she could get a grip on anything I preferred to keep to myself. She stubbornly resisted me, so I wrenched her wrist hard—much harder than I would have done to any mortal woman—and held it at an angle that might snap a bone with only a slight increase in pressure. She locked eyes with mine, showing no pain. There was only a flash of defiance, a hint of anger, at being turned down. It must have hurt—mostly her pride—but she said nothing, waiting for my next words instead. I chose them carefully.

"Goodbye, Magna."

I released her, and Magna stepped away. The fury drained from her eyes and the sly smile returned, like the moment had never happened. The way out yawned open and I advanced to make sure she took it.

"I suppose you should make an early night of it," she said dismissively. "Some of us are showing our age and need their sleep. Tomorrow is a big day, after all. The last day."

Magna stepped up on the window ledge and out the window like there was another step to receive her. There wasn't, but she committed with both feet and was free-floating in place a moment later, brandishing her stick-and-bone talisman. She pivoted to face me.

"As for me... I'm going to drift to the next window over and see if your friend is still awake and wants to play."

"Or I could just hold onto this for you tonight," I said, reaching outside and plucking the flight totem right out of her hand.

"Son of a b..." was as far as Magna got before she plummeted down the side of the building and landed flat on her back across the main-entry overhang with a tremendous thud.

"See you tomorrow!" I called down to her far below and cranked the window shut.

Magna didn't respond—either pissed off or horribly injured. It would take her a while to peel herself off the flattop. Especially if it was surfaced with gravel.

"Another murder victim?" Denise asked me as I slipped under the covers.

"She'll be fine," I said. "Short of getting burned at the stake, Magna Aslaug Holgersson abides."

I stuffed Magna's hideous totem in the end-table drawer next to the Gideon bible and turned out the light.

"You're a real bastard, you know," I heard Denise hiss at me in the dark as soon as my head hit the pillow.

"You have no idea."

"And you know what? You're proud of it. I can tell, you miserable shit."

If Denise was building up a head of steam, the insults could go on for hours, and I had another full day of making nice with passing acquaintances and total strangers waiting for me, bright and early.

"You want me to perform another ritual to take your voice away again?" I warned. "Because I'm sure I can call the front desk and get the number for a 24-hour barbecue-rib joint that delivers."

"You take my life, you take my voice! What else are you going to steal from me?"

Denise was off on another one of her accusation binges, but it wasn't up to her usual standards of vitriol. Her heart didn't seem to be in it anymore.

"You saw the thing at the rail yard," I reminded her. "If I hadn't done what I did to you, that would have been your fate. Better off all-the-way dead than undead."

Denise shut up, but not for long.

"I'm not going to thank you for killing me."

"Of course not," I said, and closed my eyes.

I thought she was done, but Denise had something else on her mind. It came out a minute later.

"But thanks for not letting me turn into one of those things."

"You're welcome," I said.

If Denise spoke again, I missed it. Sleep took me quickly that night.

Chapter Eighteen

Closing Ceremony

"HERE," I SAID, tossing Magna's totem onto the food-court table, "your twiggy, bird-head dollie thing."

A message from the concierge had informed me that Magna was expecting me at one of the eateries on the second level of the convention hall, overlooking the bustle of the floor below. I thought she might be waiting in ambush, looking to take revenge for last night, but she was too busy having breakfast.

"Did you sleep with it tucked under your arm like a teddy bear?" Magna asked, collecting her property.

"No I did not."

"Because that could have been me in bed next to you instead."

"I put it away someplace safe," I assured her.

"You didn't sleep with it under your pillow by any chance?" she asked hopefully. "Because then I'd own your soul."

"I didn't do that either."

"Pity."

I wasn't sure if she was being serious. I could rarely tell.

"Would that have really transferred ownership of my soul?"

"Nah, I'm just messing with you. Besides, I already own your soul, Rip. I keep it in a lovely clay jar back at my condo."

"Sure you do."

Her plate was stacked with enough greasy bacon and sausages to stop a heart at thirty paces. It was one of the most egregious examples of bad convention food I had ever witnessed, and none of it looked fit to eat. But Magna was never health-conscious. Whatever atrocities she subjected her body to, she'd never suffer any long-term consequences. A new trade-in or upgrade was always one human sacrifice away. She probably already had her eye on a spare or two.

"Last night," she said, after watching me dig into my comparatively modest meal of toast and coffee. "That wasn't funny."

"On the contrary, I thought it was hilarious."

"You could have really hurt me."

"After all the times you killed me? You had it coming."

"I was up half the night stitching my skin back together where it broke open. Lucky the front desk had a sewing kit I could borrow."

Magna rolled up one of her sleeves and showed me where the fall had split the skin in a spiralling pattern that disappeared up the arm of her dress. I imagine, after her pancake landing, the situation was similar all across her body. And I didn't feel the slightest bit bad about it.

"I guess they didn't have a great selection of thread," I noted.

Magna's elaborate stitchwork had been done in bright orange, hot pink, and lime green.

"I chose these colours. I think they're festive."

"Did you come up with something worth saying to me today, out in public, or am I due for another line of bullshit?" I asked.

"Oliver Franck is dead," she stated.

"Word has spread."

"It wasn't the chirping flock gathered here," Magna assured me. "I watch the news. 'The Canning Town Charnel House.' Anything to do with you?"

"Why would it?"

"Oliver was your mentor."

"He *was not* my mentor."

"Sure he wasn't," she said. "It must sting, losing him."

"I was there. I saw what did it to him."

"I know you were. There's a police sketch of a person-of-interest. Not Oliver's poor zombie slave in lockup, but you, sans the new look. An eyewitness probably couldn't pick you out of a row of suspects now, but I recognized you straight off. Be glad they're only looking locally and not an ocean away."

"I saw what it did to him, and then I saw what it was," I said, the memory still not sitting easily with me.

"Care to describe it?"

"Not while I'm eating."

"I've been trying to piece the sequence of events together," Magna said, "but the news media has all the facts twisted around in favour of catchy headlines. It takes a lot of cross-referencing and insider knowledge to figure out the specifics. It took his head, right? Ate his whole noggin, in fact."

"Oliver was trying to keep something at bay."

"Had he heard about the others?"

"The other necromancers, you mean?"

Magna, as usual, was well informed.

"That one I got from the chirping flock," she said. "What's the count up to? Ten? A dozen? More?"

"I'm next on the hit list. There's a new necromancer in play. Jeevak Menahem. Ever hear of him?"

"Isn't he that property-developer real-estate tycoon?"

"And master over death and decay."

"I guess even the super-wealthy need to moonlight."

"He's no amateur," I said. "He's the real deal. Being a tycoon is the fallback job."

"What does he want with a small-potatoes necromancer like you?"

"We're up for the same position and he doesn't want the competition. *Any* competition."

"So he's the one eliminating all the necromancers—including, apparently, Oliver."

"What's your interest in this?"

"I want to help."

"Sure you do."

"Maybe I don't want to see Rip Eulogy torn apart and eaten alive."

"Sweet of you."

"If anybody's going to do that, I'd much prefer it be me."

"Less sweet of you."

"Did you commune with Oliver's remains?" Magna asked, assuming the obvious move.

"I found what was left of his brain," I confirmed, "which wasn't much after it passed through some ravenous monster's digestive tract. I got one word out of it. A final thought. But it was gibberish."

"Try me," she said. "I was always the one with the vocabulary."

She was indeed—learned from many cultures over many years.

"It was something like 'gwyllgi,'" I said, hesitantly repeating my final word of communication with Oliver. "Don't ask me for a spell check on that. It sounded like nonsense."

"Of course it sounded like nonsense," Magna agreed. "It's Welsh."

"Is it a name?"

"More a term. You should brush up on your Welsh folklore."

"I should," I agreed, guessing, correctly, that I wouldn't.

"The Gwyllgi is one of the great black dogs of the British Isles. The myths go back thousands of years, and sightings of these dogs have occurred in every corner of the U.K. The various cultures always have their own name for it, and there's some question as to how many of these dogs—phantom hounds more like—exist. There could be a dozen different ones. There might only be one that gets around."

"Ever hear of one leaving the Isles? Crossing the ocean, for instance."

"No, it's strictly a local legend."

"Because I brought one back with me."

"What?" she asked, unconvinced. "Like a souvenir snow globe in your carry-on?"

"More like a curse that's been sniffing after me for the last few thousand miles."

"Rip, what the hell did you do to get a gwyllgi on your tail?"

"I didn't do anything!" I protested. "This happened after a very long period of inactivity. I hadn't stepped on anybody's toes in years."

"Except this Jeevak Menahem guy."

"My disagreement with him only went down after I got back."

"Maybe he knew you were coming."

"Maybe," I said. "Probably. But no necromancer can order a hound of hell to do anything, least of all kill for him. They're animals, and not even dead ones."

"A gwyllgi doesn't just decide to come after you all on its own. It certainly doesn't follow you halfway around the globe. Not unless someone is commanding it to do so."

"Who issues orders to a hellhound? Are you telling me there's some sort of hellhound whisperer with a grudge?"

"What precautions was Oliver taking?"

"He was laying salt wards at the doors, front and back."

"Salt? You don't keep a gwyllgi out with salt."

"He was keeping something out with it. At least until the ward got dispelled."

"I won't ask who did that."

"There was a miscommunication."

"Maybe there was something else trying to get in. To scout out the scene of the crime-to-come."

"You mean for the gwyllgi, before setting it loose?" I suggested.

"Like it needed to choose between one necromancer and another."

"Oliver had to have been the target," I said.

"Well he's certainly the dead one. And you're still here. Head and all."

"I guess I wasn't worth the effort."

Magna patted my hand comfortingly.

"Haven't I always told you you're not?"

"Thanks," I said, devoid of any actual gratitude.

"I miss this," she said of our spitballing session. "I really do."

It had been a long time since we'd had a meeting of the minds to try to figure out a puzzle.

"What ever happened to us?" she wondered.

"You cheated on me," I reminded her.

"I did no such thing."

"I was there, remember? I walked in and saw you at it."

"I was performing a ritual."

"You were fucking a goat."

"I was fornicating with a manifestation of my patron lord, king of the nine hells, Asmodeus."

"Fucking. A. Goat."

"Tomato, to-*mah*-to," she said with a dismissive eye roll.

I didn't want to argue with her. It's not like there was anything to gain, any sort of relationship that stood to be strengthened or saved. It was over between us. Plus, she always won all our arguments. She had a way of getting in the last word. Usually by killing me.

Θ

By the time Day Three was winding down, the mood on the floor had become a lot lighter. The desperate rush everyone felt to hustle their wares while business was hopping drained away. As soon as the first booths started to pack up, looking to get a head start for the trip home, the casuals took their cue to make their last rounds and final purchases. I spent those hours passing out my card to contacts and co-conspirators who were no longer stressed about how well they were going to do at the annual event. By then they already knew, for better or worse, where their bottom line stood, and whether this year's appearance had paid for itself. Good news or bad, they were more receptive to my pitch—either because the wad of bills in their cash box promised to see their fiscal year off to a good start, or because they were hoping to salvage something from a disappointing show. A promising contact on the necromancer front was either icing on the cake, or a better-than-nothing consolation prize.

It helped that I was a rare bird, with little competition that year. One of only three necromancers present that I knew about, I was confident I was the big fish in that tiny pond. Content I'd stuffed my card into all the pockets I could, I found my two colleagues chilling out by a booth that was being rapidly disassembled by the operators. It had specialized in parchments made from a wide variety of natural fibres and leathers including, it claimed, human flesh. I recognized the human flesh as pigskin straight away, but who am I to police a bit of false advertising? If customers wanted to pretend they were jotting down their next doodle, love letter, or laundry list on somebody's back or belly, the shop was letting them have their fun without breaking all sorts of federal laws about trafficking in human remains.

Each sheet vanished down a tube as they were rolled up, one after the other. If Khalida Swanson or Paul Berrer were there for any last-minute buys, their selection was narrowing fast. But neither of them was paying attention to the parchment-shop departure. Khalida was on a tear, commiserating about a common necromantic pet peeve.

"I know! I hate it when they pull the brains out!" she exclaimed. "What the hell for? I know some people, you're tempted to check if they have one at all, but why not just put it back once you're done?"

There were others involved in the group conversation, but Paul alone understood her complaint. Nobody else had the same sort of experience dealing with body parts and organs. Even so, I knew Paul and Khalida's curriculum vitae ran short compared to that of the old guard. All the heavy-hitters were dead and gone. It would take years for new talent to come up through the ranks and replace them, if the world even lasted that long. Such a poor showing was enough to tempt me to take on an apprentice.

"Rip!" Khalida waved me over when she spotted me.

I squeezed my way through and joined the summit.

"How long have you been here?" she asked.

"I got in yesterday," I said.

"Were you too busy competing with me to say hello?"

Khalida and I had worked a few cases together, when time was short and the bodies were stacked high. Sometimes it pays to have someone share the workload. Sometimes it's just nice to have another pair of hands to help you dig up a grave.

"I'm kidding," she said, slapping me on the shoulder before I could respond. "I've been giving seminars the whole show. Pays better than any work I'm likely to scrounge up here."

Seminars. I might have tried to grab that gig myself if I'd thought of it earlier. Not only is it a way to get yourself in front of potential clients, but you can earn a paycheck for doing it.

"Did you catch my talk by any chance?"

"No," I admitted. "I was too busy making the rounds. What was it about?"

Khalida handed me a creased and dog-eared copy of the convention program, flipping to one of the pages that was heavily marked in ballpoint pen.

"Death, Dying, and the Digital Age," I read aloud.

"Not everybody today wants to get elbow-deep in corpses," she said. "Not if there's an app for that."

"I'm sure you have your finger on the still pulse of the future," I agreed.

"You're staying for the party, I hope?" Khalida asked.

"I can stick around," I confirmed. "I'm travelling light."

Most of the hall was bound to clear out before the night's final festivities got underway. A lot of the vendors were more interested in the quick cash they could make, than participating in the bohemian after-hours activities of practitioners legitimately involved in the scene. There would be fringe magic shows of tricks that ventured into R-rated territory, incantations that hopefully wouldn't summon anything dangerous, and a certain amount of public nudity for ritualistic or exhibitionist purposes.

"Are there any surprise guests on the schedule?" Paul asked hopefully. Sometimes notable occultists and minor celebrities popped in for a visit during the closing ceremonies, when they were sure there would only be friendly insiders to greet them, and no civilian autograph hounds who would badger them because they vaguely remembered seeing them on television once. One year I'd brought Wilbur along for just such a purpose, and he'd been a big hit for those who remembered his act. But then he was eclipsed by some idiot with stupid hair and dumber ideas about ancient aliens.

"Not that I'm aware of," I said.

Paul looked disappointed, but Khalida didn't even hear me. She was too busy staring at someone who had just entered the hall, parting the sea of diminishing attendees.

"Oh shit. Who let him in?" she said.

I turned to follow her troubled stare and realized there was a special guest after all. I'd all but forgotten about him.

The sun must have been down because Marin was diving into the deep end of the social pool, just as I had promised him he could. Most people were ignoring him, figuring him for another freak in a strange costume and purposely gruesome makeup. But Khalida knew a real vampire when she spotted one. Paul was right behind her on the uptake.

"Oh shit is right," he said. "Tell me that garlic-braid shop hasn't already packed up and left!"

"Um, I hate to admit this," I said, "but he's sort of with me. And forget the garlic routine. He loves the stuff."

"Wow," Khalida noted, "I've never seen one of *them* behave around so many potential victims before."

"I've never seen one behave around a single living human," said Paul.

"Do you have him under control?" Khalida asked hopefully, like I'd come up with some innovation that had eluded our profession for centuries.

"Not exactly," I said. "It's more like he has himself under control."

Marin filtered through the crowd, politely nodding at anyone who caught his eye. No one engaged with him, even though most of them couldn't have known he was the real deal. Something in the most primal parts of their subconscious instinct was warning them to stay the hell away. Marin didn't let it discourage him. When he spotted me, he came right over and unashamedly joined our group.

"All these people!" he marvelled. "I have not seen such a gala, with so many dressed in their splendour, since the throngs would gather in San Marco to celebrate the *Carnevale di Venezia.*"

"He's not talking about a recent holiday trip, is he?" Khalida whispered at me.

"No, he would have been a local at the time. In the 14th century."

"You must introduce me to your friends!" Marin insisted, quivering with excitement. "There are so many humans to talk to...and not kill!"

He added that last part for my benefit. I nodded accordingly, assuring him he was being a good boy.

"Uh, well," I began. "This is Khalida Swanson and Paul Berrer. Fellow necromancers."

Marin bowed respectfully to them both.

"And this is Marin Venerio Grissoni, a very old vampire."

"I am at your service," he said, following my announcement.

"My, aren't you a chatty one as far as..." Khalida casually raised a hand and held it protectively over her throat, even though that wouldn't have stopped Marin from snapping at any number of other vulnerable arteries if he chose to. "...As far as your kind goes."

"I have come to appreciate that humans have so much more to offer than blood alone."

"Oh sure," Paul agreed, "we've got a whole bunch of qualities vampires never seem to appreciate."

"Blood is, of course, the finest," said Marin. "But there is more to humanity than the sweet nectar that flows through their veins, waiting to be released in a torrent of delectable nourishment, suckled through wounds deep and gaping, and savoured at length as it pools and ferments deep within, close to my unbeating heart."

Marin was lost in his memories of past feasts and more recent indulgences. Khalida and Paul waited for him to come out of it. When he didn't, Khalida asked, "Such as?"

"Oh," said Marin, remembering where he was and what he'd been talking about. He struggled to recall the next positive trait that came in at a distant second, far behind his personal favourite. "Um...good sportsmanship," is what he decided on at last.

"Really?" said Paul, unconvinced. "You join a tennis club or something?"

"He's very tall," Khalida noted. "Maybe he has a talent for basketball."

Marin held up his phone for them to see.

"I have played many a competitive match against humans in the cobwebs of the outernet," he explained. "And no matter how many times I win, there is not a single word of bitterness or anger from them in their defeat."

"I'm guessing you have the chat function off," I said.

"There is a function that permits me to speak to my opponents?" Marin said, poking randomly at icons on the screen. "How do I make it work?"

"You might want to leave that off while you're trying to discover the nobler qualities of humanity," I suggested.

"I already know that not all discourse that flows through this invention comes as glad tidings," he muttered. "And the outernet will persist to be enjoyed another day. My concern must be with present prospects. Time is short, and I wish to converse face-to-face with humans while this fleeting opportunity remains. Perhaps next I may be introduced to him..."

Marin started picking out random passing conventioneers who were staying for the after-party.

"Or her...or him...or even him..."

Each in turn recoiled in horror when the vampire selected them as a potential social target. The ones who didn't recognize him as a monster in their midst merely veered off. The ones who did, made abrupt about-faces and strode quickly away in the opposite direction, perhaps thinking better of lingering in the convention centre at all.

Marin optimistically refused to be put off and selected two more victims of his communal desire.

"These specimens appear promising," he said, as the couple in question continued to approach, oblivious to what they were about to involve themselves in. I was reticent to invite the pair into the conversation, but the options for expanding Marin's circle of associates was narrowing, and I took pity.

"Anita, Rufus," I said, "this is Marin."

"Hi," and "Hello," they said politely, not knowing enough to keep their distance.

"He's undead," I added, knowing they'd be interested in his exact classification under their cubbyhole filing system of traits and states of being.

"Ah, you identify as undead," said Rufus enthusiastically. "I identify as dead, and my friend Anita identifies as resurrected. She used to identify as dead as well, but she's been feeling better lately."

"Pleased to meet you," said Anita, offering her hand to Marin.

"I'd keep that to yourself," I interjected, gently but firmly guiding her hand away from Marin's grasp.

"How long have you identified as undead?" she asked, following her thwarted handshake.

"Since the late Middle Ages," Marin replied accordingly.

Anita looked confused, unsure if her new acquaintance was joking, lying, or delusional. I set her straight.

"He doesn't identify as undead. He's undead-undead. For real."

It was Anita I'd managed to affront this time around.

"We are all *really* what we identify as," she scolded me. "I have many friends who identify as undead, and to say that they are anything less is insensitive and offensive!"

"Okay, but Marin here is a bit more undead than someone who just goes around saying they're undead."

Anita was already onboard the outrage express.

"They don't go around *saying* they're undead. They *are* undead," she insisted. "It's a lifestyle!"

"Deathstyle," Rufus said, correcting her terminology.

"Undeathstyle," she countered, seeing his corrected speech and raising him one.

"I'm just trying to warn you, he's not pretending."

That did it. I'd crossed a line I didn't know was there. Stepped over it and straight into a pile of shit.

"It's intolerant people like you who give the community a bad name!" Anita firmly informed me.

"So I've been told."

"You're so fixated on defining everyone by their nature, or their condition, or their form, you can't see them for what they *can* be!" Rufus added.

"Maybe you're right," I conceded. "I tend to get blinded by things like facts and data and proven repeatable history."

I had to admit: Marin had come a long way. He'd tried his very best to deny his true nature and get along with the live-stock. And it had worked out so far, despite my suspicions and misgivings. My prediction of a lapse in his conviction, a return to his addictive pathology, had not panned out. Who could say he wouldn't be able to maintain this run of good behaviour indefinitely? Not me, it would seem.

"Come with us...Marin, is it?" said Anita, gathering him up. "Come and let's get you away from these toxic life-livers!"

With an activist on each arm, Marin was led away to experience a less judgmental safe space. As they departed, he looked back over his shoulder at me and flashed the closest thing to a smile his mangled mouth could manage.

"I made friends!" he said.

"Yeah," I muttered. "Good on you."

"That won't end well," Khalida said.

"You never know," I replied. "Maybe I'll give pessimism a rest. It's exhausting."

"Come on," Paul encouraged us, "the after-hours stage show should be starting soon. I hear they have an escape artist who often fails to escape from his water tank. He travels with a retired paramedic and a crash cart. Might be worth a laugh."

Θ

The Necronomi-Con Follies, as they were informally known, was an annual tradition for attendees determined to stick it out to the bitter end. The opening acts were, by design, dull and alienating, looking to convince any remaining normies to hit the road. A chanting circle usually did the trick. If not, some spoken-word gibberish by way of primal dance cleared the room. Those Wiccans sure knew how to not entertain people. The rest of us would wait them out, rudely ignoring them and talking amongst ourselves, until their allotted time was up. I think they were just happy to have their twenty minutes in the limelight while technicians made sure everything was working right for the subsequent acts more people were likely to pay attention to. Plus, every time they took to the stage, they remained eternally optimistic that maybe this year their antics would manifest something more interesting than yawns and jeers.

As the first of the professional acts tried to bring the audience to order by performing a polished routine of fire-breathing and sword-swallowing staples, Tom found me tucked in with the masses near the edge of the centre platform. I thought he'd be backstage getting warmed up for his set, but he was more

interested in pouring his performance jitters into a sympathetic
ear. It wasn't the threadbare act he'd had to cobble together in
the wake of his missing-prop fiasco that had his nerves on edge.
It was one of the other acts on the roster.

"They're putting me on after The Astounding Balzak!"
Tom fretted. "I can't follow that act! Who can one-up a guy
who lifts weights with his testicles?"

I knew the name. May have even caught the act.

"Isn't he part of that freak, geek, and gimp show?"

"They've been touring the country, getting big-time. I saw
them do a segment on that late-night talk show that comes on
after all the other late-night talk shows. It was around two in the
morning, but it was still mainstream, major-league stuff."

"They put the testicle guy on commercial television?"

"Well, okay, not him. His bit was trimmed out. But the rest
of the group got to do their act, so he's credited by association.
It makes him the most famous performer here, and I have to
follow him!"

I knew how that sort of routine went, and it didn't impress
me. Suspending irons from coat hangers hooked through scrotum piercings wasn't magic any more than circus geeks of old
biting the heads off of chickens or sticking their faces in broken
glass. Compared to that shit, Tom's act was Shakespeare.

"Balzak is a hack," I assured Tom. "Sideshow trash. You can
blow him off the stage. You're The Amazing Barfo, for fuck-
sake! Swallow your nerves and then puke them back up and
show everybody who's the boss of this merry madhouse!"

"Yeah," he said, and added more confidently, "Yeah! I've
got this."

"Of course you do."

"Thanks, Rip."

"You see, hu-man slave?" said the voice in Tom's pocket.
"Your cowardice is for naught! Even the necromancer knows
your degrading carnival exhibition is superior to the other

puerile displays of bodily functions on exhibit for these filthy degenerates!"

"His pep-talk was better," Tom told his stage partner.

As Tom and Moby-Dick returned to the talent pool, I scanned the crowd to see how Marin was doing. He was easy to spot—a gaunt grey head poking out of the rest of the fray that stood no higher than his shoulders. Anita and Rufus were busy taking selfies of themselves with their new marginalized friend, leaning in close for a three-shot, side by side. Marin was doing his best to ignore their exposed throats, so conveniently close to his mouth. They were reciprocating by politely ignoring his stink so uncomfortably close to their noses. It was a grand gesture from everyone, denying basic desires and revulsions in the name of a good trophy shot that would make for bragging rights and like-button hits on social media.

"You brought a vampire," Magna said, sneaking up behind me and reengaging in conversation like no more than a moment had passed since our earlier talk. It made me jump, which was, I'm certain, entirely her intention. "I thought you were kidding me last night."

"He brought himself. But we're...acquainted."

"You're full of surprises, Rip Eulogy. Making nice with the nosferatu."

"This one is a unique case."

"He comports himself well," she said, watching how he interacted with Anita and Rufus at the back of the gathering—stiff, awkward, but refreshingly devoid of acts of murder. "Excellent table manners."

By then, The Astounding Balzak had been introduced and had taken the stage. He wasn't wearing pants, as might be expected, allowing for his pendulous and rather calloused testicles to dangle freely. A midriff wrap, not unlike a sumo wrestler's *mawashi*, allowed him to tastefully tuck his penis out of sight, for either modesty purposes or an effort to not be gratuitously naked. His act, by its very nature, involved nudity, but there was no need to be obscene about it. This, we were assured, would be a classy set, before he proceeded to refresh some of the piercings in his scrotum by nailing flaps of excess flesh to a block of wood.

"Try not to look like you're enjoying this quite so much," I cautioned Magna. She was one of the few observers who was smiling rather than wincing.

Even Balzak's battered and abused organ was not immune to suffering fresh damage. From my vantage point, I could see a single drop of blood trickle from the renewed piercing and dribble down the side of the block of wood. Most people in the audience would have been too far away to notice it, but I knew one among them who would have spotted it from a mile away. I turned to check on Marin, and sure enough his eyes were wide and fixed. His tongue flickered out between his teeth, like a snake tasting the air, and I thought he might rush the stage. Instead, he averted his eyes, just as many others around him were doing. Unlike the others, it wasn't out of shock, empathy, or disgust at the act of self-abuse. It was out of a commitment to restraint.

"Excellent table manners indeed," Magna reiterated, following my gaze and recognizing the degree of control the vampire was exhibiting. "Your pet is keeping it together. You've trained him well."

"I didn't train him at all. This is all him."

That seemed to trouble Magna. Her jovial mood in the face of a man inflicting terrible acts of sabotage upon his own genitalia drained away as she became lost in her thoughts. It was only the appearance of Tom, several long and excruciating minutes of testicular trials later, that drew her back out of whatever she was turning over in her head.

"Ah," she commented, "your cute friend is up."

"Don't expect to find him so cute after you see his act."

There was nothing cute about The Amazing Barfo's tricks, but I'll be damned if they still didn't have the ability to amaze. His act had evolved since I last saw it. And it was, I had to admit, refined and multi-layered. Tom was no longer a silent performer, but engaged in witty repartee with his stage partner in a straight-man/funny-demon banter reminiscent of the golden age of Lewis and Martin. They traded quips and insults between masterfully performed stunts and astonishing feats of regurgitation. Even without his more advanced props, Tom had the audience in the palm of his hand, manipulating the mood in the room up and down as easily as he did foreign objects introduced to his esophagus. Even rudimentary regurgitation tricks, like linking a handful of loose paperclips in his stomach and bringing them back up as a chain, was done with a finesse that would have put his competition to shame, even in the heyday of vaudevillian regurgitators a century earlier. I'd gone hard on Tom when I first met him, but now I found myself applauding each successful feat. And it wasn't to be polite. I meant it.

I noticed Magna wasn't joining me and the rest of the appreciative crowd. She was no longer even watching the performance. Perhaps, I thought, after seeing him vomit up one thing or another a dozen times in a row, Magna's casual attraction to Tom had wavered, deciding her next fleeting act of sexual fulfillment might better be sought elsewhere. But her next words told me what was really on her mind.

"Tell me how this well-disciplined vampire came into your life."

"What? Now? We're in the middle of Tom's set."

"It's important."

Magna was serious, which was unusual for her. There was no charm, no irony, no whimsy in her tone.

"He came to me for help. We have a mutual problem."

"What mutual problem?"

"It's a long story. But the pressing issue is that other necromancer I mentioned, Menahem."

"He doesn't want you competing with him. I get that. What's his issue with the vampire?"

"Jeevak Menahem is collecting them. Draining them. Drinking their blood. Trying to sap their powers and become immortal, one sip at a time."

"He wants to *be* a vampire."

"Or something close to one. Without the negative side effects."

It was a theory that had come up more than once among occultists, and had even filtered down into popular literature. The idea that vampirism could be attained without the inconvenience of dying—and in so doing, the worst aspects of the condition avoided. But it remained only a theory. Given their formidable strength and savagery, vampire blood wasn't exactly easy to come by. And the idea of someone actually tasting it, let alone drinking the foul stuff, was something I'd only recently heard of.

"Of course he wants the blood of a master vampire."

"More power to be had," I agreed.

"It would be the quickest way to achieve mastery. A shortcut that would skip countless years of effort and experience. Your vampire there, he's old?"

"Old enough to have learned how to control himself."

"A century? More?"

"Five hundred years plus."

"A master," Magna said in a hushed tone. "Do you know how rare they are?"

"I guess that's why Jeevak Menahem wants him so bad."

"But he doesn't have him. Not yet. He hasn't drained him. Hasn't stolen his power and become a master himself..."

"Well, no. Obviously not," I said, noting that Marin remained free and fit—or at least as healthy as could be expected for someone with no vital signs and atrophied organs.

"Oh, you damn, blind idiot! Don't you see?" Magna exclaimed, loud enough to distract those around us from the show. Even Tom was momentarily thrown off his pacing as he spat up a wristwatch he'd just reset to Greenwich Mean Time inside his stomach.

"What am I missing?"

"Any run of the mill vampire can transform into a wolf. It takes a master to do a hound from hell. Like a gwyllgi, for instance. How many master vampires are currently right under your nose?"

"I already thought of that," I said, trying to allay her fears. "Marin's no devil-dog, no hellhound. He does fog, mist, light hazes. He hates transforming into animals. He says it's degrading."

"Where does he stand on commanding them?"

"Commanding them?" I repeated back at Magna with a chuckle. But my laugh sounded hollow to my own ears.

Even the youngest vampires, still tooling around on their vampiric training wheels, can command a variety of lowly vermin—not that issuing orders to cockroaches and flies will accomplish much. But this influence grows over time, and increasingly the proverbial children of the night respond. Summoning a colony of bats or a murder of crows presents more intriguing possibilities, particularly if they're whipped into a frenzy and set after someone. By the time they graduate to lording over entire packs of wolves, the strategic uses against victims or enemies become self-evident. A talented vampire, less than a century old, might manage that. Where then do the limits for one many times older than that lie?

It didn't seem possible. The sequence of events didn't match up. Marin was already shacked up in my casket thousands of miles away at the time Oliver was getting eaten alive by a gwyllgi. Harder to reconcile in my head was the betrayal. For a cold-blooded mass murderer, someone who must have killed and consumed thousands of people over the course of his long afterlife, he came off as a pitiable innocent—as much a victim of his curse as anyone he'd butchered to sustain himself. Even I had been drawn in, won over, perversely charmed, despite my best efforts to maintain and foster my natural revulsion.

My attention shifted from the stage, and my eyes leapt from one face to the next—all of them human. Marin was nowhere to be seen, either poking above the masses, or lurking below the sea of heads. It took me a few moments before I found Anita and Rufus, but their new undead representative no longer stood between them. The surrounding bodies were packed together so tightly, there was only one way the vampire could have extracted himself.

I dropped to the floor and looked through the forest of legs. It was hard to say for certain, with a view that was completely obscured not twenty feet into the tangle of limbs, but there appeared to be a certain haze clinging to the convention floor. Standing up straight again, I stood on my tiptoes and spotted a tall figure heading for a set of double doors at the far end of the convention hall, where it was possible to allow access for large display-booth segments or vehicles as big as a pickup truck, depending on the nature of the current booking. It had to have been Marin. He threw open the doors like he was leaving in a hurry, but did not pass through to the service corridor beyond. Instead, he stood there, like a posted guard, and waited.

I was so busy looking for Marin, I missed Tom's grand fin-ale. Only the thunderous applause let me know he was done. Glancing at the stage, I saw Tom taking deep bows in the face of the adulation, removing my top hat and making sweeping motions with it at arm's length. As soon as the clapping and hoots diminished slightly, Tom threw his head back and extracted Moby-Dick's pocket-watch aquarium from the back of his throat. He dangled it on the end of its chain and gestured at his partner with the hat, signalling that it was time for the audience to show their appreciation for the co-star and all the added value he brought to the show. On cue, the adulation ramped up again, higher than ever. If the demon-fish had anything derisive or condescending to bleat at the crowd in return, it was drowned out by the love.

Khalida found me in the crowd, squeezing through with her phone in hand. She was taking this opportunity of a pending intermission to share a great discovery, not realizing I was too distracted to listen.

"Oh my God, Rip! Did you see this? It's so funny!"

She stuck her phone under my nose and swiped through a series of photos that, according to the time stamp, had just been posted online. It took her a few moments to get my attention and force me to focus. At last I recognized the faces on the screen and the all-too-recent context.

Anita and Rufus beamed with their gaping-mouth smiles and hand gestures, bracketing a whole lot of empty space. Captions of "Look who we just met!" and "Our new convention buddy!" weren't stacking the accolades they were fishing for, with no icons or tags of praise. A growing list of confused comments from internet friends amounted to a collective, "Huh?"

"Think they'll be pissed when they figure out vampires don't photograph well," said Khalida, flipping through more convention pics for equally embarrassing postings, "or scared shitless when they realize they were hanging with an actual vampire?"

The screen of her phone flickered and faded, like the battery was struggling to maintain power.

"Dammit, I thought I charged this thing," she said, tapping the screen, trying to provoke the device into being more responsive.

That's when all the overhead floodlights in the hall blinked, fizzled, and went out.

We weren't plunged into complete darkness. In moments, everyone who didn't already have their phones out, recording or photographing The Necronomi-Con Follies, reached for them after a collective groan at the interruption. Hundreds of screens lit up in a row, although the illumination was uneven, like they were all having battery problems. Even as they searched for information related to the power failure—a storm brewing outside the windowless hall, or an accident at a transformer—I realized it wasn't the power that had cut out, only the lights. As Tom and several stagehands fumbled around above us, the sound system was still picking up the jostling noises and amplifying it through the speakers.

I knew what was coming, and I knew where it was coming from. Immediately, I turned to the service doors Marin had left ajar. The area was almost pitch black, but an exit sign over the passage still glowed red. I watched as it, too, flickered and died in turn. Its dim glow was replaced by a much brighter pair of crimson embers, burning directly beneath it. The gwyllgi had arrived.

So fiercely did its eyes light up at the sight of fresh prey, I could make out the figure of Marin next to it, pointing at the oblivious crowd, directing the beast to the flock of lambs. The hall was filled with confused muttering, questioning murmurs. It switched to screams a moment later as the hound bounded across the floor, closing the vast distance in moments, and plowed into the multitude of people with as much destructive force as a stampeding elephant.

I almost wished the gwyllgi's encompassing darkness that followed it wherever it went had extinguished every possible source of light. Then I might have been spared any sight of the ensuing slaughter. From the first impact, people, their phones, and their tablets went flying into the air. It was hard to tell who was who in the silhouetted tangle of limbs and bodies. Occasionally I'd get a glimpse of a face, lit by the digital glow of a nearby device, contorted in terror. Only two people in the room had any concept of what was happening, and I'd immediately lost Magna in the ensuing panic.

For the briefest of moments, I saw Tom leaping off the stage, his hand holding my hat down on his head, as he made a run for it. The gwyllgi took his place an instant later, landing on the platform on all fours with a heavy thud of its pads, and a rending of the floorboards with its claws.

The Astounding Balzak, poor bastard, had no hope of escape. He had been watching Tom's show from the wings and had neglected to free himself from the climactic gag of his own act. His scrotum remained nailed to a sawhorse, and quick extraction proved impossible, with the nearest hammer well out of reach. Under less deadly circumstances, it might have been humorous seeing him try to run away, dragging so much lumber between his legs, but there were too many fatalities happening all around us. Balzak was felled in the first minute of the attack, gored in a fury of blood and bone and wooden splinters.

By the time my eyes better adjusted to the scant light, there were bodies everywhere I looked. The dead, the maimed, were strewn around the hall. The lucky ones only had their throats torn out, or their ribs spread and their chest cavities spilled onto the floor. Others lingered with one or more limbs ripped out, remaining conscious long enough to watch their arteries hose away their lives, as if their terrified, jackhammering hearts were eager to run out of fuel as quickly as possible.

And there, in the middle of so much offal, stood Marin. He wrung his hands and clutched at his collar fretfully. Someone who didn't know him, didn't know what he was, could be excused for thinking he was having a panic attack and might swoon away at any moment. But his eyes had become giant black saucers in their sockets, dilated to drink in all the carnage, and pound all that gory input into his necrotic brain like searing hot nails.

"So much blood! So much blood!" he keened. Not in horror, but in ecstasy. There was no more holding back the passion, the inspiration to kill, the need to indulge.

Anita and Rufus had reunited with him in the chaos and were at his feet, keeping low, futilely trying to remain safe. They clung to Marin's legs like infants seeking protection from a dangerous world at the hem of their mother's dress. They might as well have sought shelter from a rainstorm by hiding under a waterfall. Marin looked down at them, the poor innocents, the well-meaning, the good-intentioned, and set upon them like a starved pig at a trough. I immediately lost track of which jet of arterial spray belonged to who as the vampire tore them open, peeling flesh and muscle from bone, and let his crimson bounty explode out.

I was knocked off my feet by the next wave of runners who didn't know where they were running to. The gwyllgi seemed to be dashing in and out of the fracas, striking a new victim and then vanishing to some other random point in the complex. Crawling along the floor in a direction I hoped was away from any feasting vampires or hellhounds, I came across Paul Berrer's remains. Only the splashes of guttered wax on his smock hinted who it was—there was no face left to recognize. Paul had run a make-your-own-candles workshop earlier in the day and hadn't changed clothes. His wax still smelled of apples, but that was quickly being overpowered by the scent of entrails as his slashed gutsack continued to split open under the weight of intestines yearning to spill free.

"Rip!" I heard a nearby voice in the dark say.

There were enough lost and abandoned phones, still switched on, scattered face-up on the floor, for Khalida and I to find each other. She was close by, lying on her side, immobile. Her neck was twisted in an oddly cocked way, and I thought she may have been paralyzed. But then she became better illuminated by a smouldering red glow inches above her face, and I understood she couldn't move because her entire head was in a vise-like grip, clenched in the jaws of the gwyllgi.

"Rip," she gasped at me, her eyes pleading, like I could do anything to stop it.

I'd seen it before. That unique look of fear that can only be found in the eyes of a necromancer—someone who truly understands death and all it entails—when they know they're about to die. Not part-time die like me, but all-the-way die. Dead-and-buried die. Or, in this case, horribly mutilated, half-eaten, closed-coffin-funeral die. There's no religious solace, no promise of eternal reward to comfort them. They know all they're losing with the end of life, and they understand where they're going. The long loneliness of the ether, the slow fade to oblivion. It's not a happy ending. And, after a necromancing career, having this truth revealed and reinforced day after day, it's suddenly upon them. No more life to live, no more days to look forward to, no more lies to tell themselves about how they might yet find a way to weasel out of this fate that stalks us all. They're out of options. They're no longer practising the business; they *are* the business. Just another pile of dead matter, and a lost spirit that's become uncoupled with its old flesh-and-blood carapace. Their eyes, in that moment, betray fear. And worse: deep, bottomless disappointment.

In the next moment, the gwyllgi bore down with its bear-trap rows of teeth, and Khalida's face cracked open like an eggshell. Her pulverized skull was torn off the stem of her neck and demolished by the pistoning mastication of a beast equally hungry for meat and destruction. The bone plates snapped and popped like brittle wood beams at first, but diminished to low crunches as the shards were reduced to a gelatin paste in the monster's furnace-hot mouth and swallowed in one final gulp.

This I watched in profile, but the single blazing eye of the gwyllgi became two as it turned its massive head and stared right at me. Its slavering lips pulled back and its forked tongue dangled precipitously over its lower teeth, dripping blood from untold dozens of victims. A single step towards me put it only a few feet away from my own fragile, delicious head. I would have run, but the moment or two it would take to get back on my feet would be all the time the dog would need to have at me.

It tried to take another step in my direction when we were both blinded by a hot white light behind me. The effect couldn't have been more dazzling if someone had set off a phosphorous shell at point-blank range. I turned over and raised my arm to shield my eyes from the merciless glare, even as I tried to spot the source. There was a silhouette in the middle of the eruption, humanoid and hovering several feet off the floor.

"Back!" thundered the voice of Magna Aslaug Holgersson, an airborne Valkyrie come to save me from my fate and the best-laid plans of my enemies.

The gwyllgi obeyed reluctantly, backing away from the solar-level illumination it was unable to extinguish, receding slowly into the shadows beyond the reach of Magna's spell, snarling at the witch who was spoiling its overindulgence.

"Get the hell out of here, Rip, I've got this," she said to me, before turning up the volume on whatever magic she was using to pierce the hellhound's aura of darkness. Even at full power, she was only managing to light a ten-foot circumference around her. Beyond that was only unknown black, but I got up and ran into it anyway, trying to navigate by my memory of the convention layout.

It didn't take long to hit a wall. I scrambled along it, feeling for any edges or feature, until I found a door handle. Pulling it down sharply, I let myself into the room beyond. It was small and empty enough to echo. I felt cold tiles against my fingertips until I found another door. This one seemed thin and insubstantial, but I figured two doors between myself and a monster out to eat me, looking to complete its necromancer trifecta of the day, was better than just the one. Past it, I found an even tighter space and nowhere else to go. I thought I might have let myself into a closet until, all at once, the lights in the room snapped on. The gwyllgi, it seemed, had been driven out of range by Magna's assault.

It wasn't a closet I was in, I discovered. It was a single stall. Men's or women's bathroom, I couldn't tell. There was only a single white toilet, and single black hat.

The hat rested upright on the floor, centrally positioned at my feet, unscathed despite how close I'd some to stepping on it in the dark.

It was my top hat.

Bending down to retrieve it, I saw a pair of feet under the divide, in the next stall over. I let myself out of my own stall and went to check on my neighbour. There was no need to knock. That door, along with all the others in the row, hung open.

The occupant was sitting on the toilet. His pants were up, but his guts were out. At some point during the attack, the gwyllgi had burst through the stall door—and an entire section of wall before it—and had eviscerated the man as he tried to hide from its wrath. Why the gwyllgi had gone out of its way for this one victim, when so many more were on offer on the convention floor, was puzzling. I'd have asked the dead man, but his head was missing. All he could tell me for certain was who he used to be. The tuxedo he wore accomplished that much, and announced that another one of Jeevak Menahem's death prophecies had come true.

Thomas Kincaid, The Amazing Barfo, Regurgitator Extraordinaire, Vomitorious Expert, Master of Expectoration, had given his final performance. So it was that a man who had spent his life spiriting away items both rare and common, out of sight among his internal organs, ended his days with those very same trick organs spilled out for all to see, emptied at last of all their contraband contents and secrets.

Part of Tom's lower jaw remained, and I could see a glint of metal around the base of one of his teeth. At first I thought it was a filling, but on closer inspection I found it was a loop of dull silver. I unhooked it and reeled in the chain, eventually drawing a pocket watch and its sole occupant out of the esophageal panic room between decapitation and disembowelment that had spared him.

"A gwyllgi devoured my minion!" decried the demon-fish as soon as he focused his one eye on the remains perched on the toilet seat.

For a moment I thought I heard sentiment, or sadness. But the regret was of a different nature.

"If it was his time to be slain, it should have been by my will, by my own fin!"

"How do you know about the gwyllgi?" I asked.

"I stared straight down its gullet as it tore away my minion's skull. Had my slave not swallowed me when he did, I might be in the beast's stomach now myself!"

"Yeah, but how do even know the term?"

"Fool necromancer! I have existed for thousands of years and have forgotten more about the underworld than you will ever know. The gwyllgi is the embodiment of vengeance! All who see the black dog will soon meet their end."

"Well no shit, if the dog goes and bites their head off the end of their neck two seconds later. That's not an omen, that's a done deal."

"The gwyllgi does not swallow heads as a matter of course! Count the decapitations among the dead and you will see the selective process."

"Why Tom? He was no necromancer."

"More to the point: why not you?"

"I got saved at the last minute."

"By who?"

As if summoned, Magna appeared behind me, looking into the entrails-spattered stall the rampaging animal had left behind.

"Ew," she said casually, too jaded to have her stomach turned by anything, "Anyone I know?"

"This was Tom," I grimly announced.

"Oh," she said, like he had slipped her mind long ago, "your cute friend."

Magna looked at the headless body—mostly headless—perched limply on the toilet.

"Not so cute now," she decided.

"What's the body count out there?" I asked, not really wanting to know the answer. One wasn't forthcoming.

"You think I want to hang around, mixing and matching limbs, trying to get an accurate total? No thanks. I'm checking out and going home. I suggest you do the same."

It was, I had to admit, a good idea. In another five minutes, the place would be packed with more cops, paramedics, and news crews than the sum total of people who had been attending the convention.

"I guess you're with me," I said to the watch-bound fish.

"Very well," he agreed. "You will make a suitable new slave-minion."

Θ

I packed quickly. There was a train to catch, and hopefully the station was far enough away from the perimeter the police were establishing for it to not be delayed by the events at the convention centre.

"Know what time is it?" I asked the only other entity in the room.

"Time you swore fealty to my Lord and Master Dagon, necromancer!" hollered the demon from the nightstand.

"You live in a pocket watch and you can't even tell time. What good are you?"

I considered opening the window and chucking him away into the night. That damned fish could live out his days in the hotel swimming pool below, annoying guests and trying not to get sucked into the filter for all I cared. But losing one companion and being betrayed by another on this trip was enough. Irritating or not, I was sentimental enough to give Moby-Dick a reprieve.

The adjoining door between rooms was open. Tom's clothes and possessions had been left behind, but his trunk was missing. Marin, it seemed, had already vacated the premises. I'd searched the baths and wardrobes of both rooms to be sure, but the vampire hadn't stayed to face me. I called the front desk to see if there were any messages. There weren't, but I did get a report that arrangements had been made to transport a single piece of luggage from Tom's room to a hired car. There was no word on the car's final destination.

The trail looked cold, but Marin had few safe harbours at his disposal. And he knew I'd be coming for him. Me, Menahem, Nocturne. We all wanted a piece of him now, and I was fresh out of pity.

The chaos at the convention centre next door was spreading. I could hear the emergency vehicles filling the street. Increasingly, there was commotion in the corridors of the hotel as word of the disaster spread. There were running footsteps passing my room, staff and lodgers alike. I'd join them soon enough. No way was I going to stick around and play eyewitness for reporters, or linger to go on record with an official statement to police.

Throwing my travel bag onto the bed, I began stuffing everything I'd come with back into it. Toiletries and dirty laundry were mixed together randomly. I wasn't tidy about it. This was a bugout, not a departure at the allotted checkout time. In my haste, I tripped over something on the floor and kicked it under the end table. Just in case it was something important that belonged to me, I took the time to reach under the furniture for it, figuring it was probably only the TV remote. It wasn't. I came up with a smartphone instead—one with a cracked screen.

Marin must have really been in a hurry if he'd left his prized possession behind. Or had he ditched it on purpose? I doubted he was tech-savvy enough to know about the tracking possibilities, but he might have decided he was done with it for other reasons.

On a hunch, I turned the phone on and flipped through his call log. He had been convincing in his act that nothing was amiss when he was first discovered to have been with us all along. Too convincing. Something had happened between then and the slaughter he orchestrated. The log was a long list of Rebecca's calls dating through to last week. There was a long gap of nothing once Marin had taken possession. But sure enough, a single number was listed as having given him a ring the previous night. And Marin, I was sure, figured out how to answer.

There was nothing to do but return the call and see what lay on the other end. I tapped the number and it was picked up after only two rings. Not by a service, but an actual person.

The voice only said, "Is it done?"

"Oh, it's done all right. And it's a fucking mess," I said. "Your mess. As for me, I'm still alive, you son of a bitch. With a head intact and on my shoulders."

"I know," said Jeevak Menahem's distant voice, unsurprised, with no hint of disappointment. "I knew it as soon as you were run through by that foolish child in the church. You were not destined to perish at your gathering, despite my arrangements. But the plans were already in motion, and a couple more dead necromancers still makes it a worthwhile endeavour. Marin did my bidding, and the beast, in turn, did his."

"What did you threaten Marin with to get him to flip?"

"Flip? He's been with me all along. I left him behind in London to take care of a small problem for me. I thought the matter might be decisively dealt with by one of the black dogs of the Isles. Only a master vampire could issue orders to such a beast."

"It was me you were trying to finish off in Canning Town. Not Oliver."

"Oliver Franck was old, tired, used up. Not worthy of my consideration. Magnanimously, I was willing to let him live out his days in retirement, even as I personally laid waste to the rest of his profession. But then I sensed your impending return, and knew he would offer you shelter."

"So you decided to kill him, too."

"His death I foresaw, once I had the notion to arrange it. Your fate was difficult to predict. The body you were regrowing was so insubstantial, I could not yet see how it would die. Had I been able to stay in London longer, I would have known for certain. But my business interests demanded my attention elsewhere, and I could not afford to waste time laying siege to some pitiable row house for months on end. My parting instructions to Marin were clear: make sure the gwyllgi took your head. Franck was a secondary concern. An afterthought. But he was a sharp enough practitioner to sense what was afoot. Even if Marin had been able to mesmerize the old man, trick him into inviting him into his home, the lines of salt would be an irresistible temptation. He would become distracted, lose focus, become engrossed in summing up the grains. And the necromancer would have a chance to counter him. Such a simple barrier kept even a master like Marin away for weeks as he waited for a lapse in security to gain access, and find a way to give the gwyllgi your scent."

"And then the ward was broken."

"Alas, that sealed Franck's end, but not your own. Marin, the worm, had abandoned his post by then. Without me there to keep him in line, he fled. Ironically, he fled seeking you out. He never realized you were right under his nose—that you were the priority target all along. The hound stood vigil, following its last orders. As Marin, its master, had been kept at bay, it followed his example. Once the ward was broken, the beast took the initiative to scout out the property on its own."

"That's two of my close, personal friends you've fed to that thing."

"Collateral damage. If only you'd kept your hat on. I took great pains to have Marin sneak his pet into my tower via the service elevator, just so it could pick up your scent again from that very item."

"All this trouble and destruction, just to see if I'll stay down if some damn dog eats my head off?"

"At the very least, it should kill you badly enough that you'll be out of contention again for a few more years. That will allow me to solidify my position. But I have a theory that getting your head torn off and devoured by one of the great devil dogs of Britannia might do the trick permanently. Don't think I've given up on seeing this experiment through."

"I'm coming for you," I told him, cold as the grave.

"No, you're not," he said. He wasn't threatened in the least. "I am the one coming for you. I have already seen it. It is how you die next."

The line went dead.

Not more than two minutes later, I was beelining through the lobby. Madness was still in command of several city blocks around the convention centre, with people wandering aimlessly, or fleeing in random directions, unsure of what they were fleeing from. Wild tales and contradictory reports abounded, some shouted, others whispered. Press crews were double-parked, blocking traffic, trying to get the story first, even though nobody had any idea what the story was. Only me. Which is why I was walking, bag in hand, the only person who knew where he was going.

Home. That's where I was headed. To take out the trash. Marin first, then Menahem.

One was already immortal and unkillable. The other had designs to become immortal, and claimed he would never die.

Killing them may have been out of the question, but that didn't mean I wasn't going to fuck them up hard.

$$\Theta$$

It seemed a lot of people were going to miss their train. Traffic was so thick with emergency vehicles and detours, nobody was getting through. I only made it because I had just the one bag and didn't even try to hail a taxi. On foot I wove through bumper-to-bumper cars until I arrived on the station. It would have been sparsely populated that late at night. With all the craziness going on, it was damn near barren. I was the only one waiting on my platform.

I was sitting on a bench, taking stock of all that had just happened, when Magna joined me. She didn't come up the stairs like I did. She floated down from the sky, bearing her hideous totem.

"Quite the closing act, wouldn't you say?" she concluded, plunking herself down beside me.

"Taking the train, too?" I asked. Magna and I had lived in the same city for years, but we'd taken pains to never bump into each other if we could help it.

"I'm flying. Obviously."

"Right," I said. "Dress warm. It's a long way and a chilly night."

"What's next for you?" she asked.

"Revenge," I shrugged.

"Against me?"

"Nah," I said. "You I should thank. You saved my butt back there. Or, more accurately, my head."

"Same difference."

I might have replied with some of my own sarcasm, but I wasn't in the mood for banter.

"Don't look so glum," Magna said, nudging my shoulder with hers. "We both survived to fight another day. Hopefully not each other, but you never know..."

"A friend of mine just died," I reminded her. "Horribly. On a damn toilet, no less!"

"This is why you don't make friends with the mortals, Rip. When are you going to learn that lesson?"

"Maybe when I meet more immortals who aren't total assholes."

I made sure the look on my face strongly suggested I was including her on the list of assholes.

The train was pulling into the station. I got up and approached the tracks. Magna called after me.

"They'll just keep dying on you," she reminded me. "None of them last."

"I think you might soon find out the immortals aren't so durable either."

The doors to my car slid open and I stepped up onto the stairs inside, letting my last thought hang in the air long enough for Magna to figure out it wasn't an idle threat. It was a statement that came from certain privileged information that I had and she didn't.

Dire as the warning was to everyone and everything I held dear, I couldn't help but feel a dose of satisfaction when Magna's face dropped and she looked deeply concerned—for the underworld she travelled in, for her own personal well-being. Worry lines became etched in the last young face she had stolen, suggesting her true age, and looked like they might stick.

"What do you mean?" she demanded to know, rising to her feet.

The train's automatic doors slid shut, separating us, and the cars started edging down the tracks with a jolt, quickly gaining speed.

Magna kept pace with the train until the end of the platform. I couldn't hear her outside the portholes, but I could see her mouthing the same words repeatedly, the wrinkles in her face becoming ever more pronounced.

"What do you mean?"

Θ

The redeye to the convention was countered by a daylight trip home. Exhausted, I pulled the window shade down and tried to get as much sleep as I could, refusing the offers of snacks and beverages from the steward. There were even more empty seats on the return trip than there had been going, but it was the vacancy next to me that weighed heavily on my conscience. Tom had died in my place, and that was never going to sit well with me.

The sun was set again by the time I got in. Rebecca was in bed, and I was eager to join her. The bright compartment on the train, the jostling on the tracks, and the recent loss on my mind had not helped me get much rest.

Brushing my teeth, I left Moby-Dick and his pocket watch resting in a glass of water next to the sink, soaking off the remnants of Tom's blood and gastric juices. Troubled as I was by his sudden death, haunted by the image of how I'd found him, the aquatic demon seemed just as affected in his own way—though his concerns were purely selfish. He wouldn't shut up about it.

"I watched the light flood in through his severed neck hole as the beast took his head," he said, relating the story yet again. "An ignoble end for my hu-man meat slave, perched atop a toilet, cowering in fear. But so was it foretold. Rest assured, necromancer, you will make a fitting minion in his stead. Perhaps you will even demonstrate yourself to be an improvement as you serve your new master."

"Right," I said, finally having heard enough on the subject. "Speaking of toilet-related departings..."

Setting sentimentality aside, I lifted the watch out of the glass of water and dangled it over the bowl. Satisfied I was on target, I dropped it with a substantial splash.

"You cannot do this to me, simpering hu-man!" the fish complained through the few inches of toilet water. "For I am Qix..."

The flush drowned out the rest of whatever he had to say. I'm sure it wasn't anything important.

Chapter Nineteen

Ebb and Flow

NIGHTMARES. All night long.

My tossing and turning had driven Rebecca out of bed early. As I staggered out into the living room, yawning and scratching my way through what was bound to be a rough morning, I found her sitting tensely on the couch. She wasn't alone.

"Look who's here to see you," Rebecca said pleasantly, through gritted teeth and glaring eyes. "Your friend dropped by for a visit."

"Hello, Mr. Eulogy. Did you have a good trip?"

Sunder Lone was on the other end of the couch, a beverage in his hand that Rebecca must have offered trying to be a good host—hoping it might get him to be a good guest.

"Is that coffee?" I asked.

"Decaf," said Rebecca.

"Good God, why?" I groaned.

"Because it's not a great idea for some of us to be caffeinated," she said, her teeth grinding twice as hard, her head nodding towards our visitor.

I turned left into the kitchen to fix myself something that would help me wake up. Rebecca launched off the couch like a coiled spring and joined me.

"There is a mass murderer in our living room," she hissed, in her lowest possible angry-voice.

"The kid?" I asked innocently.

"That's him though, isn't it?"

"Him who?"

"The..." she searched for a term. "...stabby-stabby killer dude!"

"He's put all that behind him," I said. "He's reformed."

"He's still murdered dozens of people!"

"Not *dozens*. Not even *one* dozen. Eleven," I clarified. "Eleven confirmed victims."

I didn't mention the unconfirmed ones that had come up in passing conversation. The lowballed total didn't comfort Rebecca any.

"Didn't *you* make for an even dozen?"

"That didn't stick," I said of my own untimely murder.

"What is he even doing here?"

"Well, obviously, you buzzed him in. Which is something I keep warning you about."

"No, I mean why is he trying to hang out with you?"

"I'm offering guidance to the lad. I'm teaching him the ropes."

"Oh my God, you're mentoring the psycho."

"I am not..." I started to insist, but thought better of getting into a battle of semantics so early in the morning. "I am *sort of* mentoring him. He'll learn a few basics, enough to know how not to kill the civilians, and I'll send him on his merry way."

"I don't like it," Rebecca said, glancing nervously over her shoulder.

"Besides, some extra help around here would be nice. Eulogy Undertakings could use an intern."

"So long as he's an unpaid intern," she said in her capacity as upper management, bending to the demands of the work force.

"I'll see if I can get Gladys to expense him a few bucks to keep him in ramen noodles and beans. He already has the cheap-rent part covered."

"You want to mentor him, do it off-site. I don't want him hanging out here. He gives me the creeps."

"Don't be racist," I said.

"Albinos aren't a race. And that's not what creeps me out about him. It's his résumé."

I tried to continue my foraging mission in the kitchen.

"Keep him amused for a couple more minutes while I warm up a stale muffin and make some real coffee."

"*You* entertain him. I have to pee," Rebecca announced. "I've poured two pots into the both of us, making small talk, waiting for you to get out of bed!"

She left me to it, so I put my muffin and joe on hold.

"Good news, kid," I said, getting back to Sunder, "you're hired."

"I didn't know I was applying for a job."

"I hope you got a charge from all that decaf, because you have a big first day ahead of you."

Behind the bathroom door I heard the toilet lid clack against the water tank. A moment later there was a tremendous shout.

"Wanton fleshpot! I have less than no desire to witness your puckered sphincter poised above me as the Sword of Damocles!"

Rebecca stormed back into the living room a moment later, refastening her pants.

"Rip! There's a fucking demon in the goddamn toilet!"

Sunder winced at the blasphemy, but politely stayed out of it.

"What have you been eating?" I wondered.

"What is it doing here?" she demanded.

"I guess the water pressure in the building isn't high enough to flush that hunk of metal away."

"No, I mean what is it doing *here?* In our apartment! I had enough of Qixxi-whatthefuck when I was seeing Tom. Why isn't he stuffed in one of his pockets or down his throat where he belongs?"

I considered the gentlest way I could think of to break the bad news to Rebecca. Then I went ahead and said it in the most insensitive way possible because I'm no good at kind and considerate.

"Your ex-boyfriend just became a lot more ex."

"Huh?" was Rebecca's predictable reaction.

"Tom's dead," I stated more clearly.

"What do you mean, 'Tom's dead'?"

"It's a pretty self-explanatory statement."

"How do mean, 'Tom's dead'?"

"He didn't make it out of the convention alive."

Apparently she hadn't turned on any devices since the latest news cycle broke. It was undoubtedly fuelling endless radio, television, and social-media chatter.

"He didn't survive a meet-and-greet between a bunch of magicians, pagans, and community-college dropouts?"

"Many didn't. Things didn't go according to plan. Although..." I added, trying to find a silver lining, "I did hand out a lot of copies of the new business card. Unfortunately most of the people who got one didn't survive either."

Rebecca seemed to be in brainlock. She was having a hard time processing what I was telling her, which probably had a lot to do with me explaining it terribly.

"Who's Tom?" asked Sunder, breaking the awkward silence in our domestic drama.

"You haven't met him," I explained. "And now you never will, so forget about it."

By the time I turned around again, Rebecca was back in the bathroom. The door slammed in my face and I heard muffled sobbing a moment later. I guess I'd been kidding myself when I thought she'd take the news in stride. Given how tense things had been between them, I figured any happy memories or positive associations with the relationship had been played out, and there might be a certain degree of relief in not having to deal with him anymore. Obviously I was wrong, as I so often am when it comes to other people's grief.

"Um, do you want to hear the gory details?" asked through the door, and immediately regretted my words. The details were, indeed, gory, and Rebecca probably didn't need to hear them.

"He didn't suffer. Much," I continued. "I didn't see it happen, but given the state of him, I'm pretty sure it was quick. You remember that hellhound that's been stalking me? Turns out it's called a gwyllgi and it stalked me all the way to the convention. Of course, it didn't get me. It got damn near everybody else, but I escaped. So...uh...good on me."

Again my efforts to keep positive were bombing. Rebecca's crying escalated and became a lot less muted. More subdued was the voice of Moby-Dick, who was still at the bottom of the toilet, muted by Rebecca's ass that was likely sitting on the lid.

"There, there, you poor, licentious harlot. Do not shed bitter tears from your eyelid orifices."

The fishy demon was keeping it uncharacteristically low-key. It was the closest I'd ever heard him come to speaking softly or trying to be comforting. And, considering his usual tone, the contrast seemed to be working.

"I, too, shall miss my faithful meat-puppet. He was obedient, deferent, loyal. And his stomach lining was as smooth as wet, viscous velvet."

"You really did have a soft spot for him, didn't you?" Rebecca sniffled.

"I took great pleasure in toying with his soul, using his very sanity as my plaything. Had I eventually slain him as I wished, it would have been done respectfully and with care."

There was a long silence as Rebecca composed herself.

"Is that animal still out there?" she asked me. "Still after you? Because I can't lose you again, Rip."

Women. Just when you think you know what they're crying about, they come up with a whole other thing to upset them.

"The dog isn't the problem," I said. "He was just the weapon. Marin was the one holding his leash."

Rebecca was taken aback by this. She didn't say it, but I could tell by the change in her breathing.

"Marin's been in league with Jeevak Menahem the whole time," I explained. "He played you."

"Didn't he play you, too?" she reminded me.

"Maybe. A bit. You he played like a violin virtuoso. Me, he just plunked out a few random notes. But yeah, we both got played."

The door cracked open and Rebecca looked out. Her eyes were red and wet, but I could tell she was feeling the same betrayal, the same lust for vengeance I'd been dealing with the whole trip home.

"What are you going to do now?" she asked.

I didn't want Rebecca worrying about me any more than she already was, so I told her about my plan of action in the vaguest terms I could, while still sounding like I meant business.

"I'm going to put him down."

"You're going to kill him?"

"If only that were possible… But I'm going to put him down just the same. All the way down."

"I'll help," Sunder said, rising to the occasion.

"Rip, it's never been this bad before," fretted Rebecca. "Marin, Menahem, and that dog-thing… Plus Charlie Nocturne waiting in the wings for the whole world to end."

"One unstoppable supernatural killing machine at a time," I told her, like it was as simple as making an itemized to-do list and sticking to it.

"You can't handle all this alone."

"Don't worry. Didn't you hear? I have a killing machine of my own backing me up," I said, jerking my thumb at Sunder Lone behind me. "Much more stoppable, less super and more natural, but I'm reliably informed he slays vampires in his spare time. That should come in handy."

It made Rebecca laugh. Just a little. A small chuckle, short but genuine. And it gave me strength, which was good. I needed it. I needed something. I still hadn't had my damn coffee.

☉

I led Sunder down to the basement, to my storage locker. The casket was still there but, as I expected, Marin wasn't in it. Trying to sleep off the day right under my nose would have been a foolishly ballsy play, even for an entity that can't be killed.

It wasn't the casket I was after. It was something else in the locker. Something I was starting to wish I'd tried using when I first found a nosferatu sheltering under my own roof. Even as we'd shared our first conversation, I'd been mindful that it might still be where I'd left it, within reach. A weapon designed with one purpose and one purpose only: to end vampires.

Using it was a last, desperate resort. Going hand-to-hand with Marin during our initial meeting would have been a quick way to get killed. The thing about this weapon was that it really only worked if you had the element of surprise. Otherwise, it was a heavy hindrance. I didn't look forward to wielding it, but first I had to find it. The clutter in the locker was thicker than I anticipated, and it took nearly half an hour of digging before I finally discovered it right in the back, wedged into a corner where it had been gathering dust for years. If Marin had ever suspected that such an armament lay so near, he never would have bedded down in the same building, let alone the same locker.

Victorious in my search, I came out into the concrete corridor of the storage area and presented my find to Sunder, banging the tip into the floor with a heavy clank. It was an iron spike, nearly as tall as I was, with ridges winding all the way down its length like a screw. The bottom ended in a fine point. The top was capped with a round, flat disc—a head without the groove one might expect to accommodate the giant Phillips screwdriver that would be needed to work it through some heavy timber.

Pleased as I looked to be reunited with this rare tool of the trade, Sunder was unimpressed.

"What is that? A wizard staff? You're a wizard now?"

"Nope," I replied. "Still a necromancer. A necromancer with a big iron rod."

"You trying to attract a lightning strike? That how you raise the dead?"

"I'm not raising the dead today. Quite the opposite."

"What is it?" he wondered, tilting his head to see if viewing it from another angle might give him a hint.

"It's a stake," I said, proudly.

Sunder pursed his lips and blew a raspberry.

"I have stakes!" he said. "Plenty of them. You said they were worthless."

"Those toothpicks you had made are. This, however, is a real stake for staking vampires."

"Size matters?"

I nodded. "As does the material. Wood breaks. Wood rots. This has to be durable enough to hold our boy once we pin him through the heart."

"Where'd you get this thing made?" Sunder asked, probably considering putting in an order if he could.

"I didn't. It was an inheritance of sorts. A pair of nice old ladies who used to travel around staking vampires and other undead creatures left some in storage when they retired."

"Necromancers?"

"Nuns."

"The Lord's work," Sunder nodded knowingly.

"I bought this one at a public auction, cheap. Anyone else bidding was looking to melt it for scrap. I was the only one there who knew what it was for. You have hammers?"

"A couple of mini-sledges. In my pack."

"They'll get the job done. Now it's up to us to do the hard part. We're going to end Marin's career as a vampire once and for all. And it's going to leave him in a state that will make him wish he *could* die. Even more so than usual."

Sunder looked like he was having a crisis of conscience.

"You have a problem with that?" I asked. "You, the mighty vampire hunter?"

"I don't know. He wasn't how I expected a vampire to be."

"Everyone has that reaction the first time they see a real vampire. They're much more disgusting in person."

"No, I mean he was different."

"Freaky?"

"Human."

"You're not going soft on me, are you?"

"Don't get me wrong. He's an unholy abomination before God," said Sunder. "But he was kinda cool."

"Sure, I get it. As vampires go, Marin was the nicest, sweetest nosferatu I've ever met. He was a cuddly blood-drainer if ever there was one." I handed the iron stake to Sunder, and it nearly slipped straight out of his hand from the sheer heft of it. "Now let's go utterly destroy the bastard without so much as a hint of mercy."

"You told me vampires can't be destroyed."

"No. I said they can't be killed. Destroying them though, permanently clipping their wings, fucking them up beyond recognition... Yeah, that can be done. It's just extremely dangerous. Normally I wouldn't attempt it, but I happen to be angry enough to try."

⊖

Finding Marin was strictly a best-guess scenario, but I was confident my guess was on the money. Getting invited into somebody's home is a major get for a vampire, and they don't like to let such a rare opportunity go to waste. Tom's ill-advised party invitation had served to give Marin permission to enter his apartment and make himself at home. He'd already done so once in order to stow away in Tom's prop trunk. I was betting he'd return, trunk and all, to set up shop there—at least temporarily.

Within the hour, Sunder and I were parked in the junkermobile, on another stakeout, this time across from Tom's building. There was nothing much to observe. If Marin was in there, he'd be sleeping until sundown. And I couldn't even remember for certain which window was Tom's. Mostly we were judging traffic—the comings and goings of tenants—and timing our infiltration so that the next time the front door was open, we could slip in before it swung shut again and locked. Unlike Marin, we didn't need an invite, and we didn't want to start buzzing apartments to try to get one. The fewer people who knew we were there, the fewer lies we would have to tell about what we were up to.

"Was this you?" Sunder asked me, as the headlines were reiterated at the top of the hour over his car radio that was more static than discernable voices.

The convention-centre massacre was all over the media, as I knew it had to be. On the bright side, the story was eclipsing all the other massacre stories I'd been involved in of late. The Canning Town Charnel House wasn't even worthy of an update, and the large body count and bizarre nature of the slaughter a few states over had outstripped the bloodbath at The Craven Image. That old news, as far as journalists were concerned, was a mundane mass murder, hardly worth wasting more time on. Frenz was still keeping the most unusual case details from the press, and their attention had shifted without an arrest to report. The convention centre, with all the dismemberments and conflicting testimony as to what exactly happened once the lights went out, was fodder for endless speculation. The most likely explanation yet proffered was a bear attack. How a bear managed to infiltrate a convention centre in the middle of a major metropolitan area was more fuel for baseless speculation, but animal-control units had been dispatched to find the missing mauler and put it down. Local residents were advised to remain indoors until further notice.

"Yeah, that was the one," I admitted. "The job comes with its fair share of mess, but it's never gotten messier than that."

"You think it's possible it could ever get worse?"

"Worse is exactly what I'm trying to prevent. There are forces out there that will be satisfied with a body count no less than every last living thing on earth."

"You're fighting the good fight," Sunder said.

"I guess so," I agreed, not sounding very certain of it.

"That's fine then. So long as I'm allied with the right side."

"I can't speak of moral absolutes," I told the idealistic young man next to me. "We try to do our best, as far as we can tell, with as much as we know. And we hope any gaps in our knowledge or abilities don't let us screw up everything too bad."

"Of course," he replied, like my ambiguous, uncertain take on things was the most rudimentary notion he'd ever heard expressed. "The rest is in God's hands."

"Fair enough. You handle the prayers—that's your end. I'll stick to my own area of expertise. Because if such a supreme being exists, I think I got the short end of the forsaken-stick."

Θ

Walking into a known or suspected vampire lair twice in one week was pushing our luck, but we had two key advantages. Sunder was a low-calorie snack to blood enthusiasts—the human equivalent of a rice cake—bland, unappealing, not worth the bother. And I already knew I'd get out of this scrape alive thanks to Menahem's big mouth. He'd already hinted at my next death, and this wasn't it.

Apartment 704 was at the end of the hall, as I remembered it. I had only ever been there a couple of times before—twice in the same night. Once to pick up Tom after unthinkingly saddling him with a curse that would haunt him for the rest of his days, and again to inadvertently compound the problem. The match made in hell had ultimately panned out into a new and improved stage act for Tom, but I still felt I owed him an apology which was now, officially, too late in coming.

Sunder and I stood outside the door with our respective kits. I had my medical valise, he had his backpack over his shoulder. Being the one with both hands free, he also carried the heavy spike that was so cumbersome, he could hardly wait to set it down and lean it in a corner to give himself a break from the burden.

"I'm not going to have to swing this thing in a fight, am I?" Sunder asked, flexing his hands to get some feeling back into them.

"There's not going to be a fight," I assured him.

"Are you sure?"

"No," I admitted. "But let me put it this way, if it comes down to a fight, we've already lost."

"It's two against one," he pointed out, hopefully.

"I wouldn't give us odds if we had two *dozen* on our side. The only gamble I'm willing to make is that we can surprise him."

"And if he knows we're coming?"

That I didn't respond to. I didn't want to hear whatever answer I'd come up with.

The door was locked, but my picks made short work of the pins inside. The skill came back to me as muscle memory, even years out of practice, even with a whole new set of muscles. I got it open, but only by about six inches. The chain was hooked inside, double locking the door.

"Bolt cutters would come in handy about now," I said, still missing a tool or three.

Sunder was ahead of me, and had already procured a pair from his backpack. The big-brother version of his wire cutters, this one had handles so long, it must have been a tight fit in his pack.

"Unless, of course, you have a snazzier pair in your bag," he added, not sparing me any attitude.

"Be my guest," I replied, not wanting to let him know I'd come shorthanded.

Sunder hooked the pincers around the chain and bore down on the grip. It was a struggle, but the link finally snapped in half and clattered to the floor. It wasn't a big noise, but it didn't help our attempt at stealth any. Hopefully it wasn't loud enough to wake the undead.

We put away our respective gear and collected the gigantic spike I meant to use to finish Marin's centuries-long killing spree. Letting ourselves into the home Tom would never return to, I noticed there had been a spate of redecorating since my last visit. None of it Tom's idea.

All the furniture had been moved. The large pieces were pushed up against windows that already had shades pulled down and curtains drawn. Smaller items like chairs or lamps had been haphazardly shoved aside, forming a ring around a single centrepiece—Tom's garish red trunk.

Even from a distance, I could tell it was sporting one new travel sticker from its last stop. Fresher than the rest, with glossy colours undimmed by scuffs and travel grime, it had edges that were all sharp and intact, making it stand out from the others it was overlapping. It was from this year's Necronomi-Con. Probably the last one there would ever be. A piece of memorabilia added to the collection by Tom himself, who couldn't have known that he was commemorating his final destination.

"Let's get some light in here," I whispered to Sunder.

As quietly as we could, we began to unstack the furnishings from in front of the windows, pushing aside several IKEA shelving units and one entire upended sofa. Raising the blinds and pulling the curtains open brightened the apartment considerably, but we were still on the shady side of the street. Direct sunlight wasn't going to come to our aid.

There was no hint of disturbance from inside the trunk. I'd been keeping one eye on it the whole time, waiting for a bit of noise or movement, but it had remained fixed in place, inanimate. Either Marin was sleeping deeply, or he was awake and poised to leap out at us the moment we cracked the lid.

Using only hand signals and a few mimed gestures, I instructed Sunder to get his sledgehammer and prepare to use it. I retrieved the giant iron spike, taking on the critical responsibility of getting the point on target before Sunder started raining down the blows. With a hammering motion, I reminded him of the instructions I'd given him on the way: hit hard, hit repeatedly, and don't stop for anything until I told him to let up. Sunder nodded solemnly.

There were twin latches on the trunk. Sunder popped one, then the other. Two tiny clicks that could well have served as a blaring alarm to the occupant, sealing our fate. One way or the other, we were committed.

"Now," I breathed.

Sunder drew back his hammer with one hand and flung open the lid of the trunk with the other. I instantly jammed the spike inside, but only hit the wooden base of the box. Sunder swung his sledge, but pulled his first blow and never made contact with the metal-head target. It was obvious, even in the first moment of our assault, that the trunk was vacant.

"Nobody's home," Sunder observed.

Instinctively, I looked up, which is what I should have done the moment we entered the apartment. It would be just like a vampire to cling to the ceiling, waiting for a ripe moment, when the dumb humans realized they'd screwed up, to launch an ambush. But there wasn't anything to see up there either. Maybe a strand or two of spider web between sconces on a light fixture, but nothing creepier than that.

"The trunk didn't get back here by itself," I commented.

"No," said a voice unsettlingly close. "I bore it up to Mr. Kincaid's rooms myself."

Sunder and I whipped our heads around, trying to find the source. It was Marin, and he could have been standing right next to us, so near was his voice.

"I had to scale the side of this edifice and carry it in through an unlocked window. A locked door could not thwart me, but I cannot turn a large vessel to immaterial mist as I can my own body."

There was a large armchair turned to the wall, one of the pieces set aside with no care or concern for proper placement. It hadn't occurred to me it might be in use. Marin poked his head around one side to address us, "I trust no neighbours bore witness to this strange spectacle and complained?"

He'd been watching us the whole time. Tom's television was sitting on a stand right in front of the armchair. Sunder and

I were reflected in the black screen, as was the chair. But not the one who was sitting in it.

We two would-be monster hunters stood frozen in the middle of our failed surprise attack—Sunder with his hammer in hand, me with a full-scale stake probing the interior of Marin's latest bed. The vampire couldn't have failed to appreciate our ill intentions towards him, but he didn't let on. For my part, I tried to maintain the forced casual tone.

"Hey, Marin. What have you been up to?" I asked.

"I have been watching television," he said.

"It's off," I noted.

"I like it better this way," he said, turning back to it. "I grew weary of the cacophony on display in the hotel room. Only the 'off' button on the control device brought relief and drew my attention to the real marvel that is television. It is best appreciated when it is stripped of power. Observing the stillness of the blank screen is comforting to me. It permits me to contemplate the void, and I find that soothing."

"Is that why you ditched your phone? You've upgraded?"

"The novelty of that device, and all it offers and demands, has worn thin. It provides a tether to humanity for one who is isolated, but not all social interactions are profitable, nor desirable.

"You have any particular interaction in mind?"

Marin's sunken eyes, fixed on the blank screen, looked deep inside at all that nothing.

"He called me," he said, after some contemplation.

"I know," I replied. "Why the hell did you answer it?"

"The living take such casual connections for granted, but I had never before received a telephone call from anyone. It made me feel...wanted. I was compelled to respond."

"And what did Jeevak Menahem have to say to you once he got you on the line?"

"He promised he would spare me if I once again summoned the black hound and set it loose at your gathering."

"Spare you from what? You can't die."

"There are fates worse than death. Worse than undeath."

I believed him—believed that Jeevak Menahem was sick enough to invent any number of fates best avoided, especially for an immortal. I'd been plotting one for Marin myself.

"You weren't that animal at the convention centre, were you?" Sunder asked, making the obvious connection.

"As I have said before, I refuse to transform myself into beasts or rodents," Marin grumbled, offended.

"But you can command them, can't you?" I said. "You didn't just let it off its leash. You set it after specific people. Necromancers. And one in particular. Me!"

The armchair suddenly started smoking like a fire had ignited inside it. Marin melted away to mist and vanished into the fabric, spilling out the back side of the seat between the stitchwork of the heavy, worn fibres. When he reformed himself, he was right in front of me, standing at his full height. He did this with such aggressive speed, I dropped the iron stake in surprise. It clunked heavily against the side of the box, but we both ignored it.

"Do you think my wish to ally with you against this common threat was not genuine?" he snarled, displaying more emotion than I'd ever seen out of him. "There is nothing I desire more than to be free of Menahem!"

"What about Charlie Nocturne? Isn't he the one who's really calling the shots? You help Menahem, and then Menahem gets to be his pale rider for the coming apocalypse. The big die-off."

"I have no wish to see such horror come to pass."

"Bullshit," I said. "You said as much in that sob story you strung me. You're tired, you're done. You just want it all to end. But it can't end for the likes of you. Vampires just go on and on.

Unless Charlie Nocturne succeeds and kills off everything living, barely alive, half-dead, or undead."

"It is not an agreement with Nocturne's plan that motivates me. It is a fear of Menahem and what he has done to my ilk. What he will do to me if I cease to be of use to him..."

"Oh, I get it. The allies thing was all fine and good, right up until your boss told you to stab me in the back. I already knew vampires were scum, but you...you're a fucking coward to boot!"

"You already know he has been feeding on others!" Marin raged. "Absorbing their essence, manifesting their powers! He seeks the immortality, the power, the gifts of vampirism without the curses. Already he is beyond the reach of death, and has been able to pass the curse on to human victims. It is in this way that he mints new denizens of undeath. Ones for him to bind and bleed for his own purposes. And I must not be made to join them as his chattel!"

"So long as you save your own ass, right?"

"I promise you, Mr. Eulogy, compelled to obey as I was, I wished you no harm, even as I commanded the beast to seek you out specifically. I had every confidence that your resourcefulness would prevail, and you would be spared the same fate as those of lesser consequence."

"Those 'lesser consequences' were friends of mine!"

"Have I, also, not been a friend to you?" he asked, his calm returning. True sincerity, and a certain humble neediness was written all over his grey features. The fearful, vulnerable human who was buried under the centuries of murder and mischief—the victim who never asked for this unspeakable blight that was feeding on him as surely as it was forcing him to feed on his victims—was still there, reaching out to the one person who might understand.

I considered Khalida. And I considered Paul. Not to mention all those other professional associates and thinly connected acquaintances I knew only slightly and saw rarely. It might be weeks before there was an accurate list of who made it out alive and who got cut down in those moments of dark chaos. I weighed their loss against the existence of one sentient vampire—civilized and restrained most of the time. Cultured and conscientious. Unique in my experience. And undoubtedly an unwitting, unwilling puppet of the true Machiavellian villain in this nefarious masterplan.

I considered them all.

And I also thought of Tom.

And the next words I said were precisely chosen.

"I'm not friends with a fucking vampire," I told Marin.

The words may have been selected with care, but I can't say so much for my actions. My fuming anger boiled over into a single rash act. I threw a punch. Not unlike the one I'd tossed Sunder's way in the church, but this one was born of passion, not calculated strategy. Similarly, I aimed for the nose. Marin made no move to dodge it, impotent as the gesture was.

And, despite my recent practice, I still couldn't throw a decent punch.

This one had a lot more force behind it, but my aim was off. In my defence, Marin was very tall. He must have seemed gigantic back in the Middle Ages, when the average adult height was shorter by several inches. Even by modern standards, he was towering. And as a result, I completely failed to hit my target, falling short of the mark, plowing him in the mouth instead. My balled-up fist, my row of bare knuckles, impacted against his mangled, chipped teeth. I did no damage to that hideous grill, failing to so much as loosen a single chipped tooth. But I tore open my knuckles about as well as if I'd just spent the last ten minutes boxing a sheet of sand paper. They came away bloody and I winced. Not because it hurt—which it did—but because I realized what I'd just done and how damn foolish it was.

I looked up from my wounded hand, into Marin's face, and saw my own blood smeared across his lips. At once, his eyes rolled back in his head like he might faint. His tongue flickered out, probing around the entire circumference of his mouth, lapping up the juice, licking it off his teeth, finding it to his liking.

And then his eyes rolled right back down, like a slot machine coming up jackpot. The pale white vanished, replaced by pupils black and empty, dilated to such an extent, there appeared to be two giant onyx pearls stuffed in his sockets. Those huge orbs seemed to be looking everywhere at once, taking in everything there was to see. But I knew they were staring at me and me alone.

"Oh shit," I said.

Common wisdom about vampires dictates that they have the strength of ten men. That's a load of crap. They have the strength of five men. Half a dozen, tops. Marin moving that boxcar at the yard was a matter of taking advantage of gravity and a slight slope. It had to be. Or so I told myself. Any other explanation for such a feat didn't bode well.

I backed away, sure that Marin would split me in half any second now.

"Let's try to keep calm here. Rational. Reasonable."

There wasn't far for me to go. Something hit me in the ass within a few steps. I reached behind, and felt the edge of Tom's kitchenette counter. It was blocking the way, and Marin was closing in for the kill, looking to follow up his first taste. A whole feast was in the offing—one that would reduce me to a disposable husk that wouldn't stay dead for long. I wondered if my relative immortality would result in Marin infecting me with vampirism. Just what I needed. Another curse.

The distinct possibility Menahem had lied to me about my next death just to screw with me popped into my head. It could produce a whole new vampire for him to feed off of. But I wasn't interested in turning into a lunch for both Marin and Menahem.

"Fuck it," I said, and hopped up onto the counter. I spun around on the seat of my pants, swung my legs over the top, and dove behind the collection of cupboards. Marin lunged at me, but his arms caught nothing but air.

There aren't many useful weapons against a vampire—especially when you have one that's already up and about and after every drop of your blood. The average kitchen is full of tools that might be handy for other combat situations. Knives and forks for stabbing, pots and pans for blunt force trauma. Worthless when dealing with a vampire. And it's not like I had the time to go searching through Tom's pantry for something remotely viable.

Landing on my hands and knees on the linoleum tiles, however, I spotted a promising prospect behind the fogged glass of one counter cabinet. I pulled aside the sliding door and grabbed it.

Popping back up an instant later, I pried open the cardboard box top and flung the loose contents straight at Marin. Yellow chips and shards sailed through the air and bounced off his chest, scattering everywhere, covering everything.

"Ooo! Lookie-lookie! How many is that?" I asked the hungry vampire.

I was hoping to set him to counting Corn Flakes, but Marin wasn't interested. Maybe he hadn't occupied Tom's apartment long enough to appreciate them as an additional mess worth summing. Or maybe his bloodlust was overpowering the most deeply rooted compulsions of his condition. Either way, I was screwed. The supplemental bag of rice I'd brought in my kit, waiting for me across the room, wasn't likely to occupy him either.

"Not in the mood, huh?"

With hardly a glance at the salvo of breakfast cereal, Marin advanced straight through the partition. His upper half remained solid and intact, while his lower extremities briefly turned to mist and came rolling over the countertop before reconstituting themselves on the other side. It was a neat trick. Under better circumstances, I might have complimented him on it.

Out of room, I leaned back across the stove, my fingers gripping the cold burners, waiting to be bled out. Marin was reaching for my throat, ready to tear into it, when Sunder rushed into the kitchenette and grabbed his arm. Even pulling as hard as he could on Marin's coat sleeve, he could barely keep the vampire's split nails more than an inch away from my carotid artery that was begging to be opened wide.

Thwarted for all of two seconds, Marin grew impatient.

"Away, spoiled meat!" he cursed, slapping Sunder, the inferior blood-bag, away like he was nothing. It was a blow even I felt, just witnessing it. Sunder was sent sailing over the kitchenette counter and probably would have snapped his back if the underbelly of the uprighted couch we'd pulled away from the window hadn't broken his fall. Well...half his fall. The momentum bounced him right off the springs and sent him crashing through a glass coffee table. Not a good landing for a bleeder. I expected there was a lot of triage in my future if I survived the next few minutes against Marin's feeding frenzy.

It was time to find out exactly how many times stronger than me Marin was. With nowhere else to go, I tried to swap positions with him, grabbing him by the lapels and pivoting the two of us in place. It was like moving a rooted tree, but Marin was slightly off balance after swatting away Sunder. I was able to swing him around and press him against the stove, where I'd been a moment earlier. It would be nothing for him to shove me off—or worse, pull me closer for a bite. Before he thought to do either, I solidified my position and stepped backwards, off the floor, digging my heels into the edge of the island counter so I could push forward with both arms and legs.

It was enough to get Marin to tilt back for a moment, to have to use his hands to balance himself on the stovetop. That's when I got to roll the dice on what sort of stove Tom had in his apartment. Gas or electric.

I let go of Marin with one hand long enough to reach behind him and start flipping dials. There wasn't enough time to wait for electric coils to heat up. But, as luck would have it, the stove was gas.

With a soft pop, flames erupted from each element in turn, roasting Marin's hands. He felt nothing, even as the scent of scorched flesh filled my nostrils in an instant. He might not have noticed at all if the cuffs of his coat hadn't caught fire.

It was a distraction. Not much of one, but it bought me a few seconds. There was a limit to how much damage the flames could cause him. At worse, Marin might have to get a new wardrobe after wearing the same heavy coat for the last couple of centuries. Again, he didn't have to transform his whole body into mist to deal with this petty obstacle. His arms alone did the trick, vanishing into wafts of vapour. The flames, denied more fuel, instantly extinguished themselves, and the kitchenette was momentarily filled with a mix of smoke and fog.

It was a strategy calculated out of desperation. The stove wasn't a solution, but a means to an end. With Marin unable to use his arms for a moment—a moment during which he had no arms at all—I was able to shove him off the appliance and one station farther down the kitchenette. My real target. My only hope. The sink.

Running water. It's the vampire rule that everybody always forgets about, mostly because when there's a vampire digging into your throat, you're not usually wondering where you can find the nearest river to separate hunter from prey. Like a lot of vampire rules, it's based in fact, but got screwed up in the retelling. It's not that vampires can't cross running water, it's that they won't. There's something about running water—the steady self-purifying flow perhaps—that makes it so damaging to their corrupt form. They can't stand it, they don't want to be anywhere near it, and if they come into contact with it... Well, few have witnessed the results because that so rarely happens. If there's a stream, a brook, a river, or a waterfall anywhere in the vicinity, a vampire will fight to the death to keep away from it. *Your* death.

You can't bring a vampire to running water, but sometimes you can bring the running water to them. It just has to be unexpected. Like a deluge or a flash flood. Or a common tap in a kitchen sink.

I pushed off from the counter as hard as I could, bending the armless vampire backwards over the sink. Committing to the move, I climbed right up on top of him and rammed his head down into the stainless steel basin. Hot or cold water, I didn't care. I just grabbed the nearest faucet and twisted it until the tap erupted at full flow. The blast of water rained down only a couple of inches from Marin's face. He turned to stare at it, and the expression on his face switched from one of mad desire to absolute terror.

Honestly, I didn't have the slightest idea what running water would do to him. Research as I might, I never was able to determine if anyone had ever managed to introduce a vampire to so much as a dribble with any success. Well, there was no time like the present to find out.

But before I could swivel the tap and get it on target, clammy hands were all over my face. Marin's arms had suddenly reappeared, and he was using them. In that split instant, I felt sick feeling his flesh on mine. The idea of what he was about to do to me made me sicker still. My best guess was a coin flip between him merely peeling my face off, or him tearing my whole head off its stump—possibly crushing it between his palms for good measure. Only his panic at being so close to a stream of water kept him from coordinating his efforts and choosing heads or tails.

I didn't wait for him to make the call. Snaking my own arm around his newly reformed one, I was able to reach the tap. Getting a firm grip proved impossible, but I was at least able to nudge it. A nudge did the trick.

Two inches off the mark became two inches over the target. Nothing I'd ever seen before in the necromancy business had prepared me for what happened next.

Most people are lucky enough to never hear a banshee scream. The sound Marin made would have made a banshee call the police to complain about a disturbance of the peace. The flow of water caught him straight in the eye and melted a hole through him like a wave erasing footsteps on the beach. In no more than two seconds, it burrowed through and dissolved a half-moon divot out of the entire side of his head, extending one now-vacant eye socket to the outer reaches of its bone enclave and straight through to the back of his skull.

Marin threw me off like there was nothing heavier on his chest than the air in the room. I landed hard on the kitchenette floor. The impact knocked the breath out of me, and I hit the back of my head hard enough to experience tunnel vision for a few moments. By the time the darkness receded from my peripheral vision, Marin was standing over me. He could have had his way with me—any way he saw fit—if he hadn't been so distracted by the missing chunk of his head.

The vampire staggered away into the living room. His hand hovered over his wound, sheltering it, afraid to touch it. Parts of him were phasing in and out of a corporeal state, like different extremities were trying to escape. But the rest of him wouldn't cooperate, and the timing of each individual limb was off.

My own body wasn't feeling so cooperative either. Having nearly lost consciousness from the impact, now it was arguing in favour of a good long nap. I ignored the tempting suggestion and forced myself to get back up. Grabbing the lip of the sink, my arms did the hard work, pulling the rest of my limp body to its feet. There was something else I thought I saw in that sink. Something that could finish this job before the job finished me.

And then I spotted it. The pullout faucet spray.

I seized the nozzle and yanked the hose out from its base as far as it would go. Squeezing the grip, the tap shut off and redirected the flow. Water spewed from the hose in a wide arc, and I fired it over the counter at the vampire.

Marin must have seen the first droplets coming his way. Or sensed them. His body instinctively responded to the threat, and all at once the various bits and pieces coordinated again in a joint effort. By the time the water hit him, there was nothing to hit. Marin had become a cloud, whipping around the room like its own miniature cyclone. The bank of mist darted back and forth, trying to get out of the line of fire, even as the water passed right through it and soaked everything in the place other than its intended target.

The miniature bank of fog receded, and the arc of water began to fall short. Once he was out of the range of the water pressure, Marin began to rematerialize, transforming back into something that could better defend itself, launch a counter attack, and regain the upper hand. I didn't know how he would come at me next, but I knew he would go all out. And the likelihood of me improvising another effective defence in the next few moments was thin.

Marin was so fixated on me, and what he was about to do to me, he wasn't paying attention to where he was reforming his body. Sunder, ignored and forgotten as a disposable player who posed no threat, had picked himself up out of the ruins of the coffee table and had repositioned himself right in front of Marin. And he didn't come empty-handed. He'd brought the iron stake with him.

Sunder didn't have to ram the weapon home. Marin, distracted by his pain and anger and thirst, reconstituted himself right in its path. By the time his body solidified, it was too late. The point was already imbedded in his chest.

Marin looked down and realized his blunder. The tip wasn't in very far, and it remained well short of his heart, but it was a start. He and Sunder locked eyes, and there was an awful shared moment where neither of them quite knew what had happened or how to proceed next. Marin finally reacted first, placing his hands around the threads of the giant screw and trying to extract the thing that was impaling him.

"Push!" I yelled at Sunder, dropping the hose and racing to join him in the living room.

Sunder charged forward and Marin, normally so strong, so immovable, shuffled backwards against the advance. This wasn't the feeble twig Sunder had stabbed into him days earlier, easily shrugged off. This was a real stake, designed and built to deal with vampires, by people who understood the real lore and knew what they were doing. It already had Marin weakened. Now we needed to disable him completely.

The open trunk was my destination. We'd need to contain the vampire—and a vampire's own box, coffin, or casket was usually the best bet. I shoved it across the floor as fast as I could, on a collision course with Sunder and his skewered catch. The edge of the trunk rammed into the back of Marin's legs and he folded over at the knees, collapsing into the case. Marin's ribcage remained entwined with the screw threads, and his fall nearly dragged Sunder into the box with him.

I scanned the floor and found where Sunder's hammer had fallen. Diving for it, I tossed it to the kid on the fly. There was no time for a more careful handoff. Marin wasn't going to just lie there and take it.

Even in his frightened state, Sunder remained on the ball, young and nimble. He saw the sledge coming his way, spiralling end over end, and snatched it out of the air by its handle.

"Let him have it!" I yelled, and Sunder brought the hammer down hard in one smooth movement.

Marin wailed from the base of the trunk as the stake was driven through his ribs, snapping any in its way, and perforating the first chamber of his dead heart.

"Again!"

The next blow must have worked the tip the rest of the way through Marin's heart. His arms thrashed wildly, but his cries became a high-pitched squeal that rattled the windows and made me want to stick my fingers in my ears. I didn't, only because I couldn't have Sunder follow my lead. He wasn't done yet. There was more that needed to be pierced than some ribs and a heart.

I hurried back to the trunk and grabbed the bottom corners on the side opposite Sunder. My back complained as I lifted my end off the floor, heavy with a full load of undeath.

"Again!" I grunted.

Sunder brought down another heavy blow, and I could see Marin reaching out of the box, trying to scrape the kid's pale face off. The length of the stake kept the vampire at bay by inches.

"Keep going!" I shouted.

Sunder screamed and pounded hard on the head of the stake over and over again, forcing it the rest of the way through Marin's body, out the back of his rib cage, and straight through the base of the trunk. Once I saw that enormous screw point piercing the wood, popping out another inch with each successive blow, I knew we had him. Marin was pinned like a bug in a glass display at the insectarium. He wasn't going anywhere. Not ever.

"Okay, let up," I panted, and slowly set the end of the box back down. The protruding point kept it raised off the floor at an angle, but remained firmly in place.

Sunder backed away. Whatever colour was in his albino flesh had drained away in shock at what he'd just seen and done. I joined him on the other side of the box and assessed our handiwork.

Most of the fight had gone out of Marin, and he was left feebly pawing at the stake head he was powerless to remove. He whipped his head back and forth and growled like a rabid badger, snapping at the air, robbed of his last hint of humanity. The trauma to his eye socket and skull remained, even after his recent transmogrification. This was permanent damage—worse than anything flames or direct sunlight could have inflicted. Compared to that gruesome wound, the stake seemed little more than insult to injury, but it was the *coup de grâce* that won the battle.

"I am so sorry," Sunder said to him, genuinely apologetic. His vocalized regret went ignored as Marin hissed and spat and flailed around.

A stake through a vampire's heart is useless unless it's big enough to stake him *to* something. Only now, in practice, did Sunder appreciate the difference between my stake and his.

"Through the heart like that, he can't escape, can't transform into anything that can get away," I assured the kid. And myself.

We were both exhausted and battered, with a variety of bruises and welts that were yet to fully blossom. I closed the lid of the trunk on Marin, snapped the latches shut, and left him to his eternal fit. Sunder and I took a well-deserved breather.

The kid was gushing profusely from a wide variety of cuts and scratches across his face and hands that had taken the brunt of the coffee-table landing. I found some towels in a linen closet and used them to apply pressure and soak up the blood. The wounds would have been reasonably superficial on most people, but Sunder was a prolific bleeder, and it took the better part of an hour to plug all the holes in him and get the flow to stop. We exhausted an entire box of Band-Aids from Tom's medicine cabinet patching him up. Then we helped ourselves to some leftovers in the fridge, content we'd served the late occupant of the apartment some posthumous justice.

"Are we just going to leave him like that?" Sunder asked over cold chow mein, as we were serenaded by Marin's unintelligible gibbering.

"You want to stay and keep him company?"

"Of course not. But isn't it...I don't know...cruel?"

"You know what's cruel?" I said. "Leaving that thing to walk the earth, sucking innocent victims dry."

"I still feel guilty. It's like he..."

"It," I interrupted.

Sunder looked confused.

"He's not a he. It's an it. And *it* doesn't even have a soul."

"He seemed like a real person to me."

"Don't confuse personality for soul," I said, and helped myself to another egg roll.

We ate in silence and waited for night to fall.

Θ

A couple of hours later, it was dark enough for us to sneak away for the final grim task of our errand. Locking the door behind us, Sunder and I carried the trunk down the hall and brought it to the lobby by elevator. Marin complained the whole way, inexhaustible.

"Pest control," I had to explain to one building occupant who held the front door open for us.

"Nothing that's chewed into the walls I hope," said the man, concerned he might need to break his lease if the building was infested with anything too awful.

"The guy in 704 was breeding unlicensed ferrets," I said, putting his mind at ease.

The wild noises coming from inside the box didn't sound remotely human, or even like a single breed of creature.

"Poor things sound starved," observed the tenant.

"Don't worry," I assured him, "we'll find them a good home."

We arrived on the street and packed Marin into the back of Sunder's car without further incident.

Θ

The thing in the box pounded and howled and clawed at its prison the whole way, but the stake kept him immobilized, and his supernatural abilities in check. This was as good a time as any to acquaint myself with the latest municipal graveyard that had been established to replace the venerable Algonquin Fields. That, I assured Sunder, would be our best bet for a place to dispose of a staked vampire.

"Wouldn't it be more humane to destroy him completely?" he asked, as we drove onto the grounds of the recently established, "Fairview State Cemetery."

I shook my head, already guessing what he had in mind.

"If a bit of running water could do that to his head," Sunder continued regardless, "maybe we could dissolve him completely. Kill him for good."

"I told you, there's no killing a vampire, ever."

"How do we know if we don't try?"

"Because that's not how this sort of thing is done."

"Who says?"

"I do."

Sunder gave me the side-eye so long, I thought he'd run us off of the path and get into a fender bender with a family crypt.

"I think you want revenge," he decided. "Killing him would be too merciful. You want him to suffer."

I didn't feel like explaining myself to some paranormal neophyte, half my age and IQ. As far as I was concerned, there was no Marin Venerio Grissoni left. Only unending hunger and a bottomless well of rage at not being able to feed it. He was beyond reason or understanding, and would remain so until the end of time. Or at least until somebody dug him up and pulled that hunk of metal out of him. With a fledgling new cemetery all around us, and many acres of land yet to be filled with graves, I hoped that day was one or two forevers away.

Once we were out of the car, it didn't take long to find what I was looking for. The transfer of graves from the old cemetery to the new was a long, ongoing process. Untold hundreds were probably still caught in limbo, their rotting caskets and occupants stashed in some cold-storage warehouse while remains were processed. Records of who had been in which plot had to be checked and confirmed by inefficient bureaucrats, and uprooted headstones paired with the deceased they commemorated at the new location. Inevitably, there would be some graves, dating back to early last century or before, that would leave a big question mark at the end of their incomplete file. Surprise coffins unearthed where none were supposed to be were common enough, or holes that had been filled with more than one occupant for reasons that were lost to living memory. To accommodate these outliers and exceptions, a number of graves were kept open, waiting for the next batch of unidentified remains to be processed, with simple markers already in place, offering an epitaph no more specific than an ambiguous, "Unknown."

No one was going to notice if one of the unknown graves got filled in the night.

Once we'd lowered Marin's red-trunk tomb into the first available anonymous hole, Sunder retrieved a collapsible shovel he kept in the trunk of his car, next to a jack and a lug wrench.

"Nice entrenching tool," I commented. "I used to have one just like it. Maybe an earlier model."

"It's yours if you want it," he said. "I thought I might have to excavate some graves hunting vampires, you know? But I think my vampire-hunting days are over."

"Lost your stomach for it now that you've done it for real?"

"Maybe I should take a step back. Reassess some life choices."

I let him think about it for a few moments. He'd do well to pursue a normal life. It would probably be for the best.

"You handled yourself well today," I said.

They were words of encouragement that flew in the face of what was best, but I said them anyway.

"Did I?" said Sunder, sounding surprised. "I was so scared."

"Scared is fine. Scared is healthy. You followed through with what had to be done. That's what's important."

"I barely held myself together."

"Believe me, I've seen plenty of people lose their shit when faced with this sort of thing. Your shit was not lost. You knew where your shit was the whole time, and you kept a lid on it."

"I appreciate that," he said. "Thanks. But I don't know if this sort of life is for me."

Sunder held out his entrenching tool, offering it again.

"No," I said, refusing the gift, "you hold onto it."

"Think I might need it after all?"

"I know you will," I said. "That grave isn't going to fill itself."

Sunder looked at the ton of dirt piled next to the hole.

"Put your back into it and I'm sure you can be done in an hour, tops."

☉

The winter nighttime hours started early and ran long. We were done at the cemetery and driving back to town well before midnight.

The whole way, Sunder continued down the logical path of his thought experiment about a normal life. He was openly wondering about job opportunities in mail rooms, or what chance he might have to work his way up from cashier at a big-box, big-corporate retail store to management. Give him another hour or two to think on it and he'd be fantasizing about marriage, family, and a house in the suburbs where he could spend the rest of his days mowing the lawn and trying to forget the things he knew about how the world really worked and what was crawling under the thin veneer of normalcy.

"Shut up a minute," I told him, at the first excuse to present itself.

There was a newsbreak I wanted to hear on the radio. The bleating about the convention-centre carnage, what had been the top headline all day with no fresh facts to add, had been bumped out of its position by developments in another hot story.

The lone Canning Town Charnel House suspect had been released on bail and was officially downgraded to a "person of interest" status. What sort of interest was not specified, and there was no mention of who had bailed Shambler out of lock-up. If there was any more information to be gleaned from the report, it was lost to me. Radio reception turned to crap as we entered a tunnel, on our way into the downtown core.

"As I was saying..." Sunder continued over the fizzle of broadcast static.

I sat back and let him continue to plan a mundane future, assuming such a thing was possible, assuming any of us had a future, mundane or otherwise.

Chapter Twenty

Party of One

S UNDER LET ME OFF in front of my building but didn't want to come up.

"I have a lot to think about," he said in a distant voice, staring at the road ahead.

I agreed that more thought, alone and in silence, might serve him well. I knew it would do me a lot of good.

The elevator ride up to the third floor was short, but it was the first time I'd been alone since the train ride home. And the first time I'd been alone since doing the deed. Marin had been dealt with. Permanently. Or at least as permanently as a vampire could be dealt with. That was one down. The to-do list remained in my head, but I felt like writing it down just so I could have something to physically cross out. It would have felt more like an achievement then, rather than a betrayal born of necessity, in response to a betrayal born of fear.

As I made my way down the hall, I resolved not to feel any guilt about what I'd done. He was, after all, a filthy undead parasite—feeding off of human blood and preying on our emotions. You can't suck anyone drier than that.

The crossed Band-Aids over the blown-out spyhole reminded me of Sunder Lone's face. If those cuts were the worst war wounds he would ever suffer in this struggle against true evil, then he got out at the right time. For his sake, I genuinely hoped I'd never see him again. And if I did happen to run across him one day, bagging my groceries at the end of a checkout lane, or turning me down for a business loan across a bank desk, I'd congratulate him on a clean break.

I let myself into the apartment and found it pitch black. Not a single light was on. Even when she popped out on a quick errand, Rebecca always left a light or two burning.

"Rebecca? You home?" I said aloud, expecting no response. I got one anyway.

"She's not," said a voice in the dark. "But do come in."

I recognized the speaker at once and it infuriated me. Being welcomed into my own home by an outsider was insulting enough. Considering who it was made this so much worse.

I reached for the light switch. When the overhead snapped on, I found Jeevak Menahem sitting in the most comfortable chair in the apartment. He looked cozy and at ease. I, by contrast, was put instantly on edge, ready for a fight. Despite the tension in every muscle, the tingle in every nerve, I tried to play it cool and hoped my poker face betrayed nothing. Least of all surprise.

"How did you get in here?"

"The door."

He knew damn well what I was really asking him, but Menahem was being coy. And obnoxiously smug.

"I didn't invite you in. I didn't even buzz you in. There was no invitation at all, implied or otherwise."

Having confirmed that I knew what he had become, what powers he was flirting with, learning, mastering, he copped to being subject to some of the rules and regulations that came with the package deal.

"Quite right," he said. "One of the minor inconveniences of my nascent form. By assuming it the way I did, I was able to avoid certain drawbacks of the condition. But many of the limitations still apply."

"Other than being able to win a vampire beauty contest hands down, what's the advantage?"

As someone who became a vampire in the most roundabout way possible, he had assumed his powers and immortality without ending up looking like thirty miles of bad road. Skipping the draining and death parts of the transformation had its benefits.

"The unbridled power I feel surging through me is beyond your feeble comprehension," he said. "You might know it yourself if you had the ambition to be more than human. More than an abject failure."

"Maybe I like casting a shadow, or shaving in a mirror."

"Such trivial things I will not miss."

I decided to focus on one of the bigger limitations that had apparently failed to keep Menahem out of my home.

"So how did you get into my apartment without being invited by the rightful owner?"

"Simple," he said. "I *became* the rightful owner. It was a small matter of tracking down your landlord and offering fair market value plus thirty percent. Money is no object. Especially when it comes to buying out a pitiable slum like this. How poor at your profession you must be to only be able to afford a dingy rental. And then to go and lie to me about the vast sum of money you earned on a recent job? Pathetic!"

"Are you here about me being a few days behind this month? I can write you a personal cheque made out to 'Go Fuck Yourself.'"

Menahem smiled, but it wasn't anything I said that amused him.

"If it turns out I can't kill you permanently, I may entertain myself by evicting you from every place you might seek shelter.

I figure I could have you living out of a cardboard box in the gutter by this time next week."

"So what can I do for you?" I asked, cordially but without substance. "I mean, other than drop dead forever?"

"Now that you mention it," said Menahem, "you can answer a simple query."

He extended his hand, and I saw there was a small loop of metal around the first joint of his index finger. He pointed that finger at me, like an accusation was coming, while the rest of his hand remained balled into a fist. Opening his fingers, he let Moby-Dick's pocket watch drop and dangle.

"Mercy, Lord Necromancer, Death Incarnate, Ender of Worlds, Slayer of All," pleaded the demon fish. And I was pretty sure he wasn't talking to me. Whatever Menahem had done or said to him while he was waiting, it had left Moby-Dick a rattled supplicant.

"Explain this to me," said Menahem.

I only gave a non-committal shrug.

"A harbinger, is it not? One of Nocturne's."

"Yeah," I agreed, since he already knew.

"And you put it into a reanimated fish," he observed. "Why?"

"I guess you had to be there."

"I'm grateful I wasn't."

Menahem spun the watch around on the end of its chain several times before flinging it away. It sailed through the office door behind him and hit something in the next room. Hit it hard.

"Ow!" I heard Gladys yell.

"Amusing trinkets you keep," Menahem noted.

"I no treenkit, fakker!" replied Gladys at full volume.

Menahem had not been shy about going through my personal belongings. He'd been in my office in my absence as well. And had apparently acquainted himself with Gladys.

"Osteo reanimation?" he commented.

"Yes," I said.

"Not a very good one."

"Fak yoo, I da beest eesteo rinnimashun yoo eavar seen, fakker!"

Menahem ignored the slighted skull.

"You couldn't imbue it with a more intelligible spirit? Perhaps one a tad more polite?"

"Luck of the draw," I said.

"I don't leave things to luck, chance, happenstance," Menahem stated, meaning it as an admonishment. "It's why I find myself on top of the world, while you crawl in the dirt."

"Maybe I'm bound by a set of rules, too. Ones that involve a few ethics."

"Ethics? Please! You are hardly fit to lecture me about ethics. You use and manipulate others as easily as I do. The only difference is I profit from my machinations. Your associates sacrifice themselves in your name, earning you no profit and only temporary gain at best. Like your ill-fated friend at the convention, whose death I foresaw as superfluous damage. His dying needlessly in your stead has only delayed the inevitable. The gwyllgi has grown quite ravenous since its last feast. It awaits you."

"You must already know if that works or not."

"Unfortunately, no," admitted Menahem. "That is not your next death. Nor, I imagine, the next few to follow. I'm afraid I must have my fun first. I simply can't help myself."

"I guess we all need a hobby."

"And you have become mine, Rip Eulogy."

"So what's the next death you have planned?"

"This one isn't planned. It's spur of the moment."

"Is this an impulse-control issue, or an anger-management issue?"

"Perhaps a bit of both," he said, pulling out something he'd had tucked between the arm of the chair he was in and the cushion he sat on. The item sported a forged metal hilt sticking out the end of a sheath.

"You should see somebody about that," I said, nervously eying the holstered weapon.

"I am," he said, and laid the scabbard across his lap. "I'm seeing you, right now. Who better than you to vent my ire upon?"

"Well don't keep me all in suspense. How do you do it?"

The item he'd brought with him seemed like a great big spoiler.

"I choke the life out of you," he said.

"Again? Get some new material, asshole."

"I don't know what comes over me. I suppose we'll find out. My conscious intention is to stab you with this lovely ceremonial dagger I brought, and yet that's not how I kill you next," he said, drawing said dagger from its cover. "Perhaps it is the time after that."

He turned the blade over in his hand, admiring the ornate craftsmanship. I was more focused on the shimmer of light bouncing off the curving razor edge.

"Stabbing me isn't very original either," I pointed out.

"Indeed, I know. That was your last death I foresaw. The one with the albino and the stake. The detail that interested me the most was your inability to rise again until the object piercing your heart was removed."

"So you think you can lock me out of my own body that way," I said, trying to anticipate his next move. "I can work around that. It just takes longer."

"Yes, but a bit of time is all I need. Arrangements have already been made. I only need your cooperation for a short time. You staying dead for the duration will facilitate this."

"And after you've had this bit of cooperation?"

"Oh, I have so many other deaths planned for you. Each more inventive than the last."

"So what's with the strangling routine?"

Menahem had come up short on the inventive front thus far.

"Crime of passion," he said apologetically. "It happens. I get worked up. One can't be cold and calculating all the time."

"What's the reason this time? Am I insolent again?"

"We'll find out in a few minutes."

"Looking forward to it."

"As am I. The last time I murdered you was a wonderful catharsis. I haven't slept so well in years."

"I hope you get a nice long dirt-nap real soon," I said, expressing my fondest wish for him.

"It's too late for me to die now. I have drunk from enough vampires to have achieved my desired immortality. The feeling of being beyond death, beyond even the end of all other life, is quite intoxicating. It almost makes me feel sympathy for the lives that are about to be lost. Especially the ones belonging to those who only think they are immortal, and can imagine no pending demise. As for the rest...even I feel some small pang for the fragile, feeble mortals, who were never long for this world, even at the best of times."

"You're all heart," I told him.

"Would you like to know how the rest of your purported friends die? Like those two who weaseled their way into my grand opening, for instance—the angry woman and the pompous ass with the diminishing psychic powers? I've seen it. I know the time, the place, and the set of circumstances."

"Right. The end of the world. I expect that's how most people go out."

"Most," he agreed. "But not all. Nocturne's end game is indeed in play. The knights are all gathered on the chess board, ready to ride. Csaba Szabo will be his War. You have already met Pestilence and Famine. And I—I am Death."

"His plans are subject to change, so I'll believe it when I see it."

"Your failure as Nocturne's choice of Death Incarnate was not a disruption in the plan. It only served to point the way to me as the true embodiment of the end of all things. It is I who shall lead the charge when the moment is ripe. I have already raised a personal army from the dead. They are poised to lead my advance, thousands strong."

I wondered where Menahem might have happened upon that many corpses to raise. The answer that came to me was obvious.

"The bodies from the Algonquin Fields," I said, remembering the plots I had just seen filling the replacement cemetery. "I thought they were all moved."

"So they were," said Menahem regretfully. "Sentimentality won with the recent dead, with loved ones still living, and I was compelled to have them all reburied on the new grounds. But there were others I was able to spirit away."

"The vampires," I said, of the inevitable handful that were to be found buried in any graveyard.

"Oh yes, them of course. Whenever my excavations discovered one, I saw to it that it was contained and delivered to me. But I am talking about the original occupants of the cemetery. The founders of this city, the settlers, the cholera victims of its first major die-off. They were dug up as well, a layer beneath the more recent additions. No one laid claim to those bodies, centuries old. They're mine now. Raw resources to be unleashed for the apocalypse. They will serve as my honour guard as I lead the other horsemen on our charge across a doomed world."

"It hasn't happened yet," I reminded him.

"And yet I foresee it," he replied. "Billions of times over. The entire populace of the world, wiped out. And I, alone, will be left standing. How can a pitiable amateur practitioner such as yourself hope to stop it?"

"I'm working on it."

Menahem shook his head at me slowly, like a teacher disappointed by the class moron. He'd have me standing in the corner with a dunce cap before long.

"You're a disgrace to our profession, Eulogy. A buffoon, disrespectfully meddling in forces beyond your control or understanding. How Nocturne ever sought to recruit you mystifies me."

"And yet he did," I said. "He came to me first. You were an afterthought. Second fiddle. The compromise choice. The booby prize."

It looked like Jeevak Menahem was taking my insults in stride. But looks can be deceiving, and Menahem was nothing if not deceptive. The outward calm he projected was gone an instant later, and he rose from his seat so fast he forgot to bring his fancy dagger with him. Of course he did. He'd already told me he would. It wasn't cold, calculated knife-time. It was angry, vicious strangulation-time.

His hands were around my throat again, pressing down hard, exponentially stronger than the last time he'd done this. I instinctively tried to resist, but it was pointless. He was far too powerful now; the reputed vampiric strength of ten men. Ten men, easy.

Oh, fuck it, I thought. I might have said it out loud, but my larynx was too busy getting crushed.

I stopped struggling and let him get on with it. He'd seen it coming. He probably wasn't lying.

Prophecies. I hate them.

Chapter Twenty-One

Game of Death

I CAME TO ABOUT AN HOUR LATER, across town, with a sharp pain in my chest and another ruined shirt.

Maybe I should clarify. The *second* time I came to was an hour later. My recovery from the strangulation didn't take long. Menahem was there waiting for me, timing my return on a wristwatch worth more than what I made most years in the business.

"Three minutes," he said. "You beat your previous time quite handily."

Before I could say anything crude or rude, he added, "Welcome back. And goodbye again."

With that, he brought his dagger down straight into my chest and through my heart. I got a good close look at it before the lights went out. The blade was long and wavy like a kris, the hilt exquisitely elaborate, with twisted, macabre figures carved into it—gruesomely ceremonial in a way that suggested it had probably been used in human sacrifices before. An appropriate tool and effective weapon to get the job done. Knowing how I had difficulty coming back from that sort of wound, while the foreign object was still stuck through a ventricle or two, bought him time to move my body.

I tried to force myself back inside, as I had recently done in the church, and pull the blade out myself, but it proved impossible while my corpse was in motion. No sooner had he done the deed than Menahem threw me over his shoulder and carried me away like a sack of dirt. I drifted after him, focusing my consciousness on my stolen body, but after dying twice in a row in a matter of minutes, I was slow on the uptake. By the time I pursued him down to street level, Menahem was gone, and my mortal remains with him. A car had probably been waiting, and my body was likely stashed in the trunk next to the spare tire, being whisked away to who-knows-where.

"Who was that who just took off with your body?"

The voice belonged to Denise. She was somewhere close, sharing the same stretch of ether. I didn't look for her. I could sense her proximity, which was enough for us to communicate.

"That," I informed her, "was the guy who really murdered you."

"And now he's gone and killed you, too."

"Three times so far."

"Sounds like you owe him one."

"We both do," I said.

"Want to go haunt him?" Denise asked, with mischief palpably brewing in her mind. I had more than mischief in mine.

"No. I want to do worse to him."

"Kill him?" Denise seemed to like that idea even better. But if Menahem's own forecast for himself was accurate, that wasn't going to be possible. Fine by me.

"No," I said. "Worse than that."

☉

I didn't have a plan. I didn't have any bright ideas. All I had was my anger. It would do.

Once I had a moment to collect my thoughts, I realized Menahem wasn't trying to lose me, only relocate me. Whatever he had in mind, he'd want to have it out with me on a battle-field of his choosing. And that choice was obvious.

The lobby of the Algonquin Tower was hideously corpo-rate—all black leather and chrome. After drifting across town, I found my body just inside, stretched out on a couch between two potted plants, next to a rack of magazines written for tax brackets beyond my comprehension. The knife had been re-moved, allowing for an easy revivification. The unsightly wound left behind was covered by the top hat Menahem had brought along so I could fully look the part for our final duel between necromancers. I tipped the brim up off my chest to survey the damage as soon as I resurrected myself. The slice between my ribs had been so fine, the incision was able to knit together in rudimentary fashion within the first few minutes of my return. The wound wouldn't reopen unless I exerted myself. But I expected Menahem would have me exerting myself for the rest of the night.

The express elevator—the same one that had shuttled guests up to the terrace for the grand opening—dinged once. The doors slid aside and waited for me to board. The light inside the car shone as the sole beacon in a lobby that had been dimmed to a few off-hours fluorescents. I didn't approach, knowing it could only be part of the elaborate trap Menahem had planned. Instead, I looked for other options that didn't exist. The fire exits were locked, and all the exterior windows and revolving doors were blocked off by a steel security mesh that had been lowered and bolted in place. Nobody was getting in or out, especially me.

Pinpoint red lights shone from the base of security cameras that were poised from every conceivable vantage point across the lobby. Each move I made was being watched. Once he'd let me confirm the futility of my circumstances, Menahem himself spoke to me over a P.A. system.

"Surely even a bottom feeder with no self-respect like you would want revenge by now."

He was trying to push my buttons. If you mash angrily at a keyboard enough times, you're likely to hit a few. Menahem's soothing, rich voice, even filtered through a sound system, held its veneer of cool collectedness. But I'd heard enough of it to know the boiling rage that was there, just beneath the surface. His hatred and contempt for me, for everybody, was evident. My continued existence was goading him, vexing him, and now he was trying to manipulate me into following his game plan. And if that's what it took to get face to face with the bastard again, I would let myself be goaded.

"If that's not motivation enough for you," he continued, "perhaps I can convince you to come up and see me in a misguided bid to save a special someone."

I had assumed I was the lone victim on the menu. But, of course, Menahem wanted to hedge his bets, make sure I'd jump through the hoops he'd set out for me in the precise order he wanted. A bit of additional leverage would assure my cooperation.

"You're not my only guest this evening," he confirmed. "There's someone you know with me right now."

"Who?" I asked, sure there were also microphones in the area to pick up any utterance I cared to make.

"I'll give you a hint. It's someone you've grown very close to, despite your best efforts to deny it. You've come to share an address. More recently, you've been sharing the same bed. Not intimately, of course, but I'm not one to pry."

Rebecca. The bastard. I bit my lip to keep from saying anything stupid while I collected myself.

"I need proof of life," I said.

"An interesting choice of words, one necromancer to another. I'm afraid my guest is in no condition to chat right now. If you're quick about it, you may arrive in time to exchange a final heartfelt sentiment."

Whatever he had planned for me, I knew it was going to be awful. I'd endure it just the same, if only to keep Rebecca from suffering worse. This was a sick amusement for him, but he was going to have to let me advance, one step at a time, if he was going to extract all the fun out of it. Each stage would bring me closer to the man himself. Once I had him in my sights, I'd hit him with everything I had. Admittedly, that wasn't much. Following my kidnapping, my tool kit was sitting uselessly at home. Even my magic hat was empty, armed with not so much as a single business card or talking skull. All I had was the skin on my bones, the blood in my veins, and the clothes on my back. It would have to do.

I walked across the cavernous lobby, each step an angry echo, and strode directly into the elevator. Pivoting in place, I watched the doors shut behind me.

"Let's do this thing," I said.

I didn't have to press a button on the control panel. One lit up, selected remotely. Level nine. Act one.

$$\Theta$$

I'd been this far up before, but no further. The rest of the building remained a mystery to me. With the car stopped, refusing to go any higher, I stepped out into the corridor to meet whatever Menahem wanted me to find.

The building seemed utterly deserted, with not so much as a hint of the cleaning staff. I was certain my host wanted privacy as he toyed with me, and had sent everyone home, cancelling any overnight services.

Each door I tried was locked, corralling me down the hall to the familiar lounge, which was open. Progress was slow, as I anticipated some trap or deceit with each step. The P.A. system remained silent, although I'm sure Menahem was watching and listening intently. If there was something he wanted me to discover in that place where he had first murdered me, I failed to find it. The lounge looked as pristine and unused as the last time I'd seen it. All the bottles behind the bar remained factory sealed, and the carafe of vampire blood he had been drinking from on the night of the opening was gone.

The terrace was my last option, but that was even more barren. With the catering tables removed and the throng of guests long departed, it was a featureless balcony, half a block long. And cold. The outdoor heating that had blown over the city's elite to stave off the winter was shut down, and I obviously wasn't worthy of that costly amenity. I had to be missing something. This had to be the spot where Menahem wanted me, but there was nothing that caught my eye.

Rather, it was my ear that picked up on something out of place: a tiny noise against the dwindling night traffic and the whistling wind. Close. It was a sudden, distinct metallic clank that drew my attention to the ledge. There was nothing to make out in the dark, but a slight persistent grating noise, sharp steel against polished stone, drew me in until I was able to centre on the exact spot. I approached slowly, ready for anything, and found a multi-pronged hook dug into the outer lip of the terrace. It bobbed and scratched at the smooth black surface, scraping it badly as it struggled to support a weight that might have dislodged it had it not been so well fixed. That was when I noticed the rope. It was knotted through an iron eye at the base of the hook and, after a sharp dip over the side of the tower, ran all the way across the adjacent street and up to the neighbouring building, stretching right to the rooftop that overlooked the terrace I was standing on.

"A little help here," came a small voice, trying to remain clear in the face of mortal terror. "Please."

I carefully peaked over the edge. If this was Menahem's surprise, it didn't sound as perilous as I had anticipated. Dangling a few feet below the deck, with nothing but nine storeys of open air and a concrete sidewalk waiting for him, was Sunder Lone. His grappling hook and zip-line rig was keeping him from pancaking on the street below, but he had misjudged the slack in the line, and was now stuck short of his mark, the ledge just out of his reach.

Gripping the parapet tightly with one hand, I leaned over as far as I dared and offered him the other. Sunder reached up for a firm hold, and once we were grasping each other by the wrist, I was able to haul him up and over. We sat panting on the terrace following the effort.

"How did you find me?" I asked, once we had caught our breath.

"I turned around and went back to your place to see you," he said. "To tell you I changed my mind. What I saw was you being carried out and stuffed in a trunk, so I followed you here. There was no way into this building, but the one across the street let me get all the way to the roof."

I could have hugged the pale little teenaged lunatic. It felt good to have someone with me in my corner—even an inexperienced novice filled with silly notions and outright delusions. An ally in the middle of this death trap was welcome, regardless of it putting him equally in harm's way.

"What do you mean you changed your mind?" I said, once the explanation for his presence had time to sink in.

"This is the world I want to be in," Sunder told me, his recent epiphany still fresh and passionate. "This is the fight I want to have."

"Well you're in it as deep as you can get right now."

"What are we up against this time?" was all he wanted to know.

"Jeevak Menahem. Master necromancer, newly minted vampire, and all-around piece of shit. He has it in for me. And everybody else in the world."

Sunder got back on his feet to check the state of his hook and zip line. He reached down and tugged on the rope, taking up the slack, but there wasn't much more to be done with it. It had served its purpose.

"I don't think there's any way I can reel in enough of this rope to be useful," he told me. "I tied it tight on the other end. And climbing back up to the other roof is going to be tough going if not outright impossible. I suppose if I cut it on this end..."

"Look, kid," I said, "thanks for the rescue attempt. But I can't leave."

"What do you mean?"

"If I really wanted to bail, I could just jump here and now, go splat, and then peel myself off the pavement at my leisure. Menahem wouldn't have let me out here if he thought I might do that. I have to stay, and he knows it."

"A tactical retreat isn't a defeat, Mr. Eulogy. If you need to face him, there's always another time, a better place."

"He has my friend up there with him," I said. "At his mercy. And he isn't the mercy type. I have to do this, but you don't. Do you have anything that might let you bungee the hell out of here?"

Happy as I was to see him, I didn't want to get anyone else killed. Not so soon after Tom, at least.

"If you're not running away, neither am I," said Sunder. "I told you this was my fight, too. And I'll fight by your side."

"Okay," I agreed. "Let's see what goodies you brought."

I went through his bag of gear, but I'd already seen most of it at the church. The grappling hook and zip line may have gotten him on site, but now that he was here, everything else he came armed with was useless.

"Junk, junk, junk," I said of each item in turn as I set them all out on the floor.

"You never know what might come in handy," Sunder said of his tools.

I held up a potato peeler that I found stuffed in one of the pack's pockets.

"You never know," he reiterated.

"Maybe if Menahem comes after us with a potato gun," I said, tucking it away. "But I'm pretty sure he has something more deadly planned. A lot of somethings."

"Whatever it is, we'll be ready," said Sunder, as he packed up his kit again and threw the collection of random hardware and token weaponry over his shoulder, like a Boy Scout ready to make camp at the other end of a forest hike.

Grudgingly, I turned around to lead us back indoors. Too late, I spotted a chalk mark on the terrace floor between my feet. Instinctively, I looked straight up, and caught a glint of the city lights off a metal shaft dropping straight at me from a distant, higher point in the building. It was too late to sidestep.

The harpoon caught me in the shoulder, passed through my torso, burst out the opposite thigh, and imbedded itself in the stone tiles at my feet. The wound was instantly fatal. The last thing I heard was Menahem's cackle over the outdoor speaker, reverberating across city rooftops.

Θ

Sunder let me know it took him nearly ten minutes to pry the point of the harpoon out of the floor where it pinned me, and another twenty to work it back out of my body. He eventually realized he'd have to get rid of the giant barbed head if he was going to pull the thing free without dragging half my guts with it. Luckily he had a serrated hunting knife in his pack to saw through the wooden hilt. Alive and breathing again, I reluctantly admitted that maybe not all of his commando toys were as worthless as I'd assumed.

It was a hell of an injury to walk off, but I had to get up and keep going. At least the spear had missed causing further damage to my heart, and only nicked a lung. Most of the trauma had been to my intestines, which hurt like hell, but didn't stop me from staying mobile.

"Are you sure you can keep going?" Sunder worried, lending his shoulder for support until I was limping along on my own.

"Yeah," I lied. Not to Sunder. I might have been more truthful about the state I was in to him. But Menahem was listening, and I didn't want to let on that three deaths in one evening were starting to take their toll. Of course there would be more. Menahem knew what he had on the agenda, and with me back from the dead again, he'd also know all about his next successful kill.

Back inside, at the ninth-floor landing, the elevator doors yawned open, beckoning.

"This was tied to end of the harpoon," Sunder said, holding up an electronic passkey.

There was a slot beneath the elevator-button panel that accepted the card when we tried it. Although we were locked out of selecting a floor of our choosing, the car came to life and ushered us up to the next challenge—this one on level eighteen. Menahem spoke to us over the speaker.

"I see you and the albino have become fast friends after your contentious first encounter. The third wheel is an unexpected development. I might accuse you of cheating, but I will allow it. He can help you recover from each setback I throw your way. It will keep our game from dragging on all night."

It was an encouraging sign if Menahem had failed to see Sunder's involvement in the evening's festivities. It meant he was a survivor. I had a lot of misery in store, I was sure, but apparently there wasn't a fatality in Sunder's immediate future. At least not one that Menahem had foreseen or wanted to hint at.

The eighteenth storey was blandly white-collar, with a largely featureless hall to greet us. It led to equidistant corners on both the left and right sides.

"What now?" Sunder asked, peeking out of the elevator car and checking up and down the corridor for any hint of a threat. He was waiting for me to take the lead, so I took it, stepping out.

"We see what's waiting for us," I said, and tossed a mental coin as to which way to go. Right won.

To be thorough, we checked each door we passed along the way, but like the rest, they were also locked. Our options remained narrow. Menahem was steering us towards something. He maintained radio silence, offering no hints or taunts—content, I supposed, that we were proceeding according to plan. That offered me no comfort whatsoever.

Every step, I anticipated an ambush. Something from above or below, most likely. With a brand-new building made to his specifications, the blueprints could have allowed for any number of trap doors or deadfalls justified as "security features" to the contractors tasked with installing them. Paid enough money, who would question a billionaire's need for spike pits or bladed pendulums in his otherwise innocuous office tower?

With our every sense fixated on detecting danger, Sunder and I weren't completely caught off guard when something, at last, came for us. I could smell it before I could see it. A moment later, a cloud of sickening smoke came billowing around the corner ahead, filling the hallway in front of us.

"Gas!" Sunder warned, as if it weren't already obvious.

We turned and ran back the way we came, trying the left passage that led away from the elevator. It was no good, dead-ending before we were far enough away from the choking atmosphere of the approaching cloud.

"Get your socks off!" I ordered. "Just one will do. Quick now!"

Sunder didn't waste any time questioning me. He yanked one of his laces and had his shoe and sock off in an instant.

"Now what?" he asked.

"Piss on it!"

That gave him pause.

"Do what now?"

I kicked off one of my own shoes and peeled off a sock as the cloud approached.

"Piss on your sock and hold it over your mouth and nose. The ammonia should counter the gas."

Pee in your hankies, boys! had been an uninspiring but life-saving battle cry heard in the allied trenches across France during the chlorine-gas attacks of the First World War. I didn't know for sure what sort of gas was about to hit us in the face, but this trick from obscure military history was our best hope. All I knew for sure was that the fumes stank worse than our socks ever could, urine-soaked or not. Besides, who carries hankies anymore?

Even in such a dire moment, an instinct for a certain level of privacy prevailed, and we turned back-to-back while we tried to accomplish the pressing task.

"How are you doing?" I asked, and heard a slight trickle behind me in response.

I bore down, but nothing would come. Not a drop. Concentrating, trying to rush things, only made it worse.

"I'm good to go," Sunder said, turning around, holding a warm, wet sock in his hand uncomfortably. "You?"

"Nothing's happening," I admitted, and suddenly felt the urge to cough. The gas was upon us.

"Don't wait for me, I'll manage," I said. "Cover up!"

The kid winced and then stuffed the sock in his face, covering his nose and mouth, and inhaled through the improvised gas mask. It seemed to work. Sunder wasn't overcome by the hacking fit that struck me a moment later. My lungs burned as the murderous fumes struck me like a Mack Truck, and my legs buckled under me. Knocked to the floor, I was reduced to a wheezing mass of oxygen-starved flesh in moments. The struggle didn't last long. The gas hung low in the air and finished choking me out to the sound of Menahem's cackling laughter over the speaker system.

Death by shy-bladder syndrome. How humiliating.

Θ

By the time I was able to squeeze back into my body and re-inflate my seized-up lungs, the air in the hall had cleared. I could hear overhead vents working overtime to suck away the last of the gas, though the rotten-egg smell lingered, clinging to every surface.

Sunder was standing over me. With no more need for an ammonia barrier to crystallize the poison and keep it out of his body, he had returned his soggy sock to his foot and laced his shoe over it.

"I...um...zipped you up," he told me.

There was a vague memory of me hitting the floor, still dangling out of my fly.

"Yeah," I agreed, seeing he had, indeed, zipped me up. "Uh...thanks."

Sunder took me by the hand and helped pull me to my feet. No sooner was I up than I doubled over and coughed up a hefty wad of bloody sputum. My lungs felt raw, and made unsettling wet clicking noises when I inhaled. Add that to the list of damage I would have to heal my way through if I ever escaped Menahem's game plan.

"Yuck," commented Sunder, disgusted with himself. "I can't believe that trick with the sock worked."

"Desperate times, desperate measures," I rasped. "If we survive tonight and live to tell anybody about our adventures, we'll skip this part."

"I think that would be for the best," he agreed.

"What did I miss while I was out?"

"I found this taped to the side of one of the empty gas canisters," said Sunder, holding up another magnetic-stripped card.

"Okay," I said, hands on knees, giving myself a moment to clear my head. "Let's keep moving."

The card unlocked the next stage of the elevator ride. Level twenty-seven was our predetermined destination. As we shot up another nine floors, Menahem asked a rhetorical question.

"Do you have any interesting phobias I should know about, Mr. Eulogy? Fear is such an irrational emotion. Surely one who can rise from the dead cannot truly fear death. But even you must have things that make your skin crawl. I can't wait to see if I've selected one or two demises that might set you ill at ease."

"Great," I grumbled, too low for Menahem's microphones to pick up, "what does this prick have in mind now?"

My mind rifled through all the common fears, phobias, and instinctual aversions Menahem might bring into play against me, just to make my next death particularly unpleasant. Sunder was already well down that line of thinking, and he was spooking himself with the possibilities.

"I hope it's not clowns," he said.

"Clowns?"

"Clowns are creepy."

"Clowns *are* creepy," I agreed, "but I don't think he's going to try to kill me with a clown."

"It could be a clown with a knife."

"He's already stabbed me to death once tonight."

"Sure, fine," said Sunder. "But not with a clown."

"He doesn't have a clown lying in wait with a knife."

"Maybe the clown has a gun," Sunder suggested. "Maybe it's a big gun. Maybe it's a clown with a machine gun!"

"If he wants to machine-gun me, he doesn't need a clown to do it. He could just hire any goon with a machine gun."

The logic was irrefutable, but Sunder still clung to his dread.

"It wouldn't be as scary," he muttered to himself.

The elevator slowed to a stop and the doors slid open with a soft ding.

"I guess we'll find out what it is soon enough," I said.

And, in short order, we did.

Θ

So it went, with each elevator pit stop ushering in some new death trap and indignity. There were plenty of other parts of our inglorious heroism best skipped as we made our way up the tower, nine levels at a time. The script was set, with me as the sacrificial lamb, and Sunder functioning as my personal field medic. Each time I blundered into another one of Menahem's sadistic contrivances, the kid was there to help restart my heart, patch me up, and get me back on my feet in a timely fashion. Without his assistance, the whole ordeal would have easily lasted twice as long.

Sunder's rubber-soled runners protected him from the electrified flooring we encountered on twenty-seven, whereas my new pair of steel-toed loafers turned me into an effective lightning rod. The killer bees on forty-five lived up to their name, though I found their stings somewhat redundant after the scorpions on thirty-six. By the time I was bitten by the banded elapid snake on fifty-four, poisoning had become a routine, if not an overarching theme to the evening. Of course, poison was the easiest death to come back from, and wouldn't allow Menahem to grow too impatient as I made my way towards his grand finale.

The toxins accumulating in my system were keeping me fuzzy, less focused, more likely to trip the next trap on schedule. The garrote on sixty-three almost came as a relief. It dropped from an open ceiling panel and lassoed me right off my feet in mid-step. It happened so quickly and silently, Sunder, walking only a few paces ahead of me, failed to notice my predicament until I'd been lynched to death no more than six inches off the floor. Irritatingly avoidable as that demise was if we'd been more on the ball, at least switching things up allowed me to clear my head and shake off some of the residual effects of various venoms.

"Why only nine floors at a time?" Sunder wanted to know at one point, after we collected yet another passkey and unlocked the next leg of our journey up the elevator shaft.

"Nine is the death number," I explained. "The Greek numeral for nine has symbolized it for thousands of years. It's also the number of finality or judgement in the Bible. It comes up again and again in many cultures and their myths."

"Do you believe in it?"

"No," I said. "It's occultism for math nerds. But when facing off against a numerologist, it's best to pay attention. It might be a bunch of bullshit, but if it's bullshit they buy into, keep count with them."

"How many floors does this place have?" Sunder asked, looking up at the panel above the door as we skipped ahead to the next act by a factor of nine.

"Eighty-one," I said, not having to look myself. Of course there had to be eighty-one. Nine times nine.

"Nine lives," Sunder suggested.

"Nine deaths," I agreed.

The doors kept sliding open to new perils, and I kept stepping forward to meet my fate.

Time after time I died, as planned and foreseen by Jeevak Menahem. And with each death, Menahem's sick laughter reverberated through the empty halls of his monolithic tower. My only consolation was that I was at least functioning as a meat shield, protecting Sunder from harm, keeping him in play.

Just when I was certain the pattern was fixed and the trials I faced were, if not predictable, at least similar to each other, the elevator doors opened on seventy-two. Up until then, the layout of each floor had been standard office fare. Other than being armed with tanks of gas, or crates of nasties rigged to pop open when approached, there was nothing that couldn't be stashed away and hidden by morning, before the building's growing staff of worker drones and paper pushers arrived for their nine-to-five slog behind desks and computers and copy machines. But now we were in the upper reaches of the tower—the private heart of Menahem's empire. There were no more offices and cubicles. No more staff lounges and supply closets. We were in the necromancer's private dominion, and the levels were no longer designed to be fit for public consumption.

The architecture remained consistently modern and brutalist, but the angles suddenly became sharper, the ceilings higher, and the aesthetic more severe. Gone were the rat mazes of corridors and doors, replaced by open galleries and tall arches branching into other chambers, none of them inviting.

There was nothing to do but start wandering through the interconnecting cells, hoping to stumble upon the next murder lying in wait, so we could wrap up these preliminary rounds and get to the main event. With no windows on the latest level, we might as well have been spelunking through catacombs deep underground. The lighting was dimmed to such a degree, Sunder was compelled to dig a flashlight out of his backpack.

"What do you think?" he asked, pointing the beam of light down several passages, trying to determine the most promising route. They all looked alike: potentially deadly.

"What's up there?" I wondered aloud, checking out the high ceiling and seeing an anomaly in the pattern of tiles.

Sunder pointed his beam straight up and found a series of connecting conduits that led from the elevator shaft and through the labyrinth before us, marking a clear trail. The exposed pipes would have been covered over on earlier, image-conscious levels. This high up, the design seemed to be more of a practical industrial style, with less concern for eye-pleasing finishing touches.

"Plumbing?" suggested Sunder.

"Seems so," I agreed. "Let's see where it leads."

We made our way into the heart of the level, turning this way and that as the pipes indicated, running through walls, coming out the other side, and continuing towards some unknown destination. Given the unwelcoming nature of the topmost recesses of the Algonquin Tower, I doubted they were plumbing for an executive bathroom or other such convenience.

As we approached a final chamber, wedged into what I judged to be the northeastern corner of the building, a low rumble greeted us. It was a soothing, mesmerizing groan, multiplied many times over, until the multitude of individual sources merged into a single steady drone. It wasn't a mechanical sound. It was organic in nature, yet unnatural at the same time.

"What in the name of sweet Jesus..." Sunder declared as we stepped through the threshold and into a tableau that was almost beyond our ability to process.

There were bodies. Dozens of them. All left dangling upside down, with their ankles and wrists firmly shackled in steel manacles. None of them were alive, but they weren't dead either. They were vampires. I knew they had to be when I saw what the network of pipes was feeding them. Some looked to still be standard water conduits, but the rest had been converted to keep the blood flowing.

It was blood that filled the clear rubber tubes that were attached to the pipe network above—an irrigation system for a vampire farm, with each tube pumping down a steady supply of nourishment, injecting it straight into a nosferatu's femoral artery. Slowly but steadily, gravity worked fresh blood through the stagnant guts of the undead, spoiling and putrefying it over time, until it was finally harvested out the other end. Taps had been jammed into every vampire's throat, slowly dripping their blackened bounty into waiting buckets.

The vampires didn't react to our presence, though they all stared ahead intently. It wasn't the two hapless humans in the room that drew their undivided attention. Each of them hung with their faces positioned directly in front of an hourglass. They watched, transfixed, as many tens of thousands of grains of sand slipped through the narrow passage between glass vessels. They watched, and they counted, as they were being fed and bled at once.

The noise each one made as the sands of time drained past their line of sight—obsessing them, hypnotizing them, enthralling them endlessly—was a contented, catlike purr. It filled the room and vibrated our bones.

Just as I wondered what would happen when the hourglasses ran out, one did exactly that. The vampire dangling behind it snorted and twitched as it came out of its trance. But before it could do anything about its predicament, a system of mechanical gears upended the timepiece and began the slow spill of sand all over again. The vampire's muscles relaxed and it went limp, renewing the unending count, its consciousness again reduced to a dull, mindless drone.

The entire setup was magnificently cruel. I'm not one to feel sympathy for their ilk, but if there was such a thing as vampire purgatory, this was it.

"Oh God, oh God," repeated Sunder, like he had given up Christian prayer for a Hindu mantra. "Oh God, no, no, no!"

"Take it easy," I told him. "We're way outnumbered by a room full of vampires, but they can't hurt us. They're all nicely distracted."

"No, no, no!" he continued unabated, his flashlight beam swinging back and forth, from one twisted vampire face to the next. It took a moment for me to realize he was switching between the same four faces over and over again. Menahem, the eye in the sky, spotted the pattern too.

"Do I detect a certain familiarity? A glimmer of recognition?"

Sunder ignored the taunt that came over the P.A. system. Or perhaps he didn't even hear it, unable to tear any fraction of his attention away from the four inverted figures before him.

"Joshua, Ruth..." he said, which were names I wasn't familiar with. But then he added, "Mother, Father..." and I got the picture.

"Ah, reunions," sighed Menahem. "They do bring a tear to my eye."

Sunder had fallen to his knees. In grief or prayer, I couldn't tell.

"I observe you feel the same," Menahem snickered. "Cry, boy! Cry for your departed loved ones and what they have been reduced to. There is no shame in such sentimentality."

"You killed my family!" Sunder screamed like he was on the verge of madness.

"I admit to harbouring a certain sentimentality for them myself," said Menahem. "They were my first victims, only last year, as I arrived to oversee the final details of my tower's construction and was beginning my transformation. When my taste for vampire blood began to make me ever more covetous of human blood as well."

"All of them," sobbed Sunder. "My entire family..."

"Was I being gluttonous?" asked Menahem. "One might have satisfied my fledgling vampiric thirst. Certainly two would have. But I drank from all of them in turn. Not enough to drain them completely. Just enough to make sure they would rise again as my undead offspring. You see, I needed vampires. Many more than I was able to excavate from the cemetery I built this crown jewel of my empire upon. The handful trapped in their coffins, awaiting freedom and sustenance, were not nearly enough. I pressed them into service, but there was little to be tapped from them. In the decades and centuries they had been underground, they hadn't had a drop to drink, and their veins were dry as a bone. I took to feeding them, but it takes time for the blood to age and ferment and reach the level of potency I needed to finish transforming myself. I always need more, and you can see the new sources I have amassed. You might have hung next to the rest of your family, boy, if not for that thin broth running through your veins. Eager as I am for fresh casks to tap, I must maintain a certain high standard. I'm sure you'll agree."

Sunder was inconsolable, so I didn't try. There's nothing to say in the face of such a degree of grief.

"Sick," I told Menahem. "Even for you."

"Don't assume I regard them all as mere commodities. I may drain them dry, day after day, but I like to think of them more as my pets. I feed them and care for them, but that alone is not enough. You know what a good master should provide for his pets on occasion, don't you?"

I was afraid to ask, although I knew an answer I wouldn't like was immediately pending.

"One must exercise them."

With a loud snap, all the hooks suspending the vampires released at once, dropping them to the floor, where they all landed on their heads at awkward angles that might have snapped the necks of living humans. As the undead, they were able to shrug off the impact like it was nothing. Each of them twisted and turned, still bound at the wrists and ankles, trying to find their individual hourglasses so they could resume their counts. But already all the hourglasses in the room were being retracted into their stands, until a series of lids could slide shut and shelter them from view. That's when the vampires suddenly became interested in the human meat present.

Out of practice, or too recently turned to know how, none of them changed their form into something that could easily slip out of the ties that bound their limbs. It was the only thing that saved us—or at least me—from instant death. The vampires, family or not, showed no interest in Sunder, and came crawling after me alone—the vastly preferable fountain of sustenance—en masse. Even trussed up, they made excellent time in their enthusiasm for fresh meat, for some live quarry. I presented a more novel meal than cold blood from a bank, indifferently pumped into their extremities, for the sake of later cultivation like some vampiric *foie gras*. As such, they came after me hard, skittering along on knees and elbows in rapid, purely inhuman fashion.

Sunder ran to each of his former family members in turn, trying to hold them back, trying to reason with them.

"No," he begged, "please! You're only doing an evil man's bidding! Fight him!"

"They're not your family anymore, kid," I warned him. "They're long gone. Whoever they once were left along with any sort of soul or conscience. They're nothing more than corpses that should be rotting instead of feeding. Now get the hell out of here! They don't want you. I'll deal with this myself. Somehow."

I was pleased to see Sunder run away, sprinting for the elevator, though I doubted he'd be able to get to another floor without the next passkey.

I tried a different route, retreating from the approaching brood down another series of connecting chambers. Crawling vampires kept appearing at various junctures, narrowing my choices, until my route eventually led out to the same lobby area where we'd arrived. By the time I got there, the top hatch of the elevator car hung open. So Sunder did find a way up to the next floor above us after all. Good for him. He didn't need to see what his former family was about to do to me.

The lead vampire—Sunder's father, if I remembered correctly—was in hot pursuit, with his awkward knee-elbow, knee-elbow gait. In the mere moments I'd turned away to confirm his son had vacated the level, he'd redoubled his efforts and closed the gap, tackling me to the floor. The rest of them would be all over me in a few seconds more.

Sunder's father had never had the chance to feed himself of his own volition, and the opportunity before him was exciting. I saw his long perfect teeth poised over me, ready to start biting deep and hard. My bones would be the first to chip and tangle all that fine dental work.

The vampire drew his shackled hands back, like he was about to give me a knuckle-slap across the face. But I knew he was aiming lower. He meant to tear out my throat with both sets of his long fingernails and gulp at the arterial spurt like a child drinking from a garden hose on a hot summer day. There was nothing I could do to stop him.

I closed my eyes and waited to feel the warm gush of blood erupt from my neck and splash across me. Instead, I felt a cold liquid wash over me from the opposite direction. My eyes snapped back open in time to see the vampire on top of me break apart as individual streams of water cut through him at a dozen different points at once. His raised arms withered and

melted away under a torrent that hit him full in the back, spilling out of the elevator shaft as it struck the roof of the stopped
car and flowed freely into the seventy-second floor lobby
through the open escape hatch. The body I was pinned under,
so strong and unopposable moments before, washed away like
it was barely there at all, turning into a murky silt, formless and
saturated in seconds.

Looking around, I caught glimpses of the rest of the vampire's brethren coming to pieces and collapsing into the
unexpected wave all around me. But I had no time to celebrate
my salvation. The flood of water pinned me just as firmly as the
blood-drinker had, throwing me against the nearest wall. I
struggled to keep my head up, but there was no surface within
reach, no air to fill my lungs. So water filled them instead.
When I broke out over the froth of the relentless wave, it was
only my consciousness that did so. My body remained on the
floor, pressed against the wall, drowned in the current.

It took another few minutes for an automated shutoff valve
to engage and redirect the water to an unbreached pipe in the
building's water system. Even before Sunder climbed back
down from the floor above, carrying a fire axe, I had guessed he
must have chopped through a water main to create the deluge
that had both saved and killed me. The kid had been taking
notes, and running water had certainly proved itself to be the
most effective weapon against vampires if you could rustle
some up at the right moment.

Dashing across the wet floor, splashing through the puddles
that had yet to drain away to lower levels, Sunder dropped his
axe and hurried to my side the moment he spotted me. Chest
compressions and mouth-to-mouth followed as he tried to
revive me.

I had drowned before. As deaths went, it was a convenient
way to go once you got past the natural panic of breathlessness,
and the unpleasant sensation of your lungs filling with invasive

fluid. This was only the second time someone had tried to resuscitate me with common CPR, like I didn't have a simple return covered on my end.

I remembered when it was Rebecca pumping my heart, trying to breathe life into me, while I watched from the other side and stubbornly waited for her to give up on me. But she never did. I broke first, and came back, letting her think she had saved me. And in a way, she had. Those were the early days after we first met, when I sorely lacked any connection with another regular human being. She provided me one, just when I needed it most.

I didn't keep Sunder waiting nearly so long. We had to keep moving. The thought of Rebecca somewhere above us, imprisoned by Menahem, instilled more dread in me than another thousand deaths pending.

"Get off," I gurgled at Sunder, despite a double lungful of water.

Rolling over on my side, I spat and sputtered, clearing as much liquid as I could from my brimming organs. I'd swallowed another gallon of water on top of what I'd inhaled, and that all had to come up too. It was several minutes before I was breathing properly again.

Sunder gave me my privacy while I got myself in order and finished spewing out what didn't belong in my body, along with a cup or two that did. When I rose to my feet again, I found him sitting in the wet, sullenly playing in the dirt. Heavy mounds of chalky earth, soaked through and unable to absorb a single drop more, were piled where Menahem's released vampires had disintegrated.

"This...this was my family," he said, running his fingers through one of the larger clumps of soaked clay. The wet soil leaked through his fingers and fell to the floor one dollop at a time, flattening out as formless blobs on the tiles.

"You okay?" I asked him.

"Yes," he said after careful contemplation. "Yes, I am. Their souls are at peace and they're with God now."

I didn't have the heart to tell him. Destroyed as they were at that moment, they still weren't all the way dead. Water or sunlight in quantity can leave a vampire in a terrible, unrecognizable state. But whether scorched ash or soggy sand, they'd be back eventually. I myself had been resurrected from less only recently.

"Right. Yeah," I agreed. "So you're okay? You have your shit together?"

"Together, yes," he nodded. "I'm good. I'm good. Now let's go finish this son of a bitch."

Sunder handed me the final passkey he'd discovered when I was down. The last challenge, and the final confrontation with Menahem, was waiting for us.

Chapter Twenty-Two

Fall

S UNDER BROUGHT ALONG THE FIRE AXE he'd smashed out of its emergency-only case, and it looked like he meant business. All the way up to eighty-one, he gripped the handle tightly with one hand, and tapped the other end, up by the blade, into his other, like he couldn't wait to imbed it into Menahem's face at the earliest opportunity.

"Your death by drowning was a most curious development that flew in the face of my plans. I was intrigued to see how it would play out, and now I have."

We ignored our host.

"I should be angry," Menahem told us over the elevator speaker. "You spoiled my entire distillery. It's a good thing for you I recently acquired a better vintage, or I might be tempted to get really mean."

When the elevator doors opened, Menahem continued speaking without pause. But his voice no longer came at us through an electronic relay. We were now within earshot of the real thing.

"Now, if you would care to join me for this, our final..."

Sunder didn't hesitate, didn't so much as pause to listen to the rest of what Menahem had to say, before he launched his fire axe at him, putting every ounce of strength and rage behind the swing. It flew, end over end, across the room with enough force to split a man in two. But Menahem was no longer a man. With inhuman speed, he sidestepped the missile and let it plant itself in the wall behind him.

"Nice try, boy," said our host, "but do not presume to interrupt me again."

Sunder judiciously held his tongue and advanced no further, but he glared at Menahem with a hatred beyond anything I'd ever expected to see from a good Christian youth.

The entire penthouse was enclosed in tinted glass, floor to ceiling, on all sides. Only a few steps out of the elevator, I could see myself and Sunder reflected a dozen times over. Not so, Menahem. I recalled how, in our first meeting, Menahem's image in his own tower's glass had been hazy, indistinct. Now it wasn't there at all. His transformation was complete. His immortality assured. He could never die, I could never hope to kill him, and, if he had his way, he would outlive everyone and everything on earth. Soon.

"You have my friend," I said, getting to the point that was most pressing to me.

"I do," confirmed Menahem.

There was a crimson blackout curtain behind him, blocking the view. It matched the ceremonial robes he wore for the occasion. Menahem was dressed like he was prepared to offer us, and the whole world, a barnburner of a sermon in his new capacity as Death Incarnate. I suppose it was appropriate attire for the occasion. A regular two-thousand-dollar business suit would have come across as dressing down. Grabbing one end of the curtain's fabric, he began to pull it aside across the overhead rod that suspended it.

"Allow me to reunite you," he added.

The figure behind the curtain was trussed up like a side of beef fresh off the abattoir floor. And was in about as poor a shape. Even inverted, I recognized the face at once. Or what was left of it. There was a big chunk missing, scooped out of the side of the head by a recent trauma.

"Marin?" I asked no one in particular.

Like the other vampires below, Menahem had his latest acquisition dangling in a similar predicament. An hourglass full of sand trickled away before Marin, keeping him occupied, sedated. The spike we'd run through his chest had been extracted, leaving him in much improved condition compared to how we'd left him. Nevertheless, Marin remained just as trapped, just as helpless. A tap, jammed into his throat, was slowly filling a brandy glass set under it, one drop at a time. There was already enough collected for a good, bracing belt.

"None other," Menahem confirmed. "Your favourite vampire in the world. Don't deny it. You've grown quite fond of him, I can tell."

"I melted out his eyeball, ran a giant iron stake through him, and buried him deep underground."

"A spat between friends. It happens," shrugged Menahem. "Thank you for pinning him down for me. It made it most simple to exhume and capture him. Obviously I've had you under surveillance this whole time, watching your every move. Marin was tucked under the soil for no more than ten minutes before I had him dug up again."

The oversized screw we'd used had also been retrieved and preserved. Menahem had it mounted on the wall, cleaned up and resting on a pair of brackets, right next to the ceremonial dagger he'd used to put me down. Another trophy on display.

"What was with all that intimate cuddly bullshit you were talking about?" I asked of the speech he'd given me about the hostage he'd taken.

"Have you not been living under the same roof? Does he not now occupy the casket you once used as a bed?"

"I assumed you were talking about Rebecca. I thought that's who you had."

"What? The floozy you're shacked up with? Why would I waste my time kidnapping her? She obviously means nothing to you. She certainly means nothing to me. Marin, however, is of tremendous value to us both."

"I could do without him, frankly."

"Well I can't. Drinking from the corrupted veins of lesser vampires has imbued me with much of their power. But if I am to wield all the might and potential of the nosferatu, I must consume the blood of an ancient master. Marin was useful as an agent when he would not submit to me fully. Captured, crippled, his best use now is as sustenance."

Menahem retrieved the glass and turned the knob on the tap, shutting off the flow and saving the next precious drop for a later date.

"Marin has been a slow drip," he said, "but there is enough to bring me to my final level of mastery over death."

Menahem swirled the blackened goop around in his glass, coating the sides until they were barely translucent.

"He has been indulging himself again, and recently. Where did he get this small taste that has filtered its way through him and come to my lips now? What temptation broke his fast? Was it the bloodbath I orchestrated at your pathetic trade gathering?"

He studied my face across the room with his acute, heightened senses, and smiled.

"I'm so glad," he said, contemplating the sickly ooze. "Yet more fruits of my labour."

Menahem raised the glass.

"To your very poor health," he toasted, and threw back the cocktail in one big gulp.

His head remained tilted, even after swallowing, like he was in a reverie brought on by the sheer delight of it.

"Yummy, huh?" I said flatly.

"You have no idea," Menahem sighed. "The difference is astounding. Like the gap between the finest wine from the best vinyard in the world, and a homebrewed vodka concocted from rotting roots. Your destruction of my carefully cultivated crop below means nothing to me now. I could never go back."

"It smells like fish oil gone bad from here," I commented.

"And tastes worse," added Menahem. "But it is a taste that can be embraced if there is a will to do so. A necessity. And my need is great indeed."

Jeevak Menahem threw his arms wide and released the glass. It shattered across the floor, unheeded.

"I can already feel a greater strength flowing through me, a greater command of my powers. There are no more limits to my abilities, no more restrictions. The master has become my prey, and now I stand as the one, true master!"

Sunder couldn't contain himself any longer.

"You stand as a master of shit and decay, you unholy abomination! You foul abortion of the pit! You...you...you motherless fuck!"

Such naughty language. You wonder where a religious kid like that picks it up. It would certainly give Sunder something to confess. Either to a priest if he survived the night, or his god in person if he didn't.

Menahem lowered his arms, disappointed at having his victory speech so rudely interrupted. I wondered what horrible new vampire power he would unleash in response, what terror he would select from his nefarious catalogue of supernatural skills.

"I see your insolence is catching, Eulogy," said Menahem, and pulled out a gun from under his robes.

A vampire with a gun. It looked ludicrous, but I wasn't able to dwell on it. Not for long. Menahem shot Sunder straight in the chest without hesitation. The kid collapsed backwards across the floor. It would have been an instantly fatal shot, but I noticed the feathered tuft at the back of the round that was embedded between his ribs. The projectile jutted out, rather than penetrating deep like a regular bullet would.

"He's having a short nap. It's only a tranquillizer dart," Menahem explained. "No long-term effect unless fired directly into the heart or brain. Only in such an event would it be lethal. Like so."

A split moment later, he fired a second round. This one at me. After so many deaths in a row, I was in no shape to dodge anything, least of all a high-speed dart coming right at me.

The pinprick punched through my skull and pieced my brain sack, instantly injecting its venom straight into my frontal lobe. The physical damage was minimal, but the toxin plowed through my consciousness like a rocket-fueled sledgehammer, far worse than anything inflicted by the previous rounds of snakes and scorpions. For about three seconds I was treated to the world's most intense acid hit, and then my mind fell right out the back of my body. Even dead and adrift in the ether, I was tripping my ass off for the next few minutes until my consciousness came to terms with the fact that it was no longer connected to my body, my brain, or the chemical cocktail that had killed them.

"Do you sense it now, in the room with your body, the final death I have planned for you?" I heard Menahem taunt my corpse, my soul, from the other side of eternity.

Red embers ignited, glowing in the gloom, piecing straight through the living world and the reality beyond. They rose from the floor, elevated as multiple panels slid aside, allowing a platform from somewhere below to rise into position, bearing the beast that had been on my trail for several weeks and thousands of miles. My constant companion that hungered for me in a unique way I was about to suffer, much to Menahem's delight. There was no more avoiding it.

"It takes a true master of darkness to command the gwyllgi," continued Menahem, certain I could hear him. "A master vampire, as Marin has become over centuries. Or a master vampire, as I have been reborn."

Even as the platform came level with the floor, the hellhound continued to rise, standing up and stretching to its full height. My spirit hovered close by, and it seemed to follow that essence with its blazing eyes, like I had been spotted and recognized across the great divide.

"I no longer need Marin to serve as a go-between. In this, my ultimate form, I can command the beast. To kill as I see fit, to feed when I permit. And it is a treat I offer him this night."

The gwyllgi circled around the corpse on the floor, poking at my limbs with its great snout, as though daring me to revive. Alive or dead, my body was not going to go unmolested. Just as worrying were the few probing pokes it took at Sunder's sleeping form. His blood may have made him distasteful to vampires, but the monstrous dog seemed interested in making him either an entrée or a dessert, depending on when I chose to come out and play.

"Will this kill you permanently, I wonder?" continued Menahem, enjoying every moment of my dilemma. "Can you return with a head separated from your body? A head that's been masticated, digested, evacuated? I have pondered this for quite some time, and it is an experiment I look forward to seeing played out. Even if it fails, I expect it will be most amusing to watch you try to regenerate from a mound of hellhound scat."

The beast sniffed at my head, seeing if that might rouse me. My hair rustled in the wind whenever it exhaled. It could have chosen any moment to tear my head right off, but it seemed to prefer live meat. I would have to time my return very carefully if I was going to have any chance to thwart what looked like an inevitable outcome.

"There's no mistaking your scent now. The gwyllgi will not be led astray again. Come back Mr. Eulogy. Inhabit your body one final time, and let's discover your destiny together."

Impatient, the hound continued its orbit of the penthouse. I waited until it was at the farthest point it was likely to get from my body before diving back in. My brain was still full of tranquillizer soup, but it had spread out and diluted enough over the last several minutes for me to stay sharp and focused. Mentally prepared to move quickly the moment I was back, I took my first breath and braced my palms against the floor so I could better push myself up and into action.

All the preparation in the world wouldn't have made me fast enough to beat that damn dog. In the same second I sucked in air again, the very moment my heart resumed beating, it bounded over and pinned my shoulders to the floor under its enormous paws. I hadn't been able to rise more than a couple of inches off the icy tiles before the hound was all over me. Sauna steam blasted down on me from its foul breath, making me flop-sweat. Condensation formed on the marble floor at the back of my skull and started to form a pool. All I could see inches away were rows of sharp teeth, like the jaws of a shark, and a wagging forked tongue the size and colour of a raw porterhouse steak.

Probing, the sharp forks of the creature's tongue tickled my nose before the heavy wet slab hit me in the face and licked straight up my chin, across my cheek, and all the way to my forehead, slicking back my hairline. The layer of saliva left behind felt like a hot facial at a spa of ill-repute. Instantly I was reminded of the morning I had woken up to find Oliver dead, when I'd been covered in a sticky fluid I couldn't identify. Had the gwyllgi been in my room that night? Had it panted all over me then, tasted my flesh, and spared me regardless of the orders issued? Did it consider me not to its liking, an infeasible meal? Or did it see me as something else entirely?

Was this slobbering, sickly display a carnivore toying with its food before feasting, or was it simply a big dumb dog showing affection? Sure, it took a true master of darkness to command the gwyllgi. A master vampire, like Marin, like Menahem.

Or, maybe, just maybe, a master necromancer. Like me.

"Sit!" I commanded in a firm shout.

Just like that, the pressure was off me. The heavy paws pinning my shoulders were withdrawn, and the huge animal backed off a few paces.

And he sat.

I followed suit, pushing myself up off the floor until I was in a sitting position.

"Roll over!" I ordered.

And the huge bovine-sized bulk of a canine abomination from the bowels of Hades itself did just that, shaking the floor beneath us.

I rose to my feet and tried one more.

"Play dead!"

And the gwyllgi of legend, the ancient terror of Britannia, obeyed, sticking its paws up in the air and remaining stock still, waiting for me to tell it otherwise.

"Impossible!" Menahem thundered.

"What's wrong?" I asked. "Wouldn't he listen to you when you were still human? Does he answer to you even now?"

"Get up you idiot animal! Get up and tear that fool apart!"

But the gwyllgi didn't budge an inch. The only movement on the floor was Sunder, who was just coming to. Dazed, he pulled the dart out of his chest and struggled to get up. Still fuzzy around the edges, he had a hard time focusing and figuring out what he'd missed. The monstrous mutt before us was the first thing that caught his attention, sprawled and lifeless as it appeared.

"You killed it?" Sunder asked in amazement.

"Won it over, more like," I said.

"How?"

"I guess he thinks I'm his master."

Sunder, backing away trepidatiously, nudged me.

"Let's get away from it before it changes its mind."

"No," I said, watching Jeevak Menahem's temper boiling over across the room, "I think we might need all the help we can get."

I patted my thigh a couple of times and coaxed, "C'mon pup-pup!"

The hellhound seemed to know all the basic dog commands as well as if he'd been to obedience school. Who knew where he'd picked them up over the course of untold generations haunting the British Isles, but now that someone he seemed to like was issuing the orders, he was eager to prove himself.

"Eulogy! Where do you think you're going with my gwyllgi?" Menahem growled.

Another standard command occurred to me. One from more advanced dog-training courses. I didn't know if he'd learned the word, but he was well versed in the activity. I thought I'd give it a try.

"Gwilly," I said, drawing his attention with a pet name I'd just come up with, "kill."

I only had to shift my eyes to Menahem, and the beast had his target. With a savage snarl, he launched himself across the penthouse, charging in a scramble of claws and a tide of shaggy fur that rolled in waves with each stride of its muscular legs.

My rival necromancer fumbled for his tranquillizer gun, jamming a full clip of half a dozen darts into the breach. For a moment, I thought he wasn't going to manage it in time, but the rounds clicked home and he fired wildly at the running unreal animal. Dart after dart pounded into its hide with no discernable effect.

Only a dozen feet short of Menahem, the gwyllgi abruptly face-planted into the floor and skidded to a halt. The volley of darts had finally kicked in at the last moment and stopped the giant dog cold. Fast asleep, its meat-flap lips swung and sputtered with each heavy breath. He'd be sleeping it off for a good long while.

It was disappointing to not get to see the monster Menahem had set after me turn around and bite him in the ass, but his obvious frustration at his plan not panning out almost made up for it. He angrily punched a button set in the wall, and the lift that had brought the gwyllgi up from the lower depths promptly ported him back down out of sight. The floor panels reset themselves once the failed experiment was swept under the rug. I wasn't about to let Menahem ignore his blunder.

"Shooting it was your best option? What's the matter?" I taunted. "Couldn't transform into a puff of smoke? Or an even bigger dog to counter mine? I saw you do a pretty good bat that night at the bar, but I guess that's not much of a match for a hound of hell that answers to me."

"I have the power to accomplish any of those transformations," he boasted. "The instinct to do so at a moment's notice will come with experience."

"You have any other monsters tucked up your sleeve?" I wondered. "Something else I might charm once it realizes what a swell guy I am and what a piece of shit you are?"

"What value the gwyllgi could possibly see in you escapes me. Perhaps its steady diet of your fellow morons and freaks has poisoned its mind. No matter. Now that you have returned from the dead and the hound has failed at its intended task, the limits of your life are clear to me."

I didn't know what the future had in store for me as well as Menahem did, but at least now we were working outside of his game plan. He would have to improvise.

"Would you care to know the specifics of your next death?" he asked.

"Not particularly," I said, even though I knew he was going to tell me anyway.

"Four and a half minutes from now, you plummet eighty floors to a bone-shattering demise."

Improvising or not, the forecast was doubtless correct, and it pissed me off.

"Out that very window," he added, pointing at a ceiling-to-floor panel of glass behind me that couldn't be opened. That meant it was going to get broken. Probably by me as I was tossed through it. It sounded like extra pain I could do without.

"That means five or so minutes from now," he continued, "I'll be able to foresee your death after that. I look forward to it. The one silver lining of my spoiled designs this evening is that I won't have to give up my favourite pastime of previewing your demises."

Four and a half minutes and counting down fast. The smug bastard was acting like he'd already killed me again, like I was already defeated. Well, it may have been a foregone conclusion, but I wasn't dead yet, and a lot could be accomplished in four and a half minutes.

"Step aside, kid, this is going to get ugly."

Sunder was still looking woozy from getting dosed full of sedative. He didn't argue to join me for this last round of the fight, sitting down heavily in the corner and struggling to keep his eyes open so he could at least watch what was about to happen next.

Menahem and I squared off against each other. A couple of spell slingers ready to duel, waiting to see who would make the first move. What I needed was a weapon. Something within my necrotic purview. Dead matter, ideally.

And then I had a thought: we were in a necromancer's tower, after all. One built to his own specifications, on top of a graveyard no less. There had to be something I could use. Some material. Something I could snatch away from Menahem as I'd unwittingly done with his imported devil-dog.

The penthouse was mostly one large chamber, but there were pillars all around—support columns that not only held up the top of the building, but ran down the interior, all the way to its base, keeping the structure stable and steady. My hand shot out and I planted an open palm on the nearest one. It was the physical contact I needed to help connect me to the rest of the building and its contents while my mind went searching.

I began chanting an incantation I hadn't had to resort to in years.

"Audi animae mortuorum quiescit! Tu hercle dico iuxta vel procul!"

"Who taught you to conjugate Latin?" Menahem sneered contemptuously.

"Google Translate," I informed him, in a voice I hoped sounded unashamed, and repeated the chant.

My head start was short-lived. I could tell Menahem was concerned I might stumble onto something I could use. After only a moment's pause, I heard him repeat my words in English. He didn't try to Latin it up. He certainly wasn't interested in showmanship. All he wanted to do was block whatever move I was trying to make.

"Hear me, souls departed, dead at rest. Answer my call, be you near or far," he muttered, mirroring the less jazzy version of my incantation.

It was the necromantic equivalent of an all-points bulletin. An emergency signal for anyone listening. A Hail Mary pass for those who converse with the dead. And the dead responded. I heard a distant ping on my radar. It echoed back hard. And when I looked at Menahem across the room, I could tell he hadn't heard it—would never hear it. He'd missed it entirely, even as it was so obvious to me.

"You can't feel it can you?" I said, as the realization dawned on me. "The dead buried deep below."

"The cemetery and its residents were removed before the cornerstone of this tower was even laid," he told me, like I was an idiot.

"Beneath that."

"The victims of the cholera epidemic answer to me now."

"No," I said softly, "Beneath that."

The look on his face was sweet to me. Bewilderment, befuddlement, anxiety and anger. It was the look of a narcissistic control freak who had just realized there was something in his meticulous machinations that he had overlooked. Something completely beyond his control. Something he was unable to identify, even as I stood in front of him, pointing right at it. He still couldn't see it, couldn't sense it, couldn't feel it. Because despite all his vast wealth, all his terrible abilities and influence, all his grand schemes for ever greater power and dominance, he wasn't quite the very best necromancer out there.

I was.

He didn't try to ask me what I was on about. He could see I already had my head bowed, my eyes closed, concentrating, focused, trying to make contact. He followed my example and began searching the ether with his mind, rushing to discover what I knew and what he had missed, racing to make a connection before I could. He didn't stand a chance. The race was already lost before he ever heard the starting gun, before he even knew there was going to be a race at all. My mind was underground, connecting the dots, bridging the gaps of years and centuries between them. And every one of those dots was a human corpse, lost and forgotten, neglected and disavowed by history and progress. They were down there, those dots, dismissed long ago as inconsequential, ignored for so long. Nobody knew they were there so deep, except me.

And their numbers were expansive—lying under what was once the oldest graveyard in the city, under the mass graves of cholera dead that had once filled pits beneath that, under what was now the parking garage of the Algonquin Tower. If the construction workers digging the foundation of this gleaming new skyscraper had dug just a few feet deeper three years earlier, they would have discovered it before me—the greatest archaeological find on the continent so far this century. They would have found the single most populous Indian burial ground on the entire east coast. Generations—a hundred of them or more—dating back to the first humans to migrate to these unspoiled lands, thousands of years before settlers came to pave it all over. They were still down there with their wealth of artifacts and culture. To anthropologists it would have been a priceless collection of raw history. To me, in that moment, it was a priceless collection of raw material—flesh and bone, ash and dust. It was an army of the dead, and I was calling them to war.

What I needed most now was something sharp. Anything within reach that could draw blood. I wondered if I could break a window to get a shard of glass, but then I remembered the worthless potato peeler from Sunder's kit. I recalled how I had absently stuffed it in my pocket, where it wasn't so worthless after all.

I reached into my coat and found the cheap plastic handle. The inner edge of the curved blade was small and not terribly threatening, but if it could cut through the skin of a spud, it would get the job done on some flesh. Normally I hesitate to draw my own blood unless it's a spur of the moment suicide-of-necessity. If I'm going to bleed, I prefer to be dead for it. But this was an exceptional circumstance. This was pride. I had an opponent I was working against, and I was feeling highly competitive.

I drew the blade through the palm of my hand and made a fist, squeezing a thin stream of blood out between my fingers and dripping it across the floor tiles, ritualistically calling to my recruits.

Menahem saw what I was doing and reached for the much more impressive ceremonial blade mounted on the wall. He opened up some veins of his own and assumed the same position, drizzling his black vampiric blood, a mirror-image mimic. He knew the ritual. Of course he did. But he didn't know what he was performing the ritual for. He was only acting in my wake, hoping to catch up, make contact first. And there was no chance of that. He didn't even know what he was aiming for.

I could feel those ancient warriors rising from their graves, tearing through the few feet of earth and the few inches of pavement that blocked their passage into the building. First by the dozens, then by the hundreds, this army began to fill the parking garage dozens of levels beneath us until they were shoulder to shoulder. An army at attention, waiting for their orders. I gave them one. Simple. Direct. Devastating.

"Toto dissipantem!"

Menahem didn't try to mock my pigeon Latin this time. He knew what those words meant. To him, to his empire, to his precious crown jewel.

Tear it all down.

A mass reanimation like this is no small feat. The results are short lived, and nowhere near as effective as a proper raising done to create a sole zombie. The individuals are weaker, more brittle. But in bulk, they can accomplish much. And when numbering in the hundreds, the thousands, the damage they cause can be quite devastating. Especially when they're set to the task of ripping through concrete and rebar, steel and rivets. In much the same way the tide can wear down anything eventually, so too can a relentless horde of mobile corpses, clawing and biting and pounding on a targeted structure. And they can do it much faster.

It was the building infrastructure they were throwing themselves against at my behest. And the infrastructure was winning. Relentless though they were, my army was still flesh and bone against metal and stone. The flesh and bone wore out faster. But I didn't need the dead to grind their way right through a few key support columns. I just needed them to weaken those columns enough so that the crushing burden resting atop the crippled base did the rest of the work for me.

For years I'd been misinformed about how skyscrapers collapsed. Oft-repeated footage always showed a straight drop into their own footprint. Some billowing clouds of pulverized concrete later, and what's left behind is a tidy pile of ruins, ready for the bulldozers. That, of course, only happens in the event of a controlled demolition. There was nothing controlled about this collapse. Once the first set of supporting pillars were down, the building teetered violently. I watched the penthouse jolt suddenly to a startling 45-degree angle, and I thought the whole thing would come down then and there, like a felled tree under the assault of a lumberjack's axe.

Every stick of furniture and decor not bolted to the floor came loose and flung themselves across the room, smashing into the ceiling-to-floor windows and shattering the glass. Most of the panes held, but a few exploded into the night and rained shards into the street below. Even my giant iron stake jumped off its brackets and flew tip over base across the entire length of the suite. Last I saw, it was cartwheeling straight towards Menahem's head, and I spared a moment to hope the bastard took the tip straight to an eye.

I looked for Sunder and found he'd been thrown across the room like just about everything else. And he was sleeping through the whole thing. Knocking Menahem's tower out from under him was a suicide mission for me, but it didn't have to be for Sunder as well. There was only one way to get the kid to safety.

Struggling to keep my footing on the bucking, wobbling floor, I ran across to where Marin remained dangling, so distracted counting grains of sand he had no idea what was going on around him. The hourglass was still spilling its contents from one vessel to another. We would run out of time long before it had a chance to finish.

I grabbed hold of the heavy curtain that had shielded Menahem's hostage, using it to stabilize myself, and punted the hourglass out of its moorings, sending it flying across the room, out of the vampire's field of vision. Marin snapped out of his trance almost immediately.

"Mr. Eulogy," he said, spotting me, "I must apologize for my earlier behaviour! I..."

"Shut up and make yourself useful! Get the kid out of here!"

In a gush of vapour, Marin extracted himself from his bindings and reformed in front of me, perfectly steady on the wildly tilting floor. He looked around at the ongoing disaster, the unconscious teenager siding around among the penthouse debris, and understood the mortal peril at once.

"How?" he asked.

But he knew. There was one way, and one way only. The look of revulsion on his face was unmistakable, even in the middle of the rumbling and swaying of the whole tower. But he'd do it. He owed us one.

As windows continued to shatter all around us, Marin seemed to distort grotesquely. Bones popped and reconfigured, joints turned backwards upon themselves, and appendages mutated in ways that weren't even vaguely human. The thing that emerged from this twisting vortex of flesh was a sickening atrocity—a most welcome one. If anything could be read in the feral face of Marin's new form, it was disgust. Disgust with himself and what he had become. It could best be described as a gigantic bat, a Chiroptera of the flying-fox variety, but many times larger and nowhere near as cute. Particularly with the head wound that persisted and had been translated to the new physical configuration.

Spreading his wings to their full extent, Marin lifted off the floor, disengaging from the failing structure and taking to the air. He swooped over to Sunder's prone body as it slid across the tiles, dangerously close to one of the splintered window frames, and clamped his talons around the teen's shoulders. Even in Marin's grip, Sunder continued his perilous drift towards oblivion. But as they passed through the vacant panel and out into the chill night air, the bat remained aloft, carrying its human payload safely away from the doomed tower.

There was no doubt. The whole tower was coming down. I felt like I'd been to this party before; fighting one of Charlie Nocturne's anointed horsemen, a building collapsing all around me. I didn't relish being trapped inside another structural failure, this time on an epic scale—and suddenly, I wasn't. Thrown across the room by the reeling edifice one moment, I was outside and in open space the next, cast through one of the shattered-glass vacancies that were opening up on all sides. A gaping portal to the sky outside, I found myself flying high over the downtown lights, like I might safely glide all the way to the city limits and land in a grassy field far removed from asphalt and disaster.

Instead, I fell, straight down the side of the tower. In those short moments of terminal velocity, I saw the base of the building snapping away from the top two-thirds, trying to topple over to the north. The rest of the building briefly swung back upright before the whole thing committed to a southbound collapse and came down in billowing clouds of freshly pulverized powder.

By then, I'd already hit bottom.

Spared an impact with solid pavement, I instead suffered a decidedly softer but no less fatal collision with the synthetic rubber-membrane flattop roof of a neighbouring car dealership. It wasn't long before I was able to peel myself off the sticky surface where I'd left a perfect, human-shaped impact crater. After so much practice in one night, my recovery time was improving. I hoped my healing time would similarly benefit. I was in sad shape, and as I crawled back inside my poor abused body, I could tell the fall had ruptured the few organs I had left that hadn't already had holes poked in them that night. Having landed favouring one side, half of me was broken and squashed, and I felt like I'd been slapped in the face with an anvil.

With one final act of pure will power, I was able to force myself back to my feet and limp over to a fire escape. The wrought-iron stairs led to a retractable ladder that lowered me to street level. As I dragged my way down the road on one good leg, I could feel the bones of my opposite leg, arm, and ribs crunching and complaining as they tried to reorder themselves into their correct alignment and begin fusing.

The destruction that lay ahead was enormous, but the Algonquin Tower had managed to collapse straight down the boulevard, obliterating everything in its path, but sparing the commercial buildings lined up on either side. I stopped short of the major wreckage, full of twisted superstructure and shattered rubble. The demolished contents of the entire tower lay spilled out for all to see like a gutted serpent.

And there, lying on its side in the road, was my inherited headgear.

"Huh," I said aloud. "It really is a magic hat."

Dusty with particles from all the atomized glass and concrete, it had managed to float gently down to street level, in its own due time, for a soft landing away from the major debris field. I retrieved my top hat and pushed out the single dent it had suffered in the fall, returning it to its default shape.

I spotted a figure through the haze and limped over to him. It was Sunder, sitting on the curb, holding his throbbing head in his hands, trying to shake off the lingering effects of the tranquillizer.

"What did I miss?" he wondered, still not able to take in the vista of mayhem and disaster spread out before him.

"Oh, not much," I assured him. "But you might want to thank someone for coming through in a pinch to save your life."

"Thanks," he said.

"Not me."

Marin was perched above us on a steel girder that had been bent by the collapse to such a degree, it formed an arch. His extended wings kept him balanced as he stepped off and glided gracefully to the ground. Before my eyes, his face folded in on itself, switching from a hideous rodent visage to a slightly less hideous human one. In moments, he was back to looking more or less like a man.

"I sincerely apologize for attacking you," said Marin, like no time had passed since our last civil conversation. "The hunger, when it comes, demands satisfaction and takes control over all conscious thought or intent."

"Right," I said, in a conciliatory mood after so rough a night. "Well, uh, I guess I'm sorry about melting a hole through your head."

"I have retained my vision on one side. Alas, I cannot gaze upon my reflection to assess the damage. Is it very unbecoming?"

He turned his head so I might better inspect the wound I'd given him. I could see exposed brain matter through the hole.

"You can hardly notice, really," I assured him. "Maybe wear a scarf."

"The boy is safe?" he asked.

"Yeah," I said. "The kid's going to be fine. I'm not sure how he's going to square being rescued by a vampire, but he'll get to live long enough to come to terms with it thanks to you."

"He will do well to remember that most of my kind are devoid of compassion or mercy."

The talk of other vampires brought our mutual enemy to mind. Marin seemed attuned to the whereabouts of the new undead master now that his own stolen blood was flowing through the necromancer.

"Menahem!" he hissed suddenly, looking around in fright. "I sense him...and he is close!"

None of us were in any shape to fight him, but I went looking anyway. I had to end this, once and for all. I could only hope that my last glimpse of him, with my anti-vampire weapon hurtling his way, had led to some grave injury that would put us on a more even keel.

I found Jeevak Menahem a few minutes later, not far from the ruins of his tower, shrouded by the settling particles. He didn't get it in the eye, like I'd hoped. This was so much better.

The spike's point had pierced him dead centre in the mouth, ramming straight down his throat, through any number of organs, heart included, and had shot out the other end right about where I judged his sphincter would be. The entire length of that cast-iron screw ran all the way through him, from his asshole face to his actual asshole, leaving only the final top inches sticking out of his mouth. He couldn't bend, he couldn't move, and his head was thrown back sharply to accommodate the thick metal shaft that reached down his esophagus and plumbed his necrotic gastro-intestinal system.

"Now that looks like it hurts," I commented.

"'uk 'oo!" he tried to say. I was impressed he could even make that much noise.

Θ

Marin didn't want to join us for the trip back to the cemetery but, once I told him what I had in mind, he was pleased to help us load Jeevak Menahem in the trunk of Sunder's car, lifting the incapacitated necromancer-nosferatu and the hunk of metal stuck in him like the load weighed nothing at all. Safely parked around the corner, away from the disaster, the rolling rust-bucket had survived to serve us once more. The sedative still coursing through his veins left Sunder in iffy condition to drive, but we were in a hurry to get out of the area before the invasion of emergency vehicles locked down the whole district. Already the sound of approaching sirens was deafening.

"I thank you for saving me from Menahem, even after you condemned me," said Marin in parting.

"Yeah, well, the staking and burying thing was me feeling salty about what you did at the convention. I know you were only trying to keep Menahem from turning you into a sippy sack until the end of time. I get that now."

"I do not speak of that condemnation," he said, and pointed a finger at his hollowed out eye socket. "I refer to this."

"Right," I said of a scar so bad, it would never heal. "That too."

"It is not the wound itself that troubles me. It is the nature of it. I would have preferred if you had taken an arm or a leg instead."

"What do you mean?"

"Can it not be said that you have given me The Mark of the Sighted One?"

I had to admit, it seemed I had inadvertently doled out another one of the tags that were marking the proposed horsemen of the apocalypse.

"Stopping Charlie Nocturne and putting an end to the End Times is the next priority," I said. "Top of the list, right below taking a few days off to rest, relax, and sit around in my underwear. Dying a dozen times and falling off the top of a skyscraper kinda knocks the wind out of a guy, you know?"

"Recuperate, recover, Mr. Eulogy. You have earned it," said Marin, slowly becoming transparent. "But do so in haste. The schedule for the apocalypse marches forward, and it waits for no one."

Even as he blended into the clouds of smoke rising off the ruins, a wave of tiny, shelled insects skittered past underfoot, retreating from the disaster area like rats abandoning a sinking ship. The Algonquin Tower had been an awfully new building to have been so infested by bugs. Were they the best the melted vampires of the upper floors could transform into to make good their escape, or were they still trapped under the rubble, mixed into the mess as blobs of silt? Surely nothing inside that cataclysm could have made it out intact.

A lonely howl, distant but rising in volume over the sirens of the encroaching first responders, begged to differ.

☉

Resting in the passenger seat for the lengthy ride, my broken bones worked double time to link up sufficiently to allow some use of my fractured limbs. Meanwhile my guts did their best to plug themselves and stop leaking all sorts of fluids they shouldn't have been flooding my chest cavity with. By the time we arrived back at Fairview State, I was in good enough working order to get a bit of manual labour done. Sunder still looked doped to the gills, but I'd make sure he got to throw a few shovelfuls himself. Whether he'd remember them in the morning or not, he'd be glad to know he got his licks in.

The empty grave where we had buried Marin so recently had been sloppily unearthed. I barely had to widen the hole with Sunder's entrenching tool before we were able to unceremoniously stuff Menahem's carcass down into it. He sat at the bottom of the pit, glaring up at us with spite, choking on the spike like he still had something to say.

There remained half a foot of the metal stake sticking out of his gaping, upturned mouth. I decided to remedy that. Two swings of the entrenching spade finished jamming it down his throat. The first one bashed the screw head into his front teeth, breaking them. The second drove it down a few more inches, knocking out his canines, defanging him. And he'd wanted so badly to retain his good looks, like a sexy movie vampire. Now he looked like a bloody toothless idiot.

"That ought to do it," I announced. The extra length of stake had been driven out his backside and into the earth, pinning him to the spot. Hopefully forever.

I stabbed the spade into the pile of upturned earth next to the hole and dumped the first load in his lap. Menahem feebly knocked his knees together, trying to shake the soil off. I threw the next scoop into his face and thought I heard him whimper in fear. It sounded pathetic, but I was pitiless.

"Does this seem harsh? Vindictive? Just plain mean? Well, tough shit," I said. "You say you were only trying to be top dog in the necromancy game. You were only shooting for immortality by sucking the life out of others. You were only plotting the apocalypse with an entity that's trying to put an end to all life. Fair enough. We all have our lapses in judgement. But you hurt friends of mine. And that's a 'fuck you forever' in my book. Enjoy eternity, you prick."

I moved the earth into the hole quickly, filling it and watching his body vanish from sight an inch at a time. I didn't take a break until there was little more than his head and shoulders sticking out of the mud. There was still another half of the grave to drop on him.

"You want to tip me off about how I die next before we part ways?" I asked him while any sort of communication was still possible.

He made some vague, angry noise as he gummed at the edges of the iron screw that disappeared into his mouth and wound its way through the length of his chest cavity and bowels.

"Huh?" I asked, holding my palm up to my ear. "What's that? Something caught in your throat?"

He tried again to say something at me. Probably not anything nice.

"Oh well," I shrugged. "I guess I'll just have to wait and be surprised."

It took another twenty minutes to cover him over. I relished every shovelful. Then I stamped the soil down underfoot until it looked like all the other recently relocated graves that stretched away in every direction. Just one more hole filled with dirt and bad memories.

Chapter Twenty-Three

Buried

I'D SEEN THAT LOOK on her face many times before. The day-after look. And it told me all I needed to know. Rebecca hadn't been in last night because she'd been out drinking. Hard. Tom's miserable death had shoved her off the wagon, and her grief had driven her into a late-night bender that probably left her blackout drunk. She must have come home and passed out once the bars closed, sometime while I was off playing deadly games with Jeevak Menahem.

Up and out of bed again, I could feel the migraine she was coping with, just by looking at her groggy face. She'd come from the kitchen, carrying a glass brimming with her world-famous hair-of-the-dog home brew. It was a rough morning, and it was only going to get rougher.

Poor thing. I would have expressed sympathy, but I couldn't, considering the state I was in.

The moment she laid eyes on me, Rebecca screamed and dropped her hangover cure. The glass hit the floor and shattered, splashing her concoction all over the place. Pity. I would have asked her to pour it into the soup to help fortify the broth.

I was lying in the bathtub, which was brimming with water and filthy with fresh mud and old blood. Stripped bare, the brown water preserved my modesty, and my nudity was further obscured by the collection of fruits, vegetables, and raw meat I had raided from the refrigerator and dumped in the water for an added boost of nutrients I could absorb. My whole body was a collection of piercings and perforations that went straight through most of my organs. There was hardly a square inch of skin that wasn't bruised black, purple, or green, and my flesh felt like a leaky bag that was hardly up to the task of containing all the broken, fractured, and pulverized bones that were working hard to knit themselves back into a proper human skeleton just below the surface.

She'd never seen me so badly beaten and battered. Even that time she'd found my body reduced to ashes—after a bureaucratic oversight had me cremated to practically nothing—must have seemed promising by comparison.

Rebecca's hands instinctively went to her face, cupping her mouth, stifling more shrieks, but doing little to contain the sobs and tears that erupted at the sight of me.

"Oh my God, Rip! Oh my God, oh my God, oh my God!" she babbled. "What happened?"

My energy was spent. I'd used up the very last of my reserves preparing the bath after Sunder dragged me upstairs and made sure I got into the apartment okay. All I could offer, by way of assurance, was to raise a couple of fingers into a V-shape before my hand collapsed back into the tub to soak and heal.

With my weak voice, I managed exactly two words.

"I won."

☿

There were no immediate mysteries to solve. No pressing information that had to be wrung from a departed spirit. There was only me at the grave of a friend. I wanted to talk, like so many people visiting a grave wished to talk. They all longed to be heard, and I could easily make myself heard. Yet I didn't want to be. I didn't want to disturb the peace.

"Hello, Wilbur," I said, making a conscious effort not to penetrate the ether.

"Long time," I added. I don't know what made me feel more foolish. The empty pleasantries or the awkward silence between them.

"So this is how normal people have a graveside chat," I said, partly to myself, partly to Wilbur's imagined presence. "It's weird. Very one-sided."

I'd let a few of weeks go by before returning to the Fairview State Cemetery. Rebecca was the one to suggest a visit. For a brand new cemetery, it already seemed heavily populated with both friends and enemies. Others would be added before long, I was sure of it. Hopefully more of one than the other.

Time off had given me a chance to recover and let all my wounds from my string of deaths seal and regenerate. The finale had taken the greatest toll. After my long drop from the penthouse of the Algonquin Tower, it took days for all my parts and pieces to pop back into their correct positions. Rebecca found a certain delight in informing me how I looked vaguely flat on one side of my face for the first week. She took to calling me Picasso for a while and I let her have her fun.

"Rebecca's a few rows over, visiting Tom's grave," I said to the small plot of land that contained the senior-statesman magician.

"Tom's dead," I added, by way of explanation. "Maybe you already know that. Maybe you two have bumped into each other somewhere in the great beyond."

There was more silence from the other end. It was tricky making a conscious effort not to connect, but I really wanted to leave old Wilbur alone. This visit was for me, not him.

"I saw his last show. And he was good. Really, really good. You would have loved it. I didn't get to see your last show, and

I'm sorry. But Reynaldo says there's a tape of it out there, so I'll be sure to check it out. I heard you were good too. I heard you went out on a real high note, and that makes me glad. We should all get to go out on a high note."

It was time to wrap it up before I started to feel too silly.

"I guess that's all I had to say, and now I've said it. I miss you, buddy."

I began to walk away.

"Did I mention it's weird for me to have a one-sided conversation with the dead like this? Yeah, I guess I did. Anyway, it's weird. Super weird. I don't know why anybody bothers. I guess it makes them feel better."

Did I feel better having done it? Maybe. A little.

Sunder had offered to drive us out to the yard when I mentioned the planned visit. I turned him down. The more rides people had in that car of his, the more likely someone was going to end up needlessly filling a new hole.

He'd been hanging around more and more lately, and I'd set him to work in the home office, getting the rebranded Eulogy Undertakings up and running more efficiently than its previous incarnation ever had. Gladys was already bossing him around like he was an indentured servant, but a lot of petty busywork was actually getting done. It's amazing how much more filing can be accomplished when you have a helping hand who comes equipped with actual functioning hands.

The kid's rookie faux pas at The Craven Image had vanished from the headlines as media outlets got distracted by shiny new acts of more mundane slaughter and mayhem elsewhere. The absence of any closure or arrests in the case didn't seem to bother them anymore. But the lack of a conclusion that would seal the file was a tougher sell to Frenz down at the precinct. He wanted answers and I didn't want to give him any. He had to make do with unsubstantiated assurances.

"How's the vampire situation?" was his first question when I called to report in.

"Dealt with," I said.

"Dead?"

"No, just dealt with."

"And the slayer?"

"Dealt with."

"Dead?"

"It won't happen again. Let's leave it at that."

These weren't the kind of answers that closed cases. They also weren't the kind that earned me any more billable hours beyond my basic consult, but what did I care? Gladys still had me on a fixed income, and it wasn't worth selling out a dumb kid who'd made a string of bad mistakes out of grief and misinformation. Especially when that same dumb kid saved my life—or at least helped me come back from the dead in a timely fashion—so many times in a row.

More solid was the conclusion to the Canning Town Charnel House. Oliver Franck was still being vilified as some sort of serial killer while all the body parts found in his house were being processed. Forensics might one day figure out that he hadn't murdered anybody, but it seemed he was destined to go down in history as one of the most twisted figures of London criminology since Jack the Ripper. At least I, and everyone else who knew him in our select community, understood the truth. Oliver was no villain. The man was a damn hero, and he went down fighting the good fight, even in his dotage.

Shambler provided a much brighter epilogue to the whole sordid story. It seems, left to his own devices, the reanimated servile corpse had made good. He was still an unintelligible, mindless zombie, but that had proved to be a selling point in the one field where such attributes were an enormous asset— television. No charges were ever laid against him, and any connection to Oliver remained unsubstantiated. His brief moment of notoriety, however, had drawn the attention of some enterprising BBC producer, who knew a good hook when she saw one, and had not only bailed him out, but taken him in.

Pressed into service as a late-night chat-show host, Shambler had become something of a minor sensation in the industry. Zombies were, after all, a ubiquitous pop-culture presence, and letting one interview celebrities in the middle of the night was an experiment that benefitted from having not been tried before. Few likely suspected that Shambler's shtick was genuine, particularly those watching from home, and certainly not the myopically egocentric movie actors, sports stars, and pop musicians who came on his show to plug their self-aggrandizing films, trophies, and albums.

Critics had hailed Shambler's interview style as "refreshing," "original," and "long overdue." Aside from the occasional clue-less grunt, Shambler contributed absolutely nothing to the conversation, allowing his guests to speak their mind and open up to him. He was, after all, a very good listener. The idea of a chat-show host actually shutting the hell up and letting the guest do all of the talking was a startling innovation. Audiences were astounded by what their favourite celebrities might say when not being constantly interrupted by a relentless barrage of contrived one-liners, snide zingers, and tired mugging from the master of ceremonies. Already, there were shameless imitations in development in other markets, and the phenomenon of the "silent interview" format promised to revitalize talking-head television—or, at the very least, transform it into something much more informative.

Last I heard, Shambler was being tapped to provide football commentary for the coming season. The idea was to let the events of the game speak for themselves, since viewers were perfectly capable of seeing when goals were being scored without it being pointed out to them. With Shambler's staid delivery at the helm, fans would no longer be forced to dive for the mute button as some overexcited colour commentator redundantly screamed "Goooooooooal!" His coming stint was expected to have a calming influence on The Beautiful Game, thereby making it all the more beautiful, and less prone to violent soccer-hooligan outbreaks.

"Yo, Eulogy," I heard a voice behind me say.

When I turned to see who it was, there was no one to see, only a presence to be felt.

"Oh, hi Denise," I said. "It's been a while."

Wandering through a cemetery, I'm usually the one trying to make contact. It's rare to have a ghost initiate conversation, but we were, after all, well acquainted.

"Miss me?" she asked.

"No," I answered in all honesty.

"Yeah, well I thought I'd give haunting you a rest. It got old."

"I was wondering where you went."

"They planted me a few sections over that way," she said, indicating a more distant, less easily accessed part of an adjacent field. "Pauper's grave."

"I'm sorry," I said. And I was. Pauper graves were the slums of any graveyard.

"You know how it is," she said, resigned. "Family writes you off when you're alive. They have even less use for you dead."

"How are you occupying yourself these days," I asked, knowing all too well there was really nothing for her to get up to.

"Drifting. Wandering. Just...being. Until I can disappear and stop being at all."

"You know," I said, taking pity on her purposeless existence, "the guy who killed you is right over there, in that plot."

I pointed out Jeevak Menahem's anonymous grave that had already lost itself in the middle of all the new arrivals. My late-night tampering with it had gone ignored, and now it was just one more filled hole no one remembered. I thought he might deserve at least one visitor.

"You killed him?" Denise said, glad to hear any news of vengeance.

"Oh, he's alive down there. More undead, really. But conscious, aware. And all alone. Forever."

And that bit of information seemed to brighten Denise's sad, lonely afterlife right up. I could see her spirit beam.

"No," she said, "he's not alone. Not now. Not ever again."

With no further exchange, she drifted off again, this time with a destination in mind. I waved to her as I watched her essence sink into the soil several rows over, right where I'd directed her. What I'd done to Menahem—leaving him incapacitated, horrifically mutilated, buried semi-alive—was viciously ruthless. Siccing Denise on him in that state, where he could do nothing to defend himself against her tireless torments, was cruel beyond measure. And it made me smile.

"Your victory is most decisive," came another voice. This one flat—neither sad, nor pleased. Just present.

It was a busy day at the cemetery. Walk among the dead and you never know who might turn up.

"Always happy to set you back," I said to Charlie Nocturne, not even trying to figure out which looming shadow was speaking to me.

"This is no setback," he said. "It only confirms the identity of my Death Incarnate. It is something I have long known."

"No deal," I replied. "I won't be your Death, and now you're lost your Famine as well."

"Have I?"

"He's out from under Jeevak Menahem's thumb, and now he can go wherever he wishes, whenever he wants. If he's smart, he'll keep far away from you."

"You speak of Marin Venerio Grissoni."

"Of course."

"Did Marin not tell you the nature of his business that moved him from town to town when he was a living man so many centuries ago?"

"I thought he was a merchant," I said, wondering where Nocturne was going with this.

"He was a doctor."

What Charlie Nocturne was trying to tell me suddenly became obvious.

"Marin isn't Famine," I said.

"No. Despite his attempts to slowly starve himself by not feeding as often as he needs, that is not his role. Rather, he is Pestilence. Like the plague he failed to stem when he functioned as a man of medicine, vampirism likewise persists. He is an allegory for disease that, despite his best efforts, continues to spread. Sickness compounds and multiplies through the ages, until it is everywhere, gnawing on the world as do fleas upon sickly rodents. Pestilence weakens the host, killing piece by piece, and paving the way for Death. You have given Marin The Mark of the Sighted One, just as you did Csaba Szabo. And yourself."

"This wasn't self-inflicted, you know," I said, pointing at my white eye.

"If Ms. Stone shares the blame, you should take it up with her."

"Find somebody else! I've officially taken myself off the list."

"You were never out of the running," said Nocturne patiently. "You only managed to remove yourself from contention for a short while. I knew you would return."

"How could you know that?"

"You have refined your appearance to better represent yourself," he noted.

I was wearing Wilbur's magic hat. It seemed only appropriate to bring it with me when I visited his grave. The rest of my outfit had been replaced. I was able to repair my body after an evening at the Algonquin Tower, but my wardrobe needed more than some patchwork to sew it all back together. Rebecca had already expensed suitable substitutes to the Eulogy Undertakings accounts department.

"Yeah, it's a whole new look," I agreed.

"One I have seen before," he said.

"Right. At the tower opening," I reminded him. It seemed obvious. Too obvious. His long silence after I said it troubled me.

"Where else?" I asked, then thought better of it. "When?" was the more precise question. "I thought you said my path through you—through time—had become linear."

"It has," he said. "You do not seek passage through me again."

"Then how?"

"We did, at one other point, cross paths. Many years ago. Perhaps you were on your way to some future event you have yet to experience. When this happens, we do not speak, we do not interact. You assume I do not notice you, but how could I not?"

Another hurdle I looked forward to failing to jump when I came to it.

"The speed of your recovery after so many murders and mishaps is remarkable," Nocturne commended. "You are getting most proficient at it. Swifter."

"I was cremated and scattered at sea," I reminded him. "If I can come back from that, I can come back from anything."

"What you see as a strength is, in fact, a weakness. You think you have been bestowed a great gift, but you have been levied with a terrible curse."

"You're not the first one to tell me I'm cursed."

"Then perhaps I will be the first one you will listen to."

"Is this the immortality spiel? Because I've heard it all before. Yeah yeah, everybody I know and care about is going to die and I'll still be here. Well, you know what, that sucks, but I'll make new friends."

Nocturne shook the dark void he called a head back and forth, ponderously.

"You are not thinking far enough ahead. Your inability to end holds unspeakable horrors in store. There is no hell for any of us to go to. Simply the restful void. But there is a hell reserved for you alone, and you draw closer with every passing moment. This hell lies not in death, but in life everlasting. I can only speculate about what the future holds for you after the end of all other life, but it is not difficult to extrapolate. I see a sun in supernova, and the true end of the world, not simply the occupants it once held. I see a planet burned away under you, and your body at last destroyed with no matter left to allow regeneration. And yet still you will linger, still you will suffer. A final soul, unable to fade away or depart, orbiting a dead sun as it presides over a dead solar system, spiralling though an equally doomed galaxy in an indifferent universe that constantly expands and spreads itself ever more thin, ever more distant, into infinity."

It was a mouthful. I summed it up more succinctly.

"Sucks to be me."

I saw him nod ever so slightly, and I think I could almost detect sympathy in his hollow flatline voice.

"It does, indeed, suck to be you."

Charlie turned around and started to step away.

"So who's Famine?" I called after him.

He turned back, like he was going to tell me. Instead I got hit in the face with a thick spray of liquid erupting from where his face would be if he had one. At first I thought he'd spat at me. Then I tasted the thin, non-alcoholic excuse for beer and remembered where it had come from, and the weeks-old sentiment that had launched it.

"I'll take that as invitation to mind my own business."

"I do not control the destination or schedule of who or what passes through me. And yet everyone and everything seems to end up where and when they need to be."

He turned to leave for real this time.

"The same can be said of knowledge," were his parting words. "All will be revealed. In time."

The tombstones and monuments were casting long shadows that late in the day. Before he was too many rows away, Charlie Nocturne had become just one more of them, and I could no longer tell which.

Rebecca, finished with her graveside visit and the distribution of flowers, returned to my side too late to see who or what I had been talking to. She took my hand and gave it a squeeze. I looked into her eyes.

"You're wet," she noted.

THE STORY CONTINUES IN...

THE BONEYARD

THE NECROMANCER THANATOGRAPHY
BOOK THREE

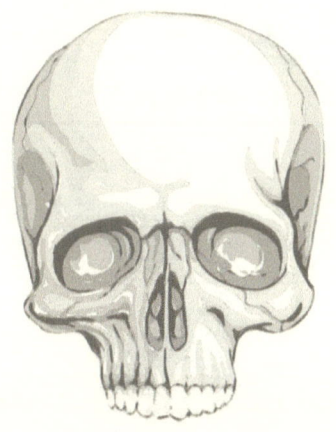

COMING SOON FROM

SHANE SIMMONS

AND EYESTRAIN PRODUCTIONS

Visit eyestrainproductions.com and subscribe to the
newsletter for other free tales from the Necropolis.

Acknowledgements

The author wishes to thank Michael Brodie, Ellie Presner, Alex Ruaux, Eric Packman, Jill Binder, and Kirsten LM for their eyes, ears, and chunky bits of brain matter that helped stitch together this literary abomination.

About the Author

Shane Simmons is an award-winning screenwriter and graphic novelist whose work has appeared in international film festivals, museums, and lectures about design and structure. His art has been discussed in multiple books and academic journals about sequential storytelling, and his short stories have been printed in critically praised anthologies of history, crime, and horror. He was born in Lachine, a suburb of Montreal best known for being massacred in 1689 and having a joke name.

Also by Shane Simmons

Novels

Necropolis
Sex Tape
Filmography

Collections

Raw and Other Stories

Booklets

Carrion Luggage
Hot Pennies
Choke the Chicken
The Red Baron: An Ace for the Ages

Graphic Novels

The Long and Unlearned Life of Roland Gethers
The Failed Promise of Bradley Gethers
The Inauspicious Adventures of Filson Gethers

Author's Note

Small-press publishers rely on reviews from readers like you to help get the word out about their books. Whether it's a simple star rating or a written critique, every bit of feedback helps convince the impersonal computer algorithms of Amazon, and other literary outlets, that the book you just read has merit and deserves more exposure. Please support independent authors, editors and publishers by taking a few moments to share your thoughts and opinions with other potential readers who may be sitting on the fence about trying an intriguing novel or collection. Your suggestions or comments can make all the difference when it comes to helping them find a new writer they'll like, or matching a struggling author with the readership he or she deserves. Thank you.